Praise for Lenora Worth and her novels

"Lenora Worth creates a character with a *Heart of Stone* that will have readers longing to melt it. Her best story yet, it is filled with spiritual depth and hidden meaning."
—*RT Book Reviews*

"In *A Tender Touch*, Lenora Worth skillfully creates a fascinating story filled with exciting intrigue and sympathetic characters."
—*RT Book Reviews*

"Lenora Worth's *A Perfect Love* is a beautiful testimony to the true meaning of family and forgiveness. The romantic pacing is just perfect, and the faith message is subtle but heartfelt."
—*RT Book Reviews*

"*Easter Blessings: The Lily Field* by Lenora Worth is perhaps the most beautiful and moving Love Inspired book I've read."
—*RT Book Reviews*

LENORA WORTH
The Carpenter's Wife

&

Heart of Stone

Steeple
Hill®

Published by Steeple Hill Books™

STEEPLE HILL BOOKS

**Steeple
Hill®**

Recycling programs
for this product may
not exist in your area.

ISBN-13: 978-0-373-65137-5

THE CARPENTER'S WIFE AND HEART OF STONE

THE CARPENTER'S WIFE
Copyright © 2003 by Lenora H. Nazworth

HEART OF STONE
Copyright © 2003 by Lenora H. Nazworth

www.SteepleHill.com

Printed in U.S.A.

CONTENTS

LENORA WORTH

has written more than forty books, most of those for Steeple Hill. She has worked freelance for a local magazine, where she wrote monthly opinion columns, feature articles and social commentaries. She also wrote for the local paper for five years. Married to her high school sweetheart for thirty-five years, Lenora lives in Louisiana and has two grown children and a cat. She loves to read, take long walks, sit in her garden and go shoe shopping.

THE CARPENTER'S WIFE

In God is my salvation, and my glory;
the rock of my strength,
and my refuge.

—*Psalms* 62:7

To my nephew Chester Howell, with love

Chapter One

Rock Dempsey loved Sunset Island.

He loved the way the small island off the Georgia coast lay tossed like a woman's dainty slipper near the mainland. He loved the way the island sat at the mouth of the Savannah River, the land caught between a glistening oval-shaped bay and the ever-churning Atlantic Ocean. He loved having the sunrise to the east over the sea, and the sunset to the west over the bay.

As he stood in the middle of his workshop, with the ocean breezes coming through the thrown-open doors from the ocean on one side and the bay on the other, Rock decided a man couldn't ask for much more in life.

Unless that man was pushing thirty-five and his whimsical mother was still asking him when he was going to settle down and produce a passel of grandchildren for her to spoil.

"Roderick, I could die and go to heaven without even a memory of a sweet baby to carry home with me," his mother, Eloise, had told him in a gentle huff just that morning when he'd stopped by for breakfast.

They had this same conversation at least once a week. It was never a good sign when his mother used his given name in a discussion. But then, his brothers Stone and Clay had to hear it from Eloise, too, each time they came to visit.

In her mid-fifties and long widowed, Eloise Dempsey kept close tabs on her three sons, properly named Roderick, Stanton and Clayton, but affectionately nicknamed Rock, Stone and Clay. She fretted that none of them had yet to make a lifetime commitment to one woman. If Rock blamed their artistic mother and her flighty ways for her sons' obvious fear of commitment, he'd never say that out loud to Eloise. She'd had enough heartache in her life, between being disinherited and then losing the man she had loved—and had given up that inheritance to be with—to the sea in a terrible storm. Even if she had sacrificed quality time with her sons to become one of the most famous sculpture artists in the South, Rock was trying very hard to come to terms with his lovable mother's flaws. And his own.

Rock reminded himself that Eloise was trying,

now that she'd found success with her art, to make things up to her children. Still, the memories of eating TV dinners and going to bed tired after watching over his two younger brothers always left a bad taste in Rock's mouth.

Growing up, he'd often dreamed of a traditional family, with a mom and dad who were devoted to family and children, with good, home-cooked meals and nights spent together watching a movie or sharing a supper out on the shore. Rock and his brothers had missed out on those things. While their mother pursued her art, they had had to find odd jobs here and there to make ends meet. The islanders had been kind and watchful, and Eloise had continued her work, unaware and undisturbed, while her children had the run of the land.

If he closed his eyes, he could still hear the hiss of her welding torch, late into the night. The glare had always been too bright for Rock, but the sound of it never went away. If he looked north toward what the islanders called the Ankle Curve, he could just make out the turret of the rambling Victorian beach house where his mother had lived and worked for so many years. He could still see her there, in the big barn settled deep in the moss-covered trees that she used as a studio, bent over yet another bust shaped from clay or an aged cross forged from wood and stone. His mother's hands had created beauty.

But he'd missed those same hands tucking him in at night.

Not wanting to dwell on his mother's shortcomings—or his own in the love department, for that matter—Rock turned back to the cabinets he'd been restoring for Miss McPherson. Now, *there* was an available single woman. She was in church every Sunday, tithed regularly, cooked everything from Brunswick stew to clam chowder and had a smile that lit up a room. Too bad she was pushing eighty.

"One day I'm going to get up the courage to ask Miss Mac why she never married," Rock said to the gleaming oak cabinet door he'd just finished vanishing.

"Do you often talk to your cabinets?" a soft feminine voice said from the open shed doors.

Rock turned to find a petite, auburn-haired woman staring at him, her green eyes slanted and questioning, a slight smile on her angular face. He stood there like a big dummy while she walked into the quiet cool of his work shed, her crisp white cotton shirt and polished tan trousers giving her an air of sophistication.

Coming out of his fog, Rock grabbed a wipe rag and ran it over his hands. "I'm afraid I do tend to talk to my creations. A bad habit." Tossing the rag aside, he leaned back on the long, dented work table. "What can I do for you?"

She pushed at a wave of burnished hair that kept falling over her chin. "I'm Ana Hanson. I just moved into the Harper house—soon to be Ana's Tea Room and Art Gallery."

"Oh." Trying to hide his surprise, Rock pushed off the table to extend a hand. "My mother told me about you."

And had urged him to get to know the *single* newcomer to the tiny island a little better. *"Ana will be lonely, Rock. Invite her to church, at least. Just as a way to break the ice."*

"Well, don't look so glum," the woman said, her head tilting in defense. "Did I come at a bad time?"

Despite his mother's very obvious suggestion echoing through his head, Rock tried to stick to the here and now. He felt horrible at the way he'd sounded. "No, no. It's just—I had expected—I thought you'd be older, more like my Mother's other eccentric friends." Feeling more foolish with each word, he quickly added, "Mom said you needed some new cabinets?"

Ana nodded through an amused smile, causing the same silky length of curls to fall right back across her face. "Yes. As you probably know, the Harper house needed major renovations. Some of the preliminary work in the upstairs apartment has been done, thanks to my sister—she's a Realtor and has all kinds of connections with carpenters and contractors out of Savannah—but I wanted someone local and more accessible to help me renovate the kitchen and main dining area."

"And that'd be me?" Rock grinned, glad that at least his mother's bragging often brought him new customers.

"You come highly recommended," Ana said as she ran a hand over a newly restored pie safe. "That's one reason I waited before finishing this part of the project. Your mother suggested we might work together on this—that you'd understand... what I expected...as far as cabinets and book-shelves go."

"That's just my mother talking," Rock responded, noting that the floral scent of Ana Hanson's perfume managed to find its way to his nose over the smell of sawdust and varnish stripper. "She thinks I inherited some of her artistic ability."

"I'd have to agree with Eloise," Ana replied, an appreciative expression on her face as her gaze moved over the many cabinets, armoires and chests Rock had either built from scratch or restored. "She seems to be a good judge of talent."

"How do you know my mother?" he asked, curious as to how Ana had found her way to Sunset Island.

"I worked at an art gallery in Savannah," Ana explained. "We exhibited some of your mother's work. I got to know her when we held a reception in her honor."

"Ah, that explains it, then," Rock said, turning to put away his tools. "My mother's reputation precedes all of us."

"You sound almost ambivalent about that."

He whirled to find Ana's luminous green eyes on him.

"It's a long story, but yes, I guess it still surprises me that she's so famous."

"She has a lot of talent."

"Yes, she does. I can't argue with that." He shrugged, brushed wood chips off the sleeve of his T-shirt. "Look, I love and respect my mother. And her designs are beautiful. But she works too hard— she's almost obsessed with it."

"Most good artists are that way, don't you think?"

Rock studied her for a minute, wondering if this cute woman was just like his mother. Would Ana Hanson put work above all else in her life? Probably, since she seemed anxious to make her tea room a success. "I guess you're right. And since you worked in an art gallery, you probably appreciate art more than I do. So why don't we stick to a subject I know best—cabinets. What do you have in mind?"

Ana had a lot of things in mind, but she didn't think Rock Dempsey wanted to hear about her hopes and dreams for this business venture. Should she tell him she'd had to sell practically everything she owned to make the down payment on the Harper house? Should she explain to him that, since college, her dream had been to own some sort of gallery? Should she go into detail about how her sister, Tara, had suggested Ana use her talent for cooking along with her good eye for art to come to

Sunset Island and open a combination tea room and art gallery?

Ana watched as Rock busied himself with cleaning his workspace. He seemed on edge, resistant to her. Maybe because his mother had sent her to him. Did Rock think Eloise was up to more than just securing him another paying customer? Well, Ana could certainly nip that little concept right in the bud. She didn't have time for matchmaking, even if Eloise meant well.

Ana had to get her tea room ready for the grand opening in a few weeks. And that opening depended on how quickly Rock Dempsey could help her.

"I have several ideas," she said in answer to his earlier question. "I want to build some cabinets and buffets in keeping with the Victorian flavor of the house. It was built around the turn of the last century."

"I'm familiar with the history of the Harper house," he said, smiling. "It's been vacant on and off over the years. When we were little, my brothers and I used to sneak in there at night, mostly to scare each other and see who would be the bravest by going into a dark, deserted house."

Ana decided Rock Dempsey seemed the type to brave any situation. He was the standard tall, dark and handsome, with fire-flashing deep blue eyes. But his face had an interesting aged look that spoke of wisdom and gentleness, the same tanned richness of the priceless wooden furniture he worked hard to restore. Did Rock need a bit of restoration himself, maybe?

"So, who was the bravest?" she asked.

He shrugged, grinned. "Well, none of us was very brave. I think I managed to sneak in a back window once, but, of course, Stone and Clay decided to come around front and jiggle the door, shouting 'Police,' which naturally made me run away in terror—terror that my mother would ground me for life, rather than fear of authority."

Ana started thumbing through a design book. "Sounds as if you and your brothers had an exciting life growing up."

"We had our moments," he said. "We've always been close—or…we were growing up. I guess we've drifted apart lately, though."

"That's too bad," Ana replied, thinking of the tenuous relationship she had with her sister Tara. Tara was hard to read at times, a type-A personality with a lightning temper and bitter memories. Ana harbored some of that same bitterness, directed toward her sister at times, toward herself at others. But she didn't want to think about that right now. She had to get back to work.

"So, anyway, I thought you might come by the house later today, if possible, to look at the kitchen and dining room. It's been completely over-hauled—painted, new flooring, but I held off on the final plans. I want it to be perfect."

Rock handed her several more design books.

"Okay, then. Why don't you glance over these—there are several Victorian reproductions and some original restoration projects in there—and I'll meet you at the house, say, around four?"

"That would be good. I have some errands to run, but I should be back in plenty of time." She extended a hand. "Thanks...Rod—"

"It's Rock," he said, wincing. "My mother's choice of given names for her sons has left us the laughingstock of the island, I'm afraid."

"I like your name," Ana said, acutely aware of the strength and warmth of his big callused hand.

"Well, around here, everyone calls me Rock," he said. "Or...Preacher Rock."

Ana jerked her hand back. "You're a preacher?"

"Just on Sundays," he said, a teasing light making his dark eyes go as blue as the ocean at night. "I got the job by being in the right place at the wrong time, or something like that."

"You're going to have to explain."

He walked with her out into the oak-shadowed yard, then pointed to the tiny whitewashed church sitting like a child's playhouse a few yards away from his cottage and workshop. "Reverend Palczynski was the island preacher for over forty years. He lived in this cottage, preached every Sunday in the Sunset Chapel. Then one day he came out to the workshop to get his volleyball equipment—he loved to play volleyball—and fell over dead right underneath this great live oak. He was ninety."

"Oh, goodness."

"Yes, *goodness* is a perfect word for Reverend Pal—as we all called him. He was a good man. I happened to come along and find him. Tried to save him, but he was already gone by the time the paramedics got here. He died with a smile on his face, but his death left a great void on the island."

"And you filled that void?"

Rock nodded, glanced out to the beach in the distance. The roar of the ocean ran through the delicate tropical breezes that moved around the palm trees and great oaks. "One of the paramedics suggested I take over, since I'd always helped out at the chapel, doing odd jobs around the place, building cabinets and such. And since I have a reputation for being a philosopher of sorts, word got out. The town gossip, Greta Epperson, wrote about it in her society column in the *Sunset Sentinel,* and next thing I knew I was standing before the church elders, being blessed as their next preacher."

Ana laughed. "Your mother warned me people on the island do things their own way."

"Yes, that's true. We march to the beat of a different drummer, I think. And Greta captures it all in her column each week."

"Do you regret being…coerced into becoming a preacher?"

"No, not at all. You see, I believe no one can make me do something I don't want to do in the first place. It seemed a natural transition, since I worked out here—I already rented this space from Reverend Pal, anyway."

"So you moved right on in?"

The look he gave her made Ana's heart lift like a surprise wave coming through still waters. His eyes were filled with a quiet determination and a firm challenge.

"I've been known to move right in on a situation, yes."

She whirled, headed to her car. "Then, I'm sure I can count on you to deliver my cabinets and shelves in a timely manner. I'd like to open by mid-May."

"You don't beat around the bush, do you," she heard him say from behind her.

She also heard the crunch of his workboots on the shell-scattered drive. "I don't have time to mess around," Ana explained as she opened her car door and tossed the design books on the seat. "This is my last chance."

"Last chance for what?"

He was right there beside her, holding the car door open.

Ana slid behind the wheel, then looked up at him through the open window. "My last chance to make it. I've wanted this for a very long time. I don't intend to blow it."

"Got a lot invested in this, huh?"

She nodded, tried to relax. "Yes, time, money, commitments to several artists, your mother included. I don't want to let anybody down."

He leaned in, his big body blocking out the sun's bright rays. Ana got a whiff of aftershave mixed with turpentine. And got nervous all over again—her heart was doing the wave thing in rapid succession now.

"Then, *I* won't let *you* down," he told her.

Ana waited a couple of beats before stammering, "Th-thank you. I'll see you at four."

He smiled, then slowly stood back from the car. "See you then."

As Ana drove away, she heard the echo of his words. *"I won't let you down."*

She'd heard that one before. Many times.

But this time, she prayed it was the truth.

Chapter Two

"So you're meeting Ana at four, then?"

Rock's mother fluttered around her kitchen, adjusting a set of wind chimes here, fixing a fresh bouquet of lilies there. She smiled and hummed as she fussed and fixed, the constant breezes flowing through the many open windows causing strands of her grayish-white upswept hair to pull away from the elaborate shell-encrusted silver combs she used to hold it off her face.

She had always reminded Rock of an elusive butterfly, never settling on just one blossom.

"This is just work, Mom," Rock replied. "Don't go reading anything else into this. It's strictly business."

"Business which I sent your way," Eloise reminded him as she poured him a glass of mint-flavored sun tea. "Want another sandwich?"

"No, but thanks for the meal—and the business. It's not every day I get two meals and a huge project from you."

Eloise stopped fidgeting. "I'm trying to make things up to you, Rock, on both scores."

Rock nodded, wished he'd learn to keep his mouth shut. "I do appreciate your efforts, Mother. I can always use the steady work. And…as long as you're willing to feed me now and again, I can work on…my other issues, too, I suppose."

"Good," Eloise said as she swished back to the sink, her multi-patterned cotton skirt lifting out like soft handkerchiefs around her ankles. "A minister shouldn't have issues."

"Ministers are only human," Rock replied. "And in spite of my faith in God, I still have questions that only He can answer."

"Well, one day you shall have all your answers," his mother said, smiling. "Rock, you know I'm so proud of you, don't you?"

"Yes."

"I'm proud of all my boys."

Eloise got a faraway look in her crystal blue eyes.

"Haven't heard from Stone lately, huh?"

"No. But you know Stone. He doesn't allow for much chitchat. And he's so busy."

"I know. Amassing his fortune."

"Don't be bitter, Rock."

"I'm not bitter. Stone has his life and I have mine. I'm content right here on the island."

Eloise pulled dead heads off a nearby pink begonia. "Stone was never content living on the island. Savannah suits him much better."

Rock took a long drink from the tea, the sweet mint taste going down smooth in spite of the turmoil he always felt when talk turned to his brother, Stone. "I'm sure it does. And we all want Stone to be happy."

"That's exactly what I want—for all my sons. At least Clay seems to be thriving with the police department in Atlanta."

"Clay has always been a happy-go-lucky, hard-working fellow."

"He has a good heart."

"I couldn't agree more. In fact, I think Clay got the heart that Stone never had."

Eloise gave him a mock glare. "Stone has a heart. He just doesn't like to show it. I only want all of you to…find love, the kind of love I had with your father."

Not wanting to get into a long discussion on that topic because talking about her late husband always seemed to upset Eloise, Rock said, "So is that why you're throwing me at your friend Ana Hanson?"

Eloise reached for a yellow watering pitcher sitting in the bay window over the sink. Outside, a seagull cawed noisily in a low fly-by. "Who said I was throwing you at her? I just suggested you'd be perfect to help design her tea room, is all."

Rock chuckled. "Mom, why didn't you tell me she was young and pretty…and apparently single?"

His mother gave an eloquent shrug, her dangling

turquoise feathered earrings brushing against the crocheted lace of her cream-colored linen tunic. "I figured if I told you about Ana, you'd clam up like a crab in a sand hole and refuse the job."

"I never turn down paying customers."

"Even cute...*available* ones?"

"Okay, I might have been a little hesitant if I'd known Ana was close to my age and single. But I have to admit, she is very pretty." He finished off the tea. "She *is* single, right?"

"Very much so," Eloise replied, her smile widening to reveal an endearing gap between her front teeth. "So, is that or the fact that she is attractive, smart, capable and...*available* going to hinder your working for her?"

"Probably," he said. "But then, it might just make it interesting, too. As Auguste Renoir said, 'Why should beauty be suspect?'"

"That's the spirit," Eloise replied, clasping her hands together. "Well, then, if you don't want some fruit and yogurt for dessert, I'll go back to my own work."

"I'm fine, Mom. Got to get moving."

Eloise whirled by, giving him a quick peck on the cheek. "I'll see you later."

Rock watched as his mother moved gracefully over the steps leading from the wraparound porch and walked down the path to what had once been a horse stable, her soft leather walking sandals making very little noise.

The gardens were in full bloom—the fuchsia bougainvillea, the rich red hibiscus trees, the crape myrtle and azaleas all splashing together like a bright abstract painting underneath the Spanish moss of the ancient oak trees. And his mother in her feathered turquoise jewelry and flowing broom-stick skirt fit right into the picture. Beautiful.

That made him think again of Ana Hanson. His mother had left out one trait he thought he recognized in the petite auburn-haired dynamo—ambition. And he remembered another favorite quote from a long-dead philosopher: "Beauty and folly are generally companions."

She'd come here for companionship. For the warm ocean breezes and wonderful, salty mist of the sea. She'd come here to put down roots and settle in like the sea oats that flowed in wheat-colored patterns down on the dunes.

"I'm going to be a success," Ana promised herself as she glanced around the large near-empty kitchen of her tea room. "I have to make this work."

"I think you're off to a good start," Jackie Welsh, her just-hired assistant said as she passed by and grabbed her purse off the counter. "I'll be here bright and early tomorrow to begin training Tina and the other servers."

"Thanks," Ana told the tall brunette. "I appreciate your help so much."

She'd hired Jackie a few days ago, and already

they were able to read each other's minds. She'd need that kind of connection when things got to hopping around here.

Glancing at her watch, she mentally went over her to-do list while she waited for Rock Dempsey. The two-bedroom upstairs apartment was done. Everything was unpacked and in place, and the entire staff had been hired. Over the next month or so, they'd help set things up and learn the menus and recipes by heart. Next week, the furnishings for the shop and tea room would start arriving. She'd have plenty to keep her busy then. Especially if Rock was here every day, measuring and building.

Just thinking of his big, muscular frame in the middle of her dainty treasures made Ana smile. It felt good to smile. She'd been so focused on this venture over the past few months, she'd forgotten how to relax. But now, she was here at last. Here in her own place, with her own living quarters—no roommates, no rent to pay—just a big mortgage that her sister had helped finance—she had no one to answer to except herself. She'd finally accomplished her dream.

Now she had to make that dream work.

She envisioned the wicker bistro tables she'd found at a clearance sale sitting here and there in what once had been the parlor of the house. She saw intimate groupings out on the long porch, where diners would have a clear view of the glistening bay down the sloping yard to the dunes.

She'd put some nice cushiony rocking chairs out there, too.

Glancing down at the big bay, Ana saw a sailboat glide by like a giant blue and white butterfly. Maybe she could go sailing herself soon. It had been a long time since she'd sailed out on the water with the sun on her face.

A knock at the stained-glass front door caused her to jump. Not one for woolgathering, Ana scooted across the room, her espadrilles barely making a click on the polished wooden floors. Adjusting her clothes and hair, she opened the door to find Rock standing there in jeans and a T-shirt emblazoned with Save the West Island Lighthouse Summer Jam Session.

"Hi," she said, smiling as she ignored the way her pulse seemed to quicken each time he looked at her. Then she pointed to the image of the old West Island Lighthouse on his shirt. "You, too, huh? Eloise told me several islanders are working to renovate the lighthouse. And I read about the jam session in that Greta woman's column. That should be a challenge, from what I hear—raising funds for renovation."

He entered the room, ran his gaze over the pale cream painted walls and the feminine wallpaper border that depicted shoes, hats and purses from the turn of the century. Then he turned to her.

"I like a good challenge."

"Well, then, you'll love the job I have for you,"

she replied, her nerves stretching as tight as the rigging on a sail. "I hope…I think I have everything in order." With a wave of her hand, she strolled around the empty rooms. "As you can see, the walls and floors are done. And I've ordered some armoires and side-buffets for displays. They should be here any day now. The major appliances are all brand-new and industrial size—those will be installed this week. Mainly, I need you to take a look at the kitchen cabinets and tell me if they can be salvaged. And I'd like you to maybe redo the walk-in pantry and build some functional shelves in the kitchen, too."

Rock stood listening, his gaze once again moving over the central hallway and two long open rooms on each side of the front of the house. "The original parlor and dining room—this will be the restaurant area?"

"Yes, diners will be seated in both rooms, but our artwork and other wares will be displayed on the walls and all around the dining tables. Then we have a room in the back for private parties, which will also display a collection of antiques and art. The cash register will be here in the vestibule by the front door. I found an antique counter in an old drugstore in Savannah. It's being shipped." She pointed to an open door off the rear of the hallway. "And I have a small office right across from the kitchen. There's a bathroom back there, too."

He nodded, made notes on a small pad. "You seem to like the Victorian era."

"I do," she said, grinning. "I've always loved old things, all periods of history. Maybe because I read a lot growing up—stories of long ago, all about valor and romance."

"Oh?" He stopped writing and glanced up at her. "I'd figure you'd have been too busy chasing off boys who wanted their own valor and romance, to sit around reading books."

Blushing, Ana shook her head. "My sister got all the boys. I got my romantic *ideas* from books."

He stopped scribbling to stare at her. "I reckon you do look like a Jane Austen kind of girl—all *Sense and Sensibility.*"

Unsure if that was a compliment, Ana replied, "I'm a little old-fashioned and sensible, but I try not to live in the past."

"'The tender grace of a day that is dead…will never come back to me.'"

Stunned, Ana shrugged. It was as if Rock had hit on her deepest, most bittersweet memories with the precision of cupid's arrow. "That's…very melancholy."

"Alfred, Lord Tennyson," Rock explained. "This house has a tender grace. Maybe it will bring you a little romance…and some comfort."

Comfort? Was that what she'd been seeking all her life? Ana pushed at the dark memories blocking out the rays of hope in her mind. "Romance I doubt.

But I guess I could use some comfort. Anyway, I love this house. And I'm thrilled to be here on the island. We used to vacation here with my parents. I fell in love with Sunset Island and I've always wanted to come back."

"You came from Savannah?"

"Yes. We lived out from Savannah, near Fort Stewart. My parents still live there in a house on the Canoochee River. Tara—that's my sister—and I attended college at Savannah State." She stopped, took a breath. "I was a senior when she was a freshman. She got married a year later and never finished college. After I graduated, I moved to Savannah to work in the art gallery." She lowered her eyes, stared at an aged spot in the floor, memories as rich as the lacquer on the wood coloring her mind. "Anyway, now I'm here. I'm moving forward, even if I do like things from the past."

Ana quieted, thinking she sounded as if she were trying to convince herself of this. And maybe she was. She still had hurtful memories from her college days, memories that had colored her whole adult life and her rocky relationship with her younger sister. But she was determined to make a new start, with both her life and her sister.

"The past can be good," Rock said, his keen eyes sweeping over her face. "As long as we keep it in perspective."

"Oh, I keep it in perspective, all right. I don't want to ever go back there."

"Bad memories?"

Ana looked up at him, saw the sincere curiosity in his beautiful eyes. "Some." *Lots.* But she wasn't about to tell him any of that. She ruffled her hair with her hand. "Do you want to see the kitchen?"

"Sure."

She started toward the back of the house, heard him behind her, then willed her heart and her head to stay calm. Ana reminded herself that she'd given her heart to a man once, only to have it returned bruised and battered.

She would never make that mistake again. Even if this handsome preacher named Rock did cause her to think of romantic things like strolling on the beach at sunset and intimate dinners by candle-light.

Ana would stick to her art, her cooking and her books. Those were safe, tangible things.

Love wasn't safe. That "tender grace," as Rock had quoted, would never come back to her again. She was all business now. And all on her own.

If only Rock Dempsey's eyes would stop looking at her with that anything-but-business gaze.

This woman meant business.

Rock had measured, suggested, tested, rearranged, gauged and decided on what could be done for the beautiful old cabinets in the long, sunny kitchen. A good stripping of old paint, some new hardware and a lot of wood restorer and varnish would make them shine like new. That part had been easy.

But testing and gauging Ana Hanson—ah, therein lay the challenge of this assignment.

She had been hurt somewhere in the past. Maybe during her childhood, maybe during her college years. But something had left her unsure and unsteady, even if she did try to present a calm, capable facade to the world.

Rock had no doubt she was capable. She seemed as intent on making her tea room a popular tourist attraction as his mother did on creating intriguing artifacts from rocks and stones. That ability to focus should serve as a warning to Rock. Ana held many of the traits he'd seen too many times in his mother—that tendency to shut everything out, that need to finish the work, create the next sculpture piece, or, in Ana's case, create a haven for fine art and good food.

There was nothing wrong with that. But Rock wondered if Ana was pouring all of her strength into this new venture because she was running from the past. Running from herself, just as his mother had done most of her life.

Turning to see where she'd flittered off to this time, Rock found Ana standing on a footstool wiping one of the big bay windows in the front parlor. He almost called out to her, but then the way the last of the sun's rays were gleaming all around her from the open west window on the other side of the room caused him to stop and just watch.

She stood in the soft wind, her dark red hair shining in the soft afternoon sun. Her skin was glistening with a golden creaminess. She'd changed clothes since this morning and now her long floral skirt moved around her like a flower garden.

Rock took this picture in, and realized it had been way too long since he'd been out on a date with a pretty woman. And taking old Miss McPherson to the seafood market once a week didn't count.

"You hungry?" he heard himself saying.

Ana turned, almost too fast. She nearly fell off the stepstool. Rock wasn't fast enough to catch her, and he was glad. That would have been a classic romantic way of getting her into his arms—too obvious.

But since he didn't want to look unchivalrous, he did step forward. "Steady there."

"I'm fine," Ana said, stepping down from the stool to turn and stare at him as she pushed her hair away from her eyes. "I must have misunderstood you, though. I thought you asked me if I was hungry."

"No misunderstanding. I did—ask you that, I mean."

She stood there with her hands on her hips, an almost doubting glare on her pretty face. "Why did you—ask?"

So she was the suspicious type. "No particular reason, other than it's getting dark and…I only had a sandwich for lunch. I was thinking about fried catfish out at the Sunken Pier. Ever been there?"

"No."

"No, you've never been there, or no, you aren't hungry, or just plain 'no, I don't want to have dinner with you, Rock'?"

"No to the first, yes to the second, and…I'm not sure to the last part."

He crossed his hands over his chest, his trusty pocket notepad clutched in one hand. Then he leaned forward, offering up what he hoped was his best smile. "Why aren't you sure? It's just a meal. We can go over the cabinet plans again."

She frowned, looked around. "I guess we do need to finalize everything—set your hours, your fee, things like that."

"Exactly. A business dinner."

"Strictly business."

"Wouldn't dream of having it any other way."

He liked the trace of disappointment that had scurried through her green eyes. But he wouldn't dare tell her that since she'd walked into his shop this morning, he had at least thought of having things another way—besides the strictly business way, that is.

"I'll freshen up and get my purse," she said, clearly as confused and unsure as she'd been two minutes ago. "We won't be late, will we? I have so much paperwork—contracts with food vendors, inventory sheets to check over—"

"I'll have you home at a reasonable hour, I promise."

"Okay, then."

"Okay, then."

"You know, Mark Twain said principles have no real force except when one is well fed."

She rewarded him with a smile. "And you are clearly a man of principle."

"That I am. And manners. My mama taught me both."

"That I can believe," she said, her expression softening. "I trust your mother's opinion and her good judgment of character, even if you are her son and she has to recommend you on that basis alone. I think I'll be safe with you."

"Completely."

But as Rock watched her hurry up the narrow staircase, he had to wonder how much *he* could trust his mother's judgment. After all, Eloise had brought Ana and him together for her own maternal reasons.

And now Rock was worried about those reasons and about how being with this shy, old-fashioned woman made him feel.

The real question was—would *he* be safe with Ana Hanson?

Chapter Three

~∽

"And that's how it got its name," Rock said, waving a hand in the air toward the old partially sunken pier just outside the wide window.

Ana watched as he smiled, but the smile didn't quite reach his eyes. They held that distant darkness that seemed to flare like thunderclouds now and then. He looked down at his plate, then shrugged. "There's a lot of history on this old island."

Ana laughed, then nibbled the remains of her baked trout. "So you're telling me that pier used to be completely safe and sturdy, until twenty years ago when a hurricane came through and almost swept it into the sea? And because of that and the restaurant's legendary name, no one wants to fix the pier now?"

Rock nodded, grabbed a crispy hush puppy, then chewed before answering. "The first restaurant got washed into the ocean. That was the original Seafood at the Pier fine dining establishment. It had been here since 1910. But after the hurricane, the only thing left was that part of the pier that's sticking up from the water now. A good place for pelicans and egrets to perch. The owner's son decided to rebuild under a new name—thus The Sunken Pier Restaurant. Been here and been going strong ever since, through storms and summer tourists alike, frying up fish and steaming up shrimp and lobster, oysters and clams—whatever bounty the sea has to offer."

Ana stared out the window at the ocean. Dusk had descended over the water in a rainbow of pastel hues—some pinks and reds here, and a few mauves and blues there. The water washed against the ancient remains of the old pier, slapping against the aged wood pilings in an ever-changing, but never-ending melody of life. And what was left of the pier looked somehow symbolic of that life. The thick beams and timbers lay at a haphazard angle, cross-ways and sideways, like a pile of kindling, stopped in time in mid-collapse.

Ana thought that her own life seemed like that— at times she felt about to fall apart at any minute, but at other times, she dug in, refusing to give up in spite of being beaten down at every turn.

She looked back over at Rock. "I guess I can understand why they left it that way. It's a reminder of sorts."

"Exactly," he said, bobbing his head, a bitter-sweet smile crinkling his dark-skinned face. "My mother even did a sculpture based on that pier. She called it *The Resurrection* because the cross-beams of some of the pilings made her think of a cross. She made it out of wood and iron, with a waterfall flowing through it to represent the ocean and life."

"Where is this sculpture now?" Ana asked. "I imagine some collector snatched it up right away, but I don't recall seeing it in any of the trade catalogues or art books."

Rock's eyes darkened again and the smile disappeared from his face. "You probably never saw it because it wasn't for sale. But someone *acquired* the piece, anyway, many years after she'd finished it. Locked it away in a garden behind his fancy mansion up on the bluffs."

Sensing that Rock didn't approve of this particular art collector, Ana leaned forward. "Isn't that a good thing? That your mother sold the piece, I mean?"

He lifted his chin. "Normally, yeah, that's good, selling a fine piece of art. But she didn't get a very good price for what she had to give up."

And that's all he said. Wondering why he insisted on talking in riddles, Ana watched as he took a long swallow of his iced tea. "Rock," she said, "did I ask the wrong question?"

Rock glanced over at her as if he'd forgotten

she was even there. "No, nothing like that. Let's change the subject."

Ana again got the impression that Rock somehow resented his mother's art. Maybe because it had taken his mother away from him and his brothers? It was a known fact in local art circles that Eloise Dempsey was a woman driven by her talent, a woman who had worked long and hard to become a successful force in the art world. It was also known, from various interviews and articles written about Eloise, that her relationship with her three grown sons was difficult. And even though Eloise knew exactly what to say in order to protect her privacy, she still managed, when necessary, to get a good sound bite on the evening news.

Deciding to venture forth, Ana said, "You know, Rock, I've read articles in the trade magazines about your mother. Being an artist is never easy. The art demands a lot, but you and Eloise seem so close. She brags on you—on all of her sons—and she did recommend you to me."

Rock held his tea glass in one hand while he watched the waves crashing against the seawall and pier outside. "We've managed to stay on good terms over the years, in spite of what the media might say. And in spite of what the world doesn't know or see."

Thinking he wasn't going to elaborate, Ana could only nod and sit silently. She didn't want to appear nosy, yet she yearned to understand what had brought that darkness to his beautiful eyes. "It must have been hard on all of you, losing your father when you were so young."

"It was tough," Rock finally said. "For a long time, we didn't understand why he had to die out there doing what he loved best, shrimping." He glanced out at the water again. "But then 'deep calleth unto deep' or so the scripture says."

"Did he die in a storm?"

"Yes." Rock nodded toward the toppled pilings. "The very same hurricane that took that pier."

Ana let out a little gasp that caused him to look across the space between them. "I'm sorry, Rock. Is that why you don't want to talk about the sculpture?"

He sighed, kept staring at her, his eyes now as dark and unreadable as the faraway waters over the distant horizon. "It's not the sculpture, Ana. It's the fact that my mother designed it out of grief and sorrow and made it into a beautiful symbol of redeeming love. She didn't sell the sculpture. She gave it to…someone who doesn't really appreciate it."

"Can you tell me who?"

Rock set his glass on the table, then folded his hands together across the white linen tablecloth. "I can tell you exactly who, and exactly why. My mother gave that sculpture to my brother Stone. And she gave it to him as a way of asking his forgiveness. Stone took the sculpture, but he has yet to forgive my mother…or me."

* * *

Ana had many more questions, but decided they had to wait. She wouldn't press Rock into talking about his obviously strained relationship with his middle brother, Stone. From what Ana knew, each of the three Dempsey brothers was successful in his own right. But Stone Dempsey was probably the most successful, business-and-money-wise. She'd read somewhere a few years ago that Stone had bought Hidden Hill, a big stucco and stone turn-of-the-century mansion sitting atop the highest bluff on the island, not far from the West Island Lighthouse. But the mansion was crumbling around its foundations, from what Ana had heard. Which meant Stone had to have a lot of money to pour into restoration and renovations, at least.

Did Rock resent his brother's success?

As they strolled along the shoreline heading back to Rock's car, Ana couldn't picture this quiet, talented man resenting anyone because of money. Rock seemed content enough. He had a lovely cottage near the Ankle Curve and he had his little church. He had his own talent, too. His cabinetry work was exquisite. His restoration of old pieces was precise and loving. Based on his ideas, he would turn her kitchen into a functional, but charming, workplace.

So what was eating at this gentle preacher? Ana wondered.

"I guess you're wondering why I said that about

Stone," Rock told her as he took her hand and guided her a few yards away from the pier and the restaurant to a craggy rock that looked like a ready-made bench.

"You don't have to explain," she said, taking in their surroundings. Seagulls lifted out overhead, searching for tidbits from the diners strolling along the boardwalk and dunes. "I have…a very delicate relationship with my sister, so you're allowed the same with your brother."

"Stone…is bitter," Rock said. "He blames my mother for our being so poor when we were growing up. You see, she gave up her inheritance to marry our father. His name was Tillman. Everyone called him Till. Till Dempsey, a kid from the wrong side of Savannah. He had the audacity to fall in love with the beautiful debutante from one of the oldest families in Savannah." He pointed to the big curved rock. "And he brought Eloise here to propose to her. It's an island tradition."

A marker sign standing beside the rock stated that this was the Wedding Rock, a place where down through the centuries, sailors and fishermen had proposed to their true loves before heading out to sea. The sign also said that often couples got married here in front of the rock, their faces turned toward the ocean as they pledged their love.

"My parents were so in love, they didn't care about all that old money back in Savannah. But when my father died, my grandparents tried to make amends. They wanted us to come live with them in Savannah, but on their terms, of course. My mother refused to conform, so we stayed here in what was once the family vacation home, the house she lives in now—the only thing she accepted from her parents—and that was just so we'd have a roof over our heads. Stone got angry with her for refusing their help and their money, and I guess he never got over it. I tried to make him see that we didn't need them, but he was just twelve years old—you know, that age where peer pressure makes life so hard.

"The other kids teased us because we wore old clothes and couldn't afford the things they took for granted. Stone resented our mother for that. I rode him pretty hard back then, trying to make him see that we were going to be okay. But we weren't okay, really, and I guess I wasn't the easiest person to live with. Stone hasn't forgotten. It's not something we like to talk about."

Ana finished reading the historical marker, then turned to Rock. "If you don't like talking about this, why did you bring me here to this particular restaurant?"

"The food is good," he said with logical clarity.

"But the memories—"

"Won't go away," he finished as he tugged her down on the smooth surface of the rock. "The memories are scattered all over this island, so I quit fighting them long ago."

Ana settled down beside him, then held her face up to catch the soft ocean breeze. The wind felt cool on her heated skin, felt good blowing over her hair. "So we both have painful memories. Why is it so hard to let go, Rock?"

"I don't know," he said, his eyes open and honest. "I read a quote once about old memories and young hope. I guess we cling to the sadness of the past in hopes that something better will come along and change the future."

"You have a good memory for quotes, at least," she said, smiling. "I like that."

"Really?" He lifted a dark brow, tilting his head toward her. "Most women find my quotes—and me—stuffy and old-fashioned."

"I'm an old-fashioned kind of girl, remember?"

"Yes, I do recall." He leaned back against the veined rock. "And I apologize. We didn't get to discuss business very much."

"We'll have tomorrow for business," she said. Then she ran a hand over the gray-blue rock formation. "The Wedding Rock—very romantic. I bet there are a lot of memories here."

He nodded, his eyes shimmering a deep, dark blue. "And young hope for new, better memories to come. Maybe that's why I keep coming back to this spot."

Wondering why he had taken Ana to that sad, old pier, Rock walked Ana inside her house, then checked around to make sure everything was intact.

"We rarely have any crime here on the island," he told her, hoping to reassure her. "We have a two-man police department and I think they mostly play cards and watch television all day. Or rescue a cat from a tree here and there." Then he grinned. "Besides, you strike me as a capable, independent woman."

"I already have a security system in place," she told him as she hit buttons on the code box on the hallway wall. "I learned the hard way in Savannah—my apartment got robbed once."

Rock waited, wondering what he should do or say. He was uncomfortable now that he'd revealed some of his family secrets to Ana. But she didn't seem to be holding that against him. Thinking it might be best if he just went on home, he said, "About those plans—I'll come by first thing in the morning with some sketches and ideas. I think we can have your cabinets renovated and your pantry shelves built right on time."

"Good," she said as she automatically checked the phone sitting lonely and misplaced on the hallway floor. "Oh, I have a message. Do you mind if I check it?"

"Go ahead. I need to be going, anyway."

He was about to leave, but she held up a hand while she waited for the recorder.

A feminine voice said, "Hi, Ana. It's me. Listen, I really need your help. I have to do some extensive traveling this summer—we're working on buying up a big spot of land near Atlanta for development. This just came up and I'm still trying to sell that land I own over near Savannah, so I was wondering if…well, I might need your help with the girls. I'll call you back tomorrow."

Rock watched as Ana's expression went from mild interest to a keen awareness. She seemed to stiffen, her eyes glazing over with what looked like dread. "Everything okay?" he asked, to break the silence that creaked through the old house.

Ana sighed, clicked the delete button on the message machine. "That was my sister, Tara," she said. "I have a feeling I'm about to be hit up to baby-sit all summer."

"And open a new business, too? That might be hard."

"Tara doesn't stop to think about things like that. She's a workaholic—so she expects everyone else to be the same. The only problem is, since her husband died, she's poured herself into her work even more, and now, I'm afraid she's neglecting her three daughters."

"Reminds me of my mother—and Stone, too," Rock said before thinking. "Not that he's married with children. But he works 24/7. Guess he did get a couple of my mother's traits."

"Maybe we should introduce Tara and him," Ana said with a skeptical smile. Then she added, "Don't get me wrong. Tara loves her girls. It's just been…hard on all of us since Chad died. I don't think Tara even realizes that the girls are still grieving, too. They are acting out in all sorts of ways, but she can't seem to connect on why."

"I'm sorry to hear that," Rock said, coming to lean on the wall opposite her. "But it sounds very familiar. Our mother at least understood…when our father died. She tried to comfort us, but then she got caught up in her work and we somehow learned to fend for ourselves most days. I don't know, though, if a child ever gets over that kind of grief."

Ana nodded. "That's the way it's been with the girls lately. All teenagers now, too."

"Wow. And she's going to pass them off on you?"

"I love them. And Tara doesn't trust anyone else. My parents are at that age where they travel a lot, when they aren't sick or volunteering. The girls can be a handful, so they can't keep them for more than a few days at a time. And Chad's parents live out in Texas—Ana won't let the girls go that far away over the summer. She's there with them now, for a short visit, but I doubt the girls will want to stay in Texas all summer. That leaves me, I guess."

"And me," Rock heard himself saying. "Listen, Ana, this is small island. Everyone knows everyone. We all watch out for each other. We can help with the girls."

She looked up at him, awe sparkling in her green eyes. "You'd do that…for me?"

"Of course. Mother would love it, too, I'm sure.

They can swim, run around the village, learn to make pottery. There's lots to entertain teenagers here."

"You haven't met these three yet—they are eleven, thirteen and fourteen—going on thirty."

Rock leaned forward, taking in the sight of Ana standing there in the semidarkness, her fiery hair wind-tossed, the scent of the ocean still surrounding her. "If they are anything like their aunt, I can't wait to meet them."

Ana moved away, ran a hand through her hair. "Well, I have to think long and hard about this, but not tonight. It's getting late. And we have lots of work to do tomorrow."

Rock followed her to the front door. "Back to business, right?"

"Yes, business is what brought me here. But I did enjoy dinner."

"Even though I told you all about the Dempsey family dysfunctions?"

"Every family has dysfunctions, as you can see from my sister's phone call."

"Maybe so. But, Ana, I want you to understand. I love my mother and my brothers—they mean the world to me. And since becoming a minister, I've learned we can't control other people. We can only control how we react to them, and we have to leave the rest in God's hands."

She glanced down at the phone. "It's hard to do that."

"Yes, it is. But we can do the next-best thing. We love them—unconditionally, sometimes with trepidation, sometimes with a bit of anger and resentment, but always, knowing that if family needs us, we have to come through."

"Like me, with my sister? I should tell her yes, bring the girls to me?"

"If that's what you want to do in your heart."

"I love those three. I've always wanted children."

"You might be the best thing for them right now. A good, positive role model."

"Me?" She scoffed, shook her head. "I'm just their old-maid aunt who loves art and reading and cooking. I'm the plain sister, Rock, in case you haven't figured that out yet."

He leaned close again, one hand on the old brass doorknob. "Oh, I've figured out a lot of things about you, Ana. And I'm looking forward to working through the rest."

He heard her sigh.

"The rest?"

"The rest of what makes Ana Hanson such an interesting, pretty woman."

"Interesting and pretty describes my outgoing, dynamic sister, not me."

"I don't recall asking you about your sister. I'm only interested in getting to know you. And you are by no means plain."

"Really, Rock, there's not much to me."

Rock reached up, pushed at a burnished curl clinging to her cheek. "There's more than you know, Ana. Much more."

Ana stepped back, away from his touch. "Remember, you were hired to work on restoring my cabinets, not me."

Rock could tell she was scared, uncomfortable. He felt much the same way. And he still wasn't sure where all of this might lead. "Fair enough," he said. "But I've learned something about restoration over the years. Sometimes, if we keep polishing and pampering, we find true treasures underneath all the dirt and dust and neglect."

"You're talking in riddles again."

"I'm telling it like it is," he replied as he backed out the door. "You are a treasure, Ana. And somebody needs to show you that."

She just smiled and said, "Thank you. You're awfully sweet to try and make me feel better."

Then she closed the door. Rock could hear the *click* of the lock, effectively shutting him out of her life for now.

"You should feel better," he thought. "Someone needs to show you how special you are." Rock decided that he was just the man for the job.

Chapter Four

"I invited Ana to dinner tonight—with you and me."

Rock stared across the workshop at his mother. "That explains this surprise visit."

Eloise rarely came to his workshop. She rarely left the compound of her home and studio. And she never cooked. Her groceries, housekeeping and other essentials, including real cooked meals, were now taken care of by a capable couple that lived in a small cottage near her property.

Rock had been pleased, but curious, when his mother had waltzed into the workshop this morning. Now he understood, of course. Eloise was up to matchmaking again.

"What if I have plans?"

"You never have plans, Rock. When was the last time you actually dated anyone?"

He had to stop and think. "I paid a visit to a single woman just the other night."

Eloise lifted a finger, wagging it at him. "You've been watching wrestling on Saturday nights with old Miss McPherson again, haven't you, son? That doesn't count."

"Okay, it's been a while. But you know how it is, Mom. I work."

Eloise picked up a plywood pattern. "Getting in your digs early today?"

"I'm sorry. Like mother, like son, I reckon. I guess I have been working too hard lately. What time is dinner? And what is Neda cooking?"

Eloise smiled at that. "Around seven, and we're having a picnic out on the grounds—barbecued chicken, potato salad, the works. Ana told me once she loved picnics."

"I'll keep that in mind," Rock replied while he set his router flush with the base of a piece of wood, then lined up for the cut. Dropping his protective goggles on, he proceeded to cut the fresh-smelling walnut wood.

Eloise waited patiently, her hands folded over the front of her long linen skirt. When Rock had finished, she said, "Is that for Ana's kitchen?"

"Yep. I'm having to replace some of the original wood—the back sections of some of the cabinets just aren't sturdy anymore. Not to mention that most of the upper units need reinforcement." He lifted his head toward the sections of what would soon be an island station in the kitchen. "Don Ashworth and his son, Cal, have been helping me with that monster. But they took the morning off— Cal's getting his driver's license."

Eloise said, "Oh, I saw Greta Epperson at the town hall meeting about the lighthouse fund-raiser. She said rumor has it you and Ana were having dinner at the Sunken Pier a couple of nights ago."

Rock lifted his gaze to the heavens. "Oh, great. I guess that news flash will grace the gossip page in this week's paper. And it probably won't matter that it was a *business* dinner."

Eloise chuckled, then eyed the pieces that had yet to be put together inside Ana's house. "Not to Greta. She loves trailing a good story and embellishing on the facts. And speaking of business, you're doing a good job, according to Ana."

"She hasn't complained so far. Besides, she's been busy training her staff and testing recipes. She's got to get her menu down just right—she's a stickler for details."

"I want to hear the details of how things are progressing between you two, and I don't mean the working relationship. I'd rather hear it from you than that pesky Greta."

Staying tight-lipped, Rock picked up a hand plane and started passing it over a piece of wood he'd shaped into a crown molding. He wasn't about to go into detail about Ana with his overly inquisitive mother.

Yet Eloise asked, anyway. "Do you like her?"

Pretending to misunderstand, Rock nodded toward the new cabinets. "This one—she's coming along nicely."

Eloise scoffed, kicked at sawdust. "You know perfectly well I'm not talking about cabinets. How are things with Ana?"

Rock stopped the pressure he'd been applying to the hand plane. "Things with Ana are... business as usual."

He wouldn't tell Eloise that the week he'd spent working for Ana had left him disturbed and excited. He liked knowing Ana was in the next room, working, sometimes humming, at her desk. He liked hearing her laughing and talking with her two capable sidekicks, Jackie and Tina. He enjoyed hearing the women talk about their families and their stressful days. He even enjoyed trying to figure out the secret codes women use to convey message. He suspected, from some of the sly, smiling looks the women gave him in passing, that some of those codes were used to throw him off. Or maybe drive him crazy.

But Rock didn't ask for explanations. He worked silently, or with Don and Cal by his side. He worked steadily, since they only had a few weeks left before the opening. He couldn't tell his mother that he went to bed each night with the scent of Ana's floral perfume wafting through his senses. He couldn't explain that when he went down to the beach for a midnight run, his thoughts always turned to the time he'd spent in Ana's kitchen, measuring and hammering, tearing out and replacing.

And the whole time, he'd felt as if he'd been tearing away at his own old hurts and replacing them with something good and pure. Only, other than cooking him wonderful, dainty lunches so she could test her menu, Ana was keeping her distance. And keeping busy.

Which meant he couldn't wait to see her tonight at dinner. But he didn't dare tell his mother that.

Eloise was watching him in that calm, disconcerting way she had. It was the same way in which she'd stare at a piece of ancient wood or jagged stone and see things no one else could even begin to imagine. Rock wondered what she saw when she looked at him.

"Mother, I'll be there. So you can quit glaring at me."

"I love your face," his mother said. "You have a noble face, Rock."

"Thank you."

"You don't want to talk to me, do you."

"I'm busy, is all. Got to finish these pieces and get started on a few others. Time marches on."

"You don't like me interfering."

"Never have."

"I've tried to stay out of your love life, but there's something about Ana."

Rock wiped the sweat off his brow, then looked at his mother. "On that, at least, we can agree."

"Then, you do…like her?"

"We're not going steady yet, but yes, I like her."

"So a mother can hope."

The old anger surfaced as quickly and swiftly as a rebel wave hitting the shore. "Why does this matter so much to you, anyway?"

Eloise's stark eyes opened wide. Rock saw the mist of tears there. "I know I failed you, Rock. I was…alone, afraid, obsessed with making a name for myself. I…believe God has given me another chance. I intend to see that chance through."

"By pushing your oldest, bachelor son off on the first woman who shows him the slightest hint of attention?"

"You've dated other women, so don't put yourself down." She shook her head. "I'm just hoping and praying that you and Ana make a good match. I want you to be happy, truly happy, and Ana seems perfect for you. Everyone should have the chance to know pure happiness in their life."

Rock saw the light leave his mother's beautiful eyes, and he knew she was remembering. He hated himself for being harsh with her. He couldn't touch her. He couldn't bring himself to hug her. But he did give her his full attention. "I'd like that, Mother. I'd like to have that just once in my life."

Eloise's expression changed to a smile. "I'll see you at seven, then."

* * *

Ana stepped out of her car, a warm apple pie in one hand and her crocheted purse in the other. Closing the car door with a sandaled foot, she stared up at the imposing Victorian beach house that sat nestled underneath billowing live oaks across from the sandy curve of the shore.

The house was an aged white, battered from years of tropical winds and salty mists. Its shutters were a muted gray, its many lace-curtained windows thrown open to the sea. Around back, past the sandy, shell-covered drive, stood Eloise's studio.

She heard laughter coming from the garden, so Ana headed through the carriage drive on the side of the house to find Eloise and Rock talking with another, older couple.

Eloise turned as she heard the crunch of Ana's footsteps. "Ana! You made it."

"And brought pie," Rock said, his smile gentle, his eyes keen on her.

Ana managed a shaky smile, and wondered why she'd gone to such great pains with her appearance. Upswept hair, a sundress with brilliant tropical flowers splashed across its gathered skirts, a dash of lipstick and perfume. From the look in Rock's eyes, she'd done a passable job, at least. That pleased and aggravated her at the same time.

But then, this past week had been full of such moments—sweet and torturing all at the same time.

She had found herself, on more than one occasion, stopping to watch Rock while he worked. He'd looked like every woman's dream in his faded T-shirt and even more faded jeans, his heavy work boots clunking on her polished floors, his dark, curling hair sprinkled with sawdust.

"Why do carpenters always look so yummy?" Jackie had asked just yesterday, grinning.

"And they are so good with their hands," Tina, petite and buxom, had said through a sigh.

"Why don't you two get back to work?" Ana had retorted, her own smile belying the stern tone in her voice. She had to agree with her new helpers. Rock looked good working, and he felt good each time his fingers brushed over hers in passing or his arm touched hers as they met in the doorway.

But what Ana had enjoyed the most didn't really have anything to do with Rock's physical appearance. It was his eyes, his facial expressions, that tugged at her heart and made her want to get to know him better. He'd go from intense concentration to thoughtful contemplation, his blue eyes changing color like a sea in the sun with each new calculation, with each touch of hammer to nail. Rock truly loved his work. And it showed in the beautiful cabinets he was recreating in her kitchen.

"Want me to take that?" he asked now, bringing Ana out of her thoughts.

She glanced down at the pie she still held in one hand. "Oh, yes. Thanks."

"Smells wonderful," he said under his breath, his eyes on her instead of the pie.

Ana allowed a little shiver of pure delight to move like falling mist down her spine. Rock flirted in such a subtle, quiet way, it sometimes took her a few minutes to even realize he *was* doing it. But he was doing it—flirting with her. And tonight, she intended to enjoy it.

"We're eating in the garden," Eloise told her as she guided Ana to a lacy black wrought-iron table and matching chairs centered near a cluster of vivid red-tipped firebush.

As Ana glanced around, a hummingbird buzzed near the tall, bright shrubs. "It's such a lovely night."

"Yes, it is," Rock said, his gaze once again moving over Ana's face and hair. "You look great."

"Thanks." She hated the way she automatically patted at her hair.

He just stood there, his hands in the pockets of his khaki walking shorts. The man sure cleaned up nicely. The light blue polo shirt only made his eyes seem darker. And he didn't smell half-bad himself—like the sea on a fresh crisp morning.

Ana swallowed, dropped her purse on the nearest chair. "What can I do to help with dinner?"

Eloise motioned to the man and woman hovering over the smoking grill. "Not a thing. Neda and Cy Wilson, meet Ana Hanson. Ana, these two are the cooks around here."

"Among other things," Rock said with a wry smile.

Ana waved to the couple. "Hello."

They both shouted a greeting.

"Hope you're hungry," Cy said, his jovial grin full of leathery wrinkles. "Neda cooked enough for a small army."

"I'll do my best to eat my fair share," Ana replied.

Neda, a short, gray-haired woman, nodded. "You look like you could use a good meal."

Rock laughed, his glance moving over Ana. "Ana happens to be a very good cook herself."

Neda came over to stand by them. "I hear you're opening a tea room. That sounds lovely."

Ana immediately felt at home with the tiny woman. "I hope it will be a hit. The island seemed like the perfect spot, based on our research."

"We get a lot of tourists, of course," Cy said as he lifted the grill lid to check on the sizzling chicken. "The ladies should like that. Shopping and lunch—ain't that what women like most?"

Eloise waved a hand. "Not all the time. Believe it or not, some women actually prefer work to shopping and eating."

"I sure hope not all of them. I need customers," Ana replied, acutely aware of Rock's gaze as he looked with a frown from his mother to her. She always got a strange, unsettling impression whenever she talked about her ambitions with him.

He seemed interested, yet she sensed a hesitation in him, as if he wasn't quite listening. Did Rock disapprove of a woman in business?

It didn't matter if he approved or not. She was in this for the duration and she had to make it work—she had to make a living somehow. She'd wagered everything on this venture, including giving in to her sister's insistence that Ana let her help finance the whole thing. Ana wouldn't be able to hold her head up if she failed Tara. In spite of their often strained relationship, she loved her sister.

That made her think about the girls.

Rock touched her arm. "Have you decided?"

"About what?"

"About your nieces coming for the summer."

"Can you read my mind?"

He gave her a long, measuring look, as if he truly were trying to do just that. "No. It's just that we talked about this earlier, after you got another phone call, remember? You were worried then, and you have that same look on your face now."

"I do remember," she replied, thinking back to her long conversation with Tara earlier today. "And yes, I guess I've decided. My sister came through for me with the financing of the tea room. I intend to come through for her and the girls. Tara needs my help now more than ever."

"You're a good sister."

"No, not really. Just trying to make amends."

"Now, what could you possibly have to make amends for?"

"You'd be surprised."

He grinned, offered her a tall glass of tea with lemon. "You do have that tendency to…surprise me, that is. Take tonight, for example. I was sure you wouldn't show up."

"And why wouldn't I?" She took a drink of the syrupy sweet tea, glad for the liquid on her suddenly dry throat.

"Business, remember?" He winked, lowered his voice. "In case you haven't noticed, my dear mother is trying very hard to throw us together. I've tried to explain we have a good, solid *working* relationship. Wouldn't want to ruin that."

His eyes indicated that he'd love to ruin that.

Ana set her glass down. She didn't miss the bit of sarcasm in his words. "So because of that, you thought I'd refuse to come to dinner? You thought maybe I'd just work straight through the weekend?"

"Yep. You've made it pretty clear—"

"A girl has to eat."

"And a girl shouldn't be all alone on a warm Friday night."

"True." She pushed at her hair, tried to hide her disappointment that he considered their relationship just *working,* that perhaps he considered her a workaholic—then reminded herself that she wanted it that way, too. "As long as we have an understanding," she said, just to back up her feelings.

"We do. Monday through Friday, we work." He leaned close, so close she could smell the scent of sandalwood and spice around him. "But come Friday night, I might be inclined to ask you to take a long stroll along the beach with me after dinner."

His words implied they'd be doing this more often—having dinner together on a Friday night. That left Ana feeling light-headed and more confused than ever. So she tried to counter. "To talk business, right?"

"No, ma'am. Just to talk—about you, about me, about anything but cabinets and remodeling kitchens and opening tea rooms."

"What if we find we have nothing else to talk about?"

"Then, we can do something besides talking, I reckon."

She swallowed again, felt the heat rising up her back in spite of the balmy breeze. "That could… be a serious mistake."

"Could be. Might be pleasant, though."

Ana watched his face—that expressive face that lingered in her mind long after the lights were out. He seemed determined to make her blush, to make her feel things she didn't need to be feeling. Yet he seemed almost to be testing her. Did he find her a challenge? Did he think he could turn her head, make her forget about work and obligations, maybe just to prove a point?

He's a distraction, Ana. A big one. A big, handsome, kind, considerate, intriguing, puzzling, distraction. You don't need that kind of distraction right now. You need to focus on the tea room.

And the girls. They'd be coming next week.

Suddenly, Ana smiled. With three rambunctious, inquisitive teenagers in the house, she wouldn't have time to dream about Rock Dempsey. Even on a lonely Friday night.

"After dinner," he whispered, making her forget everything she'd just thought, as the feather of his words moved over her ear and hair with a heart-stopping warmth.

"What?" she managed to whisper back.

"We're going for that walk on the beach."

"Are you sure that's wise? I mean, won't your mother get the wrong idea?"

"No, I think she'll get the right idea. I have to hand it to her, she's right on target with this one."

"What do you mean?"

"I mean," he said as he reached out a hand to tug her toward the wonderful-smelling food, "she said she hoped we'd make a good match. I'm inclined to agree with her on that. At least, I'm hoping, too."

Ana knew she was crossing a line here. If she let this go any farther, it would be so hard to turn back.

"And…what about our *working* relationship? What if things get messy?"

Rock nudged her toward the table. "Well, there's work and there's play. I try never to confuse the two."

Before Ana could respond, Eloise announced dinner and asked Rock to say grace. A few minutes later, Ana listened to his deep, baritone voice as he thanked God for all their many blessings, and wondered if he'd still feel the same toward her when her work started getting in the way of their play. Would she fail the Rock Dempsey test of the perfect woman?

It didn't matter if he was testing her. It didn't matter that she found him attractive. She had to put her business, and now the girls, first.

And Rock Dempsey would just have to see that, whether he approved or not.

Chapter Five

Rock stood on the steps of the Sunset Chapel, taking in the stormy morning. "Probably won't get many takers today, Lord," he said out loud. It looked like a long, rainy Sunday.

"A good day for a nap," Reverend Pal would have said.

Rock thought about the long day ahead and wondered how Ana would spend it. Now, why did he have to think of her? Why, indeed? Maybe because they *had* gone for that walk on the beach after dinner the other night? Maybe because he'd enjoyed being with her, making her laugh, watching the way the moonlight washed her copper-colored hair in shimmering hues of gold. And maybe because he had issued her a challenge of sorts, a challenge about which he was now having serious doubts.

Rock remembered the feel of her hand in his, the way her expressive green eyes lit up when she smiled. Then he remembered her dogged determination to make her tea room a success. Nothing wrong there, except that he'd vowed not to get involved with a woman too much like his mother.

But was Ana like his mother? Certainly not in looks. Ana was pretty, not in the exotic way Eloise was beautiful, but pretty in a girl-next-door kind of way that Rock liked. Ana could cook, too. That gave her points in Rock's book. But her cooking revolved around her career. He couldn't forget that.

Rock shook his head, glanced up as church members started appearing, some walking underneath umbrellas, others driving to avoid the coming storm.

Greta Epperson greeted him from underneath a bright pansy-bordered umbrella. "Morning, Preacher Rock. How's the cabinet business?"

Her sly grin told him she was fishing for more than an update on his work habits. With her big round black-framed glasses and stark white bobbed hair, she reminded him of an owl.

"Business is good," he told her, smiling. "But then, you probably already know exactly how good, right, Greta?"

"I hear things. Very interesting things." Greta grinned, shook his hand, then went on inside.

His mother walked up, smiled, patted his cheek,

then found a seat near Greta. They whispered and chuckled, their heads close together.

His mother was too smug. It irritated him that he was actually doing something Eloise approved of. Thinking that was no way for a preacher to act, Rock sent up a prayer for patience and forgiveness. He needed to cut his mother some slack. After all, she had three grown sons and wanted them all married with families.

Rock hadn't thought too much about a family. He'd pretty much given up after a few false starts with women who wanted to move to the city. Rock would never leave Sunset Island. He was too set in his ways, and too attached to this place. It would take a special woman to understand and accept that about him.

He thought of Ana. She'd left the city to come to the island. That earned her points, too. Smiling and shaking the hands of more of his congregation, Rock decided he'd better concentrate on his sermon for this morning and quit worrying about his feelings for Ana Hanson. Because right now, it was obvious Ana needed to stay centered on her business. And that made it even more obvious that Rock needed to remember his pledge to never get involved with a career woman. Or a woman in the arts, for that matter.

That was two strikes against Ana.

But when Rock looked up to find her car coming up the winding drive, he felt his heart crash against his rib cage with the ferocity of the distant thunder clashing in the sky. When she got out, all fresh-faced and dressed in a dainty white dress sprinkled with green and blue flowers, Rock couldn't seem to remember exactly why he should steer clear of her.

So he stood there, debating with his soul.

Career woman, art patron, work-focused.

Pretty woman, good cook, great smelling, great smile.

A nice lady.

A nice, available single woman.

A woman who was now smiling at him as she ignored the mist of rain falling around her. *This* version won out. How could he turn away from a woman who didn't seem to mind her hair getting wet?

"Ana," he said in a rush of breath. "Welcome."

"I hope you don't mind," she said as she came up the steps. "I was just feeling so lonely…and even though I have a ton of work to do—"

"It's the Sabbath," Rock said. "You're allowed a day of rest. And I never mind it when I get a prospective new church member."

She stopped on the steps, just underneath the overhang. Rock resisted the urge to reach up and wipe a drop of rain off her curling hair. "I've always attended church on and off," she said, smiling. "I guess I could use some encouragement in that department though."

Waving to other people, Rock guided her through the planked double doors inside the tiny chapel. "Savannah has a lot of gracious, old churches."

Ana nodded, glanced around at the simple furnishings. "This one is as beautiful as any I've seen there," she said, her words hushed, her eyes wide.

"It's been here for centuries," Rock explained. "The pews are made of cypress, as are the beams in the ceiling. If you look very closely up near the altar, you'll find bullet holes from both the Revolutionary War and the Civil War. Even though Savannah fell during the Revolutionary War, toward the end the 'Swamp Fox' outfoxed the British up and down the South Carolina coast and all around these parts. Then, almost a century later, Sherman marched to the sea, and after giving Savannah to Abraham Lincoln as a Christmas present, he allowed some of his soldiers to pass by here on their way back up north. But we're still standing."

"Amazing," Ana said, clearly impressed. "I love the history of this island."

"There's lots more," Rock said, pleased that she was indeed an old-fashioned kind of girl. That got her more points, too. Not that he was keeping a tally. Anyway, he thought to himself, the pros were fast outweighing the cons in this relationship.

Feeling a bit better now, he thought he might be able to handle this, if he kept his head. It wouldn't hurt to keep Ana company, to enjoy picnics and sitting on the beach with her. Wouldn't hurt at all.

"Why are you grinning at me?" Ana asked, causing Rock to snap to attention.

"Was I? I guess I'm just glad you came."

"Your mother suggested I might enjoy one of your sermons."

"Oh, so you only came to please my mother?"

"No. I came because I wanted to. To hear you preach."

"I don't preach, really. Mostly just spout philosophy and couple that with Bible lessons. I'll probably make you to fall asleep."

"I doubt that."

The look she gave him made Rock swallow and stall out. What if Ana took things way more seriously between them than he was planning? What would he do then?

Rock couldn't answer that question. He had to give his sermon. Beside he doubted Ana would have much time for him, what with three girls coming for the summer and Ana opening a new business.

In fact, this relationship should work out perfectly. Ana was too busy for a love life, and Rock, well, he was too wary to let down his guard. They could coast along, as friends and companions, for a very long time. He'd enjoy home-cooked meals, her pretty smile, and knowing he had a friend who would please Eloise enough to keep her off his back. Ana would get companionship, a mentor and a friend, and a man who was determined to respect the boundaries they obviously needed between them. A perfect arrangement.

Almost too perfect, Rock concluded just before he stepped up into the pulpit.

He had looked perfect and sounded even better, Ana thought after Rock had finished his sermon. Was it right and fair that a man of God could dress in a striped polo shirt and casual slacks and still look so fine? Was it good and great that what he said about the wisdom of Psalm 42—the one about hope in God's love—made sense and kept her interest even while she kept wondering what it would be like to kiss him? Did it matter that she'd seen him every day for the past week, but she had to have one more hour with him on Sunday?

Lord forgive me, but that's why I came here.

Ana wasn't proud of that confession, but it was the truth. She'd woken up this morning, restless and blue. Not even working on inventory or polishing already shining furniture had given her any peace.

She'd wanted to see Rock again. And she'd been pleasantly surprised that he had seemed pleased to see *her* again. Ana knew this was tentative. She knew that Rock had reservations about a relationship with her. Well, she felt the same—interested but cautious. Maybe that was the best way to go into this.

Thinking back over the years since she'd been

dumped in college, Ana could see that her dealings with the opposite sex had been pitiful and sad, to say the least. She'd always tried to rush things. That hadn't worked, so she'd given up. Now she was a bit rusty in the dating department. All the more reason to be cautious, but hopeful, just as Rock's sermon had suggested.

"I hope you come back."

The lilting voice beside Ana pulled her back to reality. She turned to find a tiny woman in a big straw hat with a giant sunflower on it staring up at her through eyes surrounded by wrinkles.

"I just might," Ana said, smiling. She took the aged hand the woman extended. "I'm Ana, Ana Hanson."

"The tea room lady," the woman replied, her thin lips pursing as she scrutinized Ana. "The one the preacher there's been seen around the island with."

"Uh, yes, I guess that's me, but—"

"I'm Mildred McPherson. Known Roderick Dempsey since he was knee-high to a June bug. He's a good boy."

Ana had to smile at Rock being called a "boy." "He seems like a good person."

"He watches basketball and wrestling with me on Saturday nights."

"Oh, really?" Sensing a tad of womanly jealousy here, Ana could only nod. "I...didn't realize he's a wrestling fan."

"He mostly just sits there and watches me," the

little old lady said, preening as she touched her hat. "I get a bit carried away."

"I see."

"He's probably afraid I'll have a stroke or something."

"Wouldn't want that."

"Honey, I'll be eighty-one next month. A stroke is the least of my worries. I can assure you, I am fully prepared to meet my Maker."

Completely nonplussed by this tiny dynamo, Ana glanced around, glad to find Rock walking down the aisle toward them.

"I see you've met Milly," he said to Ana.

"Yes. We were just talking about…wrestling."

Rock grinned. "Ah, yes. Milly's one vice."

"I just watch, is all," Milly said, her expression stubborn. "Besides, at my age, there aren't many vices left."

Rock patted the little woman on the back. "Ana, Milly McPherson is one of the finest Christian women you will ever meet. And she can cook like a dream." He motioned to Ana. "Ana can cook, too. You two should compare recipes."

"I'd love that," Ana said, relaxing now that Rock had joined the conversation. "I could put some of your recipes on the menu at the tea room. You'd get full credit, of course."

"I'd expect full credit," Milly retorted. "We might can talk. People do say my Brunswick stew is the best this side of Atlanta."

"Oh, that would make a great dish for winter."

"Or a rainy day like this one," Milly countered. Then she leaned close. "I just happen to have a slow-cooker full back home. You're welcome to come to Sunday dinner and try it for yourself." Then she stretched her head toward Rock. "You too, of course, Preacher."

Ana felt a sudden panic. Another meal with Rock. But then, she would like to test that stew. "That's very kind of you."

"Take it or leave it," Milly replied tartly as she started up the aisle toward the door. "Twelve-thirty sharp—that's when I eat. I have to have my beauty nap, you know."

"We'll be there," Rock called. Then he turned to Ana, a grin splitting his face. "Don't you just love her?"

"Uh…yes, sure," Ana said, smiling. "But is it just me, or does she intimidate everyone?"

"She does, indeed. Crusty and full of a viper's wit, but good as gold. Mildred McPherson was a schoolteacher—retired now, of course. But she has struck fear in the hearts of many an island child, including my brothers and me."

"But you seem close to her now." At his perplexed expression, she added, "Wrestling?"

"Oh, that. I just enjoy watching Milly enjoying herself. I get a kick out of her competitive spirit."

"She made it quite clear your Saturday nights are usually occupied—watching her watch wrestling."

"I just go by to check on her from time to time," he said as they strolled down the aisle. The chapel was empty now. Leading her out onto the porch, Rock turned to lock the door. "Miss McPherson lives down the street from me. She cooks for me, mentors me, fusses at me, and keeps me on the straight and narrow."

"Miss? She's a spinster?"

"Some would say. I prefer calling her a lovely *mature maiden.*"

"Oh, I meant no disrespect. But I can certainly understand why she might not have married."

"Think she scared all of her suitors away?"

"Most definitely."

The rain had stopped, leaving a cool mist in the afternoon air. Ana waited for Rock to finish locking up, then said, "Do you think going to her house for lunch is wise?"

"It's a necessary function of life. George Bernard Shaw said there is no love sincerer than the love of food."

Ana saw the stubborn glint in his eyes and once again got the distinct feeling that he somehow disapproved of her, even when he was flirting.

"My point exactly," she said. "You seem to migrate toward women who can feed you. Should I be worried about that?"

Rock glanced across the narrow ribbon of road between the church and the shore. "Think I'm using you for cooking purposes?"

She thought back on the past week. He'd personally tested every one of her menu recipes, and he'd asked for seconds several times. "Are you?"

He shook his head. "I can't lie. I like a woman who can cook."

Ana put her hands on her hips, a narrow thread of defiance coursing up her spine. Was this it, then? It would certainly explain why she'd felt as if she were being tested.

"Is that a prerequisite?"

"To what?"

"To…dating? Have you been testing me, Rock, to see if I fit your idea of what a woman should be?"

"What if it is? What if I have? Would that be a problem for you?"

"I don't know. You said there's work and there's play, and you never confuse the two. But I think you are confused about me. My cooking is my work. And I don't like being used…while you play."

"I didn't say that. You have misunderstood the situation. And besides, *you* offered me samples of everything you cooked. Are you mad about that now?"

Whirling in a stance of feminine fire, she said, "No, not at all, since we obviously aren't *dating*. I'm just glad I found this out now."

He was right behind her. "Good, I'm glad, too. A man has a right to demand some things in life."

She pivoted and butted right into his chest. "*Demand?* Did you say *demand?*"

"I believe so, yes."

"So you're telling me that you will demand a woman knows how to cook before you'll even consider—"

He gave a gentle tug, pulling her so close that she could see the flecks of black in his blue eyes. "Before I'd consider dating her…kissing her, maybe?"

His gaze moved from her eyes to her mouth.

Ana's breath lodged inside her throat. "What if I told you I wouldn't dream of dating, much less *kissing,* a man who'd make such a demand?"

His eyes still on her lips, he said, "I guess that wouldn't matter, since we're not dating. And since I'm not about to kiss you."

Disappointment overtook fury in Ana's heart. "Oh, well then—"

Before she could finish, he did kiss her. His mouth came down on hers like rain hitting sand, fast and swift. At first Ana tried to pull away, but his hands on her back held her still. And the feel of his lips on hers held her suspended between want and need, between rage and calm. She returned the kiss with one of her own.

Just to show him she could do more than cook.

Until Rock lifted his head and stared down at her as if she'd bitten him.

"What—" Ana asked, breathless.

"I am so sorry," he said, backing away. "I don't know what came over me."

Ana stepped back too, fists at her side. "It's all right. It...I...we...I'd better just go on home."

"What about Miss McPherson's stew?"

Just like a man to think of food—especially *this* man.

She turned, her head down in mortification. She'd certainly lost her appetite. "I'll taste the stew another time." He regretted kissing her. Rock regretted his actions. Well, shouldn't she regret it, too?

No, I can't regret something that felt so good, so right, she thought bitterly. But she knew it could never happen again. Rock obviously had some issues to work through and she didn't have time to help him.

"Ana?"

She heard Rock calling her, but Ana kept walking to her car, wet sand kicking up with each step to smear on her bare legs.

"Ana, come back, please?"

Ana couldn't look at him.

She opened the car door, only to have it slammed shut by a big, strong hand.

"Ana," he said, her name like a plea on the wind. "Ana, I'm sorry."

"Would you just stop apologizing," she said. "Look, it's bad enough that we got in a fight over who does the cooking. And it's even worse that you were forced to kiss me to prove a point."

"I wasn't trying to prove anything," Rock said,

his hand on her arm, his eyes holding hers. "Look, I'm a big dolt, okay? I'm too old-fashioned for my own good."

"Because you *demand* that a woman should cook for you?"

He winced. "You make me sound like a male chauvinist monster."

"Not a monster, Rock. And I know you're not a male chauvinist. Just a man who knows what he wants in a relationship. No shame in that."

But she could see the shame in his eyes. He looked so sheepish, Ana instantly wished she could just fall through the earth. "Honestly, it's good to know where we stand. At least now I know what to expect. Not that I expected anything."

Could this get any worse?

It did.

Rain started coming down in mean, stinging drops. Huge, mad drops. Before she even thought of getting the car door open, Ana was soaked.

"Now look what you've done!" she shouted to Rock.

"Me?" He held his hands in the air. "Believe it or not, Ana, although I might make certain demands, I can't bring about rain with the snap of my fingers."

"Well, you have connections up there, don't you?" she asked, pointing a dripping wet finger toward the dark heavens.

"Not that kind," Rock countered. Then he

reached for her hand. "Let's get inside, out of this storm, okay?"

"Good idea." She turned for her car. "I'm going home—to fix my own lunch."

Rock tugged her around. "No, come on inside, to my house."

"I will not."

"You're getting soaked."

"I don't care. I can dry off at home."

"Ana, please. So I can explain."

"There is nothing to explain. You've made yourself perfectly clear. Since I've met you, I've felt you've been judging me, testing me in some way. Now I know you were only trying to find out what I had in my pantry."

He looked dazed for a minute. "But you *like* to cook."

"Yes, I do," she said over the sound of pelting rain. "But that doesn't mean I want a man telling me I *have* to do it."

"Women," Rock said, dragging her by the hand toward his cottage. "You have to listen to reason."

"Let me go!"

"I will not let you go home mad and wet."

Stomping up onto his porch, Ana pushed drenched hair off her face. "You probably just want me to come inside to fix your Sunday dinner!"

Groaning in frustration, Rock yanked her into his arms, bringing her clinging-clothed body close to his. "I only want you here for one reason, Ana."

And then he showed her that reason.

He kissed her again, wet lips to wet lips.

Ana sighed and fell against him, a soft, radiating warmth spreading through her heart.

Well, at least he wasn't thinking about food *right now.*

Chapter Six

Food was the farthest thing from Rock's mind. But he was preparing lunch for Ana, anyway. And wondering the whole time why he'd gone and done a foolish thing like kiss the woman.

Maybe because she made him mad and glad at the same time. Maybe because he'd wanted to kiss her, even when he was trying to reason with her. And he *would* make her listen to reason, Rock thought as he slapped together bread and chicken salad.

That is, if she ever came out of the bathroom.

After their second kiss out on the porch, he'd finally convinced her to come inside, out of the cold and wet. She'd been shivering—maybe from the rain, maybe because their kiss seemed to affect her just as much as it had him—Rock couldn't be sure. And he wasn't too sure about where they might go from here. But he did know he'd made a big mess of things and he still had work to do at Ana's place. He wanted to smooth things out, so they wouldn't have any more scenes such as this.

If she ever spoke to him again.

A few minutes later, the door down the hall opened and Ana emerged, dressed in his heavy bathrobe, her damp hair combed and her face fresh-scrubbed. "Thanks...for the robe," she said timidly, her eyes downcast.

"You're welcome," he said, his eyes on her in his robe. Maybe he should have had her put on a shirt and some sweat pants instead. The faded blue robe swallowed her and made her look sweet and vulnerable. And *kissable.*

And he couldn't kiss her again.

Help me, Lord, Rock silently prayed, appealing to heaven for strength. He'd made two big mistakes today. One, implying he needed a woman who could cook for him, and two, kissing the very woman who could cook for him, but didn't want to.

And forcing her to come inside his cottage to get into dry clothes had been an even worse decision.

"Go on into the den," he said, his back turned. "I built a fire. This rain has brought a chill to the air."

"Thank you."

He didn't dare turn around. Instead he waited, holding his breath and wondering if he'd done the right thing by bringing Ana here. Then he heard her sharp intake of breath.

Rock couldn't take it anymore. Picking up the tray of sandwiches and fruit, he hurried into the wide, multi-windowed den that allowed a sweeping view of the distant ocean.

And found Ana clutching her hands to his robe as if the material were a lifeboat. She turned at the sound of his footfalls. Turned and sent him a look somewhere between amazement and frustration. "What have you done?"

Rock shrugged, wishing he knew how to handle her. "My mother told me you like picnics. So I—"

"Made a picnic," she said, finishing his sentence. "Right here on the floor in front of the fire."

"Yeah." He looked down at the checkered blanket and tattered tapestry throw pillows he'd tossed down on the wooden floor. He'd grabbed the flowers from the porch—thank goodness Miss McPherson insisted on bringing him geraniums—and he'd strewn the mismatched plates, silverware and chipped glasses in what he hoped was a passable setting. He'd finished it off with a battered, sputtering candle he'd used a few weeks ago when the electricity had gone out, as it often did during rainstorms.

"Why did you do this?"

Her question was accusing, suspicious.

Rock felt as he'd been pinned to the wall. "I…I felt bad about our…misunderstanding. I wanted to make it up to you."

She glanced at the tray of food in his hands. "What's that?"

"Chicken-salad sandwiches. Some grapefruit and orange sections. A couple of strawberries, and some cheese." He shrugged. "It's not much, but the chicken salad is fresh."

Ana eyed his concoction with a look of disdain. "Did you make it yourself?"

Rock brought the tray to the wooden coffee table. "As a matter of fact, I did. Canned chicken, walnuts and celery. A little mayonnaise and a touch of mustard."

Ana sniffed the air, her chin lifted. "Sounds okay."

"Then, have a seat on the blanket," Rock replied, knowing he sounded as curt and distant as she seemed.

The phone rang, and, glad for the distraction, Rock grabbed it from its cradle on the hallway table. "Hello?"

It was Miss McPherson. "You're late."

Rock glanced at Ana. "Uh, we had a bit of a problem. We got soaked in the rainstorm. Decided to just have a sandwich here instead. Sorry I didn't call. I got busy—"

"You like her, don't you."

He took a breath, willed himself to say the right thing. "I'm not sure about that, but we'll see."

"Yep, you got it bad. Must have put you in a regular tizzy. You never pass up my Brunswick stew."

Rock winced, wondering if Ana was right about

him, after all. Maybe he did only hang around women who could feed him, regardless of their age or status. But, stubbornly, he refused to change now.

"Save me a bowlful?"

"I'll put you a pint or two in the freezer. Goodbye."

The dial tone tolled like a ship horn in Rock's head. Replaying the phone in its cradle, he turned back to Ana. "Milly is going to save us some stew."

"That's nice."

He hated the civility of this conversation, hated the stilted way Ana was holding herself, all stiff-backed and proper. He'd much rather have her ranting at him with that green fire in her eyes. He'd much rather be kissing her again.

"Are you going to eat?" he asked, hurt by the way she kept staring at the food.

"I'm not very hungry."

Letting out a breath, Rock grabbed her by the arms. "Ana, sit down, please. I need to…explain."

She looked at him then, her eyes full of doubt. "You don't need to explain, Rock. I understand things now."

"Oh, really?"

"Yes. I've felt it, seen it in your eyes. You disapprove of me. But you have to finish the work at my tea room. I only hope you can tolerate me enough to do the job."

"I'd never leave a job unfinished," he said, affronted that she'd even suggest such a thing.

"But you don't approve of me, do you?"

"Ana, sit."

She slumped onto the blanket, pushed at the sleeves of the big robe, then stared up at him.

Rock settled down beside her, his gaze moving to the fire. "When I was growing up, my mother was always working. We missed out on a lot of home-cooked meals and time together as a family because her art always took precedence over anything or anyone else."

Ana sat very still, staring at him. "Do you think I'm like that? Because I own a business and deal in art?"

"I don't know," he said honestly. "I only know that my behavior today, my attitude toward you and what you're trying to do, has been clouded by these things I'm holding over from my childhood."

"I'm not like that, Rock," she said, her voice going soft. She looked into the fire, then said, "Can I tell you something?"

"Of course."

Picking at some fuzz on the sleeve of his robe, she said, "My sister Tara is the career woman. She's the go-getter, the assertive, modern female. Me, I'm the one who'd rather stay home on a Friday night, reading a romance novel and baking cookies. I always wanted a home and a family, and maybe a career on the side." She stopped, lowered her eyes. "Once, long ago, I actually believed I was close to having those things."

"What happened?" he asked, wishing he could

take the hurt out of her eyes. Wishing that he hadn't added to that hurt.

"The man I'd dated all through college dumped me for another woman."

"Oh." Rock hadn't thought he could feel any worse about how he'd acted, but now he did. "That must have been rough."

"It was," she replied, her eyes wide. "So I gave up—on myself, on men, on having the things I dreamed about. After college, I poured myself into my work at the art gallery, but the whole time, I held out hope for some sort of…release. Something that would fill the empty place in my heart." She turned to him, pulling the robe tight against her throat as she sighed. "Since most of my relationships in the dating department didn't work out, I came up with this plan to own my own business. To be able to cook and be with people—two things I needed in my life to fill the emptiness. I decided if I couldn't have a family, I'd bring families together at least, and share their joy—you know, birthday parties, anniversaries, weddings, births, just getting together with friends. That's why I'm opening the tea room. I'm combining my love of cooking with my appreciation for art. It's that simple."

"Not so simple," Rock said, understanding dawning in his thick skull. "Ana, I know you've worked very hard to make this happen, but I didn't know what was behind it. And I'm sorry if I implied—"

"You have implied that you don't approve of women in business, women who have careers. I can't speak for your mother, Rock, but I can say this in my own defense—if I am ever blessed with a family of my own, nothing and no one will ever come between that family and me. I'd gladly cook meals three times a day, if only I had someone to share those meals with. But that doesn't mean I can't have a career. It's all about keeping your priorities straight, I guess."

Rock looked down at her folded hands against the heavy terry cloth of his faded blue robe. Once, when the robe was new, it had held tiny bright sailboat designs. Now those designs were pale and washed out.

And that's how he felt now. Pale and washed out, so out of sync with the real world that he'd forgotten how a single woman might need a life and a career.

"Goodness, when did I become so judgmental?" he said out loud, his eyes still on those small, feminine hands clutching his old robe.

Ana lifted one of those hands to touch his arm. "Rock, have you talked to Eloise about this?"

He nodded. "Oh, yeah. We've talked for hours on end. She's trying so hard now to make amends. You know, she's always had a strong faith, but somewhere back there after our daddy died, she got lost. Her work was her salvation then. Now, she's reaping the rewards of that hard work, but she's also suffering the consequences, too."

"Is that why Stone is so bitter?"

"Oh, yeah. That and his love of money and power."

"You're bitter, too, no matter how much you try to deny it."

He grinned then, sheepish and red-faced. "Gee, you think?"

Ana leaned close, her smile as warm as the nearby fire. "I think you're struggling with this. I think you're trying. I only ask that you don't put me in the position of having to defend myself, because my choices have nothing to do with your issues with your mother."

"You're right. I'm sorry I did that." He turned to reach for the tray. "Can we become friends again, over these lovely sandwiches I made?"

She nodded, reached for a half. "I think I'm hungry now." After nibbling for a while, she asked, "So if Eloise didn't cook, who did?"

"Me," he said, the silence of the one word speaking volumes in his weary mind.

His confession must have done something to Ana's resolve, too. Either that, or she was pitying him. She dropped her sandwich and took his hand in hers. "Rock, now that we've settled this between us, I want you to know that I'd be happy to cook you a meal anytime."

He pulled his hand away. "Don't feel sorry for me, Ana. I can take anything but that. We survived, me and Stone and Clay. And our mother wasn't a bad mother—she just got distracted by grief and…the need to create something that was solely hers." He stared down at the checkered blanket, wishing he hadn't revealed so much to her. "Let's just drop it, okay."

"Okay." She got up, her sandwich unfinished. "I'm going to get my dress and change. Where did you hang it?"

Rock could see the set of her shoulders. This tension between them wasn't going to go away over a haphazard picnic by the fire. He'd messed up all the way around.

But then things got even worse.

"I put it in the dryer."

Ana spun toward him, her eyes wide. "The dryer? Rock, that dress is rayon and dry-clean only. The dryer will shrink it."

Rock felt a sinking sensation moving from his shoulders to his stomach. "I'll go check. It's only been in there—" he glanced at the clock and groaned "—over an hour."

Ana ran a hand through her curls. "Just go get the dress, please."

He did as he was told. But when he pulled the hot dress out of the dryer, he could tell it wasn't exactly the same size and shape as it had been going in. What had once been a pretty, flowing white sundress sprinkled with blue flowers, was now a short, misshaped sheath with faded, wilted flowers.

With a sigh as heated as the dress, Rock emerged

from the tiny laundry room off the back porch. "Here," he said on a low voice. "I...I think I ruined it."

Ana took one look at the dress and gasped. "Oh, oh—"

"I'll buy you another one," he said, his hands flying in the air. "Just tell me where you got it."

"It doesn't matter," she said, her voice calm in spite of the fire in her eyes. "I...just want this day to end."

"Well, so do I."

"Good. I'm going to try and get back into this so I can get home."

"I can loan you a shirt."

"No, thanks."

"Ana, I didn't mean—"

"I know," she said, her cheeks red. "You didn't mean to insult me, or judge me or ruin my dress. I know, and I understand. Let's just stick to business from now on, okay. No more meals together, no more pretense of anything other than a working relationship."

Her words stung Rock, but they also brought him back to reality. It was like being knocked down by a strong current. "Yes, ma'am," he said with a salute.

Then he cleaned up the leftovers of their meal and stalked to the kitchen. He didn't glance around when he heard the front door slam.

But he couldn't resist hurrying to the window

to look for Ana's departing back. She had the dress on, but it was inches shorter and tight in all the wrong places.

In spite of that, in spite of how mad she made him, in spite of her being so upset over a dress, in spite of all their differences and all the baggage he'd laid at her feet today, Rock decided she looked good walking away. Really good.

And he really wanted her to turn around and come back.

She'd look even better walking toward him.

Chapter Seven

Ana got up in a foul mood on Monday morning. It went from bad to worse when she saw the catty caption in the society section of the paper, under Greta Epperson's byline: "Preacher Dempsey Shares Intimate Lunch with the Lovely and mysterious Tea Room Lady."

Mysterious! The story went on to say that Greta had it on very good authority that the two were an "item."

"Ugh!" Ana threw the paper down, refusing to read the rest of the "story." If only Greta knew the truth! Not that it would probably matter.

Wishing she had someone to talk to, Ana remembered that Jackie and Tina wouldn't be in this morning. Ana had sent them and the rest of the newly hired waitstaff into Savannah to a training seminar on customer service. Thinking that in the mood she was in, she probably could have used some coaching in the "nice" department herself, Ana groaned and tried to concentrate on the computer screen.

Ignoring the hammering in the kitchen, she had come straight to her office. She'd have to forgo coffee, but it would be worth it if she could avoid seeing Rock. She was glad now that she'd given him a key so he could come and go at will while working here—but she knew he'd been here since dawn. She'd *heard* him loud and clear over the pounding inside her head.

His two helpers—that nice fellow Don and his shy, lanky son Cal—had gone off to buy more supplies. Last she'd heard, they'd be working at the shop today on various projects.

Which left Rock alone here with her.

Thinking back on the disastrous lunch they'd shared yesterday, Ana wished she hadn't gotten so mad about the dress. It was replaceable, after all. And it wasn't as if she'd paid a fortune for it. She'd bought it on a clearance rack at her favorite boutique. But…it wasn't the dress, really. It was more the way Rock seemed to take charge and just…assume things. Like, that she would willingly cook for him. Or that he knew how to handle a delicate dress better than she did. She supposed that kind of dominant attitude came from his being a bachelor. He seemed self-sufficient and capable and sure, as if he didn't really need anyone, except a cook. Why didn't the man just hire someone, then?

Oh, what did it matter, anyway? They were just as doomed as that lunch had been. *We have to cool things between us,* Ana decided. No more dinners by the bay, no more strolls on the beach, no trysts at the Wedding Rock, and especially, no more kisses. She wouldn't want dear, inquisitive Greta to get hold of that juicy bit of news.

She had to concentrate on getting this tea room off the ground. She couldn't let Tara down and she certainly didn't want to disappoint herself, either. So she pored over some order sheets, ignoring the overly loud commotion of hammer and drill in the next room, until the lack of caffeine induced a withdrawal headache and she was forced to walk across the hallway into the kitchen.

Which she immediately wished she hadn't done.

The sight of Rock standing there in a faded black T-shirt and old jeans, with his tool belt slung low over his hips, only reminded her of what a good-looking man he was. And that he'd kissed her twice the day before.

Ana took in a breath as she remembered those kisses. This man had made her a picnic in the middle of a rainstorm. That had been so incredibly sweet that she had thought she'd burst from sheer joy. But it had also shocked her.

She didn't know what Rock expected from her. Then, he'd ruined her dress. That wasn't the real issue, of course, but it sure had been a good excuse to run away as fast as she could—in the shrunken, too-tight dress, at that.

Coffee, she reminded herself. The planked floor, treacherous and rude, squeaked and moaned when she tried to sneak on tiptoe to the coffeemaker.

Rock turned from studying his cabinet plans, his gaze slamming into hers. "Oh, hi," he said, wary. "I made coffee."

"So I see." Ana beat a path straight to the pot, then poured herself a generous cup. Grabbing a big oatmeal cookie from the batch she'd made last week, she took a moment to savor the quick breakfast.

"I had a cookie, too," Rock admitted, one bronze-toned hand resting on the butcher-block work island.

"Help yourself."

"Thanks." He shifted, waved a hand toward the cabinets. "Almost done with the main wall. I'll probably be ready to install the pantry doors and the rest of the bottom units by the end of the week. And Don's going to get the island installed later today."

"That's good."

He glanced up at her. "Do you…I mean, are you satisfied?"

Shocked, Ana frowned, almost choking on a bite of cookie as she glared at him. "What do you mean?"

"About the cabinets?" He shoved at blueprints and loose nails. "Do you like what I've done with the cabinets?"

"Oh, yes. I do." She bobbed her head, flushing over her misunderstanding. "They look great. Wonderful. Perfect."

With that, she pivoted to make a hasty exit.

"Ana?"

She didn't dare look back. "Hmm?"

"Can we be friends again?"

Ana stared at a dark spot on the wood casing of the doorway, wondering how the spot had come to be there. She rubbed a finger over the aged wood. "We are friends, Rock. As well as business associates."

"Well, do you have to be so business-like?"

She turned back then, to find him standing there with his hands on his hips, all male, his presence filling the room with suppressed tension. Ana's headache beat against her brain in the same way Rock had steadily been hammering the cabinets. "How do you want me to be?"

"What kind of question is that?"

She shrugged. "I'm just trying to get through this, Rock."

He slammed his hammer down, jarring the counter. "See, that's exactly what I mean. You aren't smiling. You aren't fussing and fixing. You're just...standing there."

"I only came in here to get a snack," she said, holding up her favorite sunflower coffee cup. "Sorry I disturbed you."

"You're not disturbing me," he replied after a long-winded sigh.

"Okay, then maybe we should both get back to work."

"Ana."

He said her name as if it were something precious and rare. It sent shivers through her system.

"I'm sorry, Ana."

"If you're talking about the dress, forget it. It was old, anyway."

"It's more than your dress, and you know it," he said.

He'd somehow gotten closer. She knew this without turning around. Ana kept her eyes on the office door across the hall, ready to bolt if he tried to touch her. "I need to get back to work. I have to pick up the girls at the airport in Savannah later today."

"Want me to go with you?"

"No, thanks. I just need you to keep working on those cabinets."

"Oh, I see. Is that how it is now? Just get the job done and get out of here?"

"I didn't say that."

He moved away. Ana felt the cool breeze of him turning, even before she heard his stomping work boots.

"There's a lot not being said between us, but maybe you're right. I have a job to do, and you have other obligations."

"That's right. Best to remember that."

"Yeah."

He picked up his hammer and proceeded to knock a nail against wood. With force.

Good, Ana thought. That meant he'd be done soon.

So she could get back to matters at hand. Like her tea room and her nieces.

And her sad, empty life.

Rock finished the glass of iced tea, then set the empty plastic cup down on the porch. It was late afternoon and he was tired. He'd put in a full day at Ana's house, but he'd gotten a lot done. Another week or so, and her kitchen would be completely renovated.

He only wished he could mend this rift between them with glue and nails. Their bond seemed permanently broken. No more kisses or fights. Just civility and long, uncomfortable bouts of utter silence. It made him think of a quote by Thomas Mann: "Speech is civilization itself…. It is silence which isolates."

"You can say that again, buddy," Rock whispered.

He looked over at Miss McPherson's porch. Milly sat there in her favorite rocking chair, steadily rocking as she stared out at the sea. Deciding he needed a friend—and maybe a bowl of stew—Rock hopped off his porch to stroll over to his neighbor.

"Evening, Miss Milly."

"Evening, Rock."

"How are you tonight?"

"I'm dandy. Your stew's in the freezer."

Grimacing at his own transparency and Miss McPherson's keen awareness, Rock sputtered and stammered. "Uh, well, thanks."

Milly kept rocking, her beaded eyes on the crashing waves down the beach. "What's eating at you, anyhow?"

"Me?" Rock asked, glancing around as if someone were behind him.

"Don't see anyone else lurking about my porch."

Settling down on the wide steps of her tiny cottage, Rock stared up at his old friend. "Milly, how come you never married?"

Milly stopped rocking. "What a strange question."

"Rude?"

"That, too."

"Well, I'd just like to know."

"Think you might be headed into permanent bachelorhood? Maybe you'll wind up rocking on your porch, too?"

"Something like that."

"Have a fight with your sweetheart?"

"She's not my sweetheart."

Milly placed her hands on the arms of her rocker and eyed him. "Yes, she is."

"What makes you say that?"

"Well, everyone is talking about it. I just read in Greta's column—"

"Forget that nosy woman. What makes *you* believe that Ana and I are…close."

"Goodness, it doesn't take a news flash to see it's the truth," Milly replied. "Over the past week or so, you seemed spry and happy. Now you look so hangdog, is all."

Wincing at being called spry and hangdog in the same breath, Rock nodded. "I made a mess of things with her, that's for sure."

"Such as?"

Rock told Milly McPherson the sad tale of his rainy Sunday afternoon with Ana. "I ruined her pretty dress to boot."

"I did like that dress," Milly said, her lips pursed. "You know, I'm still pretty handy with a needle and thread."

"That won't fix this dress, Milly."

Milly leaned down, a conspiring tone in her exaggerated whisper. "You find me some pretty cotton or linen and I'll whip up another dress for your sweetheart."

"You could do that?"

"My eyesight certainly isn't what it used to be, but I reckon so."

"But…what about her size?"

"I have a good eye for that still. I'd say about a size six."

"She is slender. But womanly, too. And she did look pretty in that white—" Rock stopped when he realized Milly was watching him with those overly observant, aged eyes. "Oh, whatever you think you can do. I'll pay you to make the thing."

"Won't be necessary."

"But—"

Milly pushed up out of her chair, taking her time to stand straight. "But nothing. We'll set things right between the two of you."

"You are a kind and dear friend."

"Stop trying to sweet-talk me. Just go in and get your stew. I'm going to watch *Jeopardy*."

"Okay." Rock got up to go to the freezer that Milly kept in a shed off the garage.

"My suitor never returned from the sea," Milly said, one hand on the screen door, her back straight.

"What?"

"You asked why I never married," she said, her tone firm and controlled. "The man I planned to marry was killed out there. It's been near sixty years." She waved a hand toward the vast ocean. "Same as your daddy—working on the boats. Storm got him."

"I never knew," Rock said, a certain sadness falling over the twilight around him.

"We don't talk of such things." Milly replied. Then she went into the house and shut the door.

Rock stood there in the gathering dusk, with the sound of the swirling ocean behind him, and the moon and the stars beaming down on him from above. He wished for something he couldn't see or touch. And he knew it was there, waiting for him, just out of his reach.

* * *

Ana reached the airport in Savannah in record time, considering the rush-hour traffic, and considering her headache had turned into some kind of monster in her head.

The tension headache increased with each thought of seeing her sister again. But that stress was much easier to handle than spending the day trying to avoid Rock.

He'd gone out for lunch. That much she knew. She'd seen the remains of his chicken box in the trash.

Ana refused to feel guilty about not catering to Rock, as she'd done the week before. But she'd tested most of her recipes three times over and the menu was being printed already. No need to get overzealous about showing off her cooking skills. Especially with Rock. She wouldn't want to give him the wrong idea.

He probably got the wrong idea when you kissed him yesterday, she reminded herself as she sped into the pick-up lane at the airport. Glancing at the curb, Ana pushed thoughts of Rock out of her mind while she swept her gaze over the emerging travelers.

Then she saw Tara and the girls and immediately felt a bittersweet tug inside her heart. "Tara," she called as she stepped out of the car. "I'm here."

"Hi." Tara Hanson Parnell looked like a fashion plate in her white capri pants and black sleeveless summer sweater, her long blond hair just dusting her bare, tanned shoulders. Her strappy black sandals and matching designer bag gave her the look of a world traveler. And made Ana feel down-right dowdy in her denim jumper and T-shirt.

But Ana didn't care right now. Just the sight of her three nieces brought tears of happiness to her eyes. "Hello, girls," she called, as the three rushed to greet her.

They all started talking at once.

"Aunt Ana, Marybeth says I can't get in the ocean because of sharks."

"Laurel, would you keep your paws off my purse!"

"Amanda, give me my lip gloss back, right now."

Ana glanced from one exasperated teenager to the next, then looked over their scrawny shoulders to find their mother's frowning face.

"Laurel, please refrain from antagonizing your sisters," Tara said to her eldest daughter.

Laurel gave her mother an exaggerated shrug, shifted on her platforms and said, "Whatever," with a toss of her crimped hair.

Tara, in spite of being dressed to the hilt, looked haggard and tired up close. She dropped a silver-bangle-bracelet clad arm against her hip. "They have argued, fussed, snapped and whined for the last week. I don't know why I bothered taking them to Texas to see their grandparents. They hated the whole experience."

Ana hugged each girl, making sure each got

equal measures of squeezing and kissing. "Didn't you girls have fun with the Parnells?"

Laurel, blond and hyper like her mother, and wearing a too-short shirt that revealed her belly button, nodded. "Oh, we love Grandma and Grandpa. But they live on a ranch and they don't have cable." She rolled her eyes in horror, then glared at her mother. "And Mom expected us to just sit there, staring at chickens and cows."

"Imagine life without cable television," Ana said, shaking her head in mock concern.

"It was pretty bad, Aunt Ana," Marybeth said, tossing her golden-brown hair over her shoulder. "No movies or MTV."

"You aren't even allowed to watch MTV," Amanda piped in.

"Well, neither are you, but you sneak," Marybeth replied, sticking out her tongue.

"Do not."

"Do, too."

"Hush up, both of you," Tara said. "Now get in the car before your aunt gets a ticket."

Still catty and vocal, the girls piled in the back seat in a tangle of legs and platform shoes, while Tara and Ana finished putting their many bags into the trunk.

Tara tipped the skycap, then slid in the front beside Ana. "Thanks. This trip was tough. The Parnells are still so sad over Chad's death. They cried when the girls started packing up to leave. Then they cried again at the airport."

"How'd you hold up?" Ana asked, tears pricking her own eyes.

"I did okay." Tara stopped, took a breath. "I…I felt as if Chad's folks would somehow blame me…you know, for his death. But they were really sweet. Just a bit overprotective, given the circumstances. I did promise to let the girls come back soon." She sniffed, sighed again. "Anyway, thanks so much for…everything."

"You're welcome." Ana concentrated on getting out of the pick-up lane and back into the flow of traffic leaving the busy airport. Deciding to lighten the mood, she asked, "So…I have these three *adorable* ragamuffins for the entire summer?"

Tara smiled tiredly. "I know, I know. It strikes terror in your heart, right? I went through three nannies in as many weeks before we left for Texas. And once we got there, I knew right away the Parnells wouldn't be able to handle the girls for very long. Like I said, they were very sweet about everything, but they're old and get ornery at times, and they're still grieving about Chad's death. It was awkward, seeing them again, and even though they would have insisted on my leaving the girls there, I didn't dare ask them to help out. Plus, I couldn't bear to be that far from the girls all summer. And since Mom and Dad are traveling somewhere in Maine in that trailer-thing of theirs, you were my last hope. I was desperate, Ana."

"Must have been, to ask me to do this right in the middle of opening my tea room."

Tara pushed thick blond hair off her face, then popped her black wayfarers over her blue eyes. "You can still back out."

"I'm teasing," Ana said, acutely aware of her sister's somber mood. Tara was usually bubbly and edgy, always on the move. But now she slumped into the seat and stared straight ahead. Worried, Ana added, "Hey, you know I love the girls. And you did say you'd drive out on the weekends. They'll be safe here."

"I know," Tara said. "It's just that…" She stopped, swallowed. "I just really need them to be with someone I can trust right now. I've got so much work to do, and I worry about them. It hasn't been easy, these past few months."

"I understand," Ana said, wondering what, besides grief over Chad's death, was wrong with her sister. Tara never let anything get her down. She loved her three daughters to distraction. And since their father had died too young from a heart defect and too much stress, she supposed Tara was having anxiety attacks over the well-being of her children, just as the Parnells had probably done.

But then, they'd all been affected by Chad's death. Ana figured she herself would have to deal with that sooner or later. It would have to be later.

But the hurtful memories seemed to surround her like the cars buzzing by. Chad and Tara had started their family right away. And Tara had been so young—just eighteen. Laurel was the firstborn, then a year later, Marybeth. Then two years later, Amanda.

The family I always wanted, Ana thought. *The family I should have had.*

The old resentment returned for just an instant. Ana squelched it, her smile reflecting in the rearview mirror as she looked in the back seat at the squirming girls who resembled their father so much. She had long ago gotten over envying her sister.

But she'd probably never get over Tara's marrying the man Ana had once loved.

Chapter Eight

"I love it," Tara said, spinning around as she viewed the new tea room kitchen. They'd already toured the whole house. "Really, Ana, you've turned this old place into a showcase. You're going to be the talk of the island—and probably Savannah, too."

Ana shrugged. "I do hope to get tourists from Savannah and all over the state." Then she grinned. "Okay, all over the South would be good, too."

"You'll be a household name," Tara said, her lacquered nails drumming on the new island workstation that Rock and his two assistants had been working on for the past week. "Ana's Tea Room— it's the place for wedding showers, luncheons, or a quiet little lunch for two. Can't you just hear it?"

"Right now, I hear the sound of feet running around upstairs," Ana replied, glad that Tara approved of what she'd done, since her sister had co-signed the bank loan. "I'll order pizza for them tonight, then start them on healthier fare tomorrow."

"Good luck with that," Tara said. "They only eat junk and then complain that they're too fat. Especially Laurel. She eats in spurts."

"Typical teenager," Ana said, handing her sister a glass of mineral water. "Remember how we used to worry?"

"All through college, too," Tara said. Then, stopping, she gave Ana a flustered look before hastily adding, "But we still managed to eat a lot of pizza late at night."

"Sure we did." Ana turned away. She wouldn't let Tara see the bitterness in her eyes. That time was over and Chad was gone to both of them now. No sense hurting her sister even more with rehashed grudges. Tara would only be here a couple of days before heading off to get started on this real estate venture. Ana didn't want their time together to be awkward. "Anyway, the girls could use some meat on their bones. They look skinny to me."

"They eat all the time," Tara replied, her tone defensive in her words. "Of course, Laurel won't eat when she's in one of her pouty moods. Honestly, I hope you can bring her out of this horrible attitude she's had lately."

"I'll see what I can do to cheer her up," Ana said. "And how about you? You've lost more weight yourself."

"I'm always on the run, too busy and tired to eat a decent meal."

"Well, I'll have to remedy that while you're here, at least."

Ana knew Tara ate like a bird. She had to wonder if the girls hadn't noticed this and tried to emulate it. They were thin, but they seemed healthy. Her sister, on the other hand, looked pale and tired in spite of her expensive cosmetics.

Ana supposed being a widow did that to a person.

She dialed the pizza number, thinking the whole time that Chad Parnell hadn't stood a chance against Tara's beauty and charm. He'd loved Ana— she had to believe this. But one look at Tara and he'd been a goner. And in her heart, Ana knew that Tara and Chad had fit each other much better than she and Chad ever would have. Ana, always studious and just over a year older than her sister, had entered college at a young age and was graduating early. And because Ana had promised their parents she would watch out for her bubbly, outgoing sister, it made sense that she and Chad would tutor Tara. After a few weeks of the two seniors hovering over her freshman sister, Ana could sense Chad drifting away. Soon there were study sessions between Tara and Chad that didn't include Ana. She didn't even try to fight it. She just let him go. And yet, she'd loved him. Completely.

But she loved her sister, too. And forgiveness

was much easier and safer than bitterness and anger. So all through the years, she'd kept her distance and kept her hurt and sense of betrayal to herself. After all, Tara hadn't really betrayed her. Tara had fought against her feelings for Chad, but in the end, love had won out.

After Chad had broken things off with Ana, Tara had confessed everything to Ana in a fit of tears, one long, cold winter night. And Ana had forgiven her and told her to follow her heart. Chad had never bothered to explain, except to say he was truly sorry.

Ana could still see them on their wedding day. How could she fault either of them for being so in love, for being so happy. Except when they glanced at her. She'd hated the guilt in their eyes as much as she'd hated the hint of betrayal she felt in her heart.

So she'd tried very hard to compensate for that guilt and for her emptiness through the years. She had tried to be a good sister, but since the marriage between Tara and Chad, things had always been strained. The girls coming along had helped there, though. Ana loved them so much, and tried to be a good aunt.

She'd keep on doing that now, too. She didn't want to lose Tara and the girls. She needed them as much as they needed her. Over the years, Ana had tried to reach out to Tara. They'd gotten much closer in recent years, and that closeness had gone

one step farther when Ana told Tara about her dream to open a tea room. After that, Tara had insisted on helping Ana out financially. Then, just before Chad's death, they had finalized the loan.

Ana had to wonder if it were guilt-money, paid to soothe the stilted silence that sometimes flowed between them. But she'd accepted, thinking it would give Tara something to focus on, too. Which it had, since Chad's death.

"It's good to be here again," Tara said, bringing Ana back from her bittersweet thoughts. "Last time we got together, we were so wrapped up in setting up the contract and the construction for this place…well, it's been a while since we've had some downtime together."

"Not since the funeral," Ana said, after ordering two large veggie pizzas to be delivered. Then she turned to Tara. "How are you, really?"

"Honestly?" Tara asked, shaking her head. "It's hard to say. I miss Chad, of course. But learning the business end of things these past six months is keeping me busy. And, of course, my own work is very necessary right now, too, just to help with the bills. This deal I'm working on in Atlanta, plus the sale of the land Chad left me near Savannah—well, if both go through I can at least relax about the girls' future."

Ana frowned. "I thought you were secure, money-wise. I mean, I thought Chad had plenty of life insurance and—" She stopped. "I don't mean to pry."

"It's all right," Tara said, waving a hand in the air. "It's complicated. You know, probate and litigation, things I'm only just beginning to understand. And some surprises I didn't even know about."

"But you're okay, right?"

"I'm fine, just fine," Tara replied, laughing. "Now, Miss Ana, I want to hear all about you. Who is this Rock you keep mentioning? The carpenter, right?"

Ana dropped her eyes. Had she really mentioned Rock that much in conversation? "Yes. He's Eloise Dempsey's son."

Tara's perfectly shaped brows lifted. "*The* Eloise Dempsey?"

"The only one around these parts," Ana replied. "I met her when we displayed some of her sculpture pieces and crosses at the gallery in Savannah. In fact, she's the one who told me this house was for sale. Said it would be perfect for my tea room, and she was right. I'm planning on showcasing some of her smaller pieces, and, hopefully, selling them, too."

"That won't be a problem," Tara said. "Her work fetches top dollar among the A-list crowd. Those exquisite crosses she makes from old driftwood and stones are just beautiful."

Ana nodded. "Well, anyway, Rock is her eldest son. And an artist in his own right, even though I wouldn't say that to his face. He's worked overtime to rebuild the entire kitchen. And he's still got some work left before the opening."

"You're blushing," Tara said, grinning. "This has got to be good."

"He's just someone I hired to built cabinets," Ana said, hating her own defensive tone.

"Uh-huh. A carpenter. A man who works with his hands."

"He's also a preacher," Ana said, just to level things out in her sister's overactive mind.

"How very interesting."

Ana couldn't help but laugh at Tara's wide-eyed smile. "He is interesting. Too interesting. And... he shrunk my favorite dress."

Gasping, Tara grabbed Ana by the arm. "C'mon and sit down. You have to tell me *everything*."

"Things are coming along nicely," Rock told his mother the next morning. "I've been working day and night on the cabinets for Ana's kitchen, while Don and Cal built the workstation off-site, then brought it in piece by piece to the kitchen. Honestly, Mother, you didn't call me this much when I left home and went off to college at Georgia Tech."

"Am I bothering you?" Eloise asked, the sweet Southern lilt of her voice carrying over the phone wire.

"No. More like...amusing me," Rock retorted, his coffee cup in midair. "I've doing a job for Ana and we're just friends. That's the story, regardless of what you might read in the papers."

"Really?"

"Really."

"Well, old Miss McPherson seems to think otherwise. Caught her in the five and dime the other day, buying some pretty white and blue sprigged linen fabric. Said she was going to make a dress for Ana—to replace the one you ruined."

"Miss McPherson is a good soul, and way too innocent to encounter you. My guess is that you badgered her for information."

"I did ask a few choice questions, yes."

"Well, stop asking. And please don't fuel Greta Epperson's fire, either. Milly agreed to sew Ana a dress, that's true. But it's only because I shrunk Ana's Sunday dress in the dryer."

"And why would Ana's dress be in your dryer in the first place?"

Rock groaned, then set down his cup with such a *thud,* coffee splashed out on the counter. "We got caught in a rainstorm after church. I brought her in to get out of the cold and wet."

"And?"

"And…nothing. We had a quick lunch, then she left."

And by the way, I kissed her. Twice. Really long, sweet, life-altering kisses. But that was after I'd insulted her and implied I needed her to cook for me.

Searching his mind for patience, Rock thought of the Proverbs: "For the Lord giveth wisdom: out of his mouth cometh knowledge and understanding."

Wisely, Rock refused to give her the details.

"Okay, all right," Eloise said, letting out a mother's frustrated sigh after a moment of silence. "I have to get to work. Just wanted to check in."

"I'm fine. Ana is fine."

"You know, the lighthouse festival starts tomorrow. You could ask Ana to take a stroll with you."

"I could, except she has her three nieces here."

"Oh. Well, you'll find a way, I'm sure."

"There is no *way*, Mother. Could we just drop it?"

"Of course. Oh, I heard from Clay. He might come home toward the end of the summer. Says he needs a vacation."

"Big-city cop beat getting to him?"

"Maybe. He wouldn't say. You know he never wants to worry us."

"No, never. Clay is very thoughtful that way."

"Are you being sarcastic?"

"No, I'm being honest. I appreciate that about my baby brother."

"As compared to your middle brother?"

"Maybe."

"I'm going to hang up now, before we get into a deep discussion about Stone."

"That's probably smart. See you later, Mom."

Rock headed out the door in a dark mood. He was still as mixed up about his feelings for Ana as a jellyfish caught in seaweed. He was highly attracted to the woman, but felt he should avoid her at all costs. But his argument about her being consumed by work was fast fading. Ana wasn't unnaturally obsessed by her tea room; she just needed to make a living, and, naturally, that required a lot of work and attention to detail. He couldn't fault her for that, yet he didn't want to get caught up in something he couldn't control. He'd just have to pray his way through this, because it would be hard to spend the day hammering nails if he couldn't stop this hammering doubt in his brain.

"He sure likes to hammer a lot," Marybeth whispered to Ana around high noon. "Does he ever take a break, Aunt Ana?"

"Rarely," Ana answered, remembering the first week of sweet camaraderie she'd shared here with Rock. That bond was now shattered. And Rock was working like a man on a mission. "He wants to get finished, honey. He's a very busy man."

"And cute, too," Laurel said on a sigh. "But not as cute as Cal. How old did you say he was?"

Ana hid her smile. "Rock? Oh, he's around thirty-four or -five, I think."

Laurel rolled her big baby blues. "I meant Cal! He looks so cool in his baggy shorts."

"Oh, Cal?" Ana gave her niece a mock glare. "He's seventeen."

"I'm almost fifteen," Laurel pointed out, grinning. "Maybe I can get to know him this summer."

Ana shook her head, thinking she was going to have to watch that one. Already blossoming, Laurel was just as pretty as Tara had been at her age, and all blond-haired and blue-eyed and boy crazy, just like her mother.

"Cal works a lot with Rock, honey. He might not have much free time."

"That's a shame. This is such a neat place. When can we go to the beach?"

Relieved that Laurel's fickle mind had drifted away from the subject of Cal Ashworth, Ana said, "Maybe later today."

Marybeth slumped onto the chair next to the desk. "Aunt Ana, we're so bored. Can you take us to the mall?"

"Mall?" Ana chuckled while she shifted some papers on her desk. "We don't have a mall, sugar. Just rows and rows of boutiques and souvenir shops."

"No mall?" Amanda bounced up off the small love seat nestled underneath a long window. "But…we have to have a mall!"

"She said no mall. Are you deaf?" Marybeth stuck out her tongue at her younger sister.

"Marybeth, sweetie, I'd really like to see that tongue back in your mouth. That's not very ladylike," Ana said, her smile belying her firm tone.

"She'll never be a lady," Amanda said, plopping

back down against the fluffy pillows of the love seat. "She's a tomboy—reckless—that's what Mom says."

"Oh, I don't know about that," Ana said, glancing over at Marybeth. "I think pretty soon all of that will change."

"Just because I'm not afraid, doesn't make me a tomboy," Marybeth retorted. "I can do anything a boy does, except better."

"A feminist, too," Ana said, laughing. "No wonder your mother has her hands full."

Laurel picked at the pens and papers on Ana's desk, then motioned toward her younger sisters. "I think they're both dorks myself."

"No name-calling allowed on these premises," Ana said.

"Okay, but I can still think it."

"Hey, he's stopped hammering," Amanda said, springing up off the couch just in time to run smack into Rock as he entered the office.

"Whoa," Rock said, holding his hands on Amanda's shoulders to keep from knocking her down. "Where's the fire?"

"Nowhere," Amanda said with a shy smile. "Are you finished?"

"Just taking a lunch break," Rock said, his eyes moving over the three curious girls to Ana.

"Where's your help?" Laurel asked, craning her head around Rock.

"The Ashworths?" Rock asked, a perplexed expression on his face. "They went to lunch."

Laurel showed extreme disappointment. "Pooh! I thought maybe Cal could tell me about the island, as in what's fun and what's not."

Rock stared hard at the girl before sending Ana a profound look. "I'm sure Cal would be glad to…tell you all about the local teen scene. He's usually right in the thick of things, beginning with our youth activities at church."

"Church?" Laurel looked shocked. "Aunt Ana, you don't expect us to go to church, do you?"

"I most certainly do. And Rock is right. Cal is involved with the youth programs at Rock's church. He'd be an excellent guide in helping y'all to become part of that group."

"Great," Laurel replied, flipping her hair in irritation. "That sounds like loads of fun."

"Church can be fun," Rock said, his eyes on Ana. "Especially if you attend with someone you like and enjoy being around. It's all about… fellowship."

Ana felt the heat of his gaze and tried not to squirm against her heavy wooden office chair. "So…you headed out?"

"Actually," Rock said, his gaze moving over the girls, "I was thinking I'd take all of you to lunch. The lighthouse festival—officially called Save the West Island Lighthouse Summer Jam Session—is in full swing along the boardwalk. They've got arts-

and-crafts booths, music, and food—hot dogs, shrimp po'boys, funnel cakes, cotton candy—"

Before he could finish, he had three excited teenagers jumping in circles around him.

"Cotton candy? I love cotton candy!"

"And funnel cakes, too."

"I want a hot dog," Laurel shouted over the chatter of her sisters. "And maybe I'll buy a bracelet or some earrings at one of those booths, since there's no other place to shop around here."

Ana couldn't help but laugh. "I guess that answers your question. Girls, want to tag along with Rock for lunch before we head out to the beach this afternoon?"

"Yes," Marybeth said, answering for her sisters smugly. "But you're coming, too, right?"

Ana looked up at Rock, wondering if she shouldn't just make some sort of excuse. But Tara wouldn't be back for hours—she had a business meeting in Savannah—and it probably wouldn't do to shove the girls off on Rock, since technically he was still a stranger to them.

"Will you come?" Rock asked, the softness of the question leaving Ana breathless and warm.

"Do I have a choice?"

"No," he said at the same time the girls did. Then he leaned close, too close, and whispered, "And besides, we have chaperones. I think we'll be safe, don't you?"

Ana wondered about that. She didn't think she'd

ever be completely safe around Rock Dempsey. Not that he wasn't a gentleman or a kind, gracious man. But his kisses—she could still feel the imprint of his firm, wide lips moving over hers—were dangerous. Even thinking about that was dangerous. Wanting to kiss him again meant she wasn't safe from her own heart.

"What if Greta sees us and writes another embellished exposé?" That seemed like a good excuse not to go, at least.

Rock must have seen her turmoil on her face. "It's just lunch at a crowded festival," he said, his smile full of a dare. "Even if Greta spots us, it's for a very good cause, and…no rain predicted."

"Good," Ana replied, grabbing her straw tote bag and nodding, though against her better judgment. "Girls, go wash up. Be downstairs and ready to go in five minutes. We'll walk from here."

"Cool," Laurel shouted as she bolted up the stairs.

The other two followed, chattering like fussing seagulls about who got to wear which shoes.

"Adorable," Rock said as he walked with Ana to the front door.

"Aren't they, though?"

She found it hard to look at him. She'd missed him. She'd missed their laughing together, eating together, just being friends as they got to know each other. And she wondered what exactly she'd been so mad about.

"So they'll be here…how long?"

She managed a chuckle. "About a month." Then, just to tease him, she asked, "Is that fear I see in your eyes?"

Rock nodded. "I've never dealt with girls. Brothers, now that I can handle. But teenage girls, that's a whole different thing."

"And after you assured me that the whole island would help me with them."

"I will help you," he said, leaning close again as they waited at the bottom of the stairs. "I want to help you—that is, if you still want my help."

"I'll need all the help I can get."

"I'll take that as a yes, then."

Ana smelled him—the scent of sawdust and varnish mixed with the clean fresh scent of the sea that was in his aftershave. Trying to maintain her balance, she pushed at the balustrade at her back. Rock pushed closer.

"Nice dress," he said, his eyes sweeping over her.

"Thank you." She'd put on an old, floral sheath, thinking to get some work done. Not thinking to go to lunch with him. "It's old."

"But pretty. Burnished sunflowers to match your hair."

Ana knew he wanted to kiss her. And she knew she wanted to kiss him, too.

But the sound of flip-flops hitting wood snapped her out of that daydream. Her mind foggy with longing, she glanced up to find three inquisitive girls staring down from the upstairs landing.

"Ready?" she asked in a squeaky voice.

Laurel hopped down the stairs, a wide grin splitting her face. "Oh, yeah."

Ana knew that grin. It made her blush in spite of herself. "Then, let's go."

Marybeth and Amanda followed, giggling and whispering.

"This is bad," Ana said to Rock under her breath. "First your mother, then Greta and Miss Milly, and now the girls. The whole island is going to get the wrong idea about us."

"Would that be so terrible?" Rock asked. He wasn't joking. In fact, he seemed very serious.

But since she could never be sure of what he actually wanted or expected from her, Ana didn't know how to answer him.

She only knew that when she was around him, her heart did strange things and her head lost all logic. And she hadn't decided yet whether that was bad or good.

Chapter Nine

The smell of popcorn wafted along the air as Ana and the girls strolled through the closed-off Lady Street, the main thoroughfare that ran beside the boardwalk across the small island. A big red-and-white banner over the town square proclaimed The West Island Lighthouse Summer Jam Session and listed the dates. Off in the distance, an instrumental band played a lively tune.

All along the way, the Victorian-style shops and restaurants, once private dwellings but now commercial properties, had thrown their doors open to attract more customers. Huge stone flowerpots filled with red and pink hibiscus trees graced each doorway or porch stoop, while the white gazebo in the park boasted red and pink tea roses and creamy yellow and white Cherokee roses. The whole square, surrounded with moss-draped live oaks,

vivid azaleas and crape myrtle, and sweet-smelling
magnolias, looked festive and ready for spring. And
down the sloping shoreline, past the protected sea
oats and the planked boardwalk, the ocean glim-
mered in shades of blue and green, with sailboats,
fancy yachts and tourists boats gracing the waters
out past the breakers.

"This is awesome," Laurel said, her eyes
scanning the crowd. No doubt she was looking for
Cal Ashworth.

She'd spotted the father and son at one of the
food booths, but had lost them in the crowd. Ana
could tell Laurel was extremely interested in cute
but shy Cal. Laughing to herself, Ana decided
Laurel might be a bit too much for poor Cal. He was
used to more sedate females.

"What are you smiling about?" Rock asked a
few minutes later, as he handed her a soft drink
and a grilled chicken sandwich from a nearby restaurant booth.

"Oh, nothing," Ana replied, enjoying the balmy
gulf breeze and the gospel singers who had taken
the stage. "Teenagers, life in general, everything."

"You look content."

"I guess I am." After finding an empty picnic
table, they settled down with their sandwiches,
while Ana kept a watchful eye on the girls, who'd
all wanted hot dogs, French fries and funnel cakes.
She glanced over at Rock as she nibbled her own
French fries. "I've always wanted to live in a place

like this—small, homey, slow-paced, and near the ocean. I haven't really had time to get out and explore the island, so this is nice."

"You work too hard."

She gave him a quick look, searching for censure in his eyes. Seeing none, she relaxed. "I don't have a choice right now. Once we get established, I'll settle into a routine. I've already hired two very capable assistants to help with hostessing. And I have three waitresses lined up."

"You have been busy," Rock said. "I've been so preoccupied with getting the kitchen in order, guess I haven't notice anyone else much. But I do run into Jackie and that cute little Tina now and again. The dynamic duo, those two."

"They are worth every penny of their salaries, that's for sure. They've smoothed out the menu plans and the table arrangements while I've done a lot of work over the phone," she said. "And I interviewed several people before I even called you. I'll start training them next week. It's one thing for me to cook while you're tearing away and hammering, but I don't want the kitchen too crowded until you're just about finished. Then a couple more weeks, and we're in business."

"I don't mind you cooking." He gave her a sheepish grin. "Guess you probably noticed that, though."

"Maybe we'd better change the subject," she suggested, her grin belying her serious tone.

"Good idea." He took a long swallow of his soda. "Are you nervous?"

"Some. More anxious than nervous. I just hope this works."

"I think it will," he said, his smile warming her as much as the afternoon sun. "As you can see, this island gets very crowded during the peak summer months. And people are always hungry."

She laughed, thinking their conversations always led back to food in spite attempts to change the subject. "I'll serve a light breakfast—pastries, cookies and muffins, things such as that," she said. "Then my regular lunch and dinner menus. And on special occasions, catered private dinners."

"But you will have some nights free?"

"Yes, hopefully. That's why I hired Jackie as my assistant."

He leaned forward, his sandwich half-eaten. "I am hopeful. I hope to take you away from work on some of those free nights—a movie, dinner, dancing. I hope you and I are friends again, at least."

"Of course we're friends, Rock." She wondered if they would ever be anything but that, in spite of how the image of dancing in the moonlight with him made her feel. "And I'm sorry I got so mad about the dress."

"You were mad because I was acting like a buffoon."

She tilted her head at that. "That's a good word

for it. But I wasn't exactly acting like a lady myself."

"You are every bit a lady." He turned serious then, and she knew he had something on his mind. "'And throughout all eternity, I forgive you, you forgive me.'"

"Did you just make that up?"

"No. I have to give credit to William Blake."

"The poet?"

"The very one. It's from 'Broken Love,' if I remember correctly."

"Do you always quote poetry to find your way back to a woman's heart?"

He sighed, took her hand in his. "I wish I knew the way to a woman's heart. I seem to put my foot in my mouth every time I step on the path."

"You're getting there," Ana said, admitting what she felt without any remorse, which surprised her. She wished she hadn't done so when his eyes turned as dark as a midnight ocean.

"Am I?"

"We're friends again." She gave him a saucy smile, then bit into another French fry. "And I've learned at least this much about you—the way to your heart is truly through your stomach."

He lowered his head, then shot her a frown. "Hey, am I really that bad?"

She tossed her hair off her face. "No." Giving him a direct look, she said, "I understand…how it was for you growing up. To you, food is comfort.

It makes sense, as long as you don't confuse things…about me…about us, with all that angst from your past."

"You don't mince words, do you."

"I believe in being honest."

"Brutally honest."

"I can see the truth of the matter." She played with her paper napkin, almost fraying it in her attempt to find the right words. She'd always been able to spot the truth, which was why she'd known about Chad and Tara falling in love long before either of them had admitted it. She wanted to be straight with Rock, so there would be no misunderstandings or false expectations. "Rock, I just want you and me to…understand each other. We both have obligations, things we have to get done—that's life. But I want us to be friends, and that means being honest, too."

"Well, I'm glad for your friendship, at least." He another swallow of his drink. "And I'm glad you plan on being around for a while."

"I hope so." She stretched, tossed her head back to enjoy the sun. "This is a perfect day."

"The Lord brings them out sometimes, just to refresh us and give us new hope."

"Well, it's working." She glanced around, searching for the girls. "I guess I should get them to the beach, so I can tire them out early. Maybe then I'll get some work done later tonight."

Rock indicated with his head. "Looks like Laurel finally managed to corner Cal."

Ana saw the blonde hovering near the table where Cal and his father sat eating fried shrimp. Cal was smiling at something Laurel had said. "She is just like her mother," Ana said. "Too pretty and too full of attitude for her own good."

"Tara is lovely, from the glimpse I caught of her as she was leaving this morning," Rock replied. "But I like her older sister better."

Blushing, Ana looked over at him. "That's a first." Then she stopped, swallowed. "Actually, once a very long time ago, another man said almost the same thing to me. But…he soon changed his mind."

Rock sat studying her for a minute. "Want to tell me about it?"

Ana was about to tell him everything, when Marybeth and Amanda came bouncing up. "Can we go to the fair out on the boardwalk? Just to ride the roller coaster and the Ferris wheel maybe?"

"What about the beach?" Ana asked, glad for the interruption. It probably wouldn't be wise to tell Rock everything about her one great lost love. He might think she was self-pitying and shallow.

"We'll be back in a few minutes," Amanda said, twirling her hair in her fingers. "Please, Aunt Ana?"

"I can see I'm not going to get much work done this afternoon," Ana said. "Okay, here's the deal. You have one hour. I'm going to be around, right here near the booths, if you need me. Is Laurel going with you?"

Marybeth scoffed, then crossed her hands over her midsection. "She ditched us for that guy."

"You mean Cal Ashworth?"

"Yeah, that boy she's gone all gaga over."

Ana looked around, then saw Laurel sitting next to Cal. Mr. Ashworth was nowhere in sight. "I think your sister should go with you, to keep an eye on you two." And so Ana could keep an eye on boy-crazy Laurel.

"We're not babies," Amanda drawled.

"I know that, but you're still too young to be wandering around among strangers all by yourselves."

"Why don't *we* take them, and Laurel, too?" Rock suggested, getting to his feet. "C'mon, Ana, we haven't had an afternoon off in weeks."

"But—"

"C'mon, Aunt Ana. You can ride the roller coaster with us."

"Oh, no."

"Aunt Ana," Rock mimicked, grabbing her hand, "it'll be fun. You need to have some fun."

"But what about all that work?"

"It'll be there when you get back. And I'll work extra hours tonight to make up for my time."

"I think I'm outnumbered here," Ana said. "Well, let's go get Laurel."

"I'll tell her to c'mon." Marybeth hurried ahead of them, obviously relishing being able to boss her older sister for once.

Rock took Ana by the arm, strolling with her

toward the table where Laurel and Cal sat. "Young love. Sure does the heart good."

"You," Ana said, giving him a mock nasty glare, "are certainly no help. I can't run a business if you talk me into taking afternoons off."

"Good for the soul," Rock explained.

"But I thought you believed in working Monday through Friday, and playing only after working hours."

"I've been wrong before. I think I might be wrong on that account, too. Today is definitely a 'Let's play hooky day.'"

"I'm just not sure—"

"Do you want me to take the girls, so you can get some work done?"

Sensing the hint of frustration in his tone, Ana shook her head. "No. You're right. I deserve to spend some time with my nieces. But only for today."

He seemed content with that, but Ana once again got the impression that Rock was aggravated with her. If he was going to close up like a turtle and pout every time she mentioned work, then they did indeed have a problem.

Rock Dempsey could either accept her as she was, or he could just forget being her friend.

That thought troubled Ana more than she cared to admit. She wanted to be Rock's friend. She wanted to be with Rock, maybe as more than just a friend. But she also wanted his approval. If he couldn't give her that, then they would never see eye to eye.

Their day together was ending much too soon for Rock. The girls had enjoyed riding all the attractions at the small carnival that had come to town as part of the festival. They'd shared cotton candy and too many other sugary concoctions, and now they were ready to head down to the beach for the couple of hours before sunset.

Rock wanted to go with them.

He looked up as they were making their way back along Lady Street, to find his mother sitting in a wicker chair in front of a booth featuring some of her smaller designs.

"Rock!" Eloise waved, her beaming smile making Rock feel guilty. Hadn't he insisted to his mother that Ana and he were just *working* together? Yet here they were, in broad daylight, playing together, and for all the world to see, at that. There would be more coy comments in Greta Epperson's society column, he just bet.

Well, let them all stew. What he did was his business, as long as he held his moral ground. And Rock certainly had every intention of staying friendly and professional. As long as he didn't think about how much fun it was to kiss Ana.

His mother didn't miss any of it. As if reading his very thoughts, she asked, "Rock, what are you doing here? And Ana, too." The pleased-as-punch look she shot him made Rock groan inwardly.

"We just came to eat lunch," he said, the defensive squeak in his words ringing in the air.

"It's four in the afternoon, son."

"Is it? Wow, must have lost track of the time."

"We were only going to tour the carnival for an hour," Ana said, shaking her head.

Eloise frowned at her son, then smiled at Ana. "How are you, darling?"

"I'm good," Ana replied, her gaze straying to the pottery and ironwork displayed in the booth. "How's business?"

"I've done a fair amount," Eloise said, waving a hand at another woman who was manning the booth. "Lou here keeps track of the money, while I try to woo the onlookers and window-shoppers."

"I'd imagine people are clamoring for one of those crosses," Ana said, her hand moving over a pewter nautical-inspired cross about six inches in diameter.

"People were lined up earlier," Lou said from her spot inside the booth. "It was so gracious of Eloise to donate some of her art for the lighthouse cause."

"Glad to do it," Eloise said as she got up to straighten some of the hanging crosses, her long lime-green linen jumper falling to her ankles. "We all want to see the lighthouse restored. It's been a part of this island for over two centuries."

"Where is the lighthouse?" Laurel asked. She'd pouted for most of the afternoon, after Rock had pulled her away from Cal. But she'd wound up having fun with her sisters in spite of herself.

Eloise looked over at her, giving her a sharp appraisal. "It's on the other end of the island, near Hidden Hill. And who are you?"

Ana waved a hand at the three curious girls. "These are my nieces, Eloise. Laurel, Marybeth and Amanda Parnell. They'll be spending part of the summer with me while their mother works in Savannah."

"Charming," Eloise said, smiling at the girls.

"What's Hidden Hill?" Amanda asked shyly.

"It's a big old stone house, almost like a castle," Eloise said. "It belonged to the descendants of the first settlers on the island, and changed hands several times over the years, but now it belongs to my son, Stone."

"You have one son named Rock and one named Stone?" Marybeth giggled. "That's weird."

"And one named Clay," Eloise replied, her eyes on Rock as she spoke. "I'm a bit eccentric that way."

Trying to remain impassive, Rock said, "Our mother has a weird sense of humor, that's for sure. We actually have proper given names—which I won't reveal right now—but she nicknamed each of us after some of the things she uses in her art."

"Wow," Marybeth said, rolling her eyes. "Good thing she doesn't work with rock, paper and scissors."

Rock grimaced, then gently cuffed the girl's

arm. "You are too smart for your own good. But it might be fun to antagonize my brothers by calling them Paper and Scissors."

"Do they live here?" Amanda asked.

"No," Eloise said, her eyes growing bright. "Stone lives out from Savannah, on a golf resort. He's a real estate developer—commercial properties mostly. And Clay lives in Atlanta in an apartment. He's a policeman—a K-9 cop, as he likes to put it."

"Do they have children?" Laurel asked, her curious eyes moving toward Rock, then her aunt, her smile encouraging.

"No, none of my boys are even married yet. But I remain constantly hopeful," Eloise said, her words pointed.

"Do they come and visit?" Again, Laurel.

"Not as much as I'd like," Eloise replied, her eyes going dim for just a minute.

Rock shifted on his work boots, acutely aware of where this conservation might lead. "So you three are stuck with me—the carpenter/preacher/beach bum."

Laurel laughed, then shrugged. "You aren't so bad, Rock."

"Mr. Dempsey," Ana said.

"No, Rock is fine," he told the girl. "And thanks for the vote of confidence. I knew getting up my nerve to ride that roller coaster would pay off. You promised to come to Youth Group tomorrow night if I did, remember?"

"I remember," Laurel said, bouncing on her flip-flops. "And you promised Cal would be there, too."

"I remember," Rock said.

"Cal Ashworth?" Eloise perked up, a keen interest sparkling in her crystal eyes. "You know sweet Cal?"

"Laurel's got a crush on him," Marybeth gladly explained, her hands on her hips.

"I just like being able to talk to someone older and more mature, like me," Laurel retorted, her glare sending a warning to her sister. "We have the same interests."

That statement caused the other two girls to launch into a heated debate with Laurel about who exactly was the most mature among them, and just exactly what interests she shared with Cal.

"Hey, hey," Rock said, putting his hands together in a time-out signal at the girls' eye level, "you are all maturing in your own way and in God's own time. And Laurel's budding relationship with Cal is just that, nothing to get worked up about. Simmer down."

"Yeah, simmer down now," Laurel said, exaggerating her words to the point that they all started laughing.

Eloise quirked a brow. "I can see you and Ana will have your hands full this summer."

Rock understood perfectly the implications of that statement. Eloise was looping Ana and Rock together, as in dating, as in trying to control a family of flighty sisters.

A family.

The phrase hit Rock square in the gut, and with an instant clarity that shimmered as brightly as one of his mother's polished crosses, he knew what had been missing in his life for so long.

He glanced up to find Eloise giving him a curious look, as if she, too, had just figured this out. He hated the hopefulness in her eyes, hated that she wanted him to be happy, when for so long he hadn't actually believed she cared.

Then he looked over at Ana. She stood in a wash of late-afternoon sunshine, her wild auburn hair burning with shards of gold and red, her vivid green eyes as pure and tranquil as a forest pool. She smiled at him, a perfect smile that spoke of contentment and peace, in spite of the chaos around them.

A smile that shattered Rock's own fragile peace and shifted the very earth beneath his feet, lending that same beautiful chaos to his confused soul.

He had finally fallen in love. But he couldn't be sure if he'd fallen for Ana, or just the illusion of what having a real family with Ana might be like.

Was this a beautiful, unattainable dream? Or could it be real, at last?

Rock glanced at the girls, still whispering and fussing, then his eyes locked with Ana's. She gave him a quizzical look. Could she see his feelings on his face?

Well, he had the whole summer to test this new, disturbing theory of love. Trouble was, how was he going to keep his feelings a secret from Ana—who valued complete honesty above all things—until he could be sure?

Chapter Ten

"Hey, I found you."

At the sound of the shout, Ana turned from her spot on the blanket to find her sister strolling down the beach. "Hello," she called, waving.

Tara had changed into her swimsuit and a matching cover-up. She looked like a fashion model in her black straw hat and black-and-white bathing suit. Ana had opted for a floral bathing suit and cotton shorts to cover her thighs. And she had yet to get wet. She'd been too busy reading over the last-minute to-do lists and other paperwork she had to wade through before the tea room's opening.

"Look at that sunset," Tara said as she settled down beside Ana in a cloud of expensive perfume, her gaze moving off to the west behind the bay. "Where are the girls?"

"Beachcombing," Ana replied as she offered

Tara a bottled water from a small ice chest. "I told them to stay close. They should be back soon."

Tara let out a long sigh, then lifted the top off the water bottle. "Boy, do I wish I could stay here a few more days. This feels so good."

Ana noticed the dark circles under her sister's vivid blue eyes. "How did your meeting go?"

"Okay," Tara said, her eyes scanning the ocean before she put her shades on. Then she shook her head. "If I ever get all the bank accounts and insurance policies sorted out, not to mention the stock options and 401K account, I'll be thrilled."

"Don't you have lawyers and accountants to handle all of that?"

Tara stared straight out into the water. "Yes, but I'm trying to do most of it on my own, just to familiarize myself with it." She sat silent for a minute, then said, "You know, Chad always handled the finances. Now I wish I'd paid more attention to the details. It's like moving through a never-ending maze."

"But you're okay, right?" Ana had a strange feeling in her stomach. Tara was being evasive. "Do you need me to help?"

Tara patted her hand. "You're helping already by letting the girls stay here. And I mean it, Ana—make them work for their keep, the way Mom and Dad taught us to work. They can do odd jobs, wash dishes, help serve food."

"I intend to keep them busy," Ana replied. "But

we did take the afternoon off, since it was their first day here."

"That was thoughtful of you. So what did you do?"

Now it was Ana's turn to be evasive. "Oh, we went to the lighthouse festival—ate junk food, then went on most of the rides at that little traveling carnival on the boardwalk."

"Oh, I'm sure the girls loved that."

"They had a blast," Ana replied, leaving out the part about being with Rock for most of the afternoon. It had been such a nice, peaceful outing, even with three noisy girls in tow. Rock had been a perfect gentleman, and they'd laughed and talked about little things. Ana had refrained from talking about work, however. She supposed that had been a good idea, since Rock seemed to enjoy himself, too. Remembering how he'd held her close when the Ferris wheel had stopped them right up on top, Ana had to smile.

"What's that smile all about?" Tara asked, bringing her sunglasses down on her nose as she shot Ana a purposeful look. "Must be a man involved, since you look so dreamy."

"Not everything in life has to revolve around a man," Ana retorted, sticking out her tongue in much the same fashion Marybeth often did.

Tara grinned, then tossed her hat down. "Did Rock Dempsey just happen to tag along on this little excursion?"

"Oh, all right," Ana said, dropping her file of paperwork back in her tote bag. "Yes, he did come along. The girls seem to behave better with him around. He has a soothing...countenance."

Tara rolled her eyes. "A soothing countenance? You make him sound like a nice old uncle."

Lowering her head, Ana thought about that. "He is nice, very nice. He's dependable, solid, hardworking. Not the type I'm used to, at all."

"Not like Chad," Tara said, then instantly put a hand to her mouth. "I'm sorry. That just slipped out."

Ana thought about that. "No, you're right. Chad was a bad-boy type. We both knew that. But he had a good heart."

"Yes," Tara said, "but that heart couldn't take all the stress of his demanding job." She grew silent again. "Sometimes, I feel so guilty, as if I pushed him too hard."

"You can't blame yourself, Tara. Who knew Chad had a heart condition? You can't predict things like that."

Her sister took off her sunglasses and wiped at her eyes. "I miss him so much. Chad had his faults, but I loved him in my own way. You have to know that, Ana."

"I do," Ana said, painfully aware that even though Chad Parnell was dead, the issue of his having at one time loved both of them was still very much alive. Wanting to change the subject, she said, "Now, let's get back to Rock. You need to help me figure him out."

Tara gave a shaky laugh. "Who can figure out men?"

"Well, you're right there," Ana agreed, lying down to soak up the last rays of the sun. "But this one is different. I just don't know what makes him tick. He's old-fashioned and sweet, but I'm afraid those very things might get in the way of any kind of lasting relationship with him."

"What do you mean?"

Ana shrugged, her bare shoulders brushing against the terry cloth of the seascape beach blanket. "Rock's mother worked long hours when the boys were growing up. Being the eldest, Rock had to take care of his brothers a lot. Apparently, he cooked, cleaned, and worked odd jobs most of his teenage years. I think he still resents his mother because of that—"

"And therefore, resents working women in general?" Tara asked, hitting the mark.

"I think so." Ana waved a hand in the air. "At least, that's the impression I get. I think Rock wants a traditional kind of wife—someone who will cook, clean and provide an orderly house for him."

"That *is* old-fashioned," Tara quipped, groaning. "Funny, I tried to be that for Chad at first, but he didn't seem to notice. That's why I went into real estate. After the girls started school, I had to do something."

Ana rolled to her stomach, then placed her head on her hands. "This whole issue of a working woman—didn't we get over that in the last century?"

"You'd think."

"But you know," Ana said, her mind replaying how much she'd enjoyed being with Rock, "even if it's old-fashioned, I kinda like the idea of being a traditional wife. I like to cook and putter around the house. And I want a family."

Tara shifted on the blanket, then stared down at her sister. "You deserve that." She turned and watched the waves capping a few yards away. "I took that from you, didn't I?"

Ana shot up. "Let's not get into that, okay? Chad made his choice, and I accepted that."

"You accepted *us*," Tara corrected. "Ana, why didn't you ever scream and holler? Didn't you resent us?"

Ana thought long and hard before answering. "Of course I did. But I love you, and I loved Chad. Sometimes, because we do love so much, we also have to accept and let go. I was hurt, no doubt. But I love *you* more than I loved being bitter and hurt. I just couldn't see holding a grudge and losing my sister. We made it through."

"And now Chad is gone."

"But we have the girls."

"Yes, we do. And you are a wonderful aunt." Tara smiled then. "And an aunt who apparently is about to get a love life."

"I don't know about that," Ana said, falling back against the blanket, her eyes shut. "We'll have to see where things go with Rock."

"Hmm," Tara replied, slapping Ana on the arm. She was looking in the other direction. "I guess we'll soon find out about that. He's walking up the beach right now, with another fellow, a dog and…our girls."

Ana shot up again, her eyes scanning the horizon to the south. Behind them, the sun was setting in shades of orange and mauve. "What? Rock's here?"

"Don't hyperventilate," Tara said, swiping at Ana's back.

Ana spotted him then. He was dressed in cutoff khakis and an open, button-up shirt. He was laughing with the girls and…Cal Ashworth.

"That's Cal with him," Ana said. "Your eldest daughter has taken an immediate liking to that young man."

"Oh, great." Tara glared with a mother's intensity toward Cal. "Well, he *is* cute. But I think I might be the one to hyperventilate. Laurel and I have been at odds lately, maybe because she is beginning to notice boys. I can't stand the thought of my baby being old enough to date, and she can't stand the thought of me standing in her way."

"Actually, she's really not quite old enough for anything serious," Ana said. "But they can at least hang out together. Cal comes from a good, Christian family."

"So did Chad," Tara retorted. "Oops. Sorry again."

Ana decided there was something going on with Tara. She'd made reference to Chad's shortcomings far too many times since his death. But now wasn't the time to bring that up.

Right now, Rock was walking toward her, a lazy grin on his face and a quizzical look in his eyes.

"Hello there," Rock said, hoping he looked nonchalant. He didn't want Ana to think he was stalking her. But his next words gave him away. "The girls said I'd find you here."

"And how did you find the girls?" Ana asked as she waved at him.

"They found me," he told her while he enjoyed the view of her pretty legs underneath the baggy denim shorts. "Cal and I were finishing up some last-minute things at the shop when these three popped in."

"I saw the sign from the beach—Dempsey's Cabinetry," Laurel said, her chin jutting out in defiance. "So we walked over there." At her aunt's sharp look of disapproval, she added, "You said stay close. It's right up there." She pointed back over the hill toward the wind-tossed oak trees.

"And we found a dog," Marybeth said before Ana could protest any further.

"So I see. C'mere, boy." Tara squealed as the big, wet collie ran up and licked her face. Tara immediately began petting the animal, cooing to him in baby talk. "What a pretty boy, yes, he is."

"That's Sweetybaby," Cal said, his voice low and shy. "He's mine now. My mom's, actually— she gave him that dumb name." He shrugged. "My mom died three years ago."

"Oh, I'm sorry to hear that," Ana told the boy.

"Sweetybaby comes to the shop each day to fetch Cal home," Rock explained, changing the somber mood and hoping the friendly animal would win both Cal and him points with the womenfolk. "Somehow this dog just knows when it's quitting time."

"So why didn't you go on home?" Ana asked, a teasing light in her green eyes.

At least she seemed glad to see him. Rock relaxed. Over the past two hours, he hadn't been able to focus on work. And it was all Ana's fault. Since he'd realized right there on Lady Street that he might be falling for her, he'd wanted nothing more than to see her again. When the girls had shown up, he'd had the perfect excuse.

"We wanted him to come to the beach with us," Amanda told them in answer to Ana's question. Then she called to the dog. "C'mon, Sweetybaby, let's go play."

With that, the girls and Cal took off for the water, laughing and screaming as they tried to wet each other with the splashing surf.

Rock shrugged, then sat down on a corner of the

big blanket. "I figured you'd be worried, so I told them we'd walk them back down here. And I made Cal call his sister so she'd know where he is, too."

"How very thoughtful," Tara said, her expression telling him that she didn't believe that paltry excuse. "But then, Ana has been going on and on about how thoughtful and kind you are, Rock."

Rock saw Ana lift a bare foot to kick her sister. "Has she, now?"

"I've been telling her all about *work*," Ana said. "About how you've worked overtime to make sure the kitchen is finished on time."

Rock felt the bubble in his heart deflating a little bit. "Ah, yes, we can't forget about that, can we? Ana is on a mission to get things done, that's for sure."

"She has to be," Tara replied. "Her livelihood depends on it."

Rock thought he'd heard the hint of a dare in her statement. Were these two formidable sisters ganging up on him and his old-fashioned notions?

"Nothing wrong with an honest day's work," he replied, hoping for damage control.

"Well, I'm glad we can all agree on that," Tara said, her smile serenity itself, while her blue eyes flashed a warning.

"Just ignore her," Ana said, giving her sister her own warning look. "Tara has always worked hard herself. She's a Realtor."

"So I've heard from the girls. Sounds as if you do pretty good at it, too."

"I make a living," Tara said. Then in a rush of hands and feet, she hopped up. "Think I'll take a dip before it gets too chilly out here."

She ran down the beach and straight into the water, her girls cheering her on while Sweetybaby tried to race after her in the waves.

"Was it something I said?" Rock asked Ana when they were alone. He didn't think her sister approved of him at all.

"No. She's just having a hard time since her husband died."

"It's only been a few months, right?"

She nodded, looked away for just a moment. "Chad was a good husband, but he worked day and night. He got caught up in his career, neglected his health. He was too young, way too young, to die."

"I'm sorry. That's tough, I know. I guess Tara is dealing with a lot, especially having to raise the girls on her own."

"We're all dealing with the situation. It was rough on Chad's parents, too. They're just not able to help with the girls."

"What about your parents? You don't mention them much."

She smiled, brushed sand off her leg. "They're fine. They like to travel in their new motorhome. They go to these get-togethers where everyone has a big, silver travel trailer. It's like a sea of little houses, all lined up."

"Sounds as if they're enjoying their retirement."

"They are. And they plan on coming through here later in the summer, to visit with the girls and help out some."

"Were they close to Chad?"

She gave him a panicked look. "Of course."

Ana got such a faraway look in her eyes each time he mentioned Chad Parnell. Maybe she was still dealing with his death, too. After all, from everything she'd told him, it appeared the Hansons were a close-knit family.

Feeling like an oaf, he decided to change the subject and try again. "You got some sun. It looks nice."

Ana glanced down at her skin. "Was I too pale before?"

"No, of course not. I just mean—"

He stopped, took a long breath. "I never know the right thing to say to you." He thought he saw pity in her eyes, followed by amusement.

"What?" she asked, giving him a measured look. "No words from a dead poet? No sage advice from a philosophy book? Not even a bit of wisdom from Proverbs?"

Okay, she *was* teasing him. He could take it. And he could give as good as he got, too. "How about I say it straight? You always look good to me, Ana. How's that?"

She actually blushed. "That's...just fine, Rock."

Then she jumped up and, running toward the

ocean, tossed him a dare over her shoulder. "Bet you can't catch me."

Rock took that dare. "Oh, I intend to do just that," he said to himself as he hurried after her.

Chapter Eleven

"It was nice of your mother to do this," Ana told Rock a couple of days later. It was late afternoon and they were on their way to Eloise's studio. She had invited the girls to come and see where she worked.

"And we'll let them explore their creativity," Eloise had said over the phone.

Rock turned up the winding tree-shaded drive to Eloise's big Victorian house. "I was surprised. My mother never lets anything or anyone get in the way of her work."

"Do you think we'll bother her?" Amanda asked from the back seat of Rock's utility van, where she sat squished between her sisters.

Rock glanced in the mirror to find Amanda's big eyes on him. "Honey, she wouldn't have invited you if she didn't want you here."

Ana believed him. Rock was handling this with grace, but she still sensed the resentment in him. Obviously, he was trying to understand his mother, trying to stay close to her, in spite of what might have happened when he was younger. But then, Rock was that kind of man. A gentle soul who looked for the best in people. Rock nurtured the people who depended on him as a minister and a friend. He'd shown Ana so much about her own faith simply by talking to her and listening to her, then reassuring her. And he'd done this in spite of the rumors flying hot and heavy about their supposed love life.

But who nurtured and reassured Rock?

Don't go getting ideas, she told herself as she stayed safely in her corner of the car. It was bad enough that the whole island was involved in their personal lives, let alone her thinking they actually were more than just good friends. Still, she could be the friend he'd hoped for, if nothing else. That was a form of nurturing.

And the past few days had brought a tentative peace between them. It was a nice change— actually having the time to get to know a man before taking that next step. Perhaps that was where she'd gone wrong in all her relationships since Chad. She'd rushed things, hoping to find a perfect mate before her biological clock stopped ticking. With Rock, the slow and steady pace of getting acquainted had a very enticing rhythm. Ana prayed that she was on the right path, that she wasn't just imagining things. And she prayed that this sweet slow longing inside her heart promised something good and right.

But that slow rhythm doesn't allow for kissing him, she also reminded herself. When Rock kissed her, everything went into overdrive. Best to avoid those kisses and the feelings they provoked. Best to enjoy their friendship and the deep, abiding respect she felt for this man.

"This house is so cool," Marybeth shouted very near Ana's ear, deafening her into awareness.

"It belonged to my grandparents," Rock said as he pulled the van up underneath an aged magnolia tree.

"Do they live here, too?" Marybeth asked, opening the sliding door before the van had even stopped.

"No. They're dead now," Rock said. While the girls began piling out, he turned to Ana. "They were once the wealthiest people on the island, but when they got old, my grandfather had to sell most of their property. They wound up in a retirement home in Savannah. And that's where they died."

"That's sad," Ana said. "Why didn't they live here?"

Rock turned in the seat, waiting as Laurel took off her earphones and put away her CD player. After all the girls were out of the van, he said, "We never knew them. They disinherited my mother when she married my father. So we were never close."

Stunned, Ana looked up to find Eloise walking down a shell-covered path that ran from the main house to her studio. "Your mother gave up her inheritance for love?"

"Yeah. They had over fifteen happy years together before my father drowned. And…you know the rest."

Ana put a hand on his arm. "No, I don't know the rest. But I want to. Will you tell me about it sometime? All of it?"

"Sometime," he said, his eyes shuttered with darkness. Then he got out of the van and came around to her door before she could open it. "But not now."

Ana got out, her eyes on Rock as he greeted his mother. There was so much more to him, so many deep scars and troubling secrets hidden behind those wise eyes and that gentle smile. She wanted to know all of him.

She wanted to nurture him. That meant taking the step she'd been avoiding, that step that would take them beyond mere friendship. But it might be worth it this time. Because by doing so, she just might be able to heal her wounds, too.

Rock walked toward his waiting mother, wishing that he hadn't told Ana about his grandparents. But he hadn't told her everything. And maybe he never would.

But Ana wanted to know. Would she still look at him in the same way if she knew all about his hurts and his anger? He didn't want to lose the precious bond they'd formed.

And that was part of the reason he had brought Ana and the girls here today. Being with Ana made him a better man. It made him much more aware of his shortcomings, too.

"You're frowning," Eloise said as she reached to touch his face. His mother was a toucher. She liked to feel things, liked moving her fingers over the rough texture of life, hoping to carve the rough spots into something soft and beautiful. At least, she'd been working toward that with Rock.

Allowing her this small endearment, Rock formed the beginnings of a smile. "How's that? Better?"

"A little. You didn't mind bringing the girls, did you?"

"No, of course not." He watched as Laurel, Marybeth and Amanda glanced around the colorful, intriguing yard. "They came to conquer and explore."

"Welcome, girls," Eloise said, waving her arm in the air. "What do you think of my garden?"

Laurel shrugged. "It's weird."

Rock saw Ana cringe, but hurried to reassure her. "It's okay. She likes being weird, honestly."

"I told you, I prefer to be called eccentric," Eloise replied, her big silver hoop earrings jangling. "But these pieces are a bit different. Abstracts and modern art combined with some traditional pieces."

"I like the crosses on the tree," Amanda said timidly. "Could I make something like that?"

"Absolutely," Eloise told her. "I have plenty of scraps lying around. You can create whatever you want."

"I'm not good at art," Laurel said, sounding sullen. She was pouting because she'd wanted to go for a walk on the beach with Cal instead of coming to "make dumb artwork."

"You might just need to try something different, a new twist," Eloise said, her smile serene, her eyes taking in Laurel's stubborn stance. "You could make something special, to represent your stay on the island."

"Whatever." Laurel whirled to stare at a flower-shaped iron sculpture Eloise had created years ago. "That's cool."

"One of my first attempts," Eloise explained. "It's a lotus blossom."

"Looks like a rusty flower to me," Marybeth said. Then she put a hand to her mouth. "Sorry."

"Beauty is in the eye of the beholder," Rock said to his mother.

"And to each his own," Eloise retorted. "Now come girls. Let's see what else we can view and appreciate. We have to have art in our lives, to add human interpretation to the aesthetic beauty of God's world."

"She is weird," Marybeth whispered to Amanda. Ana shot the giggling girls a quieting glare, but they still managed to grin at each other and Rock.

Rock grinned back, then waited for Ana while

the girls took off after Eloise. "I certainly see a beauty I appreciate," he whispered in Ana's ear as he glanced down at her.

"Beauty is in the eye of the beholder," Ana mimicked.

But she blushed as she said it.

"Let's go for a walk," Rock said much later.

The girls were safely ensconced in the high-ceilinged studio with Eloise. They were making things—small creations that they could give to their mother when she returned later in the week. Or keep for themselves, to store up and treasure.

The way Rock had stored up and treasured certain little baubles he'd made in his mother's studio whenever he'd been allowed a few quiet moments with her.

Ana stretched in the lounge chair where she'd been sitting. "Okay."

"Okay?"

"A walk?"

"Oh, right." He extended a hand to her and pulled her to her feet, the sweet smell of her floral perfume merging with the scent of magnolia from a nearby tree.

"You seem distracted," Ana said. "We could go on home."

"No, I'm fine. Just remembering."

"Want to tell me about it?"

They headed down the path toward the dunes,

moonlight glistening against the sand in patterns of gray and blue. The sound of the whitecaps echoed up, calling to them in a serene melody. Rock prayed for some of that serenity.

"I have good memories," he said at last. "I don't want you to think I had a horrible childhood."

"I don't think that."

"I was just remembering once when I went out to my mother's studio late one night. She was standing there, bathed in lamplight, her hands moving and shaping a piece of clay. She looked so lovely, so at peace, her eyes flashing, her hands moving. Then she looked up at me, as if she'd known I was there."

"Was she angry at being interrupted?"

"No, she invited me in and let me work on the sculpture. She told me there was a beauty in creating something just for yourself."

"What did you create?"

"An owl. I shaped the clay into an owl. I still have that owl sitting on my mantel."

"Your mother let you keep it?"

"Yes. She said it belonged to me now. I had touched it, shaped it, made it into something entirely my own."

"That's a nice story, Rock."

They were down on the sand now. They tossed off their shoes and walked barefoot toward the sea. "That's how I feel about us, Ana." He turned to her, his hands tentatively touching her soft curls. "I feel as if each time I'm with you, I'm molding and shaping something that can become mine. Does that make sense?"

He saw the fear, the doubt, reflected in her eyes. "Ana?"

"Do you want to mold me into something else, Rock?"

He pulled her close. "Goodness, no. That's not what I'm saying."

"Then, what exactly are you saying?"

He shifted, tugged her closer. "I'm saying I like being with you. I like what being with you does to me."

"But you want to own me?"

"No." He stepped back, ran a hand through his hair. "I'm saying...you're the one, Ana. You're the one who's changing and reshaping me. You're the one who's making me see that I've been sitting in judgment against my own mother."

He felt her hand on his arm. "I don't want to change you. I just want to understand you."

He put his arms around her again, savoring the warmth of her skin, the sweetness of holding her. "I'm not telling this...I'm not explaining it right," he said. With a groan, he urged her close, then lowered his mouth to hers.

The kiss held all of his dark secrets, all of his fears and worries. As his lips moved over hers, he felt those secrets and fears being shifted and sifted, like sand moving through water, into something full of light and hope.

"There," he said as he lifted his head and stepped back.

Ana stared up at him, her eyes wide, her lips thoroughly kissed. "There what?"

"There. I hope that explained what I'm trying to say."

"That only complicated things," she said, one hand flying to her mouth. "I thought we'd decided to avoid…kissing."

"I never decided that." No, but he'd told himself a hundred times to stay away from her. From her tempting lips.

"Well, we agreed to be friends, to keep things more on a business level."

"This is a different kind of business. Personal business."

She kept staring up at him, her gaze transfixed in a wash of moonlight and night tides. "This… could ruin our friendship, you know."

"But that's what I'm trying to say. I think we might be on the verge of becoming more than friends. I don't know how to explain what you do to me, Ana."

She turned away, stared out at the water. "I can't be the woman you expect, Rock. I want my tea room."

Surprised, he felt as if she'd punched him in the stomach. "I don't want you to give up anything. I just want you to…keep doing what you're doing. To me."

"But you sound as if you're in some sort of pain."

He smiled, then tugged her around. "No. I mean, yes. It's painful to see one's own shortcomings, but it's also a good thing to find someone I enjoy being around. If it means I can be closer to you, then I'm willing to work my way through this."

"So you're saying that even though it's torture to be around me, you like to suffer?" she asked in a soft tone.

"Something like that." He stood silent, his eyes on her. Then he decided to fall back on his old ways for just a moment. "'Man cannot remake himself without suffering. He is both the marble and the sculptor.'"

Ana didn't move, didn't respond.

"Alexis Carrel," he said. "It's a quote."

"I figured that out on my own," she replied.

"Well, I was just trying to explain."

"So you're telling me you're suffering because of your feelings for me, but that's really a good thing because in the process, you're…changing… because of me?"

"Yes," he said, his hands waving in the air. "Yes. I want to be a better man, so that you'll be happy with me, so that you'll want to be with me. And that means dropping some of my preconceived notions about women in general. It also means lots of prayer—*lots* of prayer." He stopped, inhaled. "But it will be worth the price, worth the asking, worth the risk."

"You're willing to take that risk…for me?"

He nodded, the revelation washing over him like the ocean. And like those same crashing waters, it was both exhilarating and frightening.

"But that means you'd be doing all the changing, Rock," she said. "I don't necessarily want you to change. Not completely."

"I'd only change the stupid parts," he replied, hoping he wasn't scaring her away.

"And what about me? Don't I need to change some, too?"

"You're close to perfect," he blurted, then wished he hadn't said that. She looked up at him as if she didn't believe a word of it.

"Oh, no. I am far from perfect." She turned, stalked away, her feet slapping the sand. "Since college…since my heart was broken…I've searched for the *perfect* replacement. Someone I could love and have a family with."

Rock now understood the hesitancy in her, that quietness he'd seen and wondered about. She'd been in love before, he remembered. But she'd told him very little about that love or why her heart had been broken. Another revelation, but also another insight into Ana. "You thought you had that someone…in college?"

She looked out at the dark ocean. "Yes, but he fell in love with someone else, someone more outgoing and much prettier than me."

He let that soak in, mentally deciding he'd ask

her about her lost love and her broken heart later, when she was ready to tell him about it. "I'm sorry you had to go through that, but I don't want to be a replacement, Ana. I want you to see me for myself, flaws and all." And he wanted her to love him. Oh, how he wanted that.

"And will you accept me, flaws and all?" she asked, the words holding a hint of hope.

"Absolutely. If I spot a flaw in you, I'll let you know."

He heard her sigh, saw her doubt turn into a gentle smile. "We could have a chance here, Ana. A good chance, with prayer and patience, to find the things that have been missing in our lives."

"You do make it sound like business. Like some sort of contract to be ironed out and negotiated."

"I didn't mean it that way," he said, wondering when he'd started repeating himself. "Look, it just seems as if we're both scared of taking things further, for whatever reasons. I'm only asking you to meet me halfway, to be honest with me. I think you feel the same way. I just wanted you to know…I'm willing to try."

"Even though it might be painful?"

"It's a really nice sort of pain."

"Okay." She walked toward him and grabbed the lapels of his shirt, a soft sigh of release shuddering through her. "I guess it is time for the next step."

Then she kissed him, long and hard, and with

such a sweet intensity that he almost fell back into the wet, churning surf.

But Rock didn't fall. Ana caught him just in time.

She was dreaming of Rock. It was a sweet dream, muted in shades of yellow sunset and pink sky, tinged with a kind of contentment that flowed like cool water over her soul. In the dream, Rock was kissing her beside the ocean. She was wearing the shrunken dress. There was an owl sitting on a tree in the background. Ana felt safe, completely at home.

"Aunt Ana, wake up!"

The voice shrilling in her ear brought Ana out of her dreams. She sat up in bed and stared groggily out into the darkness, her breathing shallow and swift. The clock on the bedside table said four a.m. "Marybeth? What is it, honey?"

Marybeth stood fidgeting at the side of the bed, her big green eyes bright with fear. "It's Laurel. She sneaked out to meet Cal on the beach. She was supposed to be back by now, but…well, it's been hours and hours and she's not home yet. Aunt Ana, I'm so worried."

Chapter Twelve

"Start at the beginning," Ana told Marybeth. They were in the kitchen with Rock, Eloise and Cal's father, Don. It was five o'clock in the morning.

Marybeth sighed, glancing toward where Rock stood making coffee. "It's okay, honey," he said. "We just need to know the truth."

"All I know is that Laurel really, really likes Cal and he likes her, too. They decided to sneak out, to go down to the beach for a midnight stroll or swim or something." She shrugged. "I told her she'd get into trouble. Now she's going to blame me for tattling."

"It's okay to tattle when someone could be in trouble or in danger," Eloise pointed out.

Ana closed her eyes, remembering those first terrifying moments after Marybeth had told her Laurel was missing. Not knowing where else to turn, she'd called Rock first. He knew the island.

He might have an idea where Cal would take Laurel. He'd called Eloise. Ana was glad for the older woman's quiet strength.

"Cal knows better," his father, a bulky man with shots of silver in his spiky hair, said as Rock handed him a cup of steaming coffee. "That kid—he sees a pretty girl and all of the sense just leaves his brains."

Rock smiled. "It happens to the best of us," he said, glancing at Ana. "I'm sure they're okay."

"I can't stand waiting," Ana said, slipping off her stool to pace the room. "Why haven't the police called?"

"They're looking out near the lighthouse, Ana," Eloise said. "Although I must say, Chief Anderson didn't seem that concerned. That man's gotten so lackadaisical, he needs to retire." Ana didn't miss the glance that passed between mother and son.

"You think something's happened, don't you," she said, her heart fluttering with fear. "What is it, Rock?"

Rock put down his coffee, then pulled her around. "I'm sure they're okay, but…if they decided to go for a swim…well, those midnight tides can be very dangerous."

"You mean the undertow?"

"Yes, that and the fact that sharks like to troll these waters after dark."

"Sharks?" Ana sank back down against the stool. "I can't believe this is happening. Tara trusted me—" Her hand went to her mouth. "I have to call Tara."

Rock shook his head. "Let's give it some more time. If we haven't found them by daylight, then we'll call her."

Ana grabbed his arm. "Take me out there, Rock, please. Just drive me around the island. I can't stay here. I'll go crazy with worry."

Rock looked at Eloise. She nodded. "I'll stay here with the girls. Don will keep me company, won't you, Don?"

"Yeah, sure," Don said, his gray eyes widening. "Rock, you'll call us if—"

"If I hear or see anything, I promise," Rock said, already guiding Ana toward the door.

Rock had driven his small pickup instead of the big work van. Ana climbed inside, glad for the closeness the tiny vehicle allowed. "I should have seen this coming," she said, her eyes scanning the predawn darkness. "Laurel has been having a hard time dealing with her father's death. Tara told me she's been acting out. At times, she appears completely normal, then other times, she's very rude to her mother and snarly to everyone else."

"That's understandable," Rock said, his eyes on the road that ran along the beach. "I remember how confused I was at that age, especially after losing my father. I guess I've been blaming my mother for a lot of things that weren't really her fault."

"But…you're trying," Ana said, willing the chatter to calm her mind and steady her nerves so she could think. "You and Eloise seems close."

"We are now," Rock said, slowing to scan the picnic tables scattered across a roadside park. "It took many, many years and a lot of prayer, but we're making progress."

"I hope Laurel can find some sort of peace," Ana said. Then she ran a hand over her hair. "I hope they…didn't do anything stupid." She inhaled a long, shuddering breath. "Rock, she's only fourteen. I should have been more aware. I shouldn't have let things distract me—"

"It's going to be all right," Rock said, reaching across the space between them to clasp her hand in his. "And don't go blaming yourself. You've monitored those girls day and night. You have to sleep sometime, and besides, we had no inkling that she'd pull a stunt like this."

"She's so confused and hurt," Ana said, her hand gripping the handle on the truck door as she searched for movement in the trees and on the beaches as they passed. "I just wish I'd taken more time to talk with her. I've had them for two weeks, and now this."

Rock slowed the truck to search a tiny inlet where the ocean curved into the bay. "In spite of her hostility, I think Laurel has a good head on her shoulders. And Cal is a good boy. He has four older sisters who've turned out all right, and they lost their mother. Laurel probably thought she wouldn't get caught, or they could have just lost track of time."

"I hope it's that. I can handle that, but I can't handle something happening to them."

They fell silent as they searched the dunes and shores on the far west side of the island near the lighthouse, sometimes getting out to walk along the lonely, empty stretches of beach. But they didn't see Laurel and Cal.

An hour later, as the sun began to climb up over the eastern waters, Ana knew she'd waited long enough.

"I have to call Tara."

Rock nodded. "We'll make one more sweep. Let's go up Lady Street, just to see if maybe they're at one of the coffee shops. Then, if we don't find them, we'll go home and call her."

"Thank you," Ana said, sincerely meaning it. "I don't usually fall apart like this, but...she's so young and I feel so responsible." She also felt guilty, very guilty. She'd been so wrapped up in her newfound feelings for Rock that she had neglected everything else around her, first her work, and now her nieces. Maybe it was time for her to concentrate on both again.

Rock was watching her as if he could read exactly what she was thinking. "This isn't your fault, you know. Teenagers are wily, Ana. You can't predict their moves. You just have to give them guidance and hope for the best."

"But what if the worst happens?"

Rock stopped the truck in front of the closed

amusement park. "I don't know what to tell you. I don't expect the worst, but if it happens, we'll deal with it, together."

"Maybe that's part of the problem," Ana said, at her wits' end. "Maybe we've been together too much, so much that I've failed Laurel. I should have paid closer attention."

"Don't talk like that."

Ana opened the truck door and got out before he could reach for her. Her emotions had reached a fever pitch. Dashing tears away, she scanned the distant shore, her eyes touching on the Wedding Rock out past the Sunken Pier Restaurant. Remembering when Rock had brought her here, she wished she'd remembered her pledge to keep things strictly business between them. If she had, she might have been more in tune to Laurel's problems, and the girl's obvious interest in Cal Ashworth. Ana glanced back out into the muted darkness, her mind racing with the possibility of sharks and undertows.

And that's when she saw them. Laurel and Cal.

Barely visible because of the dark dawn, they were sitting up against one side of the rock, facing away from the water. Cal had his arm around Laurel and it looked as if they were asleep.

"Laurel!" Ana started running toward them, her hands waving in the air as she shouted. "Laurel?"

Her voice carried on the morning wind, echoing out over the buildings and sand. Laurel jerked her head up, saw her aunt coming, then shook Cal out of his sleep. "Aunt Ana?"

Ana cried tears of pure joy. "Laurel, are you all right?" She kept running toward them.

"I'm fine," Laurel called. Cal helped her up, and together, they started toward Ana. Then Laurel raised a hand in warning. "Aunt Ana, look out!"

It was too late for Ana, though. She didn't see the deep hole in the sand. Still running, she hit the hole and slipped, feeling nothing under her left foot. Then she fell and went rolling against the sandy, seashell-covered lane leading down to the shore.

A sharp, distinct pain burned its way up Ana's left foot and leg as one foot sank into the giant water-filled hole and she pitched forward, her face hitting the sand as she let out a tortured scream.

Rock was at her side. "Ana? Are you all right?"

"No," she said, pushing up on her hands, sand in her mouth. Her cheekbone burned from scraping the tiny shells and rocks. "I think I sprained my ankle."

Rock gently lifted her up into a sitting position, dusting off her face and clothes, while Laurel and Cal came hurrying to stand wide-eyed beside her.

"Aunt Ana?" Laurel said, her voice trembling with fear. "I'm so sorry."

Rock held Ana, then turned to the two teenagers. "You two have some explaining to do. But we need to get your Aunt to a doctor first."

"No," Ana said, trying to stand. She grimaced, the pain in her foot unbearable. "I'll be okay. Just get me home."

"You've hurt your foot," Rock said, lifting her into his arms. "I'm taking you by the medical center."

"I think he's right," Cal said, his hand in Laurel's.

Ana looked over Rock's shoulder at her niece. "Just tell me you're okay, Laurel. I've been so worried—"

"I'm fine," Laurel said sheepishly. "We went for a walk and, well, we sat down by the Wedding Rock to talk and—"

"We fell asleep," Cal finished. "We were tired and we just fell asleep. That's the truth, Ms. Hanson."

Ana didn't know if her tears were from joy or pain, or both. But she finally gave in to them. "They were tired. They fell asleep," she said through gulps as she looked up at Rock. "No sharks, no undertows...thank goodness."

"We'll either hug them or throttle them later," Rock said as he kissed her forehead. "Right now, I'm taking you to a doctor."

Ana snuggled against him, acutely aware of the strength of his arms, of the warmth of his heart beating against her ear.

This is what got you into this mess, she reminded herself. In a little while, after the pain had ebbed, after the shock of her niece missing all night had worn off, Ana would have to take a step back and evaluate the twists and turns of her mixed-up life.

In a little while. Right now, she couldn't help herself. She wanted to stay safe in Rock's arms.

The next afternoon, Tara paced the floor of Ana's long, sun-dappled second-floor bedroom. "I can't believe this."

"Believe it," Ana said, wincing as she shifted her heavily bandaged ankle. "Your daughter spent the night out on the beach with Cal Ashworth, I have a severely sprained ankle, and the tea room is set to open this weekend."

"What are we going to do?" Tara said. "I'm due back in Savannah tomorrow, for a conference on this Atlanta land deal, and I'm still in negotiation with some mystery man about that land near Savannah—extremely sensitive negotiations."

"I never expected you to help with the opening," Ana said. "I'll manage, somehow." She wanted to shake her sister into seeing that Laurel needed her right now, but decided she'd refrain from that tactic.

"How?" Tara gestured at her ankle. "You can't walk, Ana. How are you going to cook and supervise the opening? Not to mention that we now have to watch Laurel's every move, restriction or not."

Ana wondered that herself. Since yesterday, she'd been stuck here in her bedroom, with her throbbing ankle up on a pillow, encased off and on in ice packs. That meant she hadn't really had much of a chance to talk to Laurel. Then Tara had come home today, in a rage about what Laurel had done.

She'd immediately put Laurel on restriction, forbidding her to see or speak to Cal for the rest of the summer. Ana wasn't so sure that was the answer to Laurel's problems, but Tara was in such a tizzy, she wouldn't listen to Ana's pleas for mercy on Laurel's behalf.

"Jackie is capable of overseeing things," Ana said, glad she'd hired an assistant already trained in running a restaurant. "And Tina is a great hostess. Plus, my waiters and waitresses have been training for weeks now."

"But…this has to be a good opening." Tara stopped, shook her head. "I'm staying here. I'll just explain to my boss that my sister needs me."

"And your daughter," Ana said. Tara glanced down at her, perplexed. "Laurel needs you, too, Tara."

Tara sank down on a white ottoman. "I know she does. Tell me how…how can I reach her? She won't even talk to me anymore." She held her hair back with her hand. "We used to be so close and now…she's changing right before my eyes. I think she honestly hates me."

Ana moved the ice pack off her leg. "She doesn't hate you. She's just still mourning her father. She's confused and her hormones are going berserk. She might not talk to you, but if she sees that you care, that will help."

"So…all the more reason for me to stay here."

"If you do, do it for Laurel, not me," Ana said, trying to shift to a more comfortable position. "But you said yourself this deal was important. You have to decide."

"The Atlanta deal is almost done," Tara said. "I can stall them a couple of days. And as for the land I'm trying to sell—my land—well, Mr. Big Shot, whoever he is, can just stew until he gives me the asking price I want. You're right, Ana, you need me now, and so do my children. I can't leave you with my daughters and a restaurant to run, too—and with a hurt foot."

"Okay, we'll talk more about this later," Ana replied, the pain medicine Doc Sanders had given her kicking in. "I plan on being better tomorrow, anyway."

A knock at the door made Tara spin around. "Do you want visitors?"

"It's probably Jackie," Ana said, motioning for Tara to open the door. "We've got some last-minute decisions to make—a few minor concerns."

Tara threw up her hands, then opened the door. Turning to Ana, she smiled slyly. "It's not Jackie."

Before Ana could ask who was at her bedroom door, Rock walked in, carrying a tray complete with a daisy and some tea and cookies. He filled the feminine white-and-yellow room with a distinctly male presence. "Jackie said she needed someone to test the white-chocolate cookies and raspberry-peach tea."

"I've had both," Ana said, wishing she'd had time to comb her hair, at least.

"Well, now you can have both again." He set the white wicker tray across the bed. "I brought extra." Turning to Tara, he offered her a big round cookie.

"No, I don't eat sweets," Tara said, lifting a hand to stop him. "Besides, I've got things to do to get ready for the opening. I'll be downstairs with Jackie if you need me."

Ana watched as her sister beat a hasty exit. "Hyper, that one. Always in a hurry. She has it in her head to stay here and help out. She'll be bossing everyone around."

"Not like you, huh?" Rock's smile was a mixture of appreciation and admiration.

"I'm not moving very fast these days, so I can't really give anyone orders," Ana said, taking time to sip the fragrant tea. "Hmm. Jackie knows how to brew a good strong cup of tea."

"Then, I think your tea room will be a big hit."

"Good. I intend to be there for the opening."

Rock saw the stubborn glint in Ana's eyes. Shaking his head, he said, "Doc Sanders told you to rest for a few days. You're bruised and sore, Ana."

"I've rested. And now I'm ready to get back to work."

"I don't think that's wise."

"Oh, really. Well, I think I don't have any choice. The tea room opens on Saturday and I intend to be downstairs, right in the thick of things. I've worked too hard to miss this."

"But your ankle is sprained. You don't want to do permanent damage."

Ana dropped the cookie she'd been nibbling. "Rock, I have to do this. I can hobble around. I'm used to doing things my way, on my own."

Rock could relate to that. He was the same way himself. He'd had to learn to turn certain matters over to the Lord, though. Or go crazy trying to control them.

"Have you ever thought about letting go of some of that control, of trusting other people, and maybe the good Lord, too, to take care of things for you, just once?"

"Are you calling me a control-freak?"

"No, but you obviously aren't used to letting anyone help you. Maybe this is a sign you should slow down and learn to trust others."

"I do trust," she said. "I trust that my foot will be better tomorrow and I can hobble around and get things going. And I'm praying to God for that to happen."

Rock touched the daisy he'd swiped out of Milly McPherson's yard. "Look, Ana, we're all here to help."

"I appreciate that, but you have your own work."

"I don't mind pitching in."

"You don't like to cook."

"I've cooked all my life. I think I can help out in a tea room."

She laughed out loud, almost choking on her tea.

"What's so funny?"

"The image of you in a pinafore apron, serving tea to little old ladies."

"I'll do it if I must." He leaned closer. "I mean it, Ana. It's part of the new me, the better me. The me that wants to impress Ana Hanson."

He watched as his words settled over her. Ana didn't like being helpless—but then, who did? Deciding to change the subject, he said, "I had a long talk with Laurel this morning."

"Really?"

"Yep. She showed up at my shop. I think she was probably looking for Cal, but she found me, instead."

"That's good. Tara has given her strict orders to stay away from Cal."

"His daddy is handling that end of things, too. He has Cal working on a house way on the other side of the Island, pulling up baseboards and tearing out old Sheetrock. Hot, sweaty work and real torture, eight hours a day for the next two weeks."

"Well, at least Don listened when Cal tried to explain. He seems like a reasonable parent."

"He believes in love and discipline. And respect."

"I wish Tara had at least talked to Laurel. She just shouted at her and sent her to her room."

"A mistake many well-meaning parents make every day."

"So what did Laurel say to you?"

He sighed, raked a hand down his chin. "Not much at first. I made small talk, let her hammer a few nails and glue a few dadoes and tenons on a small cabinet I've been working on. She finally opened up."

"What did she say?"

"It's what she didn't say that has me concerned," Rock told her. "Laurel clearly thinks she's somehow responsible for her father's death."

Ana shot up, winced, then sank back against the pillows. "Why would she think that?"

Rock shrugged. "I don't know. She did tell me that her parents had been fighting a lot before Chad died. She said they weren't really happy. Then she said something very odd."

"What?"

Rock debated telling Ana this, but decided she had to know. And he needed some answers himself. "She said her father never really loved her mother. That he'd been in love with another woman before he met her mother. Laurel seems to think he still had feelings for that other woman."

Ana's hand went to her mouth, her face flushing hot. "Oh, my goodness. I wonder what would make her think such a thing?"

Rock leaned close, his hands on either side of Ana's lacy pillows. "I wonder that, too, Ana. And I'm really wondering who this other woman was. In fact, I've been wondering a lot of things regarding you and your sister. Care to explain any of this to me?"

Chapter Thirteen

"**I** don't know what you mean," Ana said, her heart thumping so loud that she was sure Rock could hear it.

"I remember you saying you were dumped in college. You said he fell in love with another woman."

"That's true."

"Well, I also remember you saying your sister was the pretty, outgoing one, and that this man fell for a woman who was pretty and more outgoing than you."

"That's very true."

"You've dropped enough hints, Ana. I think I have it figured out. Did your college sweetheart leave you for your sister?"

Ana lowered her gaze and stared down into her tea as if it could give her answers. "Yes," she said finally. "Chad and I had been together for almost two years. I'd never brought him home to meet my family." She stopped, set her teacup down. "Then Tara decided to attend college in Savannah, with me. Naturally, I wanted to protect her, help her around campus. Chad was more than happy to help out, too. Before the fall semester was over, he was in love with Tara. But they didn't bother telling me that until much later."

Rock lifted her chin with a finger, his eyes full of compassion and understanding. "That must have been rough on you, knowing how they felt."

"I couldn't be sure," she said, her voice shuddering. "We all kind of tap-danced around it for months. Then Chad came to me and told me we needed to break up. I didn't even question him. I just let him go."

"You didn't try to fight it?"

"No, why should I? Tara was…is so beautiful. All that blond hair and those big blue eyes. We are so very different."

He stared at her for such a long time, the heat of it sent a blush up her face. But he didn't try to argue with her. "So you thought—"

"I thought I was doing what was best for all of us. I let him go because I could tell he was in love with Tara."

Rock dropped his hand away from her face, then settled back on the side of the bed. "Did you ever question things? Did you ever talk to Tara and Chad about this?"

"No. Tara finally came to me after Chad and I broke up. She poured out her heart to me, cried with me. I forgave her, because I love her. I knew I could never be happy with Chad, knowing he'd rather be with my sister. And I couldn't find it in my heart to hate her."

"But you never talked to Chad about this?"

"No. Things were awkward after that. I tried to avoid him. The next time I saw him up close and personal was at their wedding that spring." She shifted on her pillows. "Look, it was a long time ago. We all got along fine, once things settled down. Chad and Tara had Laurel soon after they were married, and I was overjoyed to be an aunt, so I put all of that aside."

"Then, why does Laurel think her father didn't love her mother?"

"I don't know. Maybe because when she heard them fighting, it looked or sounded that way. But they loved each other. I know they did."

He leaned forward, the intensity of his gaze washing Ana in a soft, heated light. "You are a remarkable woman, Ana. You forgave your sister for taking away the man you loved. You've been a loving aunt to her children."

"She didn't take him away. I never had him."

"I wouldn't be so sure about that," Rock said, his hand moving up her arm.

"What do you mean?"

"Nothing. Never mind. Let's just concentrate on

getting you well, and getting Laurel through this rough spot."

Ana grabbed his hand, stopping him from getting any closer. "Rock, you don't think—I mean there is no way Chad still had feelings for me even after all that time. He loved me once, but not after Tara. Once they were together, he only had eyes for her."

"I don't know. I only know that Laurel heard something to trigger all of these doubts and fears. But I think there is a possibility that, yes, Chad still loved you. Maybe he loved both of you, but in different ways."

Ana had certainly believed Chad loved her once. But that was before Tara...or was it? "Is that possible?"

"Anything is possible," he replied. "But I need to know how *you* felt about Chad—how you still feel about Chad."

Ana swallowed, saw the raw need in his eyes. "Oh, Rock, I'm so sorry. All this time, you must have been thinking I've been pining away for a man I could never have."

"Have you? Are you still carrying a torch for Chad Parnell?"

Ana leaned forward, her hands clasping the front of his shirt. "No," she said, her whispered word full of longing and hope. "I accepted that he loved Tara. I'd be lying if I said I didn't think about him now and again, and I did harbor a good dose of bitterness. But I kept that bitterness to myself, to avoid hurting my family, especially my parents. They don't know any of this, and I refuse to feud with my only sister. Besides, my sister and her daughters are as close to a family—children, I mean—as I've come. I did make some bad decisions in the relationship department, I think maybe because I thought I'd lost my one chance when I lost Chad. But I stopped loving him in that way a very long time ago. We were civil to each other, friends for the sake of our family. But…I'm okay, really."

"Really?"

"Yes," she said as she put a hand on his face. "Lately, I've held out hope for another man."

His smile was soft, and filled with immediate relief. "Do I know this other man?"

"I think you do. He's a paradox, though. Always changing right before my eyes. He surprises me every day."

He scowled. "Who is this mysterious man?"

"Don't tell," she said as she leaned close and whispered in his ear. "He's a very good carpenter and he also happens to be a minister. What more could a girl ask?"

With that, she kissed him, her mouth fluttering across his face before settling on his waiting lips.

Rock sank against her, holding her, kissing her back with a gentle force that took Ana's balance completely away.

Then he released her and looked down at her. "He's one lucky man, I think."

Ana stared up at him, thinking she just might be the lucky one, the blessed one, at last. The image of that kind of intense happiness made it hard for her to find her next breath. Her fear ran deep.

"We have to take things slow," she told him, her voice ragged. "I don't want to make another mistake."

"I understand. Besides, we have a tea room to operate."

"We?" The surprise in her voice surely showed in her eyes. "This coming from a man who only wants an old-fashioned stay-at-home kind of woman?"

"I never said that. I'll admit I had these silly notions, but as you said, I'm changing all the time."

"So you're willing to…cook and wear an apron to help me serve my customers?"

"I told you I'd do it for you. And I told you when we first met, we all pitch in around here, Ana. We help each other, even if it means… wearing an apron. I intend to help you, whether you like it or not."

She was thinking she liked it. More than a lot. Ana sat in a comfortable wicker chair in a corner of the kitchen, pillows all around her, her bandaged foot elevated on a matching footstool, while she watched her dream taking shape. An added bonus, Greta Epperson was doing an exclusive story on the tea room, minus the gossip and innuendo.

"So," Greta said now, her pen in her red-lipped mouth, her big black-framed glasses sitting on top of her tuft of white hair, "where were we? Oh, yes. You met Eloise in Savannah and she persuaded you to consider opening the tea room here on Sunset Island?"

"Yes," Ana said, repeating the story of her goal to run her own business. As she talked to Greta, she smiled and sighed. Her goal, her dream was about to happen.

With the help of almost everyone she knew.

Cal and his father were busy stocking the pantry and making sure all the new cabinets were in working order, even though they'd been checked and rechecked. Cal worked silently and steadily, but Ana saw him glance at Laurel each time she passed by. The boy had it bad, apparently. And he was suffering.

Ana was reminded of how Rock was willing to suffer for her. While she didn't want either of them to suffer, Ana had to admit it was nice to know that some men would go to great lengths for their women. But was she truly Rock's woman? Contrary to what the whole island thought, she still had to wonder.

And contrary to what Laurel hoped and dreamed for, Ana knew it could all change in a heartbeat. But right now, hurt feelings and confused hearts would have to be put aside. Ana's Tea Room and Art Gallery was opening the day after tomorrow.

Eloise had formed the girls into a team. They were coming and going, setting tables and polishing glasses, placing napkins in napkin rings and making sure the menus were in their protective covers and ready to hand out on Saturday. Laurel had been especially nice and cooperative, since she obviously felt responsible for Ana's having hurt her foot.

Jackie was issuing orders to the waitstaff. "You, put that stack of napkins in the buffet drawer. Hey, you over there—Charlotte—make sure those teapot caddies are ready. And would someone please check the table arrangements one more time and make sure everyone has been assigned enough tables to wait?"

Tina ran around mostly being nervous, the stress on her face obvious as she bullied everyone into practicing being customers. "C'mon," she said, her short brown hair standing on end as she herded all the workers toward tables. "Act like you're starving and need a strong cup of tea. We'll give you free samples of lunch for your trouble."

She immediately got several hungry volunteers, especially when Milly McPherson showed up, intent on making sure that Ana's first batch of Brunswick stew, which they'd all worked on together last night, had Milly's personal stamp of approval.

"If it's going to be called Miss Milly's Brunswick Stew, then it's going to have Milly's hand in it," the old woman had stubbornly told them. In the end, all the women and the three girls, too, had a hand in Milly's stew. They'd cooked, chopped, stirred, tasted and laughed and talked about everything from flowers to men.

Sitting here now, Ana remembered last night's conversation.

"I think a wedding's coming," Milly had announced, her keen eyes on Ana as she sat with her foot propped high.

"You think so, Milly?" Eloise asked as she dumped English peas in with the pork, beef and chicken that had been slow-cooked all day in preparation for the stew.

"Preacher Rock has that lovesick look about him," Milly replied, nodding her approval at both the carrots Tara had sliced and the preacher's choice for a bride. "'Course, he's more of a carpenter than a preacher," Milly added, snickering. "God love him, he never did know how to preach a fire-and-brimstone sermon—all that philosophy and quoting poetry goes right over the head of some of us. But he's passable enough to get us into heaven, I reckon. And he's got a good steady income from his carpentry work."

"There's a certain spirituality in being a carpenter," Eloise pointed out. "Jesus was a carpenter." She stirred the stew, then grabbed a cookie. "Rock is an artist, and he does have a way with words at times. Either way, there is no shame in being a carpenter's wife, Ana."

"The carpenter's wife," Marybeth teased.

Soon, the echo had sounded throughout the kitchen as Tara and the other girls, along with Jackie and Tina, and even the timid new waitress, Charlotte, took up the chant.

The carpenter's wife.

Ana let that soak in as she now watched her family and friends put together the plans she'd held to her heart for so long.

Did she want to be the carpenter's wife? Did she want to be a preacher's wife? It would be so easy to slip into the slow, steady life here on the island. Sundays in church with Rock, Sunday dinner out on the beach, or maybe inside on a picnic blanket on a rainy afternoon. And then later—Ana stopped her thoughts right there. Rock might not be ready for a wife. Maybe he just liked having a friend, even if he had asked her to take things to the next level. A friend that he kissed now and again—more now than again, she reminded herself.

Deciding to concentrate on the here and now, rather than what might be, Ana smiled as her sister whizzed by in a huff of expensive perfume. "Slow down," she teased, laughing as Tara called out instructions to Don and Cal.

"Watch that light fixture, guys!"

Tara was in charge of making sure all the artwork and knickknacks were being displayed, paying special attention to a piece Eloise had created to celebrate the opening. It was a cutout of a little girl, her Victorian-style hooped dress and big rounded hat formed and joined by welded pieces of iron.

There were other works by Eloise, plus several beautiful watercolors and seascapes by various island artists. These were showcased among vintage hats and purses, miniature ceramic shoes, antique and art deco jewelry and a host of other items such as dishes, soaps and perfumes, candles, and dainty quilted satin walking jackets designed and hand-painted by yet another local.

"It's coming together nicely, dear," Eloise said as she brought Ana another cup of green tea. "Drink this—loaded with antioxidants."

"Will it make me walk again?" Ana asked, her sarcasm making Eloise frown. "Sorry. I just hate sitting here, doing nothing."

"You're supervising," Rock said from around the corner. He was in charge of the final kitchen details, which included everything from checking the industrial-size stove to making sure the refrigerator and walk-in freezer were stocked with the needed items for tomorrow's lunch and open house. "And may I add, you look absolutely beautiful, just sitting there." He winked, then disappeared before Ana could dispute his words.

"He's in love with you," Eloise said, clasping her hands together as if in prayer.

"What makes you think that?" Ana asked, as a warm surge of longing pierced her heart.

"Why, the way he looks at you, the way he's going beyond the call of duty to help you with this," Eloise explained. "You must have figured by now—Rock wants a traditional wife. He's always balked at career women. Too much like dear old mom. And he especially avoids anyone connected with any form of the arts—too whimsical and flighty—just like dear old mom."

"I do understand that about him," Ana said, amazed that Eloise knew her son so very well. "So…how can he be in love with me, since I'm involved in a career *and* I love art?"

Eloise sank down on the wide, cushioned footstool, careful not to bother Ana's wrapped ankle. "That's the pure beauty of it. He's fought against those things all of his life, but low and behold, you come along and…he's had to stop fighting. It's no longer an issue—what you do or don't do, whether you're a traditional kind of woman or not. You've got qualities he admires, and you've also got qualities that frighten him. Rock loves you in spite of his greatest fears. That's true love, darling."

Ana swallowed and closed her eyes, afraid to hope. "Is that how you felt about Rock's father?"

"Absolutely," Eloise replied. "I loved Tillman Dempsey from the moment I set eyes on him walking along the beach. And in spite of everything I had to endure, loving him and having him for the time I did was worth all of it."

"But you gave up so much."

"I gave up nothing. Material things only. I gained a true treasure, Ana. I had love, so much love."

Ana saw the tears well in Eloise's gray eyes. "How did you cope…after he died?"

"Not very well," Eloise said, her voice going soft. "I didn't always do things right. I had to learn the hard way. I became a success in my work, but I was a miserable failure with my sons."

"But Rock loves you."

"Yes, because Rock is noble and good and respectful. He has all the qualities that are admirable in a man."

"Do you think he loves you out of duty?"

"No," Eloise said, getting up to return to work. "Rock loves with his heart. And I know he loves you. It just might take a while for him to figure that out."

"I'm still not sure…about us," Ana said. "I don't know if Rock can handle this." She gestured to indicate the tea room. "And I can't let go. I need this."

"You don't have to give up your dream," Eloise told her. "You're much wiser than I was. You can have it all, Ana. You know how to balance love and work. I didn't."

Ana wondered if Eloise could see how scared she was. She wasn't sure she could balance anything. For so long, she'd dreamed of owning her own business. On the other hand, in her secret heart, she'd also longed for a family. A traditional family where she raised children and took care of a home and husband.

Suddenly, she could see that she and Rock weren't so very different, after all.

Eloise watched her, as if sensing her turmoil and her realizations. "It takes compromise, Ana. I never learned that. I was too wrapped in grief and ambition to see the treasures God had given me. When I think of all the times I shooed my children away so I could work one more hour, one more late night, I wish now I could turn back time and stop everything, just to see their young faces again. Those faces were so full of hope and questions, so full of need and grief. I failed my sons when they were growing up, at a time when they needed me most. I've promised God I will make it up to them now. That's why I'm pushing them so hard to find families of their own. I robbed them of that. With God's help, I aim to give back what I took away."

Eloise got up, and turned to find Rock standing there looking at her. Ana saw by the expression on his face that what he had overheard had been a revelation. He'd obviously overheard Eloise.

"Mother?" he said, his eyes misty, his voice low and gravelly.

Eloise's hand went to her throat, but she didn't speak.

Rock hurried to her, touched her face. "Mother,

you owe me nothing, do you understand? I was wrong to make you think so."

"Yes, I do," Eloise said, bobbing her head. "So much. I can never make up for all that lost time, but…I can pray that you find happiness. And that you finally forgive me."

Unable to speak, Rock pulled his mother into his arms. "I think I'm the one who needs forgiving."

Ana felt tears piercing her eyes. She'd never seen Rock show his mother this type of affection. He'd touch her face, smile at her conversation, but he'd never once reached beyond the wall he'd built around himself. Today, here in her kitchen, in the midst of all the commotion and chaos, Rock was holding his mother to his heart.

Ana bit back her own tears and quelled her worries. She knew she'd just witnessed one of God's tender mercies—the forgiveness of a son for a mother, the love of a mother for a son, the unconditional understanding that only a strong faith could bring. A light shone down on Eloise and Rock, maybe the sun streaming through the wide, shining-clean windows, maybe a ray of hope from heaven itself. But the light was there, washing them in redemption and joy.

Ana closed her eyes, let the light wash over her, too, and knew that God had brought her to this place.

When she opened her eyes, Rock was looking down at her, his expression full of tenderness and understanding.

"We've got a lot of work left to do," he said, releasing his mother with a shaky smile.

Ana got the impression he wasn't talking about just her tea room.

Chapter Fourteen

"You don't have to look so blue," Tara told Ana the morning of the tea room's opening. "Everything is in place and we're ready to go."

Ana tried to muster up a smile, but all she really wanted to do was sit down and have a good cry. She didn't understand why she felt this way. Maybe the opening was just anticlimactic after all the hustle and bustle of *getting there*. Or maybe she was just too confused about her feelings for Rock. She still remembered his words from yesterday. *"We've got a lot of work left to do."*

The way he'd looked at her, the way he'd hugged his mother, told her that Rock was going through the same doubts and fears that she was having. Love shouldn't be this complicated.

"Is it your ankle?" Tara asked, concern marring her expression. "Does it hurt?"

"My ankle is much better," Ana said, wishing this ache were from a physical pain.

Tara brushed at the bedspread. "Then, you're going to have to clue me in, sis. We can't have you looking like that with guests coming for lunch."

"I know, I know," Ana said, hobbling over to her jewelry box to find her pearl earrings. "I...can't explain it. I finally have everything I've dreamed about for so long, but—"

"But it's not enough?" Tara asked, coming to stand by her. Their eyes met in the mirror.

"Yes," Ana said, nodding. "How did you know?"

Tara shook her head, then turned Ana around. "I felt that way after I became successful in real estate. I worked so hard, stayed late almost every day, won sales awards, but one day I looked out the window of my office and noticed an ancient oak tree for the first time. I'd never even seen that tree before, hadn't even realized it was there. On this particular spring morning, that old oak was so beautiful it took my breath away. I got to wondering what else I was missing."

Ana sank on the bed, careful not to wrinkle her white linen sheath. "Did you feel as if something was wrong? As if you were having all these doubts and fears and you just wanted to run in the other direction?"

"I sure did," Tara replied, her blue eyes deepening with memories. "Chad and I...things were shaky in the years before he died. I sat there, remembering the fight we'd had the night before, and I wondered about that tree. What had that beautiful tree witnessed? What had it seen and heard? How had God protected it through the centuries? I asked myself, was God protecting me like that?"

"Did you want that—God's protection?"

"Oh, yes. I just wasn't sure how to find it. I'm still searching."

"I guess we all are," Ana said. Then she did smile. "Rock has helped me so much with that."

"Well, he is a preacher."

"Does that bother you?"

"Why should it?" Tara asked. "I can use some spiritual guidance, that's for sure. And Rock is a good, kind man. He doesn't pass judgment. He just listens. He's helped me with Laurel, with trying to understand her and not reprimand her so much. Until I sat down with Rock, I never realized that I don't actually talk to Laurel. I mostly just nag her. Rock made me see I'd get a whole lot more accomplished with my daughter if I just tried listening to her and talking to her."

"I'm glad he's helped you," Ana said, wishing she could find the courage to sit and pour out her heart to Rock.

"So what's the problem?" Tara asked, her arms crossed over her red knit dress. "I mean, Rock seems like the sort of man any woman would love to be involved with." Then she held up a hand. "Myself excluded, of course. I don't intend to go down that path again." Making a face, she added, "Besides, that man only has eyes for you."

Ana looked down at the planked floor. "I don't know what to do about him."

Tara laughed, then sat beside Ana. "Why don't you just enjoy being with him?"

"I've tried that. But…we seem to make each other miserable." Ana tucked a pillow up against the headboard. "I mean, we have fun together, we laugh, we talk. He quotes poems and philosophy and Bible verses to me. But it's as if we're dancing around the real issue."

"Which is?"

"Which is…I'm afraid I'll have to give up my identity, myself, in order to be the kind of woman Rock expects me to be."

"Has he tried to change you?" Tara asked, the protective ire in her eyes making Ana smile.

"No. That's just it. After that first horrible fight we had, he's been a perfect gentleman. He said he was willing to suffer to be with me. And that's part of the problem, I think."

Tara frowned, then touched a hand to Ana's arm. "You're not making sense."

Ana let out a sigh, then shrugged. "Rock is doing all the changing. He's willing to change for me. I'm not so sure I can allow him to do that. I don't know if I can accept that."

Tara got up, her charm bracelets dangling. "A man is willing to change for you, and you can't accept that? Ana, is there something seriously wrong with you, girl?"

"There must be," Ana said, getting up to hobble over to the armoire against which her crutches were leaning. "Maybe I expect too much. Maybe I never thought I'd find someone who'd be willing to do that."

"Is this about Chad?" Tara asked out of the blue, her hands going to her hips.

"Chad?" Ana felt the shock of his name all the way to her toes. "What does this have to do with Chad?"

"You loved him once, Ana. Before I came along and ruined things for both of you."

"Ruined things? You married him. You have three beautiful daughters. You had a life."

"Yes, I had the life *you* always wanted. Maybe this tea room has been just a substitute for all that you think you missed. Maybe that's why you're feeling so let-down now. Because, in spite of your dream, you still aren't truly happy."

Ana looked away from Tara's direct gaze. She didn't want her sister to see the truth in her eyes. This dream had been a way of coming close to all the things she longed to have. But she couldn't admit that now. "That's crazy. I have everything I've ever wanted."

"But you're so afraid of accepting Rock's love, you're sitting here in tears."

"I don't want to make a mistake," Ana said, her voice rising with each word. "And I especially don't want Rock to make a mistake. Besides, I don't even know how he really feels. Maybe I'm imagining things."

"You are not imagining." Tara shook her head. "The mistake would be to turn Rock away just because you think you have to be noble and brave, the way you were when you found out about Chad and me. Don't do that, Ana."

All of the anger Ana had held in check for so long came pouring through her. "I wasn't noble and I certainly wasn't brave. I didn't have any choice, Tara. If I recall correctly, Chad dumped me for you. End of discussion."

Tara dropped her arms to her side. "But there never was any discussion. That's just it. You held your feelings so close, Ana, so close. And I've wondered…so many times, what you were truly thinking."

"I was thinking that I had to make a life for myself, which I've done," Ana said, her heart pierced by the pain she'd tried to hide for so long. "I was trying to…let go. You and Chad were so in love—"

"We shouldn't have gotten married," Tara blurted out. "Do you understand me, Ana? *We*… were the mistake."

"What?" Ana felt the floor shifting underneath her. She had to grab for the brass handle of the armoire to steady herself. "What are you saying?"

Tara wiped tears away, then held up her head. "It wasn't so much love. It was more…lust. What you had with Chad was real love. What I had, well, it was love of a different sort. It was powerful and I was swept away by it. I thought he was my knight in shining armor. Then reality set in. He married me, Ana. But he never forgot you. I think he loved you until the day he died."

Ana's hands groped in the air until she found the nearest chair. "But you seemed so happy—at your wedding and afterwards, all the times I saw you together."

"*Seemed,*" Tara repeated, sinking down in front of Ana, her hand reaching for her sister's. "We seemed happy enough and we were at first. We were so caught up in the *notion* of being married, we truly believed everything would work out all right. But things were bad from the beginning. Then right away, I found out I was going to have a baby. Laurel came along and...I loved her with every ounce of my being. I thought surely all the nagging doubts and the little fights would disappear. But Chad—he was indifferent about having a baby. He treated Laurel the same way he treated me, like we were dolls. He showed us off, then expected us to sit on a shelf and behave."

Ana felt sick to her stomach. "What about Marybeth and Amanda?"

Tara sighed, sniffed back tears. "Marybeth was an accident. Chad was furious with me. He didn't want any more children, at least not so soon after Laurel. But he handled it with grace. He had to put up a good front for the world. After all, being a family man got him a big promotion at work. For a while, things got better. We actually planned for another baby, because Chad wanted a boy. Then Amanda came along. He was disappointed, but he hid it right along with everything else he'd managed to hide over the years."

"I can't believe this," Ana said, glancing at the clock. She needed to get downstairs, but she couldn't seem to move. "All these years—"

"All these years, we were living a lie," Tara said, shame in her expression. "We simply existed for the sake of our children. Chad did love his daughters, in spite of his initial indifference to being a father. I'm thankful for that, at least. But the worst part, the hardest part? Laurel heard us arguing about it—about our sham of a marriage. I don't know exactly what she heard, because a couple of days later, her father was dead and I never got a chance to talk to her about it. And now, she won't talk to me at all. She's closed herself off. She's repeating the same pattern. She's pretending everything is fine, when inside she's hurting. And I think she blames me for the whole thing."

Ana's heart went out to Tara. Her sister looked so miserable, so full of self-disgust. "Do you think she knows…everything? That you and Chad didn't love each other? But surely you felt something for each other?"

"We did, but we kept hurting each other. We

tried so hard to make it work," Tara said, tears in her eyes. "We tried to find a way back to really loving each other, or at least a way back to how we felt when we first married, but it just got worse. Especially right before he died."

"And you honestly think Laurel blames you?"

"And herself," Tara said. "I wish she would just talk to me."

Ana didn't tell Tara what Rock had said. His conversation with Laurel was privileged. Ana wouldn't break the trust that Laurel had found in Rock. That would only make matters worse. "Have you tried asking her what she heard?"

Tara shook her head. "I can't seem to find the courage."

Ana's initial shock had worn down to a numbing hum of confusion. She had to go downstairs and smile and greet her customers, but how, oh how, was she supposed to find the strength to keep this to herself?

"Dear God," she said out loud, her hand clasping Tara's, "we could sure use your guidance right about now."

Tara swallowed back another tear. "My daughter needs you, Lord. I need you, too." Then she smiled over at Ana. "I haven't prayed in a long time. It feels strange, as if I don't deserve it."

"Rock would tell us we both deserve it, simply because God allows us to have second chances," Ana said, rising from the chair. "I'm glad you told me the truth, Tara. Finally."

Tara nodded. "It does feel as if a great weight is off my shoulders. Maybe confession *is* good for the soul."

Ana wiped her eyes, then grinned. "If that's true, then I'm going to feel really good tonight when I open my heart to Rock."

Tara touched her arm. "You're going to tell him you love him?"

Ana nodded, her own anger and grief subdued by what Tara had told her. "I've been nursing this wound about Chad and you for so long, and if I'd only talked to you instead of trying to do what I thought was right...I could have at least helped you, maybe made Chad see that I held no resentment. I loved him once, but that was long ago. I can see that so clearly now. I don't know if talking about it would have made Chad love you any more, but I just wish you could have shared all this pain with me before now." Getting up, she brushed at her dress. "I think I need to quit keeping my feelings tucked inside. Don't you think it's about time I tell Rock how I really feel, and take my chances?"

"Long past," her sister said. "And you're right about Chad and me. We never truly talked things out, including telling you the truth. We just fussed and fought. That can't have been good for the girls. And I know it put a strain on my relationship with you. I'm sorry for that, Ana."

"No need to apologize to me," Ana replied. "Chad is gone now. I think in his way, Chad loved both of us. He tried to make it work with you, and that's something we can always remember about him." She stopped, looked into Tara's beautiful eyes. "All this time, I believed he loved you—the pretty one, the smart one."

"When he really loved you just as much," Tara finished. "I don't feel so very smart or pretty right now. But that's going to change. I'm going to focus on finding my way back to my children."

"Now, that is a smart move."

Tara laughed, swiped at the tear streaks on her face.

"Ana, you're smart and attractive and very worthy of enjoying Rock's love. Please remember that."

"I intend to," Ana said, smiling.

Arms linked, they walked downstairs. Ana grabbed her crutches, but doubted she needed them now. She had her sister and her newfound strength and trust in God to help her find her way.

Tonight, she would tell Rock that she loved him.

He had planned on telling her tonight.

But as Rock watched Ana mingling with the packed to capacity luncheon crowd, he knew he'd have to change his plans for them.

He loved her. He saw that now with a clarity as shimmering and crystal clear as the tall, elegant goblets she used to serve her lemon-mint iced tea. He saw that love in the reflection of the cabinets he'd rebuilt and created for her efficient, smooth-running kitchen. Felt that love with each home-cooked dish she urged the pinafore-dressed waitresses to take out to the eager people seated at the bistro tables and the antique lace-covered dining tables where she'd placed them for their first meal at Ana's Tea Room and Art Gallery.

Rock stood back in a quiet corner of the long, busy kitchen, watching Ana's face light up each time a waitress told her how much her table was enjoying the imported hot cinnamon-and-apple tea and blueberry scones, each time Tara rushed in exclaiming she'd just sold yet another work of art, each time Tina and Jackie whispered that the islanders were going crazy over having a place both to buy local art to and eat good food.

He stood out of the way, watching her chat with clients, watching her smile at his mother, who'd been working the crowd like the star she had become, watched as Ana fell right into step in spite of her noticeable limp, saw the way the customers gave her sympathetic pats on the arm, telling her how much they admired her working despite a hurt ankle.

Rock saw that Ana Hanson was a big success.

And as he saw that, he saw their future together slipping right down the drain with the scant leftovers being tossed from the antique china plates. Each *clink* of a glass being filled with ice, each *thump* of a plate being decorated with almond chicken salad or the fruit-and-cheese sampler, only added to Rock's woes. Each cut of the luscious key-lime cheesecake or the decadent dark-chocolate layer cake only reinforced what Rock had felt in his gut since the first day he'd met Ana Hanson.

This woman lived for her work. And it showed in every detail of her rousing debut here today.

Rock couldn't, wouldn't, pull Ana away from that. He couldn't, wouldn't, get involved with her right when she made her dream come true. He didn't expect her to give this up for him and he wouldn't allow her to think he'd want her to do so.

Even though he had.

But had he really expected her to just walk away from this to become a carpenter's wife? A minister's wife?

And good grief, when had he started thinking of her in terms of even *being* his wife?

Probably from the minute he'd laid eyes on her.

Turning away from the hustle and bustle of the kitchen, Rock stepped out onto the long, wrap-around back porch. From this vantage point, he could see the bay to the west. He could hear the seagulls cawing overhead. The sun shone down on the bay, where a slow-trailing sailboat gleamed. The huge, moss-covered oak trees mingled with the ever-waving, tall, elegant palms down toward the shore.

"Why on earth are you standing out here on the porch?" Milly McPherson asked him from the steps, causing Rock to start, his heart hammering.

"Milly? You scared the daylights out of me."

The old woman adjusted the battered, floppy straw hat on her head. "Good. You were way too far into the darkness, from that brooding look on your face."

"I was just thinking."

"About this, I 'magine." Slowly, she climbed the steps and, with a stern look on her face, handed him a white tissue-wrapped package.

"What is it?" Rock asked, taking the package Milly unceremoniously shoved at his stomach.

"It's the dress," she said, clearly offended by his lack of manners and memory. "You know, to replace the one you ruined. Ana's dress."

Ana's dress.

Rock held the soft package as if it were a life line. "I had forgotten."

"Well, I didn't. Wanted to finish it in time for her to wear it today, for the opening. But these old fingers and hands didn't want to cooperate. Arthritis ain't pretty."

Rock took one of Milly's gnarled hands in his. "These hands are very special. Milly, thank you so much for making the dress. I know Ana will be pleased." Then he kissed Milly's hand.

And was rewarded with a gasping, speechless Milly McPherson.

"Well, that's a first," he said, grinning.

"Let go of my hand, young man," Milly said, quickly hiding her pleased expression behind a tip-lipped nod. Then she batted what was left of her thin eyelashes. "It was my pleasure and a privilege to make a dress for Ana. She is a sweetheart."

She said this last with a meaningful glare at him, as in "And if you mess with her, you have me to contend with."

"That she certainly is," Rock agreed. Then he looked away again, out to the water, seeking answers.

"Are you gonna do right by her?"

Rock looked back at Milly, understanding she came from another generation, wishing he could explain. "I don't know what to do…about Ana."

Milly pushed at her hat. "Don't be daft, boy. You know what needs to be done. Why are you stalling?"

Rock knew he could trust his old friend. "Milly, Ana is happy here, doing what she's always wanted. I don't think I need to interfere with that."

"You *are* off your rocker," Milly huffed. "What makes you think Ana can't handle both you and this business? What makes men think they have to be the be-all-and-end-all for women, anyway?" Before he could defend that statement, she raised a hand. "And don't you dare tell me that you want her to stay at home and cook meals and clean house for you and only you. That would be just too stupid for words."

Feeling duly chastised, Rock cleared his throat. "Well, I *have* always wanted a traditional marriage, and so far, not a woman on this island nor even on the mainland coast of Georgia has wanted to have a second date with me because of that. Now I find Ana—she's beautiful, talented, a very good cook, and surprisingly, she *is* interested in me. We've had much more than a mere date. But she has a life already."

"And you don't think that life can include you?"

"No, I don't want to make her choose."

"What makes you think she will have to choose? Women today balance things, same as women have been doing for centuries. I did it. I balanced teaching with helping to raise my nieces and nephews and with counseling and advising most of the children on this island, including you. And contrary to what you think, your own mama tried to balance things."

Rock bristled at that. "But…you never married."

"And your mama never remarried. Ever wonder why?"

No, he hadn't. And he didn't want to delve into that right now. "I thought we were talking about you, Milly. Meaning no disrespect, but because you never married, how can you understand?"

Milly slapped at his shirtsleeve. "I *understand* that was *my* choice. Sometimes, I regret that decision. But I still had to balance things out, in my mind. And with the good Lord's guidance, of course. We all do."

"Of course," Rock said, nodding. Milly had certainly opened his eyes to why his mother had locked herself away from the world. Did she only have enough love left for him and his brothers? Maybe she was afraid to love them too much, the way he felt about Ana right now. The way Milly had felt when she'd decided to forget about marriage and a family. Had his mother finally opened her heart to them, before it was too late?

"What if I mess this up?" he asked Milly. "What if it's already too late?"

Milly squinted up at him, her small frame seeming awfully formidable. "Don't miss out on love, son. Go after that woman in there. Anyone with eyes can see that you two are sure-enough in love. I'd hate to see that get lost in the mix of trying to decide who's interfering with whose career. Ana wants to work. She wants to make a life for herself, but—and here's the part where you come in—she also wants exactly what you want—a traditional, loving marriage. Within reason, of course. That's a rare thing these days. Nothing says you can't be a part of that life. You just need to trust in God's plan for you."

"But, Milly, I've asked God to show me the way, many, many times. I just can't seem to find the answers to this dilemma."

Milly snorted, her tiny hand on her hip. "Maybe because there is no dilemma, except in your mixed-up head."

"I don't think—"

"Roderick Paul Dempsey, *don't* think, for once. Don't try to philosophize your way out of this one. Just look at what you're holding in your hand."

With that, Milly swept past him into the kitchen, then began issuing stern instructions, to anyone who happened to be passing by, on how to heat up her Brunswick stew without scorching it.

Stunned, Rock looked down at the bundle he held clutched to his stomach. Ana's dress.

Not sure what Milly had meant, he turned and stalked down the steps, headed back to the sanctuary of his little chapel and his workshop. He needed time to think, time to pray. Time to ponder what he should do next. And he needed time to hold Ana's dress close and imagine her wearing it. It might be his last fantasy about Ana Hanson.

Because in his heart, he knew that tonight he would have to tell her that they didn't have a future together. So she could have the future she'd always dreamed about.

At last.

Chapter Fifteen

At last, she could sit down and rest.

Ana smiled at the now-dark kitchen and restaurant area of the house. It was quiet now, settled, still. Like her heart.

The opening had been wonderful. The customers had promised to return and bring friends. And she was already getting calls for private parties. A wedding shower in two weeks. A birthday party next Wednesday at lunch. An anniversary party a month from now—their fiftieth—a surprise from their three children and seven grandchildren.

Ana limped out onto the front porch. A white wicker rocking chair beckoned her. Sinking into the soft flora cushions, she listened to the sound of the ocean. The moonlight cast shimmering silver shadows across the grass and sand, while the wind sang a melancholy song across the sea oats and hibiscus flowers.

She was so tired. But it was a good tired. She wanted to see Rock now. She'd called his cottage and left a message. *"Come by tonight after we close. We'll have leftovers out on the porch."*

So far, Rock hadn't come to see her.

Her heart pounding, Ana decided to take a walk along the sand. Her ankle was still sore, but if she went slowly and was careful, she could make it to the lapping waves. Just to find a refreshing breeze, just to soothe her mind.

She made it down the path, gritting her teeth each time pain shot through her leg. She'd tried to stay off her ankle today, but during the peak lunch hours, she'd overdone it a bit. She'd pay for that come morning.

"Aunt Ana?"

She heard the soft voice, glanced up to find Laurel walking toward her. "Laurel, what are you doing out here all alone?"

"Don't tell Mom," Laurel said, her voice pleading. "I followed you down here."

"What is it, sweetie?"

"I…I wanted to apologize…for causing your accident."

"It wasn't your fault," Ana said, reaching out a hand to the girl. "I should have been watching where I was going."

"But if I hadn't—"

"Laurel, that's all behind us now. And if you keep showing your mother and me that you can be trusted, she did say she'd let you go to the movies with Cal, provided you have an adult chaperone, of course."

"That's so lame."

"Yes, I suppose it does seem silly. But your mother loves you so much. She only wants to protect you."

"She doesn't care, really. If she did, she'd spend more time with us."

"She's going to do that, very soon."

"She never spent time with Daddy. And now he's gone."

Ana saw the pain and confusion in Laurel's big blue eyes. "Oh, honey, you can't blame your mother for that. Your father was sick, only we didn't know he was so sick."

"He died of a broken heart. I heard them—" Laurel stopped, clamped a hand over her mouth. "Don't tell Mom I said that."

"What did you hear?" Ana asked, though she was afraid to hear what Laurel had been holding so close. But they'd all been so intent on protecting each other, maybe it was time for a little honesty instead of the closemouthed civility that had colored the past few years between her sister and her.

"She said it had all been a big mistake. She accused him of loving someone else. But that's not true. My daddy loved my mother. I know he did. She was just never around to see that."

"Of course he did," Ana said, hoping Laurel

hadn't heard all the truth. "But…it's not all your mother's fault. Your father worked long hours, too. They probably just needed some time together."

"They didn't want to be together. They worked to stay away from each other. And from us. They didn't even want us."

Ana tugged Laurel to an old washed-up tree stump near the dunes. Urging the girl to sit down, she said, "That's not true, Laurel. Your parents loved you. I don't care what you think you heard. You have to give your mother another chance."

"You sound just like Preacher Rock."

"Preacher Rock is a very wise man. You need to forgive your mother. She didn't cause your father's death. Neither did you. And she's grieving for him, same as you." Wanting to give the girl hope and honesty, she added, "You know, honey, sometimes grown-ups fight and say things they don't really mean and then they regret them for a very long time."

"Is that why she cries…at night?"

Ana felt the shock of that innocent question all the way through her system. "Yes, I guess so. I didn't realize she was still hurting so much."

"She isn't happy," Laurel said, her head down. "She was always so cool, you know, funny, and always taking us on these adventures before—even if it was just to the mall to shop and have an ice-cream soda. Even if she'd had to work late, she tried to make time for us. I miss that. I want my mom to be happy again."

"Well, you just contradicted yourself," Ana said. "So your mother didn't really neglect you or your sisters, did she?"

"Not really," Laurel admitted. "It just seemed as if she was always on the run, always busy. But she did try to make things up to us, and I know she's trying now. She neglected Daddy, though. That's why I'm so mad at her."

"You can't stay mad forever," Ana told the girl. "Trust me, I've tried that and it doesn't work."

Laurel sat there looking out at the waves. "I want her to be happy again, the way I remember them when I was younger."

Ana's heart went out to the girl. She'd seen so much in her short years—anger between her parents and now death. "Then, help to make her happy. You can't bring your father back, but you can forgive your mother for whatever you think she did or didn't do for him while he was alive." She reached out a hand to Laurel. "I can tell you this, though, honey. Your mother cared about your father. So please stop giving her such a hard time."

Laurel didn't answer right away. They sat in silence for a while. In that silence, Ana asked God to help her family to heal.

"I'd better get back before she misses me," Laurel finally said. "You coming?"

"No, honey. I think I'll sit here a while. Tell your mother not to wait up for me."

"Okay." Laurel started off, then turned, twisting

her braid of hair as she hesitated. "Thanks, Aunt Ana. You always know the right thing to say."

"She sure does," Tara said from the shadow of the trees just off the shore.

"Mom?"

"C'mon inside, baby," Tara said, her voice raw with emotion. "I think it's time we had a long talk."

Ana watched as Tara hugged Laurel close. Then, hand in hand, the two headed back to the house.

Would her sister tell Laurel the truth? Ana knew it would be hard for a teenager to understand, but perhaps the truth was the best way.

The truth. Where was Rock? She finally had the nerve to tell him the truth and he was nowhere to be found. He'd disappeared during the mad rush and she hadn't seen him since. Had all the commotion and confusion scared him away? She could almost understand why. Today had certainly been stressful and overwhelming, which might explain why she felt like she needed a good, long cry. It was just the letdown after all the excitement, she told herself. Nothing to worry about.

And yet, she *was* worried. She was worried that Rock had decided he couldn't be a part of all that excitement and stress.

Ana sat for a while, and just when she was about to give up, she saw him. He was walking up the beach, carrying some sort of package. He wore a white cotton shirt, the long sleeves rolled up to his elbows, and khaki walking shorts. He was barefoot and his dark hair was lifting out in the evening wind.

Ana waved, then called out. "Hello there."

"Hello, yourself," he said as he made his way up the shore to her, sand squishing against his feet.

She waited for a few measured breaths, then said, "I missed you. Did you get my message? Are you hungry?"

He came to stand over her, his head down, the package held tightly in one hand. "So many questions."

Ana sensed immediately that something was wrong. "You don't have to answer my questions."

"Ah, but I owe you an answer. I owe you...so much, Ana."

"What do you mean by that?"

She didn't want him to answer that particular question. Suddenly, she knew what he meant. And her heart seemed to slip and scatter like a sand castle hit by a fierce wave.

"You left today," she said.

"Yes, I did."

"You left because you couldn't deal with what you saw. The people, the tea room, your mother. You still think I'll be like her, don't you."

"You are not, nor will you ever be, like my mother."

"But you came here tonight to tell me that you can't trust me, right? You can't trust yourself to have a future with me."

"'And in today already walks tomorrow,'" he quoted. "Samuel Taylor Coleridge."

Ana hauled herself up off the old log. "I don't need your philosophy, Rock." She swallowed, looked out at the glimmering waves. "I...need you. The real you."

"No, you don't need me at all." He let out a long sigh, pushed a hand through his scattered bangs. "I saw how happy you were today, Ana. You were in your element. You have at last realized your dream."

"And you can't accept that?"

"I don't want to...jeopardize that."

She felt a slow burning fury inside her chest. "Well, too late. You put my heart in jeopardy the first time you kissed me."

"I was wrong. I thought we could just—"

"Just what, Rock? Share a stolen kiss here and there? Keep things sensible and sane? Stay in touch and be good friends? No commitments, no attachments, no strings?"

"There you go with too many questions again."

Ana faced him, her hair blowing in the wind, her eyes clouding with tears of frustration. "Well, get used to it. I intend to keep asking questions until I have some answers."

"There are no easy answers," he said, leaning close. "There is no easy solution, either."

She backed away, throwing up her hands. "You're right there. For years, I questioned why my sister had stolen my boyfriend away. Then I find out from her that he never really loved her the way he loved me. Now I feel like the guilty one. She is hurting right now, her children are hurting right now, because of some misguided sense of love her husband thought he felt for me. If I had talked to both of them, asked the right questions, I could have told him that I stopped loving him long ago. I could have helped him find love with Tara again, the love they had to have felt when they first met and fell for each other."

"It wouldn't have changed anything."

"It might have," she said, glaring at him, hating the dejection in his words. "And will it change the way you feel right now, Rock, if I'm completely honest with you?"

"I'd like a little honesty, yes."

"Well, here's the truth. I love you. And…this morning, just before I came down to that waiting crowd, I realized that. I realized that a crowded room full of happy, laughing people can't replace a quiet room with the one person I love. I realized that having a restaurant and an art gallery can't replace a real family. I realized that at last I had everything I'd worked so hard for…and I still felt empty."

She stopped, backed farther away at his attempt to touch her. "I thought about you in your workshop. Thought about sitting in church, listening to your sweet, wonderful, quirky sermons. I thought about…what our children would look like. That's the truth, Rock. That's why I invited you back here tonight. I thought I could have it all, including you, but I guess that's not enough for you. You can't seem to let go of that image of the perfect wife you have planted in your brain. Well, I'm not perfect by a long shot, but I could have made you happy. I would have tried to make you happy."

She turned away too quickly, her pride causing her to put too much pressure on her sore foot. She tried to make it up the sloping sand, slipped, groaned and waited to hit the ground.

But Rock was right there, catching her up in his arms.

"Ana," he said, her name a whisper in the wind. "Ana."

She looked up at him, tears flowing down her face. "I could have made you happy," she repeated. "I wanted to love you. I wanted us to be a family."

"And I only want you to be happy," he said. "Ana, please…"

"I'm going home now," she said as she pulled away.

"Won't you at least let me explain?"

"What's to explain? You can't get past your notion of what a carpenter's wife should be."

"It's not that—"

"It's that and so much more. And I'm too tired and drained to deal with it tonight. I'm going home, to my house, to my tea room, to my life."

"Take this," he said, his voice hoarse and raspy. He shoved the package at her. "Just take it."

Ana took the tattered, tissued bundle and hobbled her way up the path, tears causing her to stumble again. When she reached the porch, she turned to look out at the ocean.

And saw him still standing there, watching her home.

A week later, Ana finally got up the nerve to open the package from Rock. After a busy first week at the tea room, Tara and the girls had left for a long weekend in Savannah. Tara wanted to mend things with her children, starting with Laurel.

Ana had talked to Eloise almost every day, but hadn't seen Rock. When Eloise mentioned him, Ana simply said they had decided to be friends. She hadn't gone to church this morning either. She wasn't ready for that just yet.

Now that her ankle was completely healed, she'd taken to going on long evening walks on the beach. Since she didn't provide dinner unless it was a special occasion, most of her nights were free. And lonely.

Tonight, she stared down at the tattered bundle for the last time. Whatever gift Rock had wanted to give her, she would open it, then promptly return it. She wanted no part of a man too stubborn to see life staring him in the face. A man too stubborn to fight for the woman he loved.

She stood in her bedroom with the windows

thrown open to the sea wind. She reached for the package and ripped the paper away, felt inside the bundle to pull out soft white flower-sprigged linen.

Ana gasped.

The design was old-fashioned but pretty, the blue flowers sprinkled across it reminding her of another such dress, which only reminded her of how much Rock had hurt her.

And yet, this dress beckoned her to forgive and forget. The neckline was a simple boat-cut, while the heavily gathered skirt flared from the waist into a sea of flowing tea-length folds. A huge cummerbund covered the fitted waist, its sashes falling down the sides to be tied in back.

"Oh," Ana said. "Oh, my."

She had to try it on.

She'd try it on, then send it back to him.

Hurriedly, Ana tossed off her t-shirt and shorts, then slipped the dress over her hips. With shaking fingers, she managed to get the zipper closed. With jittery hands, she managed to tie the wide crisp sashes into a bow at her back. It seemed to fit her perfectly.

Ana turned and looked at herself in the standing mirror. And at last, she saw that she was pretty.

Soon, tears were rolling down her cheeks. "Such a sweet, incredible gift," she said, wishing she didn't talk to herself so much.

Angry, she didn't stop to think. She headed down the stairs, barefoot and still in the dress. She ran out onto the beach, her tears falling in earnest now. She was so angry at Rock Dempsey that she was going to march all the way to his cottage and just tell him how she felt. Ana walked and walked, all around the perimeter of the small island, moist sand clinging and then falling away from the crisp folds of her dress. Soon, she found herself not at Rock's house, but instead, standing in front of the Wedding Rock.

"I don't want to be *here*," she said, glancing around to see if anyone was watching her. She probably looked a bit demented, in her long white dress, her hair windswept and trailing around her neck and face.

I'm going home, she told herself. It would be a long, sobering walk, but it would clear her head— prevent her from doing something stupid like falling at Rock Dempsey's feet. She started out at a brisk pace, thinking about how she'd have to have the dress cleaned. Before she returned it to him.

Then she looked up and saw *him* standing on the other side of the big rock. Waiting for her. Blocking her way home.

"Ana," he said.

Ana enjoyed the way his breath seemed to halt with the word, and the way his gaze moved over her with a sweet intensity. Let him suffer.

"Hello, Rock. I was just coming to see you, but somehow I wound up here."

"In that dress?"

"Yes, in this dress. I suppose I owe you a thanks, at least. It's…lovely."

"Milly made it for me—for you, I mean."

"Milly did a great job, considering."

His gaze took in the gathered dress with wide-eyed appreciation, then returned to her face. "The design is from another time."

Ana lowered her head. "So are your notions regarding women."

"I have no notions regarding women. Ana—"

"Don't say it, Rock. Don't tell me you're doing this for me. You're doing this for yourself and you know it. Everyone on this island knows it."

"Yes, and I've heard it enough over the past week to believe that."

"Heard what?"

"Heard that I'm a mean, stubborn, ornery, old-fashioned, pigheaded man. Heard that I've lost the love of a good woman. Heard that I'm a fool and idiot all rolled up into one. I got enough glares in church this morning to make me seriously consider going on a long sabbatical. And I have to say, I'm mighty tired of the whole of Sunset Island telling me how to fix my love life. Even if they are right."

Ignoring the "even if they are right" part, she said, "I guess I could agree with all of that."

"I don't want you to agree, Ana." He stomped toward her and then stopped, his hands at his side. Then he let out a groan. "I want…I want you to marry me."

Ana lifted her chin, her eyes locking with his. "What did you say?"

Rock came up the path then, pulling her back to the rock and into his arms with a firm, determined grip. "I said...I want you to marry me. Soon. And in this dress."

"You're proposing to me, here in front of the Wedding Rock?"

"It's a good place to propose, don't you think?"

"What if I don't want to marry you?" She did, of course, but she couldn't let him hurt her again.

"You do want to marry me," he said as he lowered his head, his mouth touching hers with the softness of moonlight hitting water. "You do want to marry me. You love me, remember?"

"I also remember that you walked away from me and my tea room, and my art and all the baggage concerning you and your mother and who knows what else."

"I came back," he said, his voice so low and pleading that Ana instantly forgave him. "I came back, Ana, because I can live *with* all that a whole lot more than I can ever live *without* you."

"You...want me?"

"Of course I want you," he said on a shaky laugh. "With my every waking breath, I want you. I love you so much it hurts."

"I don't want you to hurt," she said, touching his face. "I want to make you happy."

"Then, marry me, here on the beach, in that dress."

"And I can keep my tea room?"

"You can keep *yourself*," he said. "I don't want you to change one hair for me."

"You can live with that?"

"I can live with whatever comes our way, because I love you. Can you live with me, in spite of my old-fashioned ideas, in spite of my love of a good home-cooked meal? In spite of me being me?"

"I love you being you," Ana said. "That's all I've ever wanted."

"Are you sure?"

"Very sure," she said. Then she reached up to pull his head down. Ana kissed him, sealing their reunion with a commitment from her heart.

And from above, the moon's light touched on the Wedding Rock, its gentle beams sealing God's commitment to Ana and Rock with a glistening, glowing blessing from the heavens.

Sunset Island Sentinel Society News— reported by Greta Epperson

One month from today, appropriately at sunset, Rock Dempsey will wed Ana Hanson on the beach in front of the Sunset Chapel. Sister of the bride, Tara Parnell, and her three daughters, Laurel, Marybeth and Amanda, will serve as attendants for the bride. Clay Dempsey will serve as best man for his brother. (And rumor has it that millionaire business tycoon Stone Dempsey might make a rare appearance at the happy occasion.)

A reception will follow at Ana's Tea Room and Art Gallery, to be hosted by Eloise Dempsey and Milly McPherson, with help from the entire tea room staff, and Ms. Dempsey's capable cooks Neda and Cy Wilson. (As many of you may know, Ana Hanson's tea room has become an island favorite, among both tourists and locals alike.)

Other tidbits about the upcoming nuptials: The bride will wear a dress the groom had especially made for her by none other than our own Milly McPherson. And Eloise was happy to share that the groom also gave the bride an antique diamond and filigree wedding ring that belonged to his wealthy, deceased grandmother, Eve Blanchard.

All in all, a happy love story. Another endearing detail regarding the couple—friends and family lovingly refer to the future bride as "the carpenter's wife." But they also call Rock Dempsey "the tea room lady's soon-to-be husband." This sure isn't going to be a traditional marriage, is it, folks?

Details to follow.

* * * * *

Dear Reader,

Welcome to Sunset Island, Georgia. I love the ocean. Each spring I go to Gulf Shores, Alabama, with a group of friends I call the Surf Sisters. We spend a few days resting and walking along the beach, shopping, staying up late, eating chocolate and talking about our lives. This spring retreat renews our spirits and makes us appreciate the beauty of friendship.

While Sunset Island is from my imagination, the ocean is a true reminder of how beautiful God's world is. In this series about three brothers, I want to convey the message that God is truly our rock and our refuge, even when we've turned from Him. In this story, Rock and Ana both had mixed emotions about love and faith. Sometimes, what seems traditional and old-fashioned is really a step into the future—completely new and uncharted.

That's what taking a leap of faith can be—exciting, new, unexplored and hard to explain. And yet, taking that step brings us back full circle into a spiritual renewal of the traditional teachings of Christ. I hope you enjoyed falling in love again with Rock and Ana. And I invite you to return to Sunset Island, when Rock's brother Stone Dempsey comes home to his brother's wedding and meets a woman who might just break down the walls he's built around his "Heart of Stone."

Until next time, may the angels watch over you—always.

Lenora Worth

HEART OF STONE

A new heart I will give you, and a new spirit I will put within you; and I will remove from your body the heart of stone and give you a heart of flesh.

—*Ezekiel* 36:26

To the Surf Sisters—Cindy, Elaine, Sue, Kim, Jackie, Barbara, Julie, Tina, Charlotte, Carla, Pam and Mary Ann—friends for life, sisters forever.

Chapter One

He refused to feel anything.

Stone Dempsey watched as his older brother, Rock, kissed his new bride. They had just married on the beach right in front of the Sunset Island Chapel where Rock preached each and every Sunday, with practically the whole island population and a few tourists witnessing the nuptials. Rock looked happy and so at peace it made Stone's stomach turn. He didn't know why his brother's marriage to Ana Hanson should have him in such a foul mood.

But then, most things kept Stone in a foul mood.

He studied the happy newlyweds behind the cover of his expensive sunglasses. They protected his eyes from the glare of the late-afternoon sun, but mostly they protected his soul from any interlopers. Stone liked watching people, but he didn't like people watching him.

He'd deliberately arrived late, so he stayed back, away from the crowd, away from his mother who stood dressed in lavender and blue, away from his other brother Clay who had served as best man for Rock's wedding.

At least I was invited, Stone thought, his mind churning like the whitecapped breakers just beyond the shore. The evening tide was coming in. Soon, the wedding party would move to a small reception on the church grounds, underneath the moss-draped live oaks and centuries-old magnolia trees. The party would continue, with just family, later at Ana's Tea Room and Art Gallery.

Maybe he'd skip that part, Stone thought. After all, he had business to take care of—that was the only reason he'd even made an appearance today anyway. His business was in nearby Savannah, and since he had to be in the neighborhood...

As if on cue, Stone's cell phone rang and he turned to hurriedly answer it before anyone else got distracted by the shrill ringing. Not that anyone noticed. Everyone was clapping and cheering his brother and the bride as they headed up the path toward the church.

Stone stepped out of the crowd to duck behind a whitewashed gazebo that had been decorated with trailing flowers and bright netting in celebration of the wedding.

"Hello," he said into the state-of-the-art cell phone, the latest model on the market. "Yes? Great.

I'll be there tomorrow morning bright and early. Sounds as if our mysterious seller is finally running out of time."

Stone hung up the phone then turned as he heard a similar ringing nearby. Someone else had received a phone call, too. Someone else had slipped into the gazebo.

And that someone took Stone's breath away.

Watching as she dropped the single white calla lily she'd been carrying onto the gazebo bench, he realized she had been in the wedding party. One of the bridesmaids, maybe? She wore pale baby blue, something slinky with a gathered skirt flowing to just at her knees, and obviously with hidden pockets just right for a cell phone. Her light-blond hair was swept up in an elegant chignon that begged to be shaken and rearranged. And she wore a dainty pearl choker around her slender neck.

Stone hadn't paid much attention to any of the attendants before. But he was paying attention to this one now.

"Hello," she said into the silver-etched phone, her voice as silky soft and sultry as the magnolia blossoms blooming all around them. She was backing up as she talked, but Stone didn't bother to move out of her way. "Yes, I understand. Tomorrow morning. I'll be there. Finally, a face-to-face meeting. Thanks." Her long sigh of relief filled the flower-scented air.

Glancing up the path, she hung up the phone,

placed it carefully back in the tiny pocket of her skirts, then turned and ran right smack into Stone.

"Hi there," he said, his gaze hidden behind the safety of his shades.

"Oh, hello. I—I didn't see you there."

"Obviously not."

Surprised, and looking guilty, she grabbed up her flower and stumbled on the wooden gazebo step, but Stone reached out a hand to steady her. "Careful now."

Putting a hand to her hair, she glanced around. "I suppose you think it strange—carrying a cell phone during a wedding."

Stone held up his own phone. "A necessary evil."

She nodded. "Very necessary. I was expecting an important phone call and well...I discovered this dress had pockets, so..."

"So you tucked your phone close because you can't stop working, even for a wedding."

"Even my *sister's* wedding," she said, a trace of what might have been anger at herself causing her to emphasize the words. "I told my assistant not to call *during* the wedding, at least. And I did just turn it back on." That same anger made her look him square in the face, as if daring him to dispute her right to carry her phone. And that's when he saw her eyes, up close for the very first time. They were almost the same blue as her dress. And wide and round. And defiant.

A defiant, blue-eyed, workaholic blonde. A

blonde who felt fragile to his touch. Stone was immediately captivated. And cautious. Realizing he was still holding her bare arm, he helped her down the step, then registered what she'd just said. "Your sister is the bride?"

"Yes. Ana Hanson—well, now she's Ana Dempsey—is my sister." She stopped, adjusted her hair again. "I'm Tara Parnell."

Tara Parnell.

Stone was very glad the woman couldn't see his eyes. If she had, she would have seen the shock and recognition he was sure he couldn't hide. He knew all about Tara Parnell. At least, he knew all about her on paper. He hadn't had an inkling, however, about how beautiful and young she was. Stone had pictured a middle-aged, hard-to-deal-with widow.

She *wasn't* middle-aged, but he knew she was a widow, and he had a distinct feeling she *was* going to be hard to deal with even more once she found out why he was here. But then, she didn't have a clue as to who *she* was dealing with either, obviously.

"I'm Stone. Stone Dempsey." He could tell her his name, since he knew beyond any doubt that she didn't know who he really was. He'd been very careful up until now.

"You're Rock's brother." It was a statement, given with a look that hovered between shock and suppressed interest.

Okay, so she now knew that much at least. "One

of them. The one who wasn't asked to be a member of the wedding party."

"And the one who was apparently late getting here. Your family gave up on you even coming."

"My family gave up on me a long time ago," he said.

She frowned, then went blank. "Oh, I doubt that. But you were just running late, right? Business?"

"Guilty," he said, without giving any apologies or explanations. "I slipped in the back way."

She studied him then, giving him a direct blue-eyed look that become disconcerting in its intensity. Stone stared down business opponents every day, but he almost wanted to look away from this woman's all-encompassing blue eyes. And yet, he didn't. He couldn't.

"It's all true," he said by way of defense.

She tilted her head up. "What?"

"Everything you've heard about me, and everything you're wondering about me right now. All the bad stuff about the black sheep of the family. True. Every bit of it."

She smiled then, a soft parting of her wide full lips that made Stone's stomach do a little dance. "Oh, I've heard a lot, that's for sure. But I don't listen to *everything* I hear."

He touched a hand to her arm, then took off his shades.

"You should listen. And you should get away from me as fast as you can."

Summing him up with a sweeping look that told him there was no doubt she wanted to be away from him, she nodded. "Probably a good suggestion, since I'm sure my sister is wondering what happened to me." Then she pushed past him and hurried up the path, her high-heeled strappy sandals crunching against shell and rock.

Stone was glad he'd scared her away, glad she'd had the good sense to heed his warning. Because come tomorrow morning, she would hate him.

Tara Parnell was the business that had brought Stone Dempsey back to Sunset Island.

"He's very intense."

Tara turned from the long table where the almond-flavored wedding cake and tropical fruit punch had been set up in the front parlor of Ana's Tea Room, her gaze scanning the intimate group of family and friends that had congregated here after the wedding. Eloise Dempsey reclined on a swing out on the porch, chatting with Tara and Ana's parents, Peggy and Martin Hanson. Clay Dempsey, handsome in a boy-faced way, was sitting on the steps regaling Ana's assistants Tina and Jackie with tales about being a K-9 cop. And that society newspaper columnist, Greta Epperson, was busy taking it all down for next week's *Sunset Island Sentinel*.

Then she saw the man she'd just described as intense, standing apart from the crowd. And she remembered how he'd told her to stay away from

him. Or rather, how he'd *warned* her away
from him.

Stone Dempsey stood off to one side of the long
front porch, his hands tucked into the pockets of his
expertly tailored cream linen pants, as he looked
out past the oak trees and sand dunes at the sunset-
tinged ocean. He'd taken off his navy sports coat
and rolled up the sleeves of his cream-and-blue
striped oxford shirt. Even in the middle of the
crowd, he seemed alone, aloof, but very much
aware that Greta was dying to get some exclusive
comments from him. He continued to ignore
everyone around him, however, including the inquisitive local social reporter.

Ana whirled in her lovely flower-sprinkled
wedding dress, a gift from her new husband that
had been handmade by eighty-year-old Milly
McPherson. Her gaze followed the direction of
Tara's stare. "You mean Stone, of course?"

"Of course," Tara replied, reliving how her heart
had fluttered when he'd taken off his sunglasses
and she'd seen his eyes for the first time. She'd
never seen such eyes on a man. They were gray-
blue, at once both harsh and gentle, like cut crystal,
or perhaps more like shattered crystal. And dangerous. But it wasn't just his eyes.

Stone Dempsey exemplified the kind of controlled power that automatically attracted women.
It was a power that spoke of wealth and civility and
manners, but it was also a power that held a

tempered kind of unleashed energy, a wildness that no amount of designer duds could hide.

"He seems as if he's about to...pounce."

Ana gave her a quizzical look. "I suppose he has to be intense, being such a shrewd businessman. From what Rock tells me, Stone has accumulated a vast amount of money in a short amount of time, mostly through commercial real estate development." Taking a sip of punch, she said, "I'm surprised you haven't heard of him, since you work in the same field. Stone Enterprises is one of the fastest growing companies in the South. He buys up property, resells it to corporations to build subdivisions and resorts, then starts all over again. Rock says he's driven. He works hard, and he plays hard, by all accounts. And has women begging at his feet, Or at least according to the island gossips."

Tara gasped, her mouth dropping open. "I have heard of Stone Enterprises, but that company is way out of my league. I mean, the firm I work for is small potatoes compared to that." Pointing a finger, she said, "So you're telling me that the man standing out there *is* Stone Enterprises?"

"The very one," Ana said. "Stanton Dempsey himself, in the flesh, better known around here by his nickname, Stone. But he likes to keep a low profile." She grinned, then whispered, "Rock and I actually joked about introducing you two, since you both work in real estate, and given how you both seem to love what you do to the point of distraction." Ana indicated her head toward Stone. "So welcome to lifestyles of the rich and famous."

Immediately recognizing the matchmaking grin on her sister's face, Tara glared at Ana. "I think I'll pass. Been there, done that, don't recommend it."

Ana didn't seem convinced. "C'mon, you know you love the life to which you've become accustomed—the travel, the clothes, the perks of being such a driven, successful person. It just reminded me of you, when Rock was talking about Stone's need to accumulate more money, more material possessions."

"Do I seem that greedy to you?" Tara asked, acutely aware that she had indeed been that greedy and obsessed with work and money at one time. But not anymore.

"No, honey," Ana said. "I know you've changed over the months since Chad's death. And I'm very proud of you. Turning back to God, spending more time with the girls—that's so important. They need that kind of structure and stability in their lives."

"But I was that way once, wasn't I?" Tara asked, humiliation coloring her words. "I neglected my daughters, just to make that next big deal." And look where that had gotten her, she thought to herself.

"You have never neglected your children," Ana countered. "You just got caught up in work, Tara. It happens to all of us." Then she smiled, tugged Tara close. "Thankfully, I have Rock now to keep me grounded. And you have your girls. They've enjoyed having you around these last few weeks before the wedding. And so have I."

"I'm glad," Tara said. "And I really am trying to slow things down, to let go of that need to work so much."

Her guilt grating like sand in a sandal, she remembered her cell phone, still nestled in the deep pocket of her dress. And remembered how Stone Dempsey had caught her doing business on that very phone.

She wanted to tell Ana the truth, that she had to work, had to make the next sale, for the very sake of her daughters. But she wasn't ready for that much honesty. Instead, she turned her thoughts back to the intriguing subject still standing outside like a sculptured statue.

Stone Dempsey was obviously a very rich and powerful man, but more infamous than famous, Tara thought. Since he didn't run in the same business circles as her, she couldn't really say how she knew this about him. She just knew, somehow. Besides, she could see it in the cut of his designer suit, in the shape of his sleek golden-brown, too long hair, in the way he walked and talked. The man exuded wealth and power. She knew the type, after all. She'd been married to one.

"He seems to stand around and brood a lot," she told Ana as they both glanced out the big bay window. "He's barely been civil to anyone, including his mother and brothers."

She saw Rock approach Stone now, saw the blank, bored look Stone gave his brother even as he shook his hand and congratulated him. Saw the way Rock turned away, a confused anger in his eyes. It had been much the same when Eloise had spotted Stone earlier and rushed to hug him close. He'd barely allowed his mother to touch him before he'd held her back, his hands on her arms, his expression devoid of any emotion.

"He is different from Rock, and Clay, too, for that matter, that's for sure," Ana said, smiling the dreamy smile of a new bride. "Like night and day. Think you're up to the challenge?"

"What challenge?" Tara asked. "Look, Ana, I'm not interested in Rock's brother."

"Are you sure about that?"

"Very sure."

Ana looked doubtful. "I say go for it, but be careful."

Tara gave her sister an infuriated look. "So are you telling me to go after Stone, or run in the other direction? Honestly, Ana, I'm not ready for a new relationship."

"I'm not telling you anything," Ana said, waving to her husband through the window. "But I do want you to be happy again. You and Stone…well, you might be good for each other."

Tara didn't see how two overachievers could be good for each other, and she was surprised Ana would even push her in Stone's direction. But then, her sister was too blissful right now to think straight. Ana probably just wanted Tara to feel the way she did.

Tara watched as Rock entered the room and motioned for her sister. Ana walked toward her new husband, a brilliant smile on her face. Rock's own angered expression changed instantly as he gazed at his new wife. They were obviously happy. And Tara was very happy for them. Ana deserved this kind of love, this kind of life.

I had this once, Tara remembered, her eyes still on Stone.

Correction. She'd thought she had true happiness. But it had been one big facade. She'd married Chad Parnell on a youthful whim, thinking she'd love him forever. That had been her first mistake. And throughout the marriage, there had been other mistakes. No more marital bliss for her.

"Mom, why are you staring so hard at that man out there?"

Tara turned to find her oldest daughter, Laurel, standing there with her hands on her hips, her starkly etched brows lifted in a question.

"I didn't realize I was staring," she said, her hand automatically fluttering to her hair. "Where are your sisters?"

"In the kitchen with Charlotte putting out more shrimp canapés," Laurel said, rolling her eyes. "Can I please take this dress off now?"

"Not until all of the guests are gone," Tara said,

her gaze moving over the blue-and-white floral crepe dress Laurel was wearing. All three of her daughters had been in their Aunt Ana's wedding, but Laurel had been the only one to moan and groan about wearing a frilly dress. "Besides, you look lovely. Did Cal notice?"

That brought a smile to Laurel's sulking face. "He said I looked pretty, but I feel like such a kindergartner in this baby-doll dress."

"Well, he's right." Reaching a hand up to cup Laurel's face, Tara added, "And I agree with him. You do look pretty, baby."

"I'm not a baby. I'm almost fifteen," Laurel said, pushing her mother's hand away. "Oh, never mind. I'm going to find Grandma."

"Okay." Tara hid the pain of her daughter's rejection, but since her husband's death a few months ago, she'd gotten used to Laurel's shutting her out. Her daughter blamed her for Chad's death.

And deep down inside, Tara knew Laurel was right to blame her.

"She one of yours?"

Tara whirled to find Stone leaning against one of the open pocket doors, his coat held in his thumb over one shoulder. He stared at her with that same intensity she'd just mentioned to Ana.

"My oldest," she said, turning to busy herself with gathering napkins and punch cups. "And the reason I'm finding more and more gray hairs on my head."

Dropping his coat on a chair, Stone reached out

a hand to take the stack of dishes from her. "I don't see any gray hairs."

"Only my hairdresser knows for sure," Tara quipped, very much aware of his touch. When he'd helped her down the gazebo step earlier, she'd felt a kind of lightning bolt moving up her arm. That same jolt was back now, like a current, humming right up to her heart.

Or maybe more like another warning.

"Does your hairdresser charge you a lot for that shampoo?"

Tara felt the magnetic pull of his eyes as they traveled over her hair then came to settle on her lips before his gaze met hers. Again, she got the feeling that he would pounce on her like a lion at any minute. "Drugstore special," she managed to say. "I'm watching my budget these days."

Why she'd said that, she didn't have a clue. Or maybe she did. Tara had dealt with the whims and demands of her materialistic husband, and now that he was dead, she was dealing with the bills he'd left behind. Maybe she just wanted to set things straight with Stone Dempsey right away, so there would be no misunderstandings. So that he'd see she wasn't like him, in any way, shape or form.

But then, what did it matter? Stone would be gone come tomorrow. And she'd be in a meeting that could very well change her life and hopefully take away some of the financial strain she'd been under since Chad's death.

"It smells good," he said, no disdain for her honesty in his eyes or his words. "Maybe I should invest in shampoo stock."

Tara pulled away, dishes clattering in her hands. "Is that how it is with you? Is everything about money?"

"Yes," he said, unabashed and unashamed. "Isn't that how it is with everyone? Isn't everything always about money?"

"You *are* different from your brothers," she said, frustration and anger making her see red. His words sounded so much like Chad, it hurt to think about it. Or the fact that she'd once felt the same way.

Stone took the dishes away again, this time setting them down on a nearby side table. "And you're completely different from your sister."

"Touché," she replied, feeling the sting of his remark just as much as she'd felt the heat of his touch.

"I didn't mean—"

"I know exactly what you meant," she said, moving around the table to get away from him. Stone made her too jittery, too aware of her own shortcomings.

But there he was, right beside her before she could rush out of the room, his hand bracing against the door facing, blocking her way.

"Could you *please* be a gentleman and let me by?" Tara asked, defiance in each word.

"Could you *please* not be in such a hurry to get

away?" he countered, a daring quality in the question.

"I'm not in a hurry," Tara replied, lifting her gaze to meet his compelling eyes. "I just think we got off to a very bad start, you and me." Then she held her gaze and leaned close. "And we both know that you don't visit very often around these parts. We probably won't see each other much, in spite of the fact that my sister just married your brother, so what's the point?"

He let that soak in while he took his time searching her face. Tara dropped her eyes, wishing she hadn't said that, but when she looked back up, his expression had turned grim, as if he understood exactly what she was trying to say to him, exactly what she meant.

"Well, I did try to warn you," he said, dropping his hand away as he stepped back.

Then he picked up his coat, turned and walked out into the night.

Chapter Two

She refused to be nervous.

Finally, Tara thought as she paced the confines of the elegant lawyer's office located in what used to be a Savannah town house, she was going to meet the buyer who'd been playing cat and mouse with her over the land Chad had left her. Finally, she was going to get the price she had named, the only price she would accept for the seventy-five acres of land that was now a prime piece of real estate.

And finally, she was going to get the face-to-face meeting she had requested with the buyer as part of the stipulation for the sale. Tara had to be sure that she was doing the right thing by selling off the land that rightfully belonged to her children. She had to see this mystery man in person, to look him in the eye, to know that she wasn't selling out.

Whoever he was, he wanted this land badly. They'd been negotiating since the day she'd grudgingly decided to put the land on the market. Tara knew the buyer, who was hiding behind some massive corporate logo, wanted the land for the least amount of money possible, but she also knew what the land was worth. Situated between the Savannah River and a small inland bay, this parcel was well suited to an upscale subdivision and shopping center. If developed, it had the potential to generate millions of dollars, which was why she had wrestled with letting it go.

But Tara didn't have near the kind of capital to develop the land. That would take a lot of money, and right now she didn't have it, and she was too in debt to borrow more. What little bit she had received from Chad's life insurance was almost entirely gone. No, what she wanted, what she needed now, was enough money to get her out of debt and set up college funds for her girls.

"That's all I ask, Lord," she said, still unfamiliar with trying to pray even though she'd been doing a lot of that lately, thanks to Rock and Ana. "I only ask that my children be taken care of. I can handle the rest."

The same way she'd been handling things since Chad had died.

The door of the office opened, causing Tara to whirl around. A petite, redheaded secretary in a striped suit came strutting into the room, her smile practiced and calm. "They're on their way," the woman said. "Would you like anything to drink? Some coffee maybe?"

"No, I'm fine," Tara replied, trying to muster her own smile. Her nerves felt like ship rigging pulled too tight, but she refused to let that show.

The redhead straightened a few files, then smiled again. "Let me know if you need anything, Mrs. Parnell. My name is Brandy."

"Thanks, Brandy." Tara watched the woman leave, then sank down into a staid burgundy leather armchair, her gaze moving over the busy Savannah street just outside the tall window. Tourists mingled with businesspeople in the tree-shaded square across the cobblestone street, making Tara think she did need something after all.

What she needed was a long vacation from all the worry and stress of juggling the many financial problems Chad had left her with. What she needed was some way of lifting this tremendous guilt off her shoulders. At least her parents were staying with her and the girls for a while, now that the wedding was over and she had brought her family back to their house in Savannah. Her mom and dad loved the girls and wanted to spend time with them before school started in a few weeks. But in spite of having her folks close, Tara still felt so alone.

"Turn to God," Rock had told her after she'd blurted out the truth to him just last week. "Turn to the Lord, Tara. Give some of it over to Him. I'm telling you, it will help you get through this."

Dear Rock. He couldn't even tell Ana about Tara's troubles, since she'd told them to him as her minister. He had to keep that information confidential. Tara had needlessly begged him to do so, but he had assured he wouldn't break her confidence. He'd also urged her to talk to her sister. But Tara didn't want to worry Ana with her problems, not now when Ana had at last found happiness with Rock. Not now, when Ana had just opened her new tea room to an immediate success. Thank goodness that investment was solid, at least. Tara had managed to loan Ana that little bit of money just before Chad's death, just before the dam had burst on her finances. She didn't want Ana worrying about paying her back right now.

She'd do all the worrying. *Turn to God.*

"I'm trying, Rock," she whispered now, her fear so close she could almost taste it. This fear was born of hurt and pain, after finding out her husband had pretty much left her with nothing. It was a feeling of being helpless, of knowing she'd let Chad struggle with the finances all those years while she kept on pretending things were all right between them. She'd busied herself with work and redecorating, endless shopping, with keeping the girls active, with social responsibilities, just to hide her pain. When one charge card ran out, Chad had simply handed her another one. She never questioned him. He'd fixed it. He'd taken care of things.

Well, you didn't do that, did you, Chad? You didn't really take care of anything. And neither did I. And now, her children would have to pay for their parents' mistakes.

Now, Tara was left to deal with the debt collectors. And the shame. Lowering her head into her hands, she said out loud, "Oh, Chad, where did we go wrong?"

"*You* went wrong by trusting your husband in the first place."

Tara lifted her head, the familiarity of that voice causing the nerves she'd kept at bay to go into a spinning whirl of emotion. "You," she said as she sat there, unable to push out of the chair. "You," she repeated, realization dawning on her like a stormy sunrise.

"Me."

Stone Dempsey walked into the room and threw his briefcase on the mahogany table with the smug air of someone who'd just won the lottery. He was followed by Brandy and an entourage of lawyers and accountants, which only made Tara sickeningly aware of how she must look, slumped in the chair in utter defeat.

Well, she wasn't defeated yet. She had something Stone Dempsey wanted. And now that she knew who was behind the bid to buy her precious land, she wouldn't sell it so easily. Not until she was sure she was doing the right thing for her girls.

Rising up, she adjusted her white linen suit and looked across the conference table at him. "You could have told me yesterday at the wedding. You could have given me that small courtesy."

He calmly placed both hands on the table, then stared across at her, making her heart skip. "What, and spoil the happy occasion? I didn't want to do that." His harsh, unyielding gaze moved over her face, then he added, "And besides, as you so graciously pointed out, I probably won't stick around long enough to worry you. So what's the point?"

Anger made her look him straight in the eye. "The point is—*Mr. Dempsey*—that for months now I've been trying to sell my land, and for months now someone, somewhere has managed to squelch every other offer that's been made. That same someone, who refused to be identified, I might add, doesn't want to give me a fair amount for my land, but he sure doesn't want anyone else to get it, either." Taking a calming breath, she leaned across the table, the fire inside her belly giving her the much needed fuel to tell him exactly what she thought of his underhanded tactics. "The point is— you've been evasive and elusive, teasing me with promises all this time so I wouldn't sell the land to someone else, but never really giving me a firm answer regarding my asking price. I don't appreciate it, but there it is." Lifting away, she stood back, her eyes locking with his. "And I don't think I like you, but here you stand." She shot him a look she hoped showed her disdain. "Maybe your family was right about you, after all."

Tara realized her mistake the minute the words shot out of her mouth. Stone didn't move a muscle, but she saw the twitching in his jaw, saw the flicker of acknowledged pain in the shattered reflection of his eyes before they became as glassy as a broken mirror.

She wished she hadn't mentioned his family.

"Leave us, please," he said with a wave of his hand to the stunned group still gathered at the open double doors.

An older, white-haired man wearing a dark suit spoke up. Tara recognized him as the man she'd been doing business with up to now, the go-between, Griffin Smith. "Stone, I don't think—"

"I said leave me alone with Mrs. Parnell, Griffin," Stone replied, his firm, soft-spoken tone leaving no room for arguments.

The room cleared quickly. Brandy gave them a wide-eyed look, then discreetly closed the door.

And then they were left, staring across the table at each other.

Refusing to be intimidated by a man who had deliberately tricked her, Tara once again put her hands down on the cool smooth-surfaced table, then stared across at him, wary, half expecting him to lunge at her.

Stone did the same, his palms pushing into the polished wood as he stared at her. "I tried to warn you," he said, the whisper of the words so low, Tara had to lean even closer to hear him.

"You didn't warn me about *this*," she said,

amazed that he could be serious. "You didn't even bother mentioning this."

"I told you, I didn't want to interfere with the wedding."

"Afraid I'd burst into a fit of tears and make a scene?"

He shook his head. "No. I stayed quiet out of respect for your sister."

That made her back off. But not much. "That was very considerate of you." Turning her head, her thick hair falling across her face, she said, "Did you come to the wedding to purposely check me out?"

He stared at her hair for a minute, making her wish she could shove it away, then shook his head. "No. I didn't know who you were until you told me your name."

She let that settle, then asked, "Well, why didn't you say something, then? Why didn't you tell me who *you* were? We were away from everyone. You could have explained."

He stepped back, then crossed his arms over his lightweight gray wool suit. "Maybe I was too busy enjoying…getting to know you."

Tara laughed. "Oh, please. That dripping charm might work on socialites, but it won't work on me. You realized who I was and you didn't do anything about it. You probably even figured out what my phone call was about. Guess that gave you a good laugh."

"Did you see me laughing? Am I laughing right now?"

"No," she said, the honest intensity in his eyes making her decide to be truthful herself. "I don't think you're the laughing type. Too busy nurturing that chip on your shoulder."

"You think you have me figured out, don't you?"

"I've seen your kind before."

"Meaning, your husband?"

Remembering his words as he entered the room, she asked, "And just what would you know about my husband?"

Stone opened the leather briefcase he'd brought into the room, then tossed a heavy manila file across the table at her. "I know he owed me money. I know he owed lots of people money. And I also know that you've been frantically trying to hold several of those people off while you work on this land deal. So why don't you do us both a favor and agree to my price. It's a fair market price for that swamp."

Tara didn't know how to define the anger and hurt coursing through her system. She wanted to direct it at Chad, but he was dead. So she sent it toward Stone, who was very much alive. "Chad owes you?"

"We had some dealings through my friend Griffin, yes." He shrugged. "Savannah's business community is close-knit. And your husband was a player. Or at least, he was until he let things get out of hand."

Tara grabbed the file, glanced at the first few

documents, then carefully closed it and placed it back on the table. It was all there. All the gory details of the rise and fall of Chad Parnell.

Her heart dropped to her feet as her anger turned into dread. If Chad owed Stone money, then she'd have to practically give him the land. Besides, if she didn't sell it soon, the bank and the creditors would probably seize it anyway. That realization made her sick to her stomach. She leaned on the table again, but this time it was strictly for physical support. "How much?"

Stone stared at her, his grim expression changing to one of concern before his face became blank. "That's not important," he said at last. "I'll absorb that in exchange for the land—at the same price I've already quoted you."

Tara knew he was playing games with her, banking on her emotional turmoil to steal her land away. "That's awfully generous of you, considering you just called it swampland."

"Part of it is swamp," he said, reverting back to business with a smooth swipe of his hand through his too long hair. "We'll have to haul in dirt and rock, build restraining walls, sea walls. We'll have to build up the foundation, make sure we don't build half-a-million dollar homes in a flood zone. That's going to cost a pretty penny."

"But you still want the land?"

He gave her a long, appraising look. "Yes, I still want the land."

"Why have I never heard of you? Why didn't Chad ever mention you?"

He shrugged again. "Your husband and I never actually met each other. Griffin Smith, who I believe you've been working with, acted on my behalf with your husband. I prefer working as a consultant for other companies, like a trouble-shooter, behind the scenes."

"So you can use underhanded tactics?"

He didn't even flinch. "I use wise business tactics. I advise people on how to buy and sell vast amounts of property, and I do the same myself. That's how your husband found me—he needed to unload a few buildings, some warehouses out on the river."

Tara knew about that property—she'd already spent part of that money, too, to pay off some of the charge cards.

"And so you graciously helped him, for a small fee?"

"Actually, it was a rather large fee, which I've never collected." He looked down then. "We sold the property right before he died, so I held off on collecting my cut. And look, I'm sorry—"

She cut him off with a hand in the air. She didn't need his sympathy. "So that's when you came gunning for me, right?" She had to wonder if he'd been watching her all along, and just waiting for the right time to strike.

"I knew of your situation, yes. Then I did some research." He stopped, rubbed a hand down his chin while his eyes searched her face. "I didn't know…about you—that you were Ana's sister. I only knew Chad was married." He waited a beat, then added, "Tara, I only see what's on paper."

Deciding that statement clearly summed him up, she inclined her head. "So you heard about the land, saw a good opportunity—on paper—then bided your time until you knew I couldn't hold out any longer. Is that why you finally agreed to meet with me?"

He shifted, and sighed. "I agreed to meet with you because you were being stubborn. Griffin could have handled the contract, but you kept digging, wanting to know about the company trying to buy your land."

"You mean Hidden Haven Development Company? Is that just a name you pulled out of a hat or does it have some sort of subliminal meaning?"

"No, it's legitimate. A subsidiary of Stone Enterprises."

"And you are Stone Enterprises, of course. That much I do know."

He nodded. "Normally, I prefer to remain anonymous. It just makes things easier in the long run."

She nodded. "Easier for you. That way you don't have to face the people you've bullied and taken advantage of."

"I take advantage of situations, not people," he said, and she could see the fire of that conviction in his slate-colored eyes. He actually believed that baloney.

"Oh, good. I feel better already."

"Look," he said, impatience and irritation coloring his words. "Can we just get on with this? Do you want to sell me the property or not?"

Crossing her arms again, she asked in a defiant, split second decision, "What if I've changed my mind? What if I say the deal is off?"

And then, he did it. He pounced.

Pulling her across the table with a hand wrapped around her wrist, Stone brought Tara's face close to his, his shimmering eyes moving over her hair and lips. "Oh, no, darling. It doesn't quite work that way. Because you see, now, I want much more than that land, Tara."

"You're going to have to explain that," she said, her face inches from his. "What else could you possibly want?"

Stone stared at the woman he was holding, his thoughts going back to yesterday, when he'd first met her. That particular encounter had kept him awake most of last night. He'd come so close to calling her in the middle of the night to prepare her, but around 3:00 a.m. had decided it wouldn't matter. He'd probably never see Tara Parnell again after this sale was finalized.

If it was finalized. By the look in her cornflower-blue eyes, that might not be happening anytime soon.

But he wanted to see her again.

And what he wanted right now, right this very

minute, was to kiss her. But Stone refrained from that particular need. He had to play this cool. He had to forget about how attracted he was to Tara Parnell and remember the real prize.

He wanted that land. *And* her. But he couldn't tell her that, of course. Not yet, anyway.

"I want us to talk about it," he said, hoping she would stick around long enough for that, at least. "We need to have a calm, rational discussion."

She yanked her arm away, as if disgusted with him. "I am not *calm* and *rational* right now. And I want to get as far away from you as possible."

He didn't blame her. Stone knew he had her cornered. It was how he worked. He negotiated through his lawyers and managers, then he sat back and waited, always silent, always low-key, and always one step ahead of the rest of the pack. It drove people crazy, but it worked. But strangely, today's victory didn't bring him the usual rush of adrenaline he normally got when closing a deal. "I did try—"

Her finger in the air stopped him. "Do not tell me again how you tried to warn me. Nothing could have prepared me for this."

"I'm willing to explain it to you," he said, wishing he *could* explain his need for more money and power, his need to be successful at all costs. "If you sit down and let me bring my people back in, I can show you why this is a fair offer."

She paced the floor, giving him ample time to

enjoy the way her crisp suit fit her slender, petite body. He also enjoyed the way she tossed those thick, blond bangs out of her pretty eyes.

Except those eyes were now centered on him.

"Okay," she said, the one word calm and quiet. "Get them back in here. Where do I sign?"

Her defeat floored Stone. Literally. He sank down in his own chair, ran a hand through his long bangs, then glanced up at her. "What? No fight? And to think, I was so looking forward to sparring with you."

She turned then and he would never forget the look in her eyes. Forget disgust. She hated him. Stone could feel it to his very soul. And nothing had ever burned him so badly.

"I don't have any fight left," she said, her words devoid of any emotion. "I have to consider my children." She turned away again.

Don't let her cry, Stone silently pleaded. Although he wasn't sure to whom or what he was pleading.

But she didn't cry. She just wrapped her arms against her stomach, as if to ward off being sick, then turned to face him. "Since you know so very much about my late husband, and me, too, for that matter, Mr. Dempsey, then you probably know that I can't hold out any longer. I've used up most of my assets to pay off the credit cards and the other bills. I've used some of the life insurance to make the house payment, and while I'm trying to sell the house, I still need to buy groceries and clothes for three growing girls, not to mention school supplies and health insurance, so I've sold off everything I could to have some sort of cash flow. But soon that will be dried up, too. And my salary, as nice and cushy as it might seem, won't begin to cover the debts my husband left because my company has threatened downsizing and I won't be getting a raise anytime soon.

"So, you see, I'm tired of fighting. I'm tired of playing games. I need the money you're willing to pay for that land, even though we both know it's worth more than the price you've quoted me. And I need it now. Today." She leaned over the table again, then grabbed a pen, her hand steady in spite of the emotion cresting in her voice. "So, call the lawyers and accountants back in and show me where to sign. I want to get this over with."

Something inside Stone changed. It was a subtle shifting, much like sand flowing through a sieve. It was just a nudge of doubt and regret, coupled with admiration for her spunk and strength, but it pushed through enough to scare him to death. He couldn't go soft. Not now. Not after he'd been working this deal for months.

But he did go soft. Goodness, he wasn't such an ogre that he'd cause a woman's children to go hungry. Was he?

"Look, Tara, we don't have to do this today."

It was her turn to pounce. Tara lunged across the

table at him, her blue eyes bright with tears she wouldn't shed, her expression full of loathing and rage. "Oh, yes, we do have to do this today. Because I will not allow you to continue to humiliate or goad me. You've won, Mr. Dempsey—"

"I'm Stone. Call me Stone, please."

She gave the suggestion some thought. "Okay, then, *Stone*. You've won. You can have the land, as long as I never have to see you again. I'll deal with your middleman, and anybody else who wants to do your dirty work, but don't you ever show your face around me again. That has to be part of the deal."

Now Stone actually felt sick. Sick at himself for being so rude and ruthless. He felt deflated, defeated, done in.

By a blue-eyed blond widow who *had* turned out to be very hard to deal with. A blue-eyed blond widow who'd just told him she never wanted to see him again. Only, he *had* to see her again. Now he had to convince her of that, too.

"You're not serious," he said, giving her a half smile full of puzzlement.

"I'm dead serious," she replied, giving him a tight-lipped ultimatum. "I want it in the contract."

Stone got up, pushed at his hair. "You want me to put in the contract that you won't have to ever see me again?"

"That's what I said—but I want it worded—that I don't *want* to ever see you again."

"That won't hold up. You'll have to see me, Tara, to finish up the paperwork, at least."

"Then the deal's off. You did say you like to remain in the background, let other people handle the details. What was it—you prefer to stay anonymous?"

"But that's crazy. Once the papers are signed, that clause won't mean anything. And it won't matter."

"You're right," she said, smiling at last. "It won't matter then, because *you* won't matter. At all." She rubbed her hands together, then tossed them in the air, as if she'd just washed away a bad stain. "I'll be done with you by then."

Stone felt sweat trickling down the center of his back. This deal had all of a sudden turned very, very sour.

Surprisingly, he wanted it to matter. He wanted to matter to her. And he certainly didn't want her to be done with him just yet. Because he wasn't done with her, not by a long shot. In fact, as the famous saying went, he'd only just begun to fight.

Stone watched her, saw the agitation on her pretty face, but decided he was willing to suffer her wrath just to keep her near. "We're *not* finished here, Tara. Because I've just decided I'm not ready to sign that contract."

Her rage went into double overdrive. Giving him an incredulous look, she asked, "What do you mean?"

"I mean, I want to reconsider this deal. We've

waited this long, why not take it slow and think it through?"

"I told you, I want to get this over with."

"Yes, I heard that loud and clear. And I'm asking you to wait. Just one week."

She stomped and shifted, her taupe heels clicking softly against the carpet. "I'm agreeing to your offer on the land. You can't intimidate me or play games with me anymore. What more can you possibly hope to gain by waiting, Stone?"

He came around the table, and unable to stop himself, he pushed at the fringe of bangs falling against her cheekbone. "Your respect," he said. "I'll be in touch."

Then he turned and left the room.

Chapter Three

It had been nearly a week.

Tara stood at the window of her bedroom, looking out over the swimming pool and trees in her lush backyard. It was beautiful, and Chad had been very proud of it, but Tara didn't see the shimmering water of the pool or the tropical foliage that she'd paid a landscaper to plant in her yard.

She only saw red. Because of Stone Dempsey.

He'd said he'd be in touch, but in the four days since she'd met with him, she hadn't heard a word from the man. Even his trusted associate, Griffin Smith, wouldn't return her calls. And she'd called several times. If Stone really wanted to win her respect, he could at least return her phone calls.

But then, maybe he had decided she didn't merit any respect after all. "I guess I blew it," she said aloud, her hands going to her aching head.

"Blew what?" Laurel came sauntering into the room, the sullen look on her face indicating that her mother had messed up on several things.

Surprised by this unexpected visit, Tara smiled. "Nothing for you to worry about, honey."

Laurel plopped down on a gold brocade chaise longue set before the sliding door leading out to the pool.

"What's up with you?" Tara asked, cautious to not sound too eager.

"I want to go to a concert in Savannah tomorrow night. All my friends are going. Will you take me?"

"What kind of concert?" Tara asked, the price of the ticket already adding up in her brain. The ticket, a new outfit, food. The sum kept silently increasing.

Laurel twisted the strands of a tiny braid she'd worn on one side of her temple all summer, while the rest of her long hair hung down her back. "It's a new alternative rock band. They're awesome. Can I go, please?"

Tara ignored the pain pounding in her head. "What's the name of this awesome new band?"

"The Grass Snakes," Laurel said, hopping up, her hands in the air. "Their latest single—'Out to Get You, Girl'—it's number one this week. I'll just die if I can't go, Mom."

Already, Tara didn't like the tone of this conversation. "And what is the rating on their latest CD?"

Laurel rolled her eyes, her heavily ringed fingers

still threading through her braid. "What's that matter? I like them. C'mon, Mom, don't be such a drag."

"I'm not being a drag," Tara replied, familiar with this conversation. "I'm being a responsible mother. And until I find out what kind of music this awesome new Snake band is playing and if it's suitable for you, I can't agree to let you go to this concert."

Laurel's oval face flushed with anger. "You are so lame! Since when did you start being *responsible,* anyway?"

Hurt by the rage spewing out of her daughter, Tara could only stare. When she finally found her voice, she asked, "What does that mean, Laurel? I'm your mother. I'm trying to do what I think is best."

"Yeah, right," Laurel shouted, her hands on her hip-hugger jeans. "*Now,* Mom. *Now* you're trying to do the right thing. Now that Dad is gone and you've finally realized you have a family—"

At Tara's shocked gasp, Laurel stopped, tears welling in her eyes. "Oh, never mind. It's a dumb band, anyway. I'll just sit at home and mope, the way you do!"

With that, Laurel marched to the door, only to run smack into Tara's mother, Peggy.

"Whoa," Peggy said, her hands reaching up to steady Laurel. "Where are you going?" Seeing the look on Tara's face, she held Laurel with her hands on the girl's slender arms. "What's wrong?"

"It's her!" Laurel said, jerking away to point at Tara. "She's decided to be a real mom, only it's too late for that now."

Peggy watched as her granddaughter charged down the hall and up the stairs to her room on the second floor, then she turned to Tara as they both heard the door slamming shut. "I thought things were getting better between you two."

"Me, too," Tara said, slinking down on the bed. Her voice shaky, she said, "We had such a good talk a few weeks ago, you know, after she ran away with Cal Ashworth."

Peggy sat down next to her. "Honey, they didn't run away. They just fell asleep on the beach."

"Yes, and caused Ana to worry and then hurt her ankle looking for them."

"But…as you said, you worked through that."

"I thought we worked through it," Tara said, looking at her mother's comforting face. Ana looked like their mother. They both had auburn hair and green eyes, whereas Tara took after their father, blonde and blue eyed. "At times, we can talk and laugh, at other times, she reverts back to a little she-monster."

Her mother's knowing green eyes were appraising her now, in the way only a mother's could. "What's wrong this time?"

"She wants to go to some rock concert in Savannah this weekend. I simply wanted to know what kind of songs this bands sings, before I let her go."

Peggy smiled. "Does that sound familiar?"

Tara nodded, wiped her eyes. "I remember, Mom. My freshman year in high school. I wanted to go see some heavy metal band that was playing in Atlanta, and you refused to even consider it."

"You pouted for two weeks."

Tara took her mother's hand in hers. "Yes, and about a month later, the band broke up. Their fifteen minutes of fame was over."

"Glad you're not still pouting," Peggy said. "Honey, Laurel will be fine. She's at that age—growing up, hormones going wacky."

Tara nodded. "Yes, but it's more than that. She's still so angry at me…because of Chad's death."

"She can't blame you for that," Peggy said, frowning. "The man died of a heart attack. Granted, he was way too young, but…you didn't know. None of us knew how sick Chad was."

"Tell that to Laurel," Tara said, getting up to pace around the spacious room. "Mom, she heard us fighting the night before he died."

"Oh, my," Peggy said, a hand playing through her clipped hair. "Have you talked to her about this?"

"I've tried. We talked a little about it after…after I realized how much Laurel was hurting, and I thought we were making progress. Rock's been counseling her about forgiveness, and letting go of her anger."

Peggy's expression was full of understanding.

"Well, maybe this outburst is just because you won't let her go to the concert."

Tara shook her head. "You heard what she said. Laurel doesn't believe I'm a good mother. And maybe she's right."

"No," Peggy replied, coming to stand by her. "You have always been a good mother. You know, we all slip up now and again. The important thing is to not keep making the same mistakes. I don't think you're going to let anything come between you and your children, ever again."

"No, I'm not," Tara said, wishing she could tell her mother all of her worries. But then, her mother would just worry right along with her, and she didn't want that. "Thanks, Mom," she said instead. "I'm so glad you and Daddy decided to spend this week here."

"Me, too, honey." Peggy gave her a quick hug, then said, "Oh, by the way, Ana called earlier while you were out. She invited us to come to the island Saturday. The church is having a picnic on the grounds. Some sort of anniversary celebration."

Tara groaned. "Oh, yes. The church is 230 years old. Can you imagine that? I'd forgotten all about the celebration."

"Amanda wants to go," Peggy said, her hand on the door. "And I think Marybeth does, too."

"But I bet Laurel won't like it, as compared to going to a concert in the city."

"Cal will be there," Peggy pointed out. "You might try reminding her of that."

"Good idea," Tara replied. "And a good reason to keep her from attending that concert."

And a good reason for Tara not to dwell all weekend on why Stone Dempsey hadn't returned her phone calls.

"She's called twice today, Stone."

"Let her keep calling," Stone replied, his gaze scanning the computer screen in front of him. "That land's not going anywhere."

He stopped reading the screen, aware that his executive assistant, Diane Mosley, was still standing there, staring at him with the precision of a laser light.

"What?" he finally said, closing the laptop to glare up at the woman who had been by his side since he'd first opened a storefront office, straight out of college ten years ago, in an older section of Savannah's business district.

Diane was close to fifty, her hair platinum blond and short-cropped, her eyes a keen hazel behind her wire-rimmed bifocals. Pursing her lips, she tapped a sensible-shoed foot on the marble floor. "Why are you tormenting that poor woman?"

Stone felt the wrath of Diane's formidable reprimand. But he didn't dare let it show. They had an understanding, his dependable, loyal assistant and him. She was really the boss, but he really didn't want to admit that. So they pretended he was the boss. It worked fine most days. Unless she started mothering him or pestering him.

Like now.

"I am not tormenting Tara Parnell. I have every right to go back to the drawing board regarding that piece of property. After all, we're talking millions of dollars here. I want to make sure I have all my ducks in a row."

"I understand about your little ducks," Diane said, her steely gaze unwavering. "What I don't understand is why you've seemed so edgy since meeting with Mrs. Parnell. If I didn't know better, I'd think she got the best of you."

Stone glanced at the grandfather clock centered between two multipaned windows, then deciding it was close enough to quitting time, loosened his silk tie. Since he didn't want to go into detail regarding his wildly variable feelings about Tara Parnell, he said, "No, actually, she brought out the worst in me, which is why I'm reconsidering this whole deal."

He'd planned an overall assault. Flowers, candy, the works. He'd planned on forcing Tara to spend time with him over the last week. But somehow, that planned tactic had gone by the wayside. Each time he remembered how she'd looked at him, with all that hate and disgust, he got cold feet and decided he'd do better sticking to business and playing hardball. He'd be much safer that way, less vulnerable to a counterattack.

"You aren't going to let the land go, are you?" Diane asked, shifting her files from one arm to the other. "Stone, you've been eyeing that land for months now."

"Yes, I have," he admitted. Chad Parnell had let it slip about the land he'd bought dirt cheap from a family friend years ago, land he'd been sitting on until the right time to sell. Only, Chad had died before being able to turn a profit on the land. But Stone had remembered the land, and everything had fallen into place. "No, I'm not going to let go of the land, Diane. But if it will make you stop glowering at me like I'm an ugly bulldog, I'll tell you why I'm holding off."

Diane settled one ample hip against the solid oak of his big desk, then lowered her eyeglasses. "Do tell."

"Don't mention this to Griffin," Stone said. "But I've reached a conclusion, one I think will be beneficial to both Mrs. Parnell and me."

"What's wrong with you?" Ana asked Tara the following Saturday.

They were sitting in lawn chairs behind the tiny Sunset Island Chapel, overlooking the docks of the bay and Sunset Sound to the west. Out over the sound, hungry gulls searched the waters for tasty tidbits, their caws sounding shrill in the late-afternoon air. A fresh-smelling tropical breeze rattled through the tall, moss-draped live oaks, its touch swaying the palmetto branches clustered here and there around the property. Behind them, near an arched trellis, a gardenia bush was blossoming with sweet-scented bursts of white flowers.

"I'm okay," Tara replied, her dark sunshades hiding the truth she felt sure was flashing through her eyes. "Just another fight with Laurel."

"Oh, yes, that," Ana said. "I heard." Taking a quick look around, she added, "Well, she seems to be over not going to the concert. Look at her." She inclined her head toward the docks.

Tara leaned up, squinting, then saw her daughter and Cal, sitting on one of the many wooden docks lining the bay where luxury yachts shared slips with smaller, less impressive sailboats, shrimp boats and motorboats. They were talking and laughing, their hands waving in the air. Not far away, a long brown pelican stood sentinel on an aged pier railing.

"He is a very nice boy," Tara said, lifting a hand toward Cal. "A good influence on Laurel, if he'll stick to the rules and not sneak off into the night with her again."

"Oh, I think Cal's learned his lesson on that one," Ana replied. "His father made him work that particular crime off, sweating and painting all summer."

"What about his mother? I never hear anyone mention her."

"She died when he was seven. It's sad, really. Don has sisters and brothers who help him with his children. Cal's got two older sisters, too, who watch out for him."

"That explains a few things," Tara said, her heart hurting for her daughter. "Maybe that's why Laurel's drawn to Cal. You know, losing a parent."

"Maybe." Ana sat up, waved to someone she knew. "Oh, I need to talk to that woman. She commissioned a small sculpture from Eloise, to be delivered to my shop. I want to tell her it's ready."

"Okay," Tara said, closing her eyes as she settled back to let the sun wash over her. "I'll just lie here and vegetate a few more minutes before I find the strength to sample more of Rock's wonderful barbecued ribs."

"Yes, my husband does have nice ribs," Ana quipped, slapping Tara playfully on the leg as she hopped up.

Tara didn't bother opening her eyes. The sun felt good on her legs. She'd worn a black gauze sarong skirt, lightweight and cool-feeling, with a knit red and black flower-splashed sleeveless top. Lifting at the skirt, she kicked off her black leather thong sandals and tried for the hundredth time to relax.

But all she could think about was her money woes and the fact that her oldest daughter thought she was a horrible mother. She'd prayed that things would turn around for her family, hoped that God would see fit to give her another chance. But she still had doubts. She still needed answers, guidance, assurance.

And maybe some solid health and life insurance.

Help me here, Lord, she thought. *Help me to make my life better, for the sake of my children.* She'd tried so hard all summer, working on two different land deals. But this was about more than money. Tara needed the money those deals could bring, but she also needed to spend time with her children. She'd taken way too much time off already, and her bosses weren't too happy about that. *What am I supposed to do, Lord?*

A shadow fell across Tara's face.

Annoyed, she opened her eyes to find Stone Dempsey standing over her. She didn't know why her heart seemed to sail off like a ship leaving the cove. She didn't understand why he looked so very good in his stark white polo shirt and olive-khaki pleated slacks. Tara only knew that she needed some answers. From God and Stone Dempsey.

"Me," he said, as if to answer the one question she was about to ask.

"You," Tara replied. "What are you doing here, Stone?"

"I came bearing gifts." He tossed a bouquet of fresh cut flowers onto her lap.

Tara sat up, sniffed the lilies and roses. "How did you know where to find me?"

"I have ways of finding people," he said. "Especially when I'm in the middle of negotiating a contract."

Tara imagined he knew every move she'd made since they last talked, which was a bit too unsettling. But she refused to let her qualms show. "Well, you obviously aren't too concerned, since you refused to return my calls."

He took that in, glanced out at the harbor, then lifted his shades to stare down at her. "I've been busy coming up with another plan. And I'm here because I hope we can renegotiate."

The heat from his eyes hit her with all the warmth of the sun, causing Tara to shift and straighten her skirt. "Meaning the contract, of course?"

"Among other things."

Tara thought she knew what other things he wanted to haggle over, but she didn't dare think about that now. "What's to renegotiate? You've named your price and I've accepted it."

"With a certain stipulation, if you'll recall?"

"Yes, I recall. I never wanted to see you again. But I need to sell that property, so in spite of how I feel, I've tried calling you to discuss things. You obviously aren't in a big hurry for that land, after all."

"I'm in a hurry," he said, leaning down so close she could smell the subtle spice of his aftershave. "But I can be patient, too."

"What does that mean?" Tara said, trying to get up out of the low chair.

He reached down and pulled her out of the chair with one hand on her arm, then brought her close, his gaze sweeping her. "Careful now."

Why couldn't she be graceful around him, at least, Tara wondered. Because the man flustered her, plain and simple.

Not so plain and not so simple.

"I told you, I'm through playing games," Tara said, trying to move around him, her flowers clutched to her side.

"I'm not playing, Tara." The look in his eyes washed over her like a warm, shimmering ocean wave, leaving her both languid and alert. "Have dinner with me."

"Absolutely not."

"I won't take no for an answer."

"Oh, yes, you will. Because it's not going to happen."

"Tara, what's going on with you and Stone?" Ana asked Tara later that night. "He's called here three times." Before Tara could reply, Ana clapped her hands together. "Did you take me up on my suggestion? Is that it? Are you going out with Stone, like on a date?"

"Oh, please!"

Tara sat across the massive kitchen counter of the tea room, folding napkins for tomorrow's after-church brunch crowd. The girls and her parents were down on the beach with Rock and Cal, leaving the two sisters alone in the big Victorian house that served both as Ana's tea room and art gallery on the bottom floor and Ana and Rock"s home on the second and third floors. Business had been so good at the quaint restaurant, Rock and Ana hadn't really had a proper honeymoon—just one weekend together alone in this big old house. But Ana didn't seem to mind. She was happy. Too happy to understand this problem with Rock's brother.

Which was why Tara had debated telling Ana about Stone. Now she didn't have any choice. He'd called here, asking for Tara. Luckily, Rock hadn't answered.

"Oh, please, what?" Ana said, her hands on her hips before she went back to her bread dough. "Tell me, Tara. I mean, you two must have really clicked at the wedding, so why are you holding out on me?"

"It's business," she said finally. "Stone is trying to buy my land."

Ana stopped stirring bread dough, her mouth dropping open. "That land near Savannah that Chad bought all those years ago?"

"Yes." Tara nodded, folded another napkin, then stopped, looking down at the counter. "He wants to develop it into an upscale gated residential community, complete with shopping centers and restaurants near the river."

Ana dropped her spoon to stare at her sister. "That could mean a lot of money, right?"

Tara nodded again. "He's offering me a lot, yes, but not as much as I'd hoped to get."

"And when did all of this come about? Certainly not at the wedding?"

Tara kept her eyes down. "No, we just met at the wedding. Look, it's a long story—"

A knock on the back door stopped Tara in mid-sentence. "You've got some explaining to do," Ana said underneath her breath before she opened the door.

Eloise Dempsey whirled in, carrying a yellow-colored sealed folder in her hand, her gaze hitting on Tara. "Oh, good, you're here. I'm supposed to deliver this to you."

"What is it?" Tara asked, surprised to find the famous sculpture artist playing postmistress.

Eloise gave her a wry smile, then shook her head, her feathered dreamcatcher earrings shimmering and shimmying as she moved around the long counter to give Ana a quick peck on the cheek. "Well, it's the strangest thing," Eloise said, her eyes back on Tara. "My son Stone came to pay me a rare visit this evening. We had a nice dinner and then he said he needed me to do him a favor."

Tara's heart picked up tempo, while her sister picked up an obvious interest in the conversation. "What else did he say?" Tara asked, her eyes locking with Ana's.

"He said to tell you, actually to tell all of us, we're invited to a private dinner party next month, at his home here on the island—Hidden Hill."

"What type of dinner party?" Ana asked before Tara could say a word. "I mean, that old mansion isn't in any kind of shape for a party."

"Oh, a black-tie benefit for the lighthouse." Eloise clapped her hands together. "He implied it was by invitation only. And I think he's going to hold it in the garden, in spite of how bad the place looks. I believe we'll all receive our formal invitation in about a week or so."

Ana smirked, then rolled her eyes. "So Stone couldn't come down to the fair we held last month, to mingle with the little people?"

"I guess not," Eloise said. "But he wants to do his part—make a contribution toward the restoration."

"Of course he does," Ana said, making a face to Tara behind Eloise's back. Then, as if she regretted being so cynical, she added, "That is good news, Eloise."

Eloise nodded. "Yes, and I'm so glad I was invited. And you and Rock, too, of course, Ana. Stone was very evasive about the whole thing. An exclusive crowd, I suppose."

"You think?" Ana asked, shaking her head.

"I think," Eloise replied, calm as always, "that our Stone has come home, at last. I think his brother's wedding made him realize that he needs to settle down. I also think he needs our understanding and forgiveness."

"You're right, of course," Ana said. "And I'm sorry if I sounded a tad suspicious. I mean, I'm the one who's been encouraging Rock to try for a better relationship with his brother, so I shouldn't be doubtful."

Eloise smiled softly. "Stone hasn't given us very much reason to think otherwise. Until now."

"Yes," Tara agreed, her eyes on the fat envelope laying on the counter. "But what's that got to do with me? And what's in this envelope?"

"I don't know, dear," Eloise said, her keen gaze centered on Tara. "Why don't you open it and find out?"

Chapter Four

Tara eyed the envelope as if it were a snake.

"Open it," Ana said, her curiosity obvious in the wide-eyed look she gave her sister.

Tara reached for the envelope, turned it over. "I don't understand what this could be. And why Stone would have you deliver it."

Eloise shot Ana a quizzical look that Tara couldn't miss. "Stone and I had a good talk at the wedding the other day," Eloise said. "He promised he was going to come around more. Then, tonight he told me he was going to stay here on the island for a few weeks. He's renovating that old mansion, so he wants to be close to the work. He's a details man, my Stone. Other than learning he's going to be here a while, I'm stunned and clueless."

"So is this one of those details?" Tara asked, wondering just how much Stone really had told his mother about her. And wondering what Eloise wasn't telling her.

"I don't know," Eloise said with an eloquent shrug. "I only know that my second son seems fascinated by you, dear."

Ana cleared her throat and began briskly kneading her bread dough. "Maybe it's about the land, Tara."

Rock came into the kitchen right as the words left Ana's mouth. "What land?" Glancing down at the bright envelope, he saw the label from Stone Enterprises, then asked, "What's that?"

"Hello, Rock," Eloise said as he leaned down to absently kiss her cheek. "I just delivered this to Tara, from your brother, Stone. He's staying at Hidden Hill for a while."

Tara winced. She didn't want to bring Rock into this. His relationship with his brother wasn't the best on a good day. "It's business," she said, her smile weak and shaky.

"What kind of business do you have with my brother?" Rock asked, his expression wary.

"She was just about to explain that to me when Eloise brought this in," Ana said, pointing to the package.

Tara felt the scrutiny of everyone in the room. Taking a deep breath, she said, "I guess I'd better tell all of you everything, from the beginning."

Rock sank down on a bar stool. "That might be wise."

Tara touched a finger to the package. "I put some

land on the market a few months ago—the land Chad left me in the will."

"Near Savannah, right?" Rock said, nodding.

"Yes, centered between a tributary of the Savannah River and a marsh and pond," Tara told him. "Chad always wanted to build a house out there, a weekend retreat. Of course, that can't happen now, so I decided to sell the land."

"And Stone wants to buy it?" Rock guessed, his vivid blue eyes studying her face.

"Yes. About a month ago, I got a nibble on the land, from a man named Griffin Smith. He named a price, but I held off. I thought I could get more money for the land."

"But you can't?"

She shook her head, her gaze on Rock. "I don't think so. Anyway, I held out as long as I could, but the day of the wedding I got a call confirming a face-to-face meeting with the prospective buyer, the man Griffin Smith represented—a man who had been very secretive and hard to pin down."

"My brother," Rock said, the statement confirming his resentment toward Stone. "That's so like Stone."

Tara nodded. "I had no idea I was dealing with Stone, not even at the wedding. He never indicated it, but he recognized who I was as soon as I told him my name." Lowering her gaze, she added, "Of course, he didn't bother telling me who he was, until the meeting the day after the wedding." In his defense, and against her better judgment, she said, "He didn't want to disrupt the wedding."

Rock snorted, rolled a hand down his face. "He didn't want to make a scene? I doubt that. More like he didn't want us to find out what he was up to."

"Now, Rock—" Eloise began, only to have her son hold up a hand.

"I know, Mother, I know. Stone has the best of intentions."

Tara shot her husband a warning look, then placed her bread into a baking pan. "So…Stone and you are trying to reach some sort of agreement about the land, Tara?"

Tara rubbed a hand on her throbbing temple. "At the meeting, once I realized who he was, I agreed to his price. But I was upset. I told him I never wanted to see him again."

Rock smiled at that. "I reckon that rankled him."

"It did," Tara admitted. "He backed off the contract, and now we're back in negotiations."

"So what's this?" Rock said, holding up the envelope.

"I have no idea." Tara took it from him. "Let's get this over with."

"Maybe it's the agreement contract," Ana said, leaning close as Tara tore open the sealed package.

Tara took the thick, bound papers out of the package, then started reading. "It is a contract," she said, her eyes scanning the pages. Then she stopped reading, her gaze flying to her sister. "It's not the original contract."

"What's the matter?" Ana asked, her hands holding to the counter.

Tara couldn't believe what she was seeing on the page in front of her. "This can't be right."

"Can you tell us, or should we just mind our own business?" Eloise asked, clearly hoping Tara would share all.

Tara flipped the contract pages over so no one could see the contents. "I'm sorry. I can't discuss this with any of you. As I said, it's a business decision, between Stone and me." Then she looked at Rock. "But I can say that your brother is crazy if he thinks I'll actually go for this—this deal."

"Stone isn't crazy," Rock said. "He's very shrewd and completely ruthless. Be careful, Tara."

"Oh, I'm going to be very careful," Tara said, heading for the hallway. Then she whirled to face Eloise. "Did you say he's at Hidden Hill?"

"Why, yes, but—"

"Good. Then I can see him tonight and settle this once and for all."

"Settle what?" Ana asked, her hands falling to her side in frustration. "Tara, why can't you talk to us?"

Tara headed for the stairs to change. "Because this is something I have to take care of myself. I'll explain later."

After she confronted Stone Dempsey.

If he wanted her respect, he'd failed miserably in his attempt to show her that. She'd never agree to this kind of manipulation.

Never.

He'd never before wanted to see a woman so badly.

Stone turned from the lower terrace of the big mansion he'd bought a couple of years ago, feeling restless and caged within the confines of the stucco-and-stone walls of Hidden Hill. Staring up at the muted light shining through the doors he'd flung open from the massive drawing room, he wondered why he'd come back here.

He had planned to stay away, to stay in the city until the renovations were complete. The old house needed work from the ground up. It was literally falling apart, its thick stone walls straining and craning underneath the weight of close to a century of storm winds and salt air.

And yet, Stone loved the house.

He loved the twenty-six rooms and the many terraces and steps of the house, even when he remembered having to work here as a teenager, helping with the enormous grounds, helping with the never-ending maintenance such a house required. He hated those memories, even as he loved the house.

He turned toward the sound of the ocean crashing against the shore down below, closing his eyes as he remembered everything bad about Hidden Hill.

A wealthy Northern business tycoon named Thorgood Sinclair had owned the home back then. It had been passed to Thorgood from his million- aire father, who'd built it as a family vacation retreat back in the twenties. Thorgood had rarely stayed at the house. But Stone remembered Mr. Sinclair's fancy wife and three children. The two boys, about the same age as Stone, had taunted and teased him as he sweated away in the yards. The daughter, Ramona, had flirted with him, driving him crazy, while she dated the rich boys she brought down from New York each summer. Stone had taken a lot of heat from the beautiful young lady of the manor.

Well, now he was the lord of the manor. He could hire as many groundskeepers and mainte- nance men as he needed to turn this place back into the showcase it had once been. And it had given him great pleasure to seize the crumbling house from a washed-out, near bankrupt Thorgood Sinclair, Jr. Junior hadn't remembered who Stone was at first. But by the time the ink had dried on the sale, Junior had not only remembered, he'd sunk down in a chair to stare after Stone as he'd walked out the door with a smug smile on his face. Since the day he'd stood on this very terrace listen- ing to the beautiful Sinclair children frolicking in the pool, Stone had vowed to come back rich and successful himself. And since the day the Sinclairs

had put the house up for sale, Stone had dreamed
of renovating this old mansion.

Tonight, that dream was very near.

Except that tonight, the dream seemed hollow
and lacking. And Stone felt very much alone in the
house on the bluff.

Because of her.

Tara Parnell's image shot through his mind as if
illuminated from the once beaming glow of the
nearby old lighthouse. She'd refused to have dinner
with him, and Stone wasn't used to being refused.

So he'd tried another tactic—one she'd probably
find just as underhanded as his other modes of operation. He'd sent his mother as envoy, with the one
thing that would get Tara's attention.

A revised contract.

Now, he would wait. But he didn't want to wait.
Stone was ready for the fight, welcomed the battle
he knew was coming. It was the only way to get to
see her again. Even if it meant she would be thoroughly angry with him.

Tara was so angry, she could barely see to find
the secluded gate leading up to the big square
mansion. Stopping the car at the end of the long,
tree-shaded drive, she stared up at the imposing
house, taking a minute to calm herself.

The old mansion was impressive. The stark
golden and bronzed stone walls stood out in the
moonlit night, while a solitary light from a second

floor room seemed to be the only illuminated object inside the decaying walls.

Was that where he was waiting? she wondered as she got out of the car and slammed the door, the roar of the ocean matching the roar of slow rage building in her mind. Holding on to the skirts of her flowing sundress, Tara wound her way up the cracked steps leading to the second level terrace. The wind picked up as she moved, causing her hair to lift out around her face. Impatiently, Tara brushed the hair away as she hurried up the stairs toward that light.

As she reached a small landing, she stopped to look toward the terrace. And that's when she saw him. He was waiting, all right. He stood there, as solitary and sad as the house, his hands in the pockets of his trousers, his face in the shadows.

Clutching the contract with one hand, Tara dashed up the remaining stairs, her eyes scanning the construction scaffolding and various tools scattered about the grounds and house. She hated being so predictable, but if Stone wanted to see her, then this latest trick had worked remarkably well in getting her here. She'd tell him off, tell him no, then leave with some dignity intact, she hoped.

Gasping, she reached the terrace then stopped to breathe deeply. She wouldn't give him the satisfaction of seeing her rattled. But when Stone turned to face her, the look in his crystalline eyes only added to Tara's woes.

It was not the smug, ruthless, victorious look she

had expected. Stone was looking at her as if he wanted to pull her into his arms and kiss her.

That look, that all-consuming, all-encompassing inspection that swept her from head to toe, caused her heart to beat in a panicked, trapped effort. Stone looked ready to pounce at any time.

"You're here," he said, as if in awe of the fact that she was standing ten feet away.

"Did you really expect me to just sign this?" Tara asked, regaining control of her heart and her head as she stalked toward him, the contract crushed in her hand.

"Yes," he said, the one word calm and calculated. "It's a good compromise, don't you think?"

"I think you're trying to manipulate me," Tara replied, her eyes scanning his face. "What happened to the original contract?"

"I tore that one up."

"Did it ever occur to you to discuss this with me, before you destroyed the other contract?"

"No."

The wind lifted his hair away from his brow, making him look like a golden lion standing there. Deciding she needed to quit imagining Stone as some jungle cat, Tara advanced a step. "I won't sign this, Stone. In fact, you can just forget the whole thing. I'll find another buyer for my land."

"Do you hate me that much?" he asked, his hands still in his pockets as he rocked back on his expensive loafers.

"I don't know you well enough to hate you," Tara admitted, "but from what I do know, I don't like you very much right now."

He pushed at his hair, looked off toward the distant shore. "Tara, this is a good deal. You told me you had to think of your children. Well, this way—"

She tossed the contract at him. "This way, you win, Stone. You get the land…and…the rest, well, that's charity. And I'm not so destitute that I'll take charity yet, especially from the likes of you."

She watched as he leaned down to pick up the contract. "It's not charity. I am not a charitable man, or haven't you noticed that?"

Tara waved a hand in the air. "All the more reason to suspect you. Why would you want this? Why are you being so—"

"Nice?" He came so close, she could see the perfect shape of his wide lips, could feel the heat from those shattered eyes that refused to stop staring at her.

"You want to give me a signing bonus," she said, stating the terms of the contract, "and then make me a partner in the development corporation for this project." Groaning, she added, "Stone, you're offering to pay me almost exactly the amount of money I need to get out of debt, and you're willing to give me a job, at a salary that will more than pay my bills, and make me a partner? I think, considering the first offer you made, that yes, this is charity, and yes, it's way too nice. You obviously have some other motive."

In a move that had her back against the cold bricks of the terrace wall, Stone tossed the contract on a nearby wrought-iron table, then pulled Tara into his arms. "And what if I do have another motive?"

She couldn't move, couldn't find her next breath. "I don't like this," Tara managed to whisper. "I don't like—"

"Me," he finished for her just before his mouth came down on hers. It was a tentative kiss, completely out of character for a man who obviously took what he wanted when he wanted it. The kiss was soft and quick, like a butterfly tickling against her lips, but it left a definite impact on her heart. Then he lifted his mouth, his eyes holding hers. "You don't like me. I think we've established that much. So because you don't like me, you're refusing my offer? Not a very wise business decision, Tara."

Tara found the strength to look him in the eye. "I don't take charity, Stone."

"It's not charity," he said, his hand moving over her cheekbone. "It's a good deal."

"For you?"

"Especially for me. This way, I don't have to honor that first contract—you know, the part about you never wanting to see me again."

"I still feel that way," she told him, even while her lips still tingled from his touch. Closing her eyes, she willed his soft, tender fingers on her face to stop making her feel things she didn't need to feel. "I can't do this, Stone."

His hand lifted her chin. "Open your eyes and tell me why you can't."

Tara did as he said, her eyes flying open to find him right there, his face inches from hers. "Because I don't trust you," she admitted.

Stone backed away as if she'd slapped him. And Tara immediately felt raw and exposed, standing there in the misty night wind.

"No respect, no trust," he said, the words hitting her as he tossed them over his shoulder. "I've really got my work cut out for me."

Tara hated the trace of regret in his words. But she had to stand firm. "Can't we just go back to the original deal? I'm willing to take a cut and accept your offer now."

"Rather than having to deal with the likes of me?"

He still had his back to her, and Tara felt the pull of that broad back, felt the need to touch him, nurture him, tell him she understood. But she didn't understand.

"Look," she said, letting out a long sigh, "this would be very awkward. I mean, I'm Ana's sister and you're—"

"The black sheep brother," he said, whirling around, his eyes flashing like shards of white fire. "My reputation precedes me."

"I don't want to make things difficult for Rock

and Ana," she tried to explain. "They just got married. They don't need us complicating their lives."

"Oh, no," he said, raking a hand through his hair. "My brother is so noble and good, so sanctimonious and pure. We can't mess with that, can we?"

"You're wrong about Rock," Tara said, wanting to defend her friend. "He is a good man, and he loves you."

"Oh, really?"

"Yes, really. He talks about you and Clay all the time. He mentioned his family a lot, when he helped me sort through my problems."

"I'll just bet he did."

"He's working on some of his own issues, too, from the past. I don't want to complicate that."

"And you owe him now, right? So you don't want to add to those problems by agreeing to come and work for me."

"Yes, I owe Rock, at least my consideration," she said. "He's brought my life around." She turned to look out over the horizon. Off in the distance, she could see the white-and-red stone of the old lighthouse, and beyond that, the dark, rolling sea. "Rock has shown me how to pray again, how to turn to God for help."

Stone came to stand by her then, his hands digging into the thick terrace railing. "Well, since you've got Rock and God, you certainly don't need me, right?"

"I didn't say that," Tara replied, her gaze touching on his face. He looked as if he'd been carved and shaped, like one of his mother's sculptures. And she wondered what had made him such a hard man. "What I need is to earn a good living for my children. What I need is some peace and quiet, some semblance of order and calm in my life. And I don't think accepting the terms of your offer would bring me that."

"You're afraid of me," he said, pivoting to touch a hand to her arm. "Just be honest, Tara, and admit that, at least."

She nodded. "Yes, you do frighten me."

"I'm offering you enough money to more than take care of your girls," he said, the words echoing out over the night. "Why would you turn that down?"

Tara didn't pull away. Instead, she turned to touch a hand to his face. His skin was soft and warm, a sharp contrast to the hard-edged look in his eyes. "Because over the last few months, I've found out life is about more than money. I know we need it to survive, and I could use enough to get out from under the debts Chad left me, but I have to do it my way this time. I lost control completely, being married to Chad. I won't ever let that happen again."

Stone leaned into her touch, then took her hand and kissed the inside of her palm. "Is that what this is all about? Are you afraid you'll lose control with me, Tara?"

Tara knew the answer to that question already. She felt it in his touch, in his eyes on her, in the way his kiss had made her come alive. "Yes," she said.

Then she turned and ran back down the steps.

When she reached her car, Tara looked back up at the terrace. And saw Stone standing there, almost in the same spot and in the same way in which she'd found him.

It was as if he'd never moved.

As if she'd never been there in his arms at all.

Chapter Five

"So what have you decided?"

Ana handed Tara a second cup of coffee, then sat down for a minute to catch her breath. The Sunday afternoon brunch crowd had packed into the restaurant just after church, and today had been Ana's one Sunday to work. Ana had insisted when they opened, that she wouldn't make her staff work every Sunday, so they all rotated, allowing for each of them to have a couple of Sundays a month off to be with their families. She'd also insisted that they didn't open during church hours, so that meant rushing to the restaurant just after Rock's sermon to get things in gear. Tara had to wonder if Ana adhered to her own rule, though. Her sister always seemed to be here in the kitchen, day and night.

"I haven't decided," Tara replied in answer to Ana's question. "There's nothing to decide. And

I'm leaving today, anyway. I have to remind myself my life is back in Savannah."

"You're not telling me everything, are you?" Ana asked, pushing a plate of sweet corn muffins and mixed fruit across the counter to her sister. "Eat. You helped serve, so now have some lunch."

Tara picked up a piece of cantaloupe, nibbled on it, then put it back on the plate. Glancing around to make sure none of the staff was nearby, she said, "My life is a mess."

Ana's green eyes widened. "You're still grieving. It's not even a year yet, Tara."

Tara nodded. "Yes, but it's more than just dealing with Chad's death."

"Can you tell me?" Ana asked, her expression full of sisterly concern. "Look, I know you've been confiding in Rock—that's part of his job as a minister—but I'm your sister. Didn't we agree to never again keep any secrets from each other?"

Tara lowered her head, her appetite gone. "Yes. And I do need someone to talk to, another woman."

Ana nodded, let out a sigh. "Even my adorable husband, as sweet and understanding as he is, can't seem to be impartial when it comes to his brother Stone. But I'll try to be, for your sake."

"Why do they hate each other?" Tara asked, memories of Stone's bitter comments about Rock coming to the surface.

"I don't think they hate each other," Ana replied, getting up to stack dishes and put away food. "They're brothers with an eccentric, artist mother who became a widow at a very young age." She gave Tara an apologetic look. "As you know from personal experience, that complicates things right from the start. They resent each other, but you know something I've noticed? Even when Rock is lamenting Stone's transgressions, he still seems to hold a certain amount of respect for Stone's accomplishments."

"The same with Stone, regarding Rock," Tara said, amazement coloring the realization. "Respect—that's what Stone told me. He wanted to earn my respect."

Ana sat back down, then picked up a tiny muffin. "Respect is hard to come by. Stone has become very successful, but his motives aren't always so pure, according to what Rock has told me. I think Rock just wants his brother to be happy, and when I say that, I mean happy in his faith, in finding love, in life in general. Stone, for all his riches, seems like a very miserable, lonely man."

Tara tilted her head. "Is that why you wanted to fix us up? Misery loves company?"

Ana shrugged, bit into her muffin. After chewing a while, she said, "At first, I just thought you two could share companionship, go out together, have some fun. Now, I'm beginning to doubt the wisdom of that particular suggestion. Stone has the power to hurt you, Tara, and I'd never want that."

Tara knew that to be the truth. Stone did have the

power to hurt her, but then last night, he had seemed so alone, so vulnerable. As if he were the one who could be easily hurt.

Ana leaned forward to wave a hand in her face. "Hello? Where'd you just go?"

Tara put her elbows on the counter, then laid her head in her hands. "I'm confused about Stone. He's not the hardened man everyone makes him out to be."

"Hmmm." Ana leaned back in her chair, her eyes centered on her sister. "Are you falling for him, already?"

"No," Tara said, jumping up to busy herself with putting away silverware. "I don't even know him. But he just seems so…lost."

"He is lost," Ana said. "He's lost in that big old mansion. He's lost in a world of greed and money. Rock worries about… Well, he worries about Stone's soul."

"He does have one," Tara said, too defensively.

"Of course he does, but you're not willing to do business with the man, so there must be something about him that scares you."

"There's a lot about Stone Dempsey that scares me, but none of it has to do with business."

"I see." Ana remained quiet for about two seconds. "You are interested in Stone, in more than a business way, aren't you? And that scares you, right?"

Tara nodded. "He kissed me last night."

"Uh-oh. He works fast." Ana came around the counter to stare at Tara. "That is definitely more than business."

"And he offered me a job—he'd still get my land, but he'd hire me on as a partner and pay me a very large salary to be the spokesperson for this new development. I'd deal with selling the acreage to clients, then help them with designing and building their houses to meet the specifications of the overall requirements. Stone plans to build a very exclusive, upscale residential area and a ritzy shopping center. Almost like a private town—a country club behind closed gates."

Ana stood back, letting what Tara had just told her sink in. "He's got it all figured out, hasn't he? He gets the land and you—a package deal. No wonder you refused his offer."

"I can't accept it," Tara said. "Plus, he's offering me this enormous signing bonus. It's just charity, plain and simple. Stone feels sorry for me."

Ana's head came up. "And why would he feel sorry for you? You're successful yourself. You've got a nice house in Savannah and a good job. Plus, the assets Chad left you—" She stopped, her brow lifting. "Is there more to this, Tara?"

"Chad didn't leave me any assets," Tara blurted out, glad to have her horrible secret out in the open. "He left me a little bit of life insurance and a tremendous amount of debt. And…Stone knows exactly how much I owe. Chad even owed Stone money—that's how Stone got wind of the land being up for sale."

"What?" Ana sank down on a counter stool, shock registering on her face. "But I thought—"

"I didn't want to tell you," Tara explained. "I didn't want you to worry."

"How bad is it?"

"Pretty bad. I used the life insurance money to pay off the worst of the debts. I'm barely holding on to the house in Savannah. And I don't have anything set aside for the girls' college fund." She lowered her head again. "I can barely buy them school clothes. Plus, things are bad at work. There's talk of layoffs. And since that deal near Atlanta fell through, I'll probably be one of the first to go. My boss wasn't too happy that I didn't stay on top of that this summer."

"You were spending time with your children," Ana said. "Did you tell your boss that?"

"Oh, he knew. I tried to explain things to him, but he didn't care." Tara shook her head. "It gets tough out there sometimes."

"I know," Ana replied, sympathy in her eyes. "But Tara, you insisted on loaning me money to start the tea room. How could you do that?"

"It's okay," Tara replied. "That was money already set aside before Chad died. Somehow, he managed one last noble act. He secured the loan for your tea room."

"Oh, my." Ana pushed at her hair. "I can't believe this. There is so much about Chad and you

I never knew. First you tell me your marriage was a sham—that Chad still loved me. Now you tell me that your whole lifestyle was a sham, too."

"I told you I was a mess," Tara replied, the words a whisper. "But I don't want my girls to suffer because of my mistakes."

Ana gave her a long, penetrating look. "Maybe you should consider Stone's offer."

"I can't."

"Why? It's a good offer. And it would solve a lot of problems."

"But it could create even more. Think about Rock, Ana."

"I am thinking of Rock. Maybe it's time to put the past behind us. We're doing that, by being honest with each other. Don't you think Stone and Rock need to do that, too?"

"But how can my working for Stone help that?"

"You said he seemed lost," Ana pointed out. "Maybe Stone needs someone like you in his life."

"I'm as lost and miserable as he is. You said so yourself."

"I never said that," Ana replied, shaking her head. "And besides, you've made great strides in your life, and you've done it in spite of all your financial troubles."

Tara bobbed her head, pivoted around the kitchen. "Yes, exactly. Which is why I don't need to be the one to save Stone. I'm having enough trouble just trying to save myself."

"You can't hold out forever," Ana said. "How are you going to pay off the debts?"

"I'm working on finding another buyer for the land."

"But Stone's deal is a good compromise."

Tara finished taking dishes to the big industrial-size dishwasher. "Ana, I've learned a lot about myself over these last few months. Chad kept secrets from me. He was ruthless and he worked all the time—day and night. So did I. I lost him and I've come close to losing my children. Laurel barely speaks to me and Marybeth and Amanda go around dazed and confused. I won't give in to the whims of another powerful man. I can't do it. I'll just have to come up with something else, some other way."

"You could work here part-time, if that would help," Ana suggested. "Just weekends. I'll pay you what I can. A salary coupled with the money I've been paying you back for the loan might help some."

"That's a nice offer, but how would that help with me spending time with my girls?" Tara asked, her gaze moving over the oaks and pines outside in the sloping backyard.

"Well, the girls love it here, so they could come with you."

"No, we won't pile in here on you and Rock every weekend. You're still newlyweds."

"You can stay in Rock's cottage," Ana said,

clasping her hands together. "It's vacant now that he's living here. And Milly McPherson would love to have you as a neighbor. Think what a great influence she'd be on the girls."

Tara stood there thinking it through. "Well, if I do sell the house in Savannah, I'll need a place to stay—but until then, it'd just be for weekends. Of course, I'd have to drive back and forth into the city to work each day, if I did decide to rent the cottage full-time. And Ana, I do mean rent. I won't stay there without paying Rock something."

"But that would cancel out most of your salary," Ana said. "Tara, let us help you. You helped me when I wanted to buy this place. Don't be so stubborn."

Tara saw the determination in Ana's eyes. "You're right, of course. It would be silly to turn around and pay you back money I need for other things." She held up a hand. "But I'm only going to use the cottage on a temporary basis—just until I can do something about my finances."

"Fine. I'll talk to Rock tonight. Once you get back on your feet, you can make a donation to the church to show your gratitude."

Tara smiled. "This might work. I can use the extra money and the girls will love coming out to the island each weekend. And since I've always set my own hours at the real estate office, I can probably get out here early on Fridays to help you with the occasional dinner crowd, too."

"That would be great. Jackie will be thrilled. She says you know how to sell the artwork better than she does, anyway."

"I do enjoy that," Tara replied, feeling as if a weight had been lifted off her shoulders.

"Of course," Ana said, "I can't pay you nearly what Stone Dempsey is offering."

"No, but you're giving me something much more important than money," Tara said, reaching out a hand to her sister. "You're giving me a chance to redeem myself and help my girls out, too."

Ana laughed. "Now why is that so very different from what Stone was offering you?"

"The difference is," Tara replied, "I can trust you."

"And you'll be safe here," Ana said, her eyes glowing. "Plus, you just might run into Stone here and there, since he'll be staying on the island a while. You might even get him to come to dinner, or better yet, to church one Sunday."

Tara glared at her sister in astonishment. "Ana Dempsey, did you just set me up?"

"I'm only trying to help," Ana said, grinning.

"And I thought I could trust you." Tara grinned, too, then hugged her sister close. "You're every bit as ruthless as Rock's handsome brother."

"Don't tell Rock," Ana whispered. "He thinks I'm perfect."

Stone glanced up from where he'd been scrubbing down the weathered walls on the west side of the mansion, to find his brother Rock headed toward him. "Perfect. Just perfect."

"Good to see you, too," Rock said as he came up one side of the double-sided stone staircase leading from the pool house and gardens. "I thought you hired people to do the grunt work around here."

"It's Sunday," Stone countered, taking time to wipe sweat from his face with an old towel. "The workers have the day off and I needed some time alone, to think."

"Meaning I should leave?"

Stone turned back to the wall. "Suit yourself."

Rock picked up a long-handled scrub brush and dipped it into the big bucket of bleach and detergent sitting next to Stone's workspace. "Mind if I help?"

"Suit yourself," Stone said again. "But don't you have a sermon to preach or something?"

"Already did that this morning," Rock replied before he pushed the wet broom up against the glinting gray-washed stucco wall. "You might try coming to church sometime."

Stone tore at some clinging ivy with his gloved hands. "I'll pass. You preached to me enough growing up, or have you forgotten?" He heard the tinge of broom brush against aged brick and mortar walls. Apparently, he'd struck a familiar cord.

"I remember," Rock replied, the effort of his work causing him to sound winded. "And obviously, it didn't work. Maybe you should turn to a higher source."

Stone threw down his own scrub brush then turned to face his brother. "What do you want, Rock?"

Rock stopped scrubbing, too. But he held his broom handle near his chest as he stared over at Stone. "Now, that's the question I need to ask you, brother. What exactly do you want from Tara Parnell?"

"Oh, I get it. This is a fact-finding mission," Stone retorted, disgust and frustration causing him to rip away a particularly stubborn vine. Turning to look for his water bottle, he took a long swig, then grudgingly handed it toward Rock. "Thirsty?"

"Thanks." Rock took the water, sipped it, then put it down on a nearby work table. "I don't mean to pry, Stone. But Tara is a nice woman. And she's been through a lot lately."

"Meaning, she doesn't need me complicating her life?"

"Meaning, she doesn't need you in her life, period."

His brother's automatic condemnation rankled Stone beyond measure, but he hid his discontent behind a blank wall of indifference. "Would I be so bad for Tara? I'm offering her a way out of her situation."

"Are you?" Rock said, leaning back against a granite banister to stare over at Stone. "She didn't really explain your revised contract to any of us."

Stone plopped down on a wide step of the ladder

he'd been using to climb up and tear away vines and bushes. "Maybe that's because this is just between Tara and me."

"That's true," Rock said, nodding. "I don't need to know the details, but whatever you offered sure upset her the other night."

Stone felt the weight of a thousand burdens on his back, much like this sinking old house. He'd rather spit nails than ask his brother for advice, but he was becoming desperate. He didn't like that feeling. "I don't want to upset Tara. And I didn't come back here to make trouble for you and Ana. So here's the deal—Tara thinks I'm offering her charity."

"Are you?" Rock asked, all his animosity gone.

Stone looked out over the dense foliage of the overgrown gardens. Tall palms trees and lush wild ferns swayed in the afternoon wind. "I thought I was offering her a solution to all her problems. I don't know how much Tara has told you, but she's not doing so well financially."

"I know," Rock admitted. "She's come to me for counseling."

Stone took that as a given, even though it got to him in more ways than one. He wanted to be the one Tara came to for help, for a shoulder to cry on. He still didn't know or understand why, but his competitive nature told him he didn't like his brother consoling Tara Parnell. Not one bit. So he took up the indifferent attitude again.

"What do you suggest, preacher?"

Rock gave him a long, hard look, then said, "I suggest you back off. Give Tara some space and give her the price she needs for that land so she can get on with her life."

But that would mean he'd also have to let her go, out of his life. And Stone wasn't ready to do that.

"Hey, man, I just saw this as a sound business deal. That land is prime for development, and I've offered a reasonable price. Plus, I've offered Tara a good job that I happen to know she's qualified to handle. She needs to get away from that rinky-dink real estate office and use her talents to make some real money for a change."

Rock pushed off the banister, his face marred with a frown. "It always goes back to money with you, doesn't it?"

Here it comes, Stone thought. The famous Rock Dempsey lecture. "I like money, yeah. And I've got lots of it now. What's wrong with wanting to help someone else make it?"

Rock picked up his scrub brush again. "There is more to life—"

"I know, I know," Stone interrupted, turning to get back to work himself. "There is more to life than money. You've told me that since the day our daddy died." He turned to stare over at Rock. "But you know what, when you don't have money, it becomes the most important thing in the world. And when you do have it—"

"You still can't buy happiness," Rock finished for him.

"I'm happy," Stone said to hide the hurt he felt rising up inside him like a fast-crashing tide. Throwing his hands out in the air, he added, "Look around, Rock. Look at what I've accumulated. Why shouldn't I be happy?"

Rock did look around, at the overgrown garden, at the empty, cracked swimming pool covered with water lilies and morning glory vines. At the rose-encroached fountain that no longer flowed with clear, clean water, at the ivy and kudzu threatening to overtake the whole estate. A cherub with a broken wing looked down on the dry fountain, as if waiting for someone to bring the water back. "I see what you've accomplished, Stone. And I am proud of you for persevering. But I feel sorry for you, too. 'Thy own reproach alone do fear.'"

Stone let out a groan that echoed over the trees. His brother, ever the philosopher. "Don't go quoting things to me, Rock. You know that drives me crazy."

"That quote was on the wall of Andrew Carnegie's private library. Can't remember which house, but it was one of his many castles."

Stone watched as his brother's gaze traveled over the old mansion. "Well, obviously I'm not Andrew Carnegie."

"No, he did good things with his vast fortune. Built libraries and set up foundations."

Stone put his hands on his hips. "How do you know I'm not doing good things?"

"I truly hope you are, Stone. And I'm not judging you. I actually came here today to offer you my help, with this house, with anything else. No strings attached. That's what the quote means—I think you worry so much about failure, that you're your own worst critic."

Surprised, Stone decided maybe Ana was good for his brother. Maybe being happily married had some merit after all. "Hey, don't go soft on me, brother. *You've* always been my worst critic, remember? But I don't need your sympathy or your constant reminders of my shortcomings. I told you, I'm doing just fine. I don't need your help."

Rock slowly put down his brush, then turned to stare up at Stone, his blue eyes full of regret. "Yeah, I can see that."

"You don't see anything," Stone called after his brother's retreating back. "You just don't get it, Rock."

Rock turned on the weed-infested walkway. "No, you're the one who doesn't get it, brother. But I pray that you will one day, before it's too late."

Angry and defensive, Stone shouted after Rock. "Don't waste your prayers on me. I learned a long time ago that praying doesn't work."

Rock didn't answer him.

But then Stone hadn't expected an answer.

From either his brother or God.

Chapter Six

"You have a knack for selling my work."

Tara looked up from the handful of cash register receipts she'd been sorting to find Eloise Dempsey smiling over at her. "Well, hello. It's very easy to sell your art, Mrs. Dempsey. Your pieces are exquisite."

"Call me Eloise," Stone's mother replied, her cup of hot tea in one hand. "And you're very kind to say that."

"I'm not just being kind," Tara said as she came around the counter and waved to some departing lunch guests. "Having your pieces in the tea room has been a major coup for Ana. Just about half the profits come from the artwork alone, most of that yours. In fact, I just sold that bronze brown pelican to a woman from New York."

"How lovely. I guess they don't see many pelicans in the city."

"I wouldn't think so. She said she'd heard about your sculptures through a friend from Atlanta. Word is getting out about you."

"Well, don't underestimate the other artists around here," Eloise said as she settled back on a wicker chair in a corner, just underneath a Victorian birdhouse. "The art council meets once a month. You should come to a meeting. We could use some fresh, young ideas."

"I'd like that," Tara said, pushing at her bangs. "But as you can see, I'm pretty busy holding down two jobs now."

Eloise nodded, then smiled. "Yes, Ana told me you're helping her out for a while. Splendid idea. And we love having the girls around. That Marybeth, what a doll. Did you know she has a talent for drawing and painting?"

Glancing around to make sure no customers were waiting at the antique counter, Tara sank down on a bistro chair. "No, I didn't. I mean, she's always doodled and colored, but my Marybeth—an artist?"

"She shows tremendous potential," Eloise replied, obviously delighted. "And Amanda wants to learn to play the guitar. I had an old one of Clay's lying about, so I let her fiddle with it. She has a natural ear for music."

Tara didn't know what to say. "Can you explain Laurel to me?"

"Oh, that one." Eloise's hand fluttered out. "Laurel is growing up. She reads a lot. I think she likes to scribble poetry now and again. I've seen her sharing it with that adorable Cal Ashworth."

Tara lowered her head. "I didn't know that. How can I not know these things?"

"Daughters don't always confide in their mothers," Eloise said, taking a sip of her tea. "Nor do sons, for that matter. And speaking of sons, what's going on between you and Stone?"

A bit flustered by Eloise's directness, Tara shrugged. "Nothing. Nothing at all. We came close to agreeing on a business deal, but it stalled out. Your son wants to buy my land, but I can't accept the offer he made."

"Not generous enough?" Eloise questioned, her brilliant silvery eyes, so like Stone's, moving over Tara with a questioning appraisal.

Tara didn't want to go into detail with Stone's mother. "It wasn't that. Stone made me a generous offer, but it had stipulations I couldn't accept."

Eloise sat silent, letting that sink in. "Stone always expects stipulations, I'm afraid. He was a challenge as a child and now he's even harder to deal with as an adult."

"A challenge. Yes, that just about sums him up," Tara replied, glancing at her watch. "Oh, I hate to rush, but I promised the girls we'd go into the city to do some school shopping. And then I think I'll drive them out to the land, let them see the place their father left to us. I don't want to sell it, but I don't know what else to do.

I'm sorry you and I can't spend more time talking together."

Eloise waved a hand, her silver bangle bracelets tinkling like chimes as they fell down her arm. "No need to apologize. I'm being nosy, anyway. It's just that Rock and Ana are so happy, and Rock and I are closer than ever. I credit your sister with much of that. She is a gentle force, a good influence on my son. I wish the same for Stone. And he seems smitten with you, dear."

Tara felt a heat rush up her skin as she remembered Stone's kiss. "Oh, I think your son is smitten with making more money, with getting the best deal. He seems driven."

"He is driven. And that's why I pray he'll find someone, the way Rock has, and settle down to the simple pleasures of life." She got up, placed a hand on Tara's arm. "You know, it took me a long time to realize what really matters in this world. You go for that drive with your girls. And while you have them, talk to them. But more important, listen to them. I wish I'd done more of that." Then she gave Tara a soft smile. "Enough unsolicited advice from me. I've got to get home."

"Work to do?" Tara asked, still in awe from this entire conversation.

"No," Eloise said, running a hand through her short, grayish-white hair. "I'm going to go for a long walk, maybe over to the other side of the island. To Hidden Hill."

Tara nodded her understanding. "To see Stone?"

"He needs me," Eloise said. "I think that's why he's come home. He doesn't realize it, but he has always needed me. And his brothers."

And me? Tara had to wonder as she waved goodbye to Stone's mother. Then she quickly put that thought out of her mind. And for the last two weeks, she'd tried to put Stone Dempsey out of her mind, too. But it seemed he was always there, the sweet intensity of his touch just a breath away from her dreams.

"Are we all done?" Ana called from the kitchen.

"Yes, thankfully," someone called back.

Tara could hear Jackie and Tina laughing and chatting with Charlotte in the background. Most of the other workers had already gone home for the day. Ana had a wonderful, well-trained staff. They had served a record crowd for lunch and were now shutting down for the day. The Saturday night tourists tended to head to more exciting nightlife than a tea room could offer. But Tara had an idea for something special to draw in people on Saturday night, maybe a nice jazz or classical ensemble playing in the garden.

"What are you dreaming about?" Ana asked from the hallway, jarring Tara out of her musings.

"Oh, just thinking maybe we could hold some Saturday night concerts here, in the garden."

"Hmmm, sure sounds romantic. Girls, what do you think?"

They heard a random groan from the kitchen.

"I'm not sure, but I think that was Charlotte," Ana said with a grin.

"It was Tina," Charlotte called. "We're just too tired right now to think of more work."

Ana leaned into the doorway. "Then go home and soak your feet while my smart sister and I plot more ways to torture you."

"Slave driver," Jackie called as she grabbed her purse. But she was smiling as she said it. "Anything for you, boss."

"Sure," Ana replied, laughing. "Whew, I'm tired myself. I'm looking forward to a nice quiet evening with my husband." Then she turned to Tara. "What are you going to do for the rest of the afternoon?"

Tara finished closing down the cash register. "I'm going to take the girls for a drive, out to our land. I don't think they've ever been there. Then we might do some shopping in town."

"Do you need any money—for clothes, I mean."

"I'm not that destitute yet," Tara replied, hating the sympathy in Ana's eyes, even if she did appreciate the gesture.

"Okay. Just checking. Is everything all right?"

"I'm hanging on by a thread," Tara admitted. "The extra money I'm making here has helped so much already. And the girls love their new weekend retreat. Even Laurel seems to be having fun." She grinned. "Of course, Milly McPherson is trying to teach them manners. She said they need to learn how to be proper ladies."

Ana laughed. "Did she suggest they wear hats and gloves to church?"

"Yes, I think she did," Tara replied. "Laurel went running in the other direction."

"Well, they do have some manners. They were a big help around the kitchen today," Ana said as she took off her ruffled apron and hung it on a peg by the back door. "They're good girls, Tara."

"I know. And Rock is such a sweetheart to take them off my hands for a while this afternoon. That poor man must think he's a built-in baby-sitter."

"Hush, he loves being with the girls. And teaching them to fish—he couldn't be any happier on a pretty Saturday afternoon."

Tara nodded. "Well, I'd better go down to the dock and gather them up. Maybe we'll have fish for supper, huh?"

"Maybe." Ana waited for Tara to gather her tote bag before letting her out the back. "Have you heard anything else from Stone?"

"Not to change the subject," Tara replied, her smile teasing. "No, I haven't heard anything else from Stone and if I get another offer on the land, I'm taking it. I can't hold out forever."

"You could just accept his offer, stipulations and all."

"Trying to get rid of me already?"

"No, not at all. I love having you help out around

here. You've freed up the wait staff to concentrate on the food and you're very good at persuading the customers to buy our artwork. I just… Well, Rock has always indicated that Stone is selfish and hostile. I just wonder why Stone would make you such a strange and generous offer. Maybe you should talk to him about it a little more."

"Are you still trying to fix me up with Rock's brother?"

"Maybe," Ana admitted as they strolled down the steps toward the dock at the end of the property.

"You don't think I'm selfish and hostile, do you?"

"No," Ana said, taking in a deep breath of the fresh tropical air. "And honestly, I don't believe Stone is any of those things, either. Rock just worries about him. I don't know why, but my instincts tell me you and Stone would be right for each other."

"Your instincts also told you to break up with Chad way back in college, so he could be with me, remember?"

Ana cringed. "Okay, point taken. I'll try to stay out of it."

Tara touched a hand to her sister's arm. "I appreciate your trying to find me a new man, Ana. But I'm not ready for anything serious just yet. I have to get my life straight, first."

"You're right, of course. You've been through a lot. And I need to remember that."

"Thanks for caring," Tara said, meaning it. She and Ana had grown close over the summer, thanks to some heart-to-heart talks and Rock's gentle urgings that Tara and the girls get involved in church.

Having Ana and Rock to confide in had helped Tara deal with Chad's death and the fact that their marriage had been in shambles long before he died. As Tara saw her girls laughing and talking to Rock, she couldn't help but think of all they were missing, not having a father to love them. Chad had loved his daughters. That much, at least, Tara knew to be true.

That made her think of Rock and Stone, and their brother Clay. They'd had to grow up without a father, too. Rock had been the oldest, the one who had to stay strong for everyone else. He'd carried the weight of the entire family on his shoulders. Stone was the middle child. The one who got lost in the shuffle of the bossy firstborn and the sweet, lovable baby brother, Clay. No wonder Stone had a chip on his shoulder. He'd probably never felt truly loved, even though it was obvious Eloise loved each of her sons equally.

But how did a parent prove that love to a child? How did a parent show that love to a grown man?

I won't feel this way, Tara told herself as she waved to the children and Rock. I won't feel sorry for Stone Dempsey. I won't feel anything.

But each time she remembered his eyes, his touch, his kiss, she felt funny little sensations, starting with a tingling on her skin, then moving to a gentle fluttering inside her stomach, then finally causing a slight acceleration in her heartbeat. Just nerves, she thought. She'd been wise to turn down Stone's offer.

"Mom, I caught a fish!" Marybeth exclaimed, holding up the fishing line to show her mother her prize. "But I'm gonna throw him back. I don't want him to die."

"That's very sweet, honey." Tara whispered to Ana, "Marybeth is my environmentalist. She believes in taking care of Mother Earth."

"A very noble cause," Ana said, smiling over at her husband.

Rock grinned the goofy grin of a man in love. "What brings you two lovely ladies down to the water?"

"I came to collect my children," Tara said, her gaze moving over Marybeth's dark hair and eyes, so much like her aunt Ana's. Laurel and Amanda had the blond hair and blue eyes of Tara and their grandfather, Martin. But Marybeth looked a lot like Ana and Grandmother Peggy. All of the girls had their father's distinctive characteristics, too—tall, lanky, big toothy smiles.

"My children are so beautiful," Tara said, again under her breath.

"Yes, they are." Ana moved toward the dock, then sank down beside Rock. He gave her a quick peck on the cheek.

"Want to fish?" he asked, offering her the pole, a mischievous look in his blue eyes.

Ana leaned close to nudge his side. "I just might, at that."

Tara took that as a good sign that her sister and brother-in-law wanted to be left alone. "Okay, girls, let's load up. If you want to make it to the mall before it closes, we'd better hurry."

"I need new shoes," Laurel said, her sulkiness just a tad above tolerant.

"And I need some jeans and shirts," Marybeth explained, tossing her bobbed hair off her face.

Tara sighed, then turned to Amanda. "What do you need?"

"I'm fine," Amanda said, her big eyes on her mother. "I can wear whatever doesn't fit Laurel."

"Don't be silly," Tara said, frowning. "You can get some new things, too."

Amanda shifted on her feet, digging her sneakers into the planks of the weathered dock. "But...I don't want you to have to spend extra money on me."

Tara glanced over to Rock and Ana. Her sister shot her a sympathetic look. "Honey, I have some extra cash, thanks to working for Aunt Ana. We'll be fine. You can buy a few things, too, okay?"

"Okay," Amanda said, smiling at last. "If you're sure."

"I am sure," Tara replied, not really sure at all. But she'd make do. She had a closet full of designer clothes she could wear for many years to come. Her children were growing, though. They needed new clothes. She had enough money tucked back to buy them a couple of outfits each, at least.

"We're going," she said to Ana. "We're just going to stay in town tonight, since it'll be late when we leave the mall. So I guess I'll see you again next weekend."

"Okay," Ana said as she baited a hook with a squirming worm. "Thanks for the help yesterday and today."

Amanda ran over to Ana and Rock, her arms going around both of them. "Thank you, Aunt Ana, for paying us a salary, too."

"Shhh," Ana said, her gaze catching Tara's. "You weren't supposed to tell." She shrugged, a sheepish look on her face as she looked up at Tara. "I gave them each a tip. They worked hard, so that's fair."

Tara shook her head and mouthed her own thanks. Her sister had come through for her, even after all these years, even after the way things had turned out in college when Tara had practically stolen Ana's boyfriend Chad Parnell away from her.

Somehow, Tara would repay Ana and Rock for their kindness. Somehow.

It occurred to her that if she took Stone up on his offer, she'd have the money to do that and more. Maybe it was time to put pride and personal feelings aside, for the sake of her children.

* * *

Stone stood on a high bluff overlooking the land he hoped to buy from Tara Parnell. To the north, the Savannah River glistened and flowed off in the distance, headed toward the outer banks and on to the Atlantic Ocean. To the south, a vast forest and marshland grew up around a small freshwater lake. White ibis birds strolled in the reeds and bushes on the salt marsh, while overhead a flight of brown pelicans moved in perfect symmetry out toward the sea.

Stone stood and waited.

His mother had told him Tara would be coming here today. Since Stone believed in available opportunities instead of destiny or coincidences, he'd talked politely to his mother and bided his time until he could drive the hour or so to get here.

And wait.

He wanted to talk to Tara again. About the land, about the plans he had, about her working for him to make those plans happen, about him and her and where they might be headed. Stone had lots to discuss with Tara Parnell. And he wasn't leaving until she listened to him.

It was time to put everything out on the table. Time to make one last play for the intriguing woman he couldn't seem to get out of his mind.

So he stood, listening, waiting, anticipating.

Stone heard a movement to his left and turned to find an old black man walking toward him. The man wore a battered straw hat and overalls. He walked with the help of a huge carved walking stick. Stone stared at the man, wondering where in the world he'd come from. This land was empty, vast, hidden away from the world.

"Hello, young fellow," the old man said, waving a withered hand in greeting. "Nice day for a walk, ain't it?"

"Uh, yes," Stone replied, once again glancing around to look for another car back on the sandy dirt lane. But Stone only saw his own sturdy SUV. "Do you live around here?" he asked the old man.

The man stopped to catch his breath, then leaned heavily on his walking stick. Slowly, he took off his hat and shook it out in his hand. His face was wrinkled and wizened, like a raisin dried by the sun. His hair was completely white and tightly curled. It sat against his rounded head like cotton tufts falling away from a brown bale. But his eyes, they held Stone's attention.

The man had old eyes, big and black and all-seeing, in spite of the watery age spots clouding his pupils. Those eyes seemed to see right through Stone's soul.

Finally, the man answered. "I live back there in the marsh," he explained, indicating with a thumb over his shoulder. "Near the chapel."

"Chapel? What chapel?" Again, surprise caused Stone to glance around.

"It doesn't really have a name," the man said, his

grin revealing a gold tooth right in the front of his mouth. "We've just always called it the chapel. It's been here since the beginning."

"The beginning?"

"When the first slaves came over," the man said, no censure or condemnation, just acceptance, in his rich baritone voice. "They built it right there between the marsh and the sand dunes. It only holds about twenty people. But it's still a house of God."

Fascinated, Stone asked, "And this chapel is still standing? It must be over two hundred years old, at least."

"At least," the man repeated, grinning again. "Would you like to see the place?"

Stone glanced at his watch. What if he missed Tara?

"In a hurry to get somewhere?" the old man asked.

"No. Just...I was planning on meeting someone here. But I'm probably early anyway."

"Is this someone important to you?"

"You could say that."

"A woman, maybe?"

"How could you know that?"

"Son, it's written all over your face," the old man said. "And me, I can see things. Signs of things to come."

"Oh, really." Stone doubted that. Maybe he should just leave. And yet, something told him to stay. "Who are you, anyway?"

"Samson Josiah Bennett," the man proudly said, extending a gnarled hand toward Stone. "I'm the preacher."

"At the chapel?" Stone asked, thinking this was getting more strange by the minute.

"Yep. Call me Josiah. Everybody does."

Again, Stone nodded. "And Josiah…you live on this land?"

"Lived here since the day I was born. Most folks have moved away, but I stayed. Married in the chapel, raised a family right here, but now it's just me. I like the peace and quiet of the marsh."

"And you preach in the chapel each Sunday?"

"Yep. Sometimes, I get two or three people. Sometimes, I just sit and talk to the Lord."

"I see." Stone was beginning to wonder if he'd stumbled across an escaped nursing home dweller.

"Do you want to see my church, or not?" Josiah asked, still leaning on his walking stick.

"Are you sure you're okay?" Stone moved toward the man. In spite of being old, he looked in pretty good health.

"I'm fine, just fine," Josiah said. "I don't get many visitors, is all. When I heard your vehicle pulling up, I came to investigate."

"You know this land is up for sale, don't you?" Stone asked as he strolled along to accommodate the man's snail pace.

"Yep."

"Where will you go if someone buys the land?"

Josiah chuckled, waved a hand in the air. "That's for the Lord to decide, I reckon."

Stone shook his head. "I don't depend on the Lord in life. I make my own way." And he didn't usually discuss religion with strangers.

"Do you now?" Josiah said, bobbing his head like an old turtle.

Stone glanced back toward the empty land. Where was Tara?

"She'll wait for you," Josiah said, as if reading Stone's mind.

"It's a business deal," Stone felt obligated to explain. "I might buy this land."

"I figured as much." Josiah replied, his face perfectly serene in spite of the wrinkle traces dragging his skin down.

Stone wanted it understood. "You'd have to leave."

"Maybe. Or maybe you'd let me stay."

Oh, great. Not only was he dealing with a stubborn, beautiful woman, but now Stone had to try to persuade this ancient preacher to pack up and move. "You wouldn't be able to stay," he tried to explain. "We'd be putting in a new development."

"I see new development out here in these woods and marshes every single day, son."

"I don't understand," Stone replied, perplexed.

"I know you don't," Josiah conceded. "That's why you need to visit my chapel."

Chapter Seven

"I don't get why we have to come out here," Laurel said as Tara turned her car up the dirt lane toward the property. "This is so lame."

"I told you, I wanted you to see this place," Tara replied, tired of explaining herself.

"But the mall will close," Laurel whined, her arms crossed in a rebellious tightening over her midsection.

Tara glanced across at her daughter. "The mall stays open until ten o'clock, Laurel."

"I want to see the land, Mom," Amanda said, leaning over the seat to stare ahead. "Wow, this is sure out in the country."

Marybeth leaned forward, too. "It's so pretty."

"It's hot and full of bugs, and probably lots of snakes, too," Laurel told her sisters with a tart tongue. "You two are such losers."

"Hush," Tara said, glaring at Laurel. "You will not speak to your sisters that way."

"Well, it's true," Laurel said, raising her voice. "We're all losers. You think we don't see, Mom. But we do. You're working now more than ever, when you promised you were going to spend more time with us. We can't even buy decent clothes for school. And all my friends keep asking why our house is up for sale."

"Laurel, that is enough," Tara said, bringing the car to such a fast halt, the tires skidded on the sandy dirt. "I am doing the best I can. And I am spending time with you. That's why I brought you here."

"Just so we could see this?" Laurel asked, her hand on the door handle. "Just so you could tell us how much our daddy loved us, then turn around and sell the land he left us? That makes perfect sense, Mom."

Tara sat with her hands on the steering wheel, clutching it as if it were a life preserver. Her two younger daughters had now slumped into their seats, their eyes wide, their faces devoid of any smiles.

She wouldn't break down. She couldn't do that in front of her children. She'd gotten them into this mess, and she'd have to be the one to get them out now that Chad was gone. "I'm sorry," she said, the whispered apology laced with a plea. "Things are going to get better, I promise."

"We don't believe your promises," Laurel said. Then she got out of the car and slammed the door.

"I believe you, Mommy," Amanda said, her voice sounding small and far away.

"Me, too," Marybeth chimed in. "Laurel is so weird. Don't listen to her, Mom."

Tara swiped a tear from her face. "Thanks for the support, you two. Do you want to do this? We could just go on to the mall."

"I want to see this place," Marybeth replied, her eyes capturing Tara's in the rearview mirror. "If Daddy loved it, then we will, too."

That simple declaration almost broke Tara's heart, but she regained control and got out of the car. That's when she spotted the sleek black SUV parked off the road, underneath an aged live oak.

The girls got out, too. "Who's here, Mom?" Amanda asked, glancing over at the SUV.

"I don't know," Tara said. "I haven't had any calls from prospective buyers, so I wasn't supposed to meet anyone out here."

"Maybe somebody saw your ad in the paper," Marybeth reasoned. "They might have just decided to look on their own."

"That could be it," Tara replied, careful to glance around. They were in a very remote location. She wouldn't want any harm to come to her daughters.

They walked up on the slight incline that allowed a view of the marsh and forest. This was the spot where Chad had always talked about building a cabin or cottage. Tara turned to Laurel to tell her that, but the teenager hung back, her face sullen, her whole body rigid with anger and pain.

Tara wanted to run to her daughter and take Laurel into her arms and tell her it would be okay, but she didn't do that. Instead, she just stood looking out over the quiet marshland.

Then she heard laughter and voices coming from the lane that followed the course of the river to one side and stayed high above the marsh to the other. "I guess we do have visitors, girls."

Tara waited to see who would emerge from the woods around the bend. And wondered if she really did want to sell this land after all.

He had to wonder now if he should even buy this land.

Stone stared over at the intriguing man who'd taken him on a journey that had revealed more than just the marsh and a tiny ancient chapel.

The chapel was amazing. It looked like a little dollhouse, sitting among the old live oaks and cypress trees. It was painted a bright white with red shutters and a matching red door. A crudely made cypress cross was centered over the door. Inside, the chapel was quiet and cool, the scent of vanilla candles long since burned down wafting out into the small aisle. Josiah had invited Stone to sit up front, close to the petite altar, but Stone had hung back while Josiah piddled with clearing away cobwebs and dusting off the pulpit.

And Josiah had not bothered him.

Stone had sat inside that little clapboard building, in the peace and quiet that had endured through slavery and a great war, and somehow, had touched on the shackles and wars of his very own soul. And to think, no one believed he actually had a soul.

But Josiah had seen inside his soul.

Coincidence? Or an opportunity? An opportunity for what, Stone thought now as he strolled along, listening to Josiah's aged Southern drawl. There couldn't be any opportunity in taking a man from his home. Stone was accustomed to corporate raiding, but he'd never intentionally raid the home of someone so innocent and centered, so grounded in a simple way of life.

Stone decided he wouldn't worry about that until he'd signed on the dotted line. He'd make sure Josiah got to a safe, nice new home. He'd also make sure the old preacher wanted for nothing, ever again.

But Josiah seemed to have everything he needed right here, a little voice nagged in Stone's head. The old man had his chapel and he had his tiny, gray-washed shack that sat precariously close to the marsh. Josiah lived mostly off the land and the kindness of the few who still came to hear him preach the gospel each Sunday.

Wouldn't the old man be better off somewhere safe and warm, Stone wondered. Josiah whistled as they walked, making Stone think that maybe the old man would never willingly leave the marsh.

For the first time, Stone had doubts about his grand plans.

Then he looked up to the bluff and saw Tara standing there with her three daughters. The wind was playing through Tara's hair as she held her arms on one of the girl's shoulders. She looked down at him, their eyes locking, and Stone felt something break loose inside his very being, as if a strong wall had cracked open to reveal the secret places of his heart. And suddenly, he felt as if he were the one without a place to call home.

"Is that her?" Josiah asked, the words falling across the wind like a butterfly's flutter.

"Yes." Stone couldn't take his eyes off her.

"She's a pretty little thing."

"Yes," he repeated, sounding stupid and redundant in his own mind.

"Got a family already, too."

"Yes," he said again. "She's a widow."

"I know who she is," Josiah replied just before they reached the copse of trees on the bluff. "That's Chad Parnell's widow."

"You knew Chad?" Stone asked, completely surprised by this new information. But then, this day had been full of surprises.

"Known him since he was a boy," Josiah said. "Chad used to come out here…a lot. He'd fish and hunt with his daddy. He'd come to my chapel, too."

"Chad Parnell attended church?"

"He didn't attend church, son. He came to talk to a friend about all his troubles."

"And you listened and gave him advice?"

Josiah chuckled and shook his head. "No, young fellow, *God* listened…and gave him solace."

Stone turned to face Josiah at last. "I didn't think Chad Parnell was a godly man."

"Did you ever think to ask him?" Josiah shot back.

"Well, no. I mean, I didn't know him that well."

"Some things are kept close to the heart," Josiah replied. "Chad knew the Lord. He just didn't know how to accept all the Lord's blessings."

"I guess he didn't," Stone replied, his gaze moving back to Tara.

Josiah motioned toward Tara. "You might be able to do a better job than Chad."

Stone wished the old man was right. But the concept was so foreign to him, he didn't even know how to begin to ask for God's blessings. Especially regarding Tara Parnell.

Again, it was if Josiah had read his mind. "Ask and ye shall receive. Knock and He will answer."

Stone knew what Josiah was saying. After all, Rock had often coaxed him to turn his life around by turning back to the God that Stone had abandoned. Or rather, the God that Stone believed had abandoned him and his family.

Suddenly, Stone felt so very tired. Tired of

fighting against his brother's constant suggestions and gentle admonishments, tired of fighting against the God he didn't want to accept or acknowledge. And yet, he realized he needed some sort of acceptance, some sort of solace, himself. Meeting Tara had brought out all the loneliness he tried so hard to hide.

"I've been knocking, Josiah. It's like beating my head against a wall." This time, he wasn't just talking about Tara. It seemed as if Stone had been knocking against a brick wall most of his life.

"Then it's time to bring that wall down," Josiah said on a calm voice. "Starting right now, I think."

Stone stared up at Tara. She hadn't moved, hadn't said a word in greeting. Her three girls stood there with her, staring at him as if he were a marsh monster.

He turned to say something to Josiah, but the old man was already walking away.

Which left Stone alone in the middle of the marsh, alone and more confused and afraid than he'd ever been in his life.

She'd never expected to find Stone Dempsey here.

Tara's heart took flight like the big heron the two men had scared away with their conversation.

"What are you doing here?" she asked Stone as he strolled toward them. "And who on earth was that man?"

"Hello to you, too," Stone replied, smiling down at Amanda. "My name is Stone."

"You're Rock's brother," Amanda announced, her eyes going wide as she glanced over her shoulder at her mother.

Stone nodded, grinned. "Yes. What's your name?"

"Amanda." She pointed a finger. "That's Marybeth." Then she rolled her eyes toward Laurel. "And that's Laurel."

"Hello, Amanda, Marybeth and Laurel," Stone said, taking the time to shake each girl's hand, even though Laurel just glared at him. "I saw you at the wedding, but didn't get a chance to speak to any of you. Y'all are just about as pretty as your mom."

Tara had her guard up. This was no coincidence. Stone had obviously planned to find her here. "Hello," she said finally. "Now tell me what you're doing here?"

"I came out to look over this property once again. You know, just biding my time until you make a decision."

"I won't be making any decisions, at least not regarding you," Tara said, careful that she kept her tone very impersonal and businesslike. Laurel was already giving her keen, condemning looks.

Stone stood silent, letting her curt words wash over him. "Did you know about Josiah?"

"Who's that?" Marybeth asked.

"The man I was with," Stone explained. "He came walking up the lane when I first arrived. He has a cabin back in the marsh. And the tiniest little chapel."

Tara was surprised to hear that. "What are you talking about? This land is vacant."

"No, not quite," Stone replied. "Samson Josiah Bennett lives on the edge of this land, near where the river and the marsh merge. Apparently, he's lived here all of his life and your husband knew him."

Tara glanced in the direction the old man had gone. "Are you serious?"

"Very," Stone said. "He kind of took me by surprise, too. Apparently, Chad knew Josiah lived here when he bought the land years ago, but he let Josiah stay. This adds a new wrinkle to things."

"It sure does," Tara agreed. "Why didn't Chad ever mention him?"

Laurel stalked close then. "Maybe because you were never around to talk to Dad."

Tara whirled to her daughter. "Did you know about this man?"

"No," Laurel admitted. "But Dad never talked to us about anything, either." She shrugged and went back into full hostile mode.

"Mom, if you sell the land, that old man will have to move," Marybeth said, worry clouding her green eyes.

"I know, honey. I'll have to think about what needs to be done."

"Let's think about it together," Stone suggested. "Over dinner."

"I can't," Tara replied, disappointment warring

with common sense. "I told the girls we'd go to the mall out on the interstate."

"I'll go with you then."

Tara stood back, baffled by both his tone and the soft warmth in his eyes. That warmth took her breath away more than his cold, icy stares ever could.

And she wondered what had come over the man.

Laurel shuffled in the background, bringing Tara to full alert. "Mom, if we don't hurry, we won't get dinner or shopping. And why does he have to come along?"

"Don't be rude," Tara said on a low warning.

"I won't be too much of a bother," Stone said, giving Laurel a brilliant smile. "And I'm buying. Just name the restaurant."

He got at least two different choices. "Pizza," Amanda shouted, dancing around. "Hamburgers," Marybeth said at the same time.

"How about we go where they have both?" Stone asked, his eyes on Tara again. "Laurel, where do you want to eat?"

"I don't care," Laurel said on a huff of breath. "I'm not even hungry."

"What's your favorite dessert?" Stone asked, stepping so close Laurel had to acknowledge him.

Laurel hesitated, tried to keep the pout on her face, then finally said, "Chocolate pie."

"Okay, then. It's chocolate pie for dessert. I know a great little pie shop right in the heart of Savannah."

"I haven't said we'd go to dinner with you," Tara reminded him, eternally thankful in spite of her qualms that he was being so thoughtful toward her girls.

His silver eyes held her spellbound. "But you will, won't you?"

She thought about it for a minute. They did need to talk, about a lot of things. She had almost convinced herself to give in to his offer, but now they had Josiah Bennett to worry about. And she wanted to know more about Josiah's relationship with Chad.

She turned to the girls. "Do you want Stone to take us to dinner?"

There was a chorus of voices. Two yeses. One no.

"Two out of three isn't bad," Stone quipped, giving Laurel a wink. Then he looked back at Tara. "I didn't hear your vote."

"Okay, we'll go," she said finally. "But only if we can let the girls shop first. If you don't mind?"

"I don't mind one bit," Stone said, his smile sincere and full of hope. "Why don't I follow you to your house and then we'll head to the mall in my vehicle?"

"All right," Tara said, nodding. Then she stopped, "Girls, I'm sorry. I brought you out here to see this land because…well, selling it is your decision, too."

"Funny you never bothered to ask us about that

before," Laurel said, tossing her hair as she stomped toward the car.

Tara looked over at Stone, the heat of her shame rushing up her face. "She's right. I never stopped to consider how they would feel."

"Do we have to sell it, Mom?" Marybeth asked, her green eyes moving over the lush marsh. "Look at the birds. Where will they go if you build houses here?"

Stone touched on Marybeth's ponytail. "We'd make sure we leave plenty of trees and bushes for the birds, honey. They'll be safe. We wouldn't touch the marsh. We just want to build houses up on the bluff here."

"Why?" Marybeth asked.

Stone gave Tara a helpless look that caused her to smile in spite of her embarrassment. He obviously hadn't had many dealings with teenaged girls.

"Well," he said, "it's a good investment, for your mom and for my company."

"Mom could use a few good investments," Amanda volunteered. "We're flat broke."

"Amanda!" Tara's felt sweat trickling down her back.

"Well, it's the truth," Amanda replied, her gaze moving from her mom's face to Stone. "But can't you find some other way to make money? I like this place just the way it is."

Stone let out a long breath. "Let's talk more

about it over dinner," he suggested as a means of stalling.

"Good idea," Tara said, watching as he walked to his SUV. He looked good in his faded jeans and soft yellow polo shirt. Too good. She got in the car, turned it around on the road, then headed toward the highway that would take them into Savannah.

"Why are you seeing him?" Laurel asked, her harsh gaze full of accusation.

Not wanting to get into another argument, Tara thought about her answer to that question. "I'm not *seeing* him. We are conducting a business deal. And he is Rock's brother, after all, so we'll probably see him a lot from now on."

"I don't like him," Laurel replied.

"I didn't ask you to like him," Tara countered. "I only ask that you treat him politely. I did teach you manners, remember, Laurel."

"He seems nice," Marybeth said from the back seat.

"How do you know that?" Laurel said over her shoulder. "You just met the man."

"I saw him at the wedding," Marybeth reminded her.

"Me, too," Amanda said. "He's handsome."

"Oh, please!" Laurel let out a groan then reached for her ever constant headphones.

Tara didn't stop her. She had enough to deal with. Stone was following her home. Chad had kept yet another secret from her. And her oldest daughter obviously hated the world in general. Wondering when she'd ever find some peace in her life, Tara sent up a little prayer for God's guidance. *Show me the way, Lord. Help me to understand what I'm supposed to do next.*

Tara felt tired, so tired. She needed some rest, some solace. And she decided in a fit of defeat, she needed that job Stone had offered her. She'd tell him tonight that she'd sign the contract. He could have the land to develop, and she could finally have some peace of mind.

And together, they'd have to figure out what to do about Josiah Bennett.

Chapter Eight

"What's it like, having three daughters?"

Stone watched Tara's face light up before she answered his question. They were sitting in the food court at the mall, in a spot where Tara could see Marybeth and Amanda looking over clothes in the boutique next door. Laurel had taken off to another store across the way, with strict instructions from Tara to stay close.

"It's a challenge," she said through a soft smile. "It's been hard since Chad died. The girls loved their father."

Stone felt the cut of that declaration down to his bones. He certainly understood that feeling. "And you...you loved Chad? I mean, did you have a good marriage?"

She looked across the table at him, the shock on her face causing her to frown. "Of course I did."

Then she lowered her head. "That's not exactly true. We married soon after we met, mostly on impulse and a physical attraction. Then we drifted apart after the girls were born. We had some problems toward the end—lots of problems. He had become withdrawn, quiet." She stopped, took a sip of her soft drink. "I thought…I thought he regretted marrying me. But looking back, I think he was just worried about our finances. I wish he'd opened up to me about that. But Chad kept it all inside. I think that's probably why he had a heart attack."

Stone could see the regret and sadness in her blue eyes. She wasn't telling him everything, but then, he didn't expect her to. That was her business. "You blame yourself, don't you?"

She didn't look up. She just nodded. "And Laurel blames me, too. She's so angry."

Stone had to swallow back his own burning anger. "I know exactly how she feels. I felt the same way when my father died. It's not right, it's not fair, but there it is."

Tara lifted her head, her gaze locking with his. "Is that why you aren't close to your family now?"

"I'm not close to anyone," he said, the bitterness creeping into his voice in spite of his low tone. "My father's death has colored my whole outlook on life. I blamed my mother most of all, and Rock, too." At least he could admit that now. And only to her, even though Stone knew it was fairly obvious in his family.

"But why?" Tara asked, her eyes wide with concern and questions. "Why would you blame them for something that was beyond their control? And why does Laurel blame me?"

"I can't speak for Laurel," Stone said, wondering if he even wanted to go down this road, "but as for me, I blame my mother for her pride. We could have had a better life if she'd only turned back to my grandparents for help. If she had accepted their help, my father might not have been out on that shrimp boat during that hurricane."

"But I thought they disowned her."

"They did at first. But after we all came along, they tried to get involved in our lives again. Our mother refused their overtures of help. Said they'd just try to mold us into what they thought we should be."

Tara gazed at him for a long time, then said, "Ana told me about them. They were wealthy?"

"Yes. They owned homes in Savannah and the house my mom lives in on the island. They disinherited her when she married my father, but as I said, they did offer her money through the years—for the sake of the children, they would tell her—and after his death they tried to make amends. My mother just kept refusing their help. She only accepted the island house, so we'd have a place to live. But it was rundown and old."

He shifted on his seat, his discomfort stifling him. Stone had never talked to anyone about his childhood. But being around Tara was making him see things in a different light. "I remember when the storms would roll in off the Atlantic. My bedroom leaked—a spot right over my bed. I'd have to climb in bed with Rock in his room, just to stay dry and warm. On those nights, I always thought of my father and how much I missed him. Rock tried hard to replace him." He had a flash of memory, a memory of Rock reaching out an arm to him as lightning flared through a window, telling him not to worry, he'd take care of him.

"So you and Rock were close back then?"

He shrugged, let the memory sink back into a veil of bitterness, then settled back on the metal chair. "Yes and no. We fought like most brothers do, but as we got older, something changed. Rock was always the protector. He was the oldest, so he felt like he had to prove something to the rest of us. But he started bossing us around. I resented that, so I did whatever I could to revolt against his authority."

"And you're still doing that?"

He chuckled. "I guess I am."

"What about Clay?"

"Clay is as good as gold. We get along just fine. But I don't see him very much."

"Sounds like he works a lot of long hard hours in Atlanta."

"He's a K-9 cop and Atlanta is a big place."

"I didn't get to talk to him very much at the wedding."

Stone leaned forward then. "Well, maybe you'll get to know him more when he comes home for vacation in a few weeks."

"Will you still be around then?"

"Is that a trick question?"

He waited as she gave him a long, searching look. "Stone, I've been thinking about your proposal."

His heart hammered against his chest. He ignored it. "And?"

"I think I should accept it."

He didn't want to appear too anxious. So he just tapped his fingers against the red metal table. And watched her face. And remembered how soft her lips were.

"That is, if you still want to do this," she said, her eyes flashing with worry and wonder. "Stone?"

He stopped drumming his fingers. "Oh, absolutely. I'm just curious. What made you change your mind?"

Tara glanced up to see her children walking toward the table. "Them," she said on a whisper. "And something you just said. Sometimes we need to swallow our pride for the sake of our children. I need to take care of my girls."

It occurred to Stone as to why he might be trying to help Tara Parnell. It was because as a child he had longed to hear his own mother say those exact same words. He had wanted his mother to care about them. He had wanted her to put aside her pride and her ambition for the sake of her children. But she hadn't done that. And now, she was trying very hard to make amends. Too late, in Stone's book. But he could be civil. He could be courteous and polite. While deep inside, he still longed to hear those words. And he longed to be a real son to a real mother. A real brother to Rock and Clay, not just a polite stranger who wandered in now and again.

If he couldn't do that, he could at least do the next best thing. He could save Tara's children from the same fate. "Your girls will be taken care of," he said, meaning it. "You have my promise on that."

"I don't want charity," she reminded him. "But I'm not as strong-willed as your mother apparently was. I can swallow my pride to help my girls, but I don't want a handout."

"This isn't charity, Tara. This is a good business move." Then he touched a finger to her hand. "And this is between friends."

"Are we that? Friends?"

"I'd like to think so. But I meant what I said. I want you to respect me, too."

"I believe you. But can I trust you?"

He got up, threw his drink cup in a nearby trash container. "That's up to you, isn't it?"

"I think we need to set a few guidelines," Tara told Stone later that night. "And we've got to decide what to do about Josiah."

They were back at Tara's house in Savannah. The girls had found a few things for school and were now upstairs trying on clothes. Tara could hear them giggling and talking.

Except for Laurel. She'd bought one outfit that had turned out to be much more provocative than Tara normally allowed. They had argued about returning it, so as soon as they'd gotten home, she'd stalked up to her room and slammed the door. Tara could only guess her eldest daughter was now listening to loud music with her headphones.

To shut out the pain, Tara thought.

"Hey, where'd you go?" Stone asked as he handed her a cup of coffee.

Tara glanced around to find him leaning on her kitchen counter. It seemed strange to see another man standing there in the spot where Chad had moved and lived. But it was also comforting. Too comforting.

"I'm just worried about Laurel. She's so lost and confused."

"She's a teenager," Stone reasoned. "Hard to figure out on a good day."

Tara decided to bring the subject back around to business. "That's why it's important that we have an understanding, Stone. If I work for you—"

"When you work for me," he corrected, "you will have control over your time, Tara. Since I know everything—all about your debts, your need to spend time with your children, and that you have the prettiest blue eyes I've ever seen, I think we can work on all the details as we go along."

"But you can't do that," she said, lifting a hand in the air.

"Do what?"

"Tell me I have pretty eyes. Flirt with me. I can't have you hovering about if you're my boss, Stone."

"I'll stay away during business hours, then. Unless, of course, we have business to discuss. Oh, and speaking of that, don't worry about Josiah. I'll make sure he has a safe place to live."

"He might not want to leave."

"I've thought about that. We'll have a Plan B."

"Was he close to Chad? Did he talk about him?"

Stone watched her, as if trying to decide how much of the truth she could handle. "He said Chad had a good heart, but that he didn't know how to appreciate all his blessings."

"That sounds about right. We didn't realize we had so much, and I don't mean material things."

"He also said Chad came to his little chapel to pray and talk to God."

"My Chad? He never attended church. We never had time."

"Apparently, Chad did have a relationship with Christ. At least Josiah implied that."

Tears brimmed in Tara's eyes. "That brings me some comfort at least. I just wish he could have talked to me."

"Stop tormenting yourself," Stone replied.

"Let's change the subject. I think we just had our first business discussion, if you don't count the part about your deceased husband. Josiah will be okay."

Tara appreciated the way he steered her back to the task at hand. "And you'll respect this—that I need to keep things strictly business?"

"Absolutely."

But the look in his eyes indicated he had more than just business on his mind.

"And what about after hours?" she asked, her emotions warring between accepting this attraction and fighting it with all her might.

He set his coffee cup down and came around the counter to where she perched on a bar stool. Touching a hand to her arm, he said, "That, too, will be up to you."

"Oh. Why?"

"Why what?"

"Why will that be up to me?"

Stone turned to lean back on the counter, crossing his arms over his chest, an amused look on his face. "Well, I'm trying to gain both your respect and your trust, Tara. I won't do a very good job at either if I come on too strong, now will I?"

"But..." She sighed, attempting to regain control of her equilibrium. "I don't want you to even try, Stone. I was married to a man very much like you. That marriage almost failed because it was based more on lust then love."

He lifted a hand to his face, then brushed it down

his chin. "Is that what you think? That I've just got the hots for you?"

She saw the disappointment in his eyes and wished she didn't have to be so honest. But if she'd been honest with Chad, things might be different now. "I just need to know that you'll do the right thing. That you'll respect my wishes regarding this whole arrangement."

Somehow, he'd managed to get even closer, the look in his eyes going against everything she'd just said. "And what are your wishes?"

Right now, she wished she could kiss him again. For a very long time. But, reminding herself that her next relationship with a man would have to be sincere and built on trust and love rather than just a physical attraction, Tara quickly pushed that fantasy away. "I wish that you'd understand I'm not ready for anything other than a business arrangement. A job."

His eyes searched her face. "That's all you need from me, right? A job. And a big check for your property."

"Yes," she said, trying to nod her head, trying to find a good, strong breath to push at the denial. "I'm too tired and confused to deal with anything emotional right now."

"Do I make you emotional?"

He was doing it. Right here in her kitchen. He was pouncing on her without even touching her. Tara felt the heat from his eyes, saw the way his nostrils flared slightly as he leaned close.

"You…you make me crazy," she said.

"Define *crazy.*"

"I don't know. The way you look at me. The way you kissed me the other night makes me think crazy things. Why are you doing that when we both know it can come to no good?"

"No good? Is that what you think being with me would be like, Tara? No good?"

Not really. She thought it would be not only good, but great. Wonderful. If she just leaned forward, she could be in his arms, safe and warm and overcome with a sense of belonging. But she couldn't do that. Not yet. Maybe not ever. "I just think we shouldn't rush into something we might regret," she tried to explain. "It's bad timing. I have to get my children back on a structured, calm routine. I have to pay off debts, think ahead to the future."

"I'm thinking of the future right now," he said, his hand snaking out to grab her arm. "The immediate future."

"Stone, don't. We can't."

He had her off the stool and in his embrace. "We can't what? Touch each other? Hold each other? Want each other?"

She tried to shake her head. "It's wrong."

"Why? Why is this wrong?" He pulled her close, but he didn't kiss her. "Is it wrong to want to *feel* something, Tara? Is it wrong to want something I can't even explain? Is it wrong to finally find a wonderful, interesting woman, a woman who outranks anyone I've ever known, and to want to get to know that woman, to help that woman, to protect that woman? Is that wrong?"

"Is that what you want?" she asked, her eyes touching on his. He looked so sincere, so secure in his longing, that she almost believed him. "Do you really want to get to know me, or do you just find me interesting and a challenge because I have something you want?"

"You mean the land?"

"Exactly."

He didn't answer her with words. He just pulled her close and kissed her. This kiss was slow and sweet and flowing, like a soft waterfall. She felt his hands in her hair, felt his touch on her lips, felt his need in the tender way he moved a finger down her face.

Then he lifted away and looked down at her. "I told you, I want more than just land now, Tara."

Tara whirled, then found her way to the other side of the counter. "And I'm telling you I can't give you anything more right now. I need a job. I need money. I need some peace of mind."

"But you don't need me, right?"

She did need him. But she couldn't let that happen right now. So she tried to explain. "I don't need the complications you bring, Stone." Lowering her head, she said, "I made a big mistake in marrying Chad too quickly. I just don't want to rush into another mistake. I won't do that again. And I won't put my children through that again."

"Okay." He backed up, swept a hand through his hair. "I'll expect a signed contract on my desk Monday morning. It'll take a few weeks to process the sale, but you can start to work right away. Give your boss two weeks' notice, Tara. Then report to work for me by the end of the month. You won't see me again until then, unless you decide you want to see me again. As I said, that's entirely up to you." He turned toward the back door. "Oh, and I had a nice time with you and the girls tonight. Tell Laurel I hope she'll eat a slice of that chocolate pie I put in the refrigerator."

Tara watched as he opened the French door, then closed it softly behind him.

Already the big spacious kitchen seemed empty with his leaving.

As did her heart.

"How could you do this to Daddy?"

The question, posed by Laurel at the breakfast table the next morning, threw Tara into a tailspin.

"What are you talking about?"

Laurel rolled her eyes, then threw down her half-eaten piece of toast. "I saw you last night, Mom. With *him.*"

Her heart accelerating, Tara motioned to Amanda and Marybeth. "Go get your backpacks. It's almost time for the bus."

"But—" Marybeth protested, staring intensely at Laurel.

"No buts," Tara replied. "I need to have a word with your sister, in private."

"Great," Amanda said, getting up from the table. "We never get to hear the good stuff."

"Just go, now," Tara ordered with a finger pointing toward the stairs.

The two girls stalked away, whispering to each other as they tossed curious glances over their shoulders.

"And don't try to listen on the stairs," Tara called.

Then she turned back to Laurel. "What do you think you saw, Laurel?"

Laurel sent her a chilling look through eyes made up too heavily with kohl liner and dark blue eye shadow. "I saw you kissing that man."

"Stone? You saw me kissing Stone?"

"Yes. He was all over you, Mom! And you won't even let me near Cal without a chaperon!"

Tara took time to count to ten and calm her nerves. "Were you spying on me, Laurel?"

"No!" She got up to slam her dishes into the sink. "I came downstairs to show you my outfit, to prove to you that it wasn't too skimpy. But when I got to the bottom of the stairs, I saw you with him."

"And what did you do then?"

"I watched, then I turned and ran back upstairs." She whirled to grab her suede purse. "You sure didn't waste any time."

Tara reached out a hand to her daughter. "Hold on. First of all, I am an adult and I have every right to date other people. Second of all, nothing is going on between Stone and me. I purposely told him last night that can never happen again."

"You mean, you won't kiss him again?"

"Yes. That's what I mean." Tara motioned for Laurel to sit down. "Honey, Stone and I are getting to know each other, and we're doing business together. He wants to buy my land—"

"Our land," Laurel said, her eyes flashing.

"Okay, *our* land," Tara corrected. "And he's offered me a job."

"A job?" Laurel jumped up again. "Mom, you can't work for him."

"And why can't I? It would mean more money for us, a way out of our debts. I might be able to keep this house."

"I don't care," Laurel said, her hands waving in the air. "I don't want you around Stone Dempsey."

Tara felt the weight of that demand down to her very bones. Laurel would never accept another man to replace her father. Which was why Tara could only concentrate on the job Stone had offered, and not the man who'd given her the job. "I don't have a choice. I need to make enough money to take care of us, honey. Stone has offered me a good salary."

"And what else is he offering, Mom?"

The sarcastic tone and the look her daughter sent with it only added to Tara's woes. "Stone is trying to be a friend to us. That's all I can allow right now. But that doesn't mean you should be rude and disrespectful to either me or Mr. Dempsey."

Laurel put a hand on her hip. "Well, then, that also means you don't have to go around kissing him, either. I hate him! I hate my life! And I hate—"

"Me?" Tara asked, tears brimming in her eyes. "Do you hate me, Laurel?"

Laurel grabbed her tote and books. "I have to go. The bus will be here soon."

"Laurel?" Tara called. "Laurel, we need to finish this conversation."

"I'm through talking to you," Laurel replied over her shoulder.

The next sound Tara heard was the slamming of the front door.

Shaking, Tara sank down on a kitchen stool, her head in her hands. "Lord, I can't do this anymore. I don't know where to turn. I don't know what's best for my family anymore. I need help."

She prayed that she was making the right decision regarding the new job at Stone Enterprises, working for Stone Dempsey. Working with Stone.

Tara realized she could be falling right back into the same pattern, the same trap that had brought her so much unhappiness in her marriage—being too ambitious and impulsive. Was she really taking this job for her family? Or was she taking this job just to be near him?

Chapter Nine

"Thank you for seeing me."

Tara waited for Rock to sit, then sank down on the wicker chair across from him. They were on the back porch of Rock's quaint cottage, which now served as a weekend home for Tara and the girls. Tara had left the girls in town with a neighbor so she could drive out here and have some quiet time with Rock.

Tara waved to the neighbor, Milly McPherson. Milly was out digging in her flower garden, a large straw hat plunked down over her gray bun. The old woman waved back, then went back to her task, her head down and her mind on the mums and pansies she was planting for some fall foliage.

"You sounded so upset on the phone," Rock said, his keen blue eyes moving over her face. "What's wrong?"

"Everything," Tara admitted. "I've tried to pray, but I can't seem to find the answers."

"Tell me," he said, his tone kind. "You know you can tell me anything."

"Yes, and I appreciate that," she said. "I hope my confiding in you hasn't put a strain on things with Ana."

He chuckled. "Ana knew she was marrying a preacher. I get phone calls night and day, from church members and people who want something fixed or built. Sometimes I fix cabinets, sometimes I try to fix confused souls." He shrugged, glanced out at the water. "I carry a lot of secrets close to my heart, Tara. But then, the Bible says 'for he knoweth the secrets of the heart'."

Tara looked out over the waters of the bay. It was a beautiful day, warm and humid, but with a gentle sea breeze. A colorful skiff sailed by like a quiet bird on the brilliant blue waters. "Does He know my secrets, Rock? Does God know that I'm trying to do what's best for my children?"

"I'm sure He does. What's this all about?"

"I'm going to take the job with Stone."

Rock's questioning expression changed to a frown. "Oh, I see. Have you told Ana?"

"No, not yet. But I told Stone yesterday. I won't start for a couple of weeks. I'll help Ana until the summer season is over."

"I'm not worried about you working weekends at the tea room," Rock said. "But I am worried about you working for Stone."

Tara knew Rock still had reservations regarding his

brother. Well, so did she. "That's why I wanted to talk to you. Why wouldn't you want me to work for him?"

"Oh, I think that's fairly obvious," Rock said, his hands on the arms of his chair. "My brother and I have never seen eye to eye on things. Stone doesn't share my faith. He blames God for a lot of his misery."

"We've talked about that," Tara replied. "I think you're right, but I also think Stone is changing. He seems to be searching for something to fill his life."

Rock sat up, his eyes wide. "Are you telling me you've had a spiritual influence on my brother?"

"I'm not sure," Tara admitted. "But since we got past that first awkward, horrible meeting and all the contract negotiations, he's been nothing but kind to the girls and me—almost too kind. He could have demanded that I pay him the money Chad owed him. But he's willing to write that off as part of the package for the land."

"That and he gets you as part of the deal."

"That's why I needed to talk to you," Tara said. "Do you think, knowing Stone the way you do, that he's just using me to get at the land? Do you think he's being ruthless? Or is he being generous? He says it's not charity, but business. But could he really care about what happens to me and my family?"

Rock considered her questions a while before answering. "How important is this to you? I mean, how close have you and Stone become?"

"We're friends, business associates right now."

Rock leaned forward then. "I'm going to tell you this as a brother-in-law, not a minister. I don't trust Stone. I've seen him in action before, and I've tried to give him the benefit of the doubt. But when Stone sets his mind on something or someone, he goes for it. And he doesn't stop to think of the consequences."

"How can you be so sure?"

"Well, look at him. He's rich, and he didn't get that way by sheer luck. He has a reputation for leaving beautiful women along the path. He's been called hard-hearted by all the gossips, and he's been called the same thing by the entire Southern business community."

"I never heard that," Tara said. "I've lived in Savannah for fifteen years and I never heard of him. Of course, I was lost in my own troubles during most of that time."

"That's the other thing," Rock said. "Stone keeps a low profile. Doesn't it concern you that you didn't even know him before now?"

"A lot of businesspeople do that, Rock. They delegate jobs so they don't have to be everywhere at once. And I get the impression that Stone does that so he doesn't have to answer to the press or a lot of other people. Maybe so he doesn't have to answer to his family, either."

"Well, shouldn't someone hold him account-able?"

Tara let out a sigh. "You know something? I asked

you here to get advice regarding Stone. But I think you might be the wrong person to help me here."

"Why would you say that?"

"Well, look at you. You're all in a fluster just discussing your brother. Rock, you are a kind, caring man, a minister to most of the people on this island. Why can't you be the same with Stone? Everything you've just told me about your own brother is based on gossip and speculation. You should know the real Stone in your heart, shouldn't you? Or do you think you already do?"

He looked at her, realization dawning in his eyes. "You're right, of course. Goodness knows, I've tried to get past my resentment of Stone. I truly want him to be happy, Tara. But maybe I need to fix what's wrong inside myself before I condemn Stone any further."

"How can you do that?"

Rock shrugged. "Prayer. And I did offer to help him with Hidden Hill. I hear he's planning this elaborate dinner party to raise funds for the lighthouse, but honestly, I don't see how he'll pull it off. That house needs a lot of work."

"Oh, the fund-raiser. I'd forgotten all about that," Tara said. Just the thought of getting all dressed up to be with Stone caused her to go warm and soft inside.

"Are you going?"

"I hadn't given it much thought. But I guess if I take this job, he'll expect me to be there."

"Stone will expect a lot of things from you, Tara. Just remember that."

"You still don't trust him?"

"Do you?"

"I'm trying. He told me he wanted me to respect him and trust him. And he's not pushing for anything else right now." If she didn't count the way he kissed her.

Rock got up, put a hand on one of the porch railings. "Well, it seems you already believe in Stone enough to defend him against me. And maybe you're right. Ana says I have a blind spot regarding Stone. I'm beginning to think maybe she's got a point."

"You know she wants to get us together— Stone and me?"

"Oh, yes. She's mentioned it a few times. At first, I thought she just felt guilty. You know, since we're so happy—"

"I know. My sister and I have this history with Chad that won't let us give up completely on the past, but we've come a long way in being honest about that. Ana has a good heart—that's why she wants me to be happy. She wants me to find the kind of love she's found with you."

"I honestly don't know if Stone can give you that. I don't know if my brother is capable of real love and commitment."

Tara got up to stand beside him. "Well, I know I'm not going to rush into anything. You know about my life with Chad. I loved him, but it was more of a physical attraction. Our marriage wasn't built on solid ground and it almost destroyed us."

"You thought he was still in love with Ana."

"Yes, but…Chad loved me, too. I can see that now. I just didn't give him much of a chance to prove it. And, I was the same way you are with Stone. I didn't look deeply enough to even know my own husband. I regret that so much. I guess that's why I'm curious about Stone. He reminds me so much of Chad at times."

"So now you're afraid to fall for someone who is so much like your late husband?"

"Yes," she said, bobbing her head. "You do understand."

"Of course. And I think you're wise to take things slow." Placing a hand on her arm, he added, "I'll make you a promise. I'll try to extend the olive branch to Stone and look for the good that you see in him, if you'll be very careful and very honest in your relationship with him. Don't let him hurt you, Tara."

"I won't," she said. "But I worry about Stone getting hurt, too."

"That's a first," Rock said as he started down the steps. "And I have to admit, I've never thought of it in that way." Then he stopped to look back at her. "I've hurt my brother all these years, haven't I?"

"I think so," she said, hoping she was doing the right thing by telling him that. "I think Stone needs a brother—not a preacher, not someone to tell him what he's been doing wrong, but just a brother."

"I can try to be that," Rock said. "If it's not too late."

"God gives us second chances. That's what you told me, remember?"

"Oh, I see," Rock said, grinning. "You're using my own platitudes to get back at me."

"No, I'm giving you the same good advice you gave me. You've helped me so much, Rock. Why not do the same for your brother?"

"Ah, but *you* needed my help," Rock pointed out.

"So does Stone," Tara replied. "Even if he won't admit it."

"I'll see what I can do," Rock said, waving to her as he walked toward the chapel.

"See what you can do about that broken tree limb," Stone told the men he'd hired to clear the gardens at Hidden Hill. "This place has to be ready in two weeks."

"You gotta be kidding," one of the workers said to no one in particular.

"I'm serious," Stone explained in a calm, authoritative voice. "The house won't be finished, of course. That could take years. But I intend to have the gardens in some sort of shape for this gala." Then he smiled. "Relax, it's a garden party. And it will be at night, underneath the stars. We just have to pull out the bramble and brush and make sure we have things cleared for the tents and the stage."

"You're hauling a stage in here?" the supervisor asked.

"For the musicians," Stone explained, his patience stretching thin. "Just do it, guys. You'll get paid extra if you just follow orders and stop asking questions."

"Yes, sir."

"You have a way with words," a voice from behind him said.

Stone turned to find Rock standing by an ancient camellia bush. "Oh, great. You again." At least his brother didn't have the usual look of disgust on his face.

"Yep," Rock said as he strolled through the patches of limbs and shrubs the men had already cleared away. "Do you think you'll actually have this place in shape for a big party in two weeks?"

"I'm planning on it," Stone replied, the list in his head reminding him to check and see if Diane had consulted with the caterers and florists on all the last minute details. He braced himself for the onslaught of his brother's disapproval, but was surprised by Rock's next words.

"How can I help?"

Stone held a hand to his ear. "Excuse me? I don't think I heard you right. Did you offer to help me?"

Rock looked down at the ground. "I've offered before, haven't I? I'd really like to help, Stone."

"Okay." Stone turned back to supervising the tree cutters so his brother wouldn't see his surprise and doubt. "Go ahead and take down that pine, too, Mike. Looks like the pine beetles got to it."

Mike nodded, then started issuing orders.

Satisfied, Stone pivoted back to face Rock. "Want to see the house?"

"Sure."

He took his brother up the winding stone staircase to the second-floor terrace. The wide terrace formed a cover over what had once been a carriage drive leading to the back of the house where the kitchen and servants' quarters had been built on the bottom floor.

Stone waved a hand down toward the sounds of power drills and hammering. "I'm redoing the kitchen, then turning the rest of the lower level into an office and game room."

"With a pool table?" Rock asked, hopeful.

"Of course. But I'll still beat you at eight ball."

"Probably. I'm a bit rusty since our days at the arcade on the boardwalk."

"Is that place still there?"

"No. Now there's some sort of galactic bowling and several fancy computerized game machines. The kids love it."

"I loved the arcade," Stone said, remembering how they'd hung out there during the summer when they weren't working.

"Why did you buy this place?" Rock asked as they entered through the open paneled doors.

"I wanted it," Stone replied. He didn't owe his brother any explanations.

"Remember washing all this glass?" Rock asked as he lifted his head up to the ceiling. "I think I counted all the panes in this room once—let's see, twenty panes per door and window times ten."

"Two hundred," Stone said, nodding. "I never counted them, but I've had to replace about half of them." Then he put his hands on his hips and stared at his brother. "I can promise you this. I will never have to wash them again."

"Then you bought the house out of revenge?"

He shrugged. "Maybe. Look, Rock, did you really come here to help, or to question my motives again?"

"A little of both," Rock admitted. "I had a long talk with Tara yesterday afternoon."

Stone hid his concern by holding up a hand. "Spare me the lecture, then."

"I didn't come to lecture. I said I came to offer my help. Didn't I already tell you that?"

"Let's get something to drink," Stone suggested, just to take the edge off seeing his brother here. Just to take the edge off knowing that Tara had talked to Rock about him.

Rock followed him through the drawing room—what was now going to be a huge den—and over to a massive Rococo sideboard that Stone had had restored to its former gilded glory. "Want mineral water or a soft drink?"

"Water," Rock said, his gaze moving over the high, mirrored walls. "This place always was excessive."

"And I aim to keep it that way. I'm living in these two rooms right now." He waved a hand over the big den. "I have a cot in the room that used to be the library."

"So you're The Great Gatsby now?"

Stone had to laugh at that. "Okay, maybe not quite that rich and forlorn, but I'm comfortable. Plus, I don't plan on winding up dead in the swimming pool."

"Let's hope not," Rock said as he took the crystal goblet of water from Stone. "About Tara—"

"We're going into a business arrangement, nothing more."

"Are you sure?"

"Is it any of your business?"

"She came to me for advice—"

"And you told her to steer clear of me?"

"No, as a matter of fact, she turned the tables on me and gave me some solid advice."

"To mind your own business?"

Rock shook his head, took a sip of his water. "She told me that I should give you the same consideration I do the rest of my congregation. That I shouldn't listen to the gossips. She said I should start being a brother to you again."

Stone gave Rock a long, direct look while he let that soak in. *Tara had defended him.* It was such a foreign concept that it took him a minute to realize the implications. She cared. About him. Maybe. "And did you set her straight? Did you tell her that you have always and will always disapprove of me?"

"No, but she pretty much pointed out the fact that I act that way. I guess I have been full of sanctimonious pride when it comes to you."

"That's a good word for it," Stone said, not even daring to hope that Rock might actually be trying to make amends. "Mind telling me why you feel that way about me?"

Rock glanced around. "Can we talk?"

Stone pushed a hand over his hair. "Brother, that's all I've ever wanted to do." He indicated a long brown leather couch centered in front of the huge fireplace. "Have a seat."

Rock sank down on the couch, while Stone took a matching overstuffed chair. "Stone," he began, his hands clasped together, "I haven't been a very good brother to you. All these years since you left to make your way, amass your fortune, whatever you want to call it, I've resented you."

"You resent my money?"

"No," Rock said and Stone saw the sincerity in his eyes. "I thought about it after I talked with Tara, prayed about it, and now I can see I resented that you left. That you went away, to begin with. I guess I wanted you to stay and fight right along with me."

"Fight what?"

"Our mother, our life. Our childhood," Rock said on a shrug. "I don't know."

"Clay left," Stone pointed out. "You still get along famously with him, don't you?"

"Yes, but Clay never rebelled the way you did. I always felt so responsible for you."

"Hey, I take responsibility for my own actions." Rock looked up then. "I think that's what I resented the most. You were free, Stone. Free to go. Free to explore that big world out there. You didn't let our childhood woes hold you back."

"While you felt trapped?"

He nodded. "I'm not very proud of it, but after I talked to Tara, I realized that has to be it. I don't begrudge you making a living. I just begrudge that I never had the guts to try that myself."

Stone shook his head, his soda bottle dangling from one hand. "Rock, you've made a name for yourself here on the island. Man, you're a great carpenter and furniture maker, and what I hear, a passable preacher. And you are married to one of those pretty Hanson women. What more could you want?"

"I am happy now," Rock said, his eyes lighting up. "And I have Ana to thank for that. She makes me a better person, which I guess is why I'm here. She's been encouraging me to talk to you. And now Tara's done the same." He paused long enough to inhale a deep breath. "Sometimes, God sends us answers to our prayers. But not always in a way we want to hear. I've been blind and stubborn, but now I can see clearly. I want to make things better between us, Stone. Will you let me try again? Will you give me a second chance to be your big brother?"

Stone sat there, leaning back in his chair, his eyes centered on his brother. After a long silence, he said, "Wow, those Hanson sisters are a force to be reckoned with. They actually have us in the same room, talking instead of fighting."

"Does that mean you're willing to meet me halfway?" Rock asked, extending a hand.

Tara had fought for him. The least Stone could do was make her proud, show her her efforts had not been in vain. Stone reached across and shook his brother's hand. "That means I'm glad you stopped by. But it also means the subject of my relationship with Tara is off-limits, agreed?"

Rock shifted, sighed, then nodded. "I think I can live with that. Just—"

"I won't hurt her, Rock."

Rock finished off his water. "Okay, then. End of discussion. But if you need me—"

"I'll let you know," Stone said, still on shaky ground.

They sat in silence for a few minutes, the sounds of construction echoing up to them through the open doors. Off in the distance, Stone could hear the sea crashing against the shore. He felt like that beachhead out there. Since he'd met Tara, he felt as if he were being assaulted and rearranged, then shifted and washed clean again.

"Nice mantel," Rock finally said, nodding toward the bronzed marble over the fireplace.

Relaxing, Stone said, "Thanks. It has a certain quaintness about it."

Rock grinned then. "So you do have a sense of humor after all."

"There's a lot about me that you don't know," Stone pointed out.

"Ah, but there's a lot about you I do know, too," Rock said. "I remember how you used to catch blue crabs and steam them up for dinner on those nights when Mother was out in her studio."

"When was Mother *not* out in her studio?"

"Good point." Rock sat silent for a minute, then said, "And I remember how one year you wanted to grow the perfect orchid, for Mother's Day."

Stone lowered his head. "I was hoping she'd notice."

"But we couldn't get it to bloom."

"Nope. It just sat there, all green and spindly."

"And you never even showed it to her."

"Can I show you something now?" Stone asked, his heart pounding with the force of a breaker as that memory came crashing down on him. That Rock had remembered, too, only added to his confusion. Was God trying to send him a message?

Rock lifted his brows at his request. "You don't have a mad wife in the attic, do you?"

He laughed. "No. As the rumors go, I leave behind a trail of broken hearts in my wake, but I haven't resorted to locking women in the attic."

"Okay, so what do you want to show me?"

"C'mon," he said, lifting off his chair to take Rock's empty water glass. "Now, try to keep an open mind about this, okay?"

"Sure," Rock said as they entered a long wide hallway. "Are you taking me to the dungeon?"

"No, the solarium in the south wing."

"What's it like to live in a house that actually has wings?"

Lonely, Stone wanted to say. But he didn't. "Don't know. This is the first time I've actually stayed here since I bought the place."

"'A house is not a home'," Rock said, then winced. "Sorry."

"I figured you'd start quoting somebody or something sooner or later," Stone said, wondering why it had taken a word from Tara to bring his brother to visit. And wondering, too, if maybe she could bring some good to his life simply by being in it. "You're right, though. This is a long way from being a home."

"So I'll ask it again. Why did you buy this place?" Rock said as they entered the square, arched solarium.

"'I had a lover's quarrel with the world'," Stone responded.

"Robert Frost," Rock noted with a wry smile. "Not bad."

"You're not the only one who reads books, Rock." Enjoying the awakening expression on his brother's face, he pointed toward a long potter's bench nestled underneath a row of windows across the way. Lined up on the bench in varying stages of growth, sat several exotic orchids from around the world, some bright with flowers, some waiting to bud and open. "And you're not the only one who remembers that orchid that never bloomed."

Chapter Ten

"So this is it?" Tara asked a few days later.

"This is it," Stone replied.

They were back out at the land. They had decided to meet here to sign the initial contract. There would be other papers to sign later back at Stone's office, with Griffin Smith and Diane Mosely as witnesses. But right now, Stone wanted Tara all to himself.

This seemed like the best place to guarantee that.

"I see you didn't put in that clause I had requested," she said as she skimmed the papers in her hand through a chic pair of black retro reading glasses.

Stone enjoyed just looking at her. She was like a ball of golden fire, very elegant and sophisticated, but all action, always moving. Today, she wore crisp baggy olive green pants and a stark white cotton button-up shirt. Her blond hair fluttered in the humid breeze.

"Stone?"

"Hmmm?" He refocused then remembered her statement. "Oh, if you mean the clause about you never wanting to see me again, no, I definitely did not put that in the contract. I'd rather give up this land then have that happen."

Tara took off her glasses, her sky-blue gaze hitting him square in the face. And the gut. "You don't mean that."

He moved to where she leaned against her car. "Yes, I do."

She began to fidget, her hands moving through her hair. "You *can't* mean that."

"Why can't I?"

"Because we had another agreement, remember? To keep things professional. Stone, if you're going to make moves on me, then I won't come to work for you."

He did make a move toward her, his hands locking over each of her wrists as he urged her to him. "I want you to come and work *with* me, Tara. *With* me. There is a difference."

"Not really," she said, a little breath leaving her body. Then she looked up at him, her eyes open and questioning. "Why, Stone?"

"Why, what?"

"Why are you doing this?"

"You mean this," he said as he lowered his head

to nuzzle her jawline. "Or this maybe?" He kissed her with a slow, steady, lingering touch. Then he lifted his head. "I would think that is obvious. I like kissing you."

"But you can't, we can't—"

Frustrated, and knowing she was probably right, Stone backed away. "Okay, okay. But I have to tell you, Tara, it's going to be extremely hard to work with you every day and not want to touch you or kiss you."

"Then maybe I'd better not sign this. You can have the land, Stone. But maybe you'd better not include me in this package deal."

"Is that what you think about me?" he asked, the old hurts surfacing. "You think I'm using you to get to the land or something?"

"Are you?"

His short laugh was brittle with anger. "Tara, think about it. It's more like I'm using the land to get to *you*." Raking a hand through his hair, he said, "Up until I met you, I always let Griffin and other qualified people handle the details for me. It was all about the quest. I always went after projects, then sat back to watch what I wanted to happen become a reality. But not this time. This time, I've put myself on the line. I'm finishing what I started, Tara. With a hands-on approach."

"You can say that again," she told him, looking down at his hands as if remembering how they'd just touched her. Then she turned to stare out over the marsh. "I just don't know what you want, Stone."

Stone stood there, staring at her back. "Honestly, I don't know what I want, either," he finally said. "I used to know exactly what I needed. I set out to make a living for myself after college. I worked hard to form Stone Enterprises. My companies have a solid reputation in the construction and commercial real estate market. I have money, power." He stopped, a rush of breath leaving his body. "I *had* control." Then he touched a hand to her arm, forcing her back around. "But I don't have control with you, Tara."

"So it's the thrill of the chase?" she asked, the pain in her eyes making him flinch. "Once I sign on the dotted line, you win and the game's over?"

"No," he said on a soft plea. "That's my whole point. This isn't a game." He dropped his hand away. "I just want to get to know you. Now you tell me, why that can't happen? Is it that you don't feel the same, that you don't want me around? Is it that I remind you too much of your husband? Or is it just that maybe you're a lot like me? That you have to be the one in control?"

"Maybe so," she said, her weariness apparent in the way she slumped back against the car. "I thought I was in control all during my marriage, but I wasn't. And now I'm finding out even more things I never knew about my own husband. It wasn't enough that I believed he was in love with another woman."

"Wow, back up," Stone said, throwing up a hand. "You need to explain that for me. Did Chad…did he have an affair?"

She shook her head, dread evident in her eyes. She didn't want to tell him anything more about her marriage. She still didn't trust him, obviously. But she surprised him with her next words. "Chad didn't cheat on me. But I had my doubts about him just the same. He dated Ana in college, before I came into the picture."

"And?" Stone waited for her to finish the story.

"And I wasn't sure if he ever got over her." She sighed, shifted her feet. "Look, that's another story. It's just there was so much about Chad that he kept hidden. He kept it all inside." Glancing around, she said, "I never even knew there was a chapel on this place. And now I find out Chad used to visit it on a regular basis. He never even told me that, Stone. We never communicated. Neither of us was ever in control." She looked up then, a hand to her mouth as tears started misty in her eyes. "I'm so afraid I'll make another mistake. My children can't afford another mistake."

Stone put a hand to her hair and pulled her close. Although he was beginning to see why her trust was so hard to come by, he wouldn't question her anymore about Chad right now.

His eyes centered on hers, he said, "I promise you, this won't be a mistake. And if it means keeping your children safe and cared for, then I'll

step away. I'll give you the job, with no strings
attached. We'll develop this land together, no
strings attached. But don't shut me out of your life.
Just do the right thing. Sign the contract and I'll
back off." He brushed a tear off her cheek, then
added, "I know what it's like, Tara. I know what it's
like to be a child and to be scared, with no money
and no way out."

She didn't pull away as he'd expected. Instead,
she started to cry. "Stone, I—"

He took her into his arms and held her and let
her cry. "It's okay. It's okay. I can't explain my
actions, but I will honor my promise. I won't push
you anymore. Okay?"

She nodded against his cotton shirt and Stone
felt the damp mist of her tears flooding right over
his heart.

Then she pulled away, turned and signed the
contract.

Tara felt drained. She'd cried so many tears and
she didn't understand why, today of all days, she'd
had to fall apart. And she didn't know why it felt
so good to have Stone holding her, letting her cry.
He hadn't made any demands, hadn't tried to kiss
her again. He'd just held her. That meant more to
Tara than anything else he could have done.

"I'm sorry," she told Stone as they started back
toward their cars.

"For what?"

"For being such a big baby. I don't usually resort to tears when trying to make a decision."

Stone opened her car door for her. "I don't remember ever seeing my mother cry. Don't apologize for being human, Tara."

Thinking that was an odd statement, Tara didn't question him. She let her gaze roam over the marsh and woods. "Well, now, I guess this is one burden lifted off my shoulders. But you know something, I kind of hate to see this land changed. Chad loved it the way it is now, wild and free. He wanted us to build a house right here on this bluff."

"We'll build lots of houses here," Stone said. "Together."

"So, do I report directly to you next week?"

He nodded. "Unless you'd feel more comfortable working with someone else."

Tara thought the last place she needed to be was near Stone Dempsey. He was confusing her with his words and his promises. He was such a paradox. At times, ruthless and direct, at other times vulnerable and evasive. Fascinating. And too dangerous. "I'll be all right," she said. "Just as long as you understand—"

"I do," he said, but the look he gave her was filled with regret. "I gave you my word."

"Okay, then. I'll see you soon."

"We have to finish up the paperwork back at the office. Say, Friday afternoon?"

"That's fine." She started to get in the car, then

glanced down the trail leading to Josiah's house. "What about Josiah?"

"I don't know yet," Stone said. "I thought I might walk back there and talk with him."

Surprising herself, Tara said, "Maybe we should go see him together."

Stone looked at his watch. "I've got some time right now. Want to see if he's around?" He glanced down at her shoes. "It's not a long walk."

"In high-heeled pumps, you mean?"

He grinned. "Well, they're pretty but they sure don't look sensible."

Tara laughed, glad to be back on safe ground. "Women never buy sensible shoes. Don't you know that?"

"Know it and appreciate it," he said, his eyes still on her feet. "But don't expect me to carry you all the way back here if you get blisters."

Knowing he'd have no qualms about doing just that, she said, "I won't."

She locked the car then followed him to the trail. They walked along in silence for a few minutes, the heat of the afternoon filtering through the shade of old, moss-covered oaks and knot-kneed cypress trees. Up ahead, a spray of tiny black insects whirled by like a cyclone. The marsh was filled with sounds and sights—insects buzzing, birds calling, fish jumping. Tara didn't want to think about snakes and alligators.

"Stone," she said after they rounded a curve, "thank you."

"For what?"

"For agreeing to my terms."

"Oh, that." He gave her a sideways look. "I'm regretting that already. But I'm learning to be patient."

"It's going to be a long haul," Tara said, wishing she could just let go and enjoy being with him. "But it's really important to me to learn restraint."

"Guess I need to learn that myself." Then he stopped in the road to look over at her. "And I owe you a thank-you, too."

"It's my turn to ask what for."

"For standing up for me to my brother."

"Oh, Rock told you that?"

"He didn't divulge any confessions, but yes, he told me that you defended me. No one's ever done that for me, Tara. Thank you."

Tara's heart soared with hope. "Maybe we can work together and be good friends, after all."

"If that's what you want."

"I'm like you. I don't know what I want."

"Then we'll go slow and figure things out together. And when you're ready—"

"I know where to find you."

And she would find him, Tara thought. She'd be very careful in discovering the real Stone Dempsey. She'd learn all about the man behind the myth. Maybe then she could regain some of that control she lost each time he looked at her. Maybe then, she could follow her heart and grow closer to Stone.

Dear God, show me the way, she prayed. *I need to do the right thing this time. No more mistakes, no more regrets.* She'd married Chad on impulse, and while she regretted that, she couldn't regret the life that had brought her three beautiful children. But Tara refused to be impulsive again.

"There's Josiah's house," Stone said, bringing Tara out of her silent prayers.

She glanced up to find a weathered shack on stilts sitting haphazardly out over the marsh. "He lives in that?"

Stone nodded. "And seems to love it."

"But it's barely standing."

"It has a small bathroom of sorts and running water, but he doesn't have electricity. Says he doesn't need it."

Tara shook her head. "I didn't know people still lived this way."

Stone guided her toward the rickety porch. "Over there is the chapel."

She turned to the right and saw the small white building. "How quaint. It looks like a child's playhouse."

"And not much bigger," Stone said. "But it's a pretty little thing. Very peaceful."

"You've been inside?"

"With Josiah."

Needing to know, Tara asked, "What did you feel when you went into the chapel?"

Stone smiled. "I felt a sense of peace. I felt as if everything would be all right."

"But you don't—"

"Attend church? Believe in God?" He shrugged. "God didn't do me many favors when I was growing up. I've had a grudge against Him ever since."

"And now?"

"And now, I think maybe it's time for God and me to come to terms." Stepping on the cracked concrete block that served as a porch step, he said, "I have everything a man could ask for, except someone to share it with. That gets a man to thinking, you know."

Tara nodded, feeling the sweet intensity of his words. "And you and Rock...have you made your peace with each other?"

"I think so," he said. "He's coming out to the mansion this weekend to help us get things cleared and cleaned for the benefit."

"About that—"

"You will be there. As a representative of Stone Enterprises, of course."

She accepted the order of boss to employee, even if she didn't trust his motives in using it. "Of course."

As if reading her mind, he said, "And you will be there on your own. I won't force you to be my date for the evening."

The sense of disappointment she felt was acute but necessary. She'd asked him to give her some time. He was only doing what she had requested.

Stone waited, as if expecting her to protest. When she didn't, she saw a flash of disappointment moving like a cloud cover over his silver eyes. He went up onto the porch and knocked on the door. "Josiah, are you in there? It's Stone Dempsey. We need to talk."

Then Tara heard it. A soft moan, coming from behind the house. "Stone, did you hear that?"

Stone was down the steps before Tara could turn around. Together they raced to the back of the tiny house.

"Stone, look," Tara shouted as she spotted Josiah lying in the duckweed at the water's edge. "It's Josiah."

"He's hurt," Stone said, running to the shoreline. He dropped on his knees in the mud beside Josiah, then pulled his cell phone out of his pants pocket. "Please, please let there be a tower somewhere out here," Tara heard him whispering.

Tara waited for Stone to speak into the phone. And while she waited, she prayed for Josiah Bennett to be all right.

"I can't get a signal," Stone said, throwing his phone down in disgust. "And he's hurt bad." He held up a hand to show Tara blood. "He must have hit his head."

"Josiah?" Tara said, leaning down beside Stone. "Can you hear me?"

Josiah tried to speak. "Fell down. Slippery."

Tara glanced around, seeing the marks of where the old man must have slipped in the treacherous mud. Then she saw the jagged piece of concrete beside Josiah's still body. "Stone, there's blood on this broken block. He must have hit his head on that."

Josiah managed a nod. "My fault. Left the thing there. Stepping stone."

"We'll have to get him to a doctor," Stone said, already reaching to scoop up the frail body.

"Wait," Tara cautioned. "Josiah, where do you hurt besides your head?"

Josiah swallowed, grimaced. "My insides."

"That's not good," Stone said, feeling for a pulse in Josiah's neck. "I don't know. His pulse seems weak."

"Okay, how do we get him out of here?" Tara asked, looking around.

"You stay with him," Stone said, getting up, his trousers muddy. "I'll go get my SUV and bring it back here."

"Okay," Tara said. "Just be careful. It's muddy in places along that lane."

Stone nodded, tossed her the phone. "Keep trying, just in case."

Tara took the phone, her hand still on Josiah's arm. "It's okay, Josiah. We're going to get you to a hospital."

"You're Tara."

The statement made Tara stop punching buttons on the useless cell phone. Surprised, she said, "Yes, I am. Sorry to meet you like this, though."

Josiah managed a weak smile. "God sent me two angels."

Tara didn't know about that. It seemed highly unlikely that God would choose Stone and her to be angels. But she supposed stranger things had happened. If they hadn't been here today, who knew how long Josiah would have lain here, hurt and weak. And with all sorts of predators creeping around. She took a deep, calming breath and blocked out what might have happened if they hadn't found him. Then needing to talk, she asked, "How long have you been lying here?"

"'Bout two hours, I reckon."

She fanned a hungry mosquito away. "Have the bugs been bothering you?"

"Snake crawled across my foot," Josiah answered, causing Tara to jump. He actually chuckled. "He's long gone."

"Oh, good," Tara said, looking around in the weeds and grass. "At least you still have a sense of humor." To keep him still and awake, she asked, "Did a snake really crawl across you, or are you just joking with me?"

He grunted. "Snake came and went. Slid right over my foot. Big water moccasin, I think. I played dead and he kept on movin'."

"Let's not talk about that," Tara said, wishing Stone would hurry back. "How are you holding up?"

"Good, all things considered."

"How did this happen?"

Josiah swallowed again, pain etched in his face. "Old man, not watching where he was headed."

Went he started to cough, Tara hushed him. "Don't try to talk. Let me do the talking. You just nod, okay."

Josiah nodded, his chocolate-colored eyes on her face.

"The chapel is so pretty."

He nodded.

"It must be very old."

"Built by my ancestors."

"I told you not to talk," she gently chided.

His defiant grin was too weak to suit Tara.

"My husband Chad, he came to the chapel?"

Another nod. "He was lost."

Understanding what kind of lost Josiah meant, Tara felt tears pricking her eyes. "I wasn't a very good wife."

Josiah shook his head, his eyes widening. "Loved you."

Tara thought she hadn't heard him correctly. "Chad? Did you say Chad loved me?"

"Loved you. Didn't know how to show you."

"We should have talked more," Tara said, memories of their many quarrels echoing in her mind. "I should have been more considerate of his feelings."

Josiah grunted. "A hard case."

"You mean, Chad and me?" Tara lowered her

head. "We lost something, something that we could never get back. Now I'm afraid to ever go through that again."

Josiah stared up at her, his aged eyes seeming to see right through her fears and flaws. "Sow in tears, reap in joy. God gives second chances."

It was the same thing Rock had been telling her.

"I sure hope so," she said.

"You and Stone, reap in joy."

Tara wanted to set the old man straight, but then she heard the roar of an engine coming up the lane. "Josiah, Stone is back with his SUV. We're going to get you some help."

She felt Josiah's grip tighten on her arm. "God is helping all three of us today."

Tara didn't take the time to figure out what that statement meant. Stone parked the SUV, leaving the engine still running, and leaped out of the vehicle to open the door to the spacious back seat. Tara stood and watched as he lifted Josiah, careful not to hurt the old man, then gently lowered him onto the long seat.

"How you doing?" Stone asked Josiah.

Josiah grimaced again, then grunted. "Better now that I know."

"You're safe now," Stone said.

"Not just me," Josiah replied, a satisfied look replacing the pain in his eyes.

"What's he talking about?" Stone whispered to Tara as he rounded the truck.

"I have no idea," Tara replied.

But she was beginning to think she did have an idea.

Josiah was a very wise man. A man who listened to God and followed the word of the Lord. Somehow, she got the feeling that they had not only rescued Josiah, but that maybe they'd both been rescued by God and given that second chance everyone kept telling her about.

Chapter Eleven

The emergency waiting room at Saint Joseph's was clean and white-walled, with bright blue chairs centered at the information windows and bays of silk floral plants cascading from sleek countertops and tables along the walls.

Stone and Tara sat in two of the blue chairs now, waiting to find out about Josiah Bennett.

Tara nervously twirled the braided leather strap of her purse. "It's been a while, Stone. What could they be doing in there?"

Stone took her hand to stop her from fraying her expensive purse. "They're probably giving him a thorough examination." Then to take her mind off Josiah, he asked, "Did you get in touch with Laurel?"

Tara nodded. "They all made it home from school. I told her to sit tight until she hears from me again. And I called my neighbor and asked her to go and check on them."

"You don't like leaving your girls alone?" Stone asked, remembering how he and his brothers had often been left to their own devices while their mother worked.

"Not unless it's an emergency," she answered, waving her hands in the air to indicate this was just such a time.

Stone grabbed one of her hands, taking it in his again. "Calm down. He's going to be all right."

"I know," she said, weariness apparent in the dark smudges of fatigue underneath her luminous eyes. "I just don't like hospitals."

"Who does?" Stone asked. "I guess you're remembering Chad, right?"

Tara nodded. "They…they brought him here, too. I sat right over there by the door, waiting for the rest of the family to get here. He died before the girls got to see him."

Stone shut his eyes for a minute, the pain on her face too much to bear. Maybe because he was remembering that same familiar pain himself. "A child never understands death, no matter how hard people try to explain. I never got to tell my father goodbye, either." He didn't tell her that he often stood up on the terrace of Hidden Hill looking out to sea because that's where his father's remains rested, somewhere out there in that dark ocean. It was something that gnawed at Stone like unfinished business.

"I'm so sorry." Tara gave him an understanding look that only added to his woes, then pulled her hand away and shot up out of her chair. "I can't go through this again. I mean, I don't even know Josiah that well, but he knew Chad. And he's lived on that land for such a long time. It's as if—"

"As if we were meant to know him?"

"Yes, yes," she said, pacing on the tiled hallway. "It's just odd that Chad never mentioned him, or that I didn't know he lived on the land." She stopped, pushed at her bangs. "But Josiah sure seems to have me pegged. He seems to think…Oh, never mind. I'm just so worried and tired, I can't even focus."

Stone stood, then pulled her back against the wall. "I told you, I'll take care of him. If he doesn't want to move off the land, we'll let him stay."

Tara lifted her head, her expression questioning. "And how will we do that? Build half-a-million dollar mansions around his little shanty?"

Stone shook his head, the image of that contrast somehow making him feel strange and disoriented. "No. I've thought about it. We can leave him a spot there by the river. We'll put up a security fence, to protect Josiah and the chapel—"

"And keep him and his chapel members out of the fancy neighborhood? That should go over well with the homeowners association."

Sighing, Stone lowered his head. "Can we not discuss this right now? Josiah is hurt. We'll figure out the rest later."

Tara nodded, her hands fluttering to her side. "I'm sorry. I sound petty, but honestly, I'm more worried about an old man living out in the marsh by himself than I am about how the homeowners are going to feel."

"I know that," Stone replied, loving the compassion in her eyes, which surprised him. He'd never been one for too much compassion before, or for believing in fate. "And I feel the same way. We'll figure out something. Now, will you please come and sit back down."

Tara followed him back to the chairs. Stone knew her well enough to tell by the way she kept pushing at her hair and adjusting her clothes and purse that her mind was racing.

"What?" he asked, his fingers laced with hers. "Look, if it helps to talk about mundane things so you can take your mind off being here again, then talk away."

"I've got so much to do," Tara admitted, obviously glad for the distraction. "I have to tell Ana that I'll only be working at the tea room through August. School starts soon and I don't want to have to cart the girls back and forth between the island and Savannah. At least now, with the new job, I won't have to work weekends."

"Ever again," Stone said with such conviction, her head shot up. "Not as long as you do the job I'm paying you for," he quickly amended.

"Okay." She gave him a lame smile. "It's going

to be a challenge, working for you. You'll keep me on my toes, that's for sure."

Glad to see her smiling, he nodded. "You can count on that. I'll keep you busy—which seems to be the way you like to stay."

"I get jittery when I have nothing to do."

"We'll have plenty to do. First thing, I'll show you the preliminary plans for the subdivision and shopping complex."

"A perfect upscale world."

"You say that with a bit of distaste."

"It's just that Chad and I lived in that world. And it came tumbling down pretty fast."

"I won't let our new world tumble," Stone said. "I only invest in solid acquisitions, Tara."

She looked over at him with such a pensive gaze, Stone thought she might start crying again. "Do you ever wonder if we're doing the right thing?"

He saw the worry centered in her eyes. "You mean with the land or us?"

"The land. I know all about us and that can never happen."

"Oh, the land." He wouldn't argue about the other right now, but it would happen. He'd see to that, too.

"That land needs an overhaul. It's got potential. Lots of potential."

"Then why didn't I have more offers for it?"

"Maybe because others couldn't see that potential the way I do."

"So you see potential where most folks don't think there is any?"

"I do." He let his gaze move over her face. "Maybe that's why I'm so attracted to you."

She frowned. "Is that supposed to be a compliment?"

"In the best possible way. You've been down on yourself since Chad died, probably long before he died. Don't you think it's time you realized your full potential, too?"

Stone saw something change in Tara's vivid blue eyes, something subtle but sure. "Maybe you're right," she said finally. "I've always whizzed right through life, with very few downfalls or roadblocks. But all of that changed when Chad died. I had to face things I didn't want to face. And I lost my confidence. I felt like a failure, like I couldn't trust anyone to help me through the mess my life had become."

"And now?"

"And now," she said, her eyes full of sincerity, "I think I'm beginning to trust again."

"Me?" he asked, the one word full of hope.

"You," she answered softly. "And myself. And God."

Stone nodded, smiled. "Good. Then trust me in this one other thing, Tara. I will take care of Josiah. I won't let anything happen to him, okay?"

"Okay." With that she leaned back against the wall to wait for the doctors. And took Stone's hand back in hers while she waited.

That one small gesture of assurance and trust caused Stone to experience a flow of overwhelming emotions, emotions to which he couldn't yet put a name.

Except that…he thought it meant he might be falling in love.

"Wow, I can't believe that poor man lay there for hours," Ana said late the next afternoon.

Tara had come by the tea room to tell her sister that she could no longer help her on weekends. But first, she'd told Ana about finding Josiah out in the marsh. "I've never been so scared," she said now. "But thankfully, he's going to be okay. He has a concussion and two broken ribs, but no internal bleeding."

Ana turned around in her desk chair to stare at her sister. "And he has family coming to watch out for him?"

Tara nodded. "He has four children. Two sons who are both in the service—they can't get home right now. But the two daughters live pretty close—one in Atlanta and one in Tennessee. Thelma is coming from Atlanta tomorrow to take care of him for a while."

"That's good," Ana said. "Is he going back out to the marsh?"

"Thelma didn't seem to want him to do that. She told me on the phone that they've tried to get him to move since their mother passed away ten years ago. Can you believe Josiah and Dorothy raised four children in that tiny little house out on the marsh?"

"People do that all the time," Ana said, shrugging. "We just tend to not think about it or hear much about it,"

Tara nodded. "But Josiah is different. I mean, to us, it looks as if he's living in poverty out there. But he seems perfectly content. He kept telling Stone and me that he had to get back to the chapel. He watches over that little church."

"Maybe that's why he doesn't want to leave," Ana said as she turned off her computer and called it a day. "Want a cup of cinnamon-apple tea?"

"That sounds so good," Tara said, following her across the hall to the kitchen, her mind still on Josiah. "Stone said he will provide for Josiah, no matter what."

"He did?" Ana asked, her brows lifting. "Well, how about that."

Her defenses rising, Tara asked, "Does that surprise you?"

"It does, in a way," Ana admitted. "I guess based on what Rock had told me, I imagined Stone to be cold and self-centered."

"He's not," Tara said, too quickly.

Her sister stopped measuring out tea leaves to give her a long, hard stare. But instead of questioning Tara's declaration in favor of Stone, she asked, "So, do you think you'll enjoy working for Stone?"

"I think so," Tara replied, "now that we have an understanding."

"Oh, what kind of understanding?" Ana asked as she set out a tin of fresh tea cakes.

"We've agreed to keep our relationship strictly business."

"Really?"

"Yes, and don't give me that look."

"What look?"

"The look that says you don't believe me."

"Well, I don't believe you because I think there is much more to you and Stone besides work. But I promised Rock I would stay out of it."

"Thank you," Tara said, her smile soft. "And speaking of Rock, did he tell you that he and Stone resolved some of their differences?"

"Yes, he did, and I'm very happy about that. And Eloise is beside herself with joy, knowing that those two are finally coming around. Rock even went up to Hidden Hill yesterday to help the workers. He said the gardens look a lot better now that Stone brought in landscapers and hired a tree and lawn service to clean the place up."

Tara took a sip of her tea, then broke off a piece of buttery cookie. "Stone wants this gala to be a big event."

"So you're going?"

"As an employee of Stone Enterprises, yes."

"Oh, I see."

"You're giving me that look again."

Ana grinned. "Am I?"

Tara chewed the rest of her cookie, then got up. "Look, Stone and I are attracted to each other—"

"Gee, you think?"

"Yes, okay, but I'm not ready for all of that yet."

Ana turned serious then. "You mean because of Chad?"

Tara nodded, then looked down at the tile on the counter. "There's so much inside me, Ana. Guilt, frustration, fear, pain. I don't want to make a mistake."

Ana patted her hand. "That's probably wise. You don't have to rush anything."

"I'm not," Tara explained. "And Stone has agreed to honor my request for time and space."

Ana looked skeptical, but said, "Maybe he is changing for the better. Rock seems to think he is, and Rock credits you with making that happen."

"Me?" Tara felt the shock of that down to her toes, right along with a warm feeling that left her both confused and elated. "I haven't done anything but try to be a friend to Stone, now that I've gotten to know him better."

Ana smiled, then bit into a cookie. "Well, maybe that's exactly what he needed, someone to believe in him, someone who sees his potential."

Tara remembered Stone's words to her at the hospital. "Stone told me I need to realize my full potential," she said. "Ana, do you think it's possible that God puts two people together to make them both better as a whole?"

Rock came into the kitchen before Ana could answer. Walking to his wife, he kissed her on the cheek. "So here you two are. What are you talking about—world peace or how to take over mankind?"

"A little of both," Ana said, grinning. "Tara just asked me a question I think only a preacher can answer."

Rock laughed, grabbed a cookie. "I'm not really a preacher, I just play one on Sundays. But I will try to answer your question."

Tara smiled. "You are more of a real minister, Rock, than some preachers who've been trained and earned their doctorate in religion, I think."

"Well, I'm honored you think that," Rock said, his eyes crinkling as he smiled. "What's the question?"

Tara repeated her question. "Do you think God has a hand in placing two lost souls together to find their way back—to make them better people?"

"Better as a whole," Ana added, repeating Tara's original question.

Rock glanced from his wife to his sister-in-law. "Is this a trick question?"

"No, I really need to know," Tara said, smiling at Rock's look of fear and dread. "Is it that hard to answer?"

Rock shook his head. "No, it's just that you two are a formidable duo. I don't want to say the wrong thing."

Ana patted his arm. "Relax, you're perfectly safe with us. I was just telling Tara that you think Stone has changed for the better, because of her. I think she's not quite ready to accept that she has made a difference in his life."

"It's just that it wasn't all me," Tara said. "Josiah made a strong impact on Stone, too."

"But you were there when Stone met Josiah, right?" Ana asked.

"Yes, but Stone and Josiah have a very unique relationship. It didn't include me until I agreed to work for Stone and then Josiah got hurt."

Ana waved a hand. "Okay, I can accept that. But let's get back to the question at hand." Turning to her husband, she asked, "Don't you think Tara has changed Stone?"

"Oh," Rock said, relief clear on his face. "The answer to your question is yes, absolutely." He paused a moment, then added, "My brother has been so distant and hard to deal with for so very long, both my mother and I are amazed that he's even speaking to us again."

"But wouldn't he have maybe started coming around, anyway?" Tara asked, wanting to make sense of things. "I mean, he was planning the gala for the lighthouse before I came into the picture. He would have had to run into both of you on the island anyway."

"True," Rock answered, "but before he was planning the gala for all the wrong reasons—he wanted to impress everyone on the island and he wanted to get next to my mother and me."

"And now?"

"And now," Rock said, taking another cookie in his hand, "Stone has truly changed. We've talked on several occasions since Ana first forced me to go out and see him at Hidden Hill, and especially since you and I had our own conversation about Stone. He's different now. He has more compassion for his fellow man. And he has a warmth in his voice whenever he mentions you, Tara. So yes, I'd say you've made a good impression on my brother. And I'd say God did have a hand in that, and in his meeting with Josiah, too."

Tara sank down on her chair. "But why would God choose me? For so long, I didn't put God at the center of my life. Why would He use me to change Stone for the better?"

Rock looked at Ana, then pulled his wife close. "Tara, think about it. When your life started spiraling out of control, what did you do?"

Tara sat there, seeing the happiness and contentment on their faces. Then it hit her. "I turned back to God. I turned the control over to Him." Tears springing to her eyes, she asked, "Rock, do you think because of that, he allowed me to help Stone, too?"

Rock nodded. "You opened your heart to God and now God is rewarding you by using you to help Stone. Tara, you've managed to do something I've been trying to do for years. You've made Stone more humble, more compassionate, more caring.

And my mother and I are very thankful for that. I tried so hard, but something was blocking my heart. I still held resentment toward Stone. You could have felt that way, too, when he went after your land. But instead, you turned that around and tried to reach a compromise that worked for both of you. And the result is that you've become closer."

Tara felt such a lump in her throat, she couldn't speak. Finally she said, "But what if this backfires? What if Stone and I... What if he resents me for changing him?"

"Why would he resent you for making him a better person?" Ana asked.

Rock nodded his agreement. "Tara, Christ went out among the worst of society and brought blessings to those who thought they had nothing left in this world to give. They thought no one cared about them. But Christ did. Because you believed in my brother when others, including me, doubted him, he's seen something inside himself that he's kept hidden all these years."

"Don't give me so much credit," Tara said, getting up to pace the room. "Stone always had good inside him. He was just hiding it."

"Exactly," Rock said. "The scripture says no one should hide his light under a basket or in a secret place. By offering to defend Stone, by seeing the good he was trying so hard to hide, you've opened him up to the light."

"The light inside him?" Tara asked, smiling at last.

"Yes," Rock said. Then he lowered his head. "Sorry, I didn't mean to give a sermon right here in the kitchen, but it's true."

Tara turned to face them again. "It is true. Stone has promised me he won't push me toward a relationship we might both regret. And he's promised me he'll take care of Josiah. I know there is good in him. I've seen it."

Rock came around the counter and hugged Tara close. "Actually, I've seen it, too. Stone showed me something out at Hidden Hill the other day— well, I won't say what, but it really made me see I was wrong about so many things. My hard-hearted brother does have a few soft spots." He shrugged, lowered his head. "Miracles happen when we turn control over to God, Tara. And yes, I believe God brought you and my brother together for a reason. Now whether that leads to the two of you grower closer or just staying friends, I can't say. That will be up to you."

"With God's help," Tara replied.

"With God's help," Rock answered.

Later that night, Stone stood on the terrace at Hidden Hill, looking out at the sea. He could hear the waves crashing against the dark shore, could see the whitecaps glistening in the moonlight just as they broke and lifted in a foamy song of never-ending anger and turmoil.

Stone felt some of that same anger and turmoil

inside his heart. It was the same anger, the same turbulence he'd carried inside his soul since the day his father had disappeared out in those dark, unforgiving waters.

But tonight, right this minute, his heart felt a different kind of emotion, an emotion that softened the anger like the sea calming down after a violent storm.

Because of her.

Stone thought about Tara and wondered what it was about her that made him do things he'd never dreamed of doing before. She made him feel things he'd never felt before.

"Why is that, Lord?"

Surprised that he'd made that plea out loud, Stone glanced around. But he knew he was alone here in this big, old house. And he knew with a revealing intensity that much in the same way he was working to restore this house, someone, something inside him, was working toward restoring his own lost faith and crumbling, weak, foundation.

Then Stone heard it as if it had been spoken on the wind. Words his father had told him one day when he'd been allowed to go out on the shrimp boat.

"Why do you fish?" Stone had asked his dad.

And his father had answered, "'Come after me and I will make you fishers of men'."

Stone heard that verse now, clear and concise, as he stared out to sea. And he thought about the conversation he'd had with his father there on the boat, just a few weeks before his father had died.

"Do you know what that means, son?"

Stone had answered no.

His father had explained, "It means that Christ wants us to follow Him always, and to feed the souls of men, not just with fish or bread, but with the word of God. That's why I fish. I believe in God's bounty and I believe in sharing that bounty. It provides me with a good living and it provides nourishment for my table and for my soul. When I go shrimping, I provide a practical food for people to eat, but I also bear witness to the grace and goodness of God's vast ocean. Always be a fisher of men, Stone. Remember that."

Stone stood there in the darkness, a piercing pain of longing hitting him right in the heart. "I had forgotten, Daddy," he said to the wind. "I had forgotten."

And he'd blamed everyone, including God, for taking his father from him, for keeping his mother from him, for forcing Stone and his brothers to live in poverty, for making his childhood so hard and miserable.

But that was changing. Stone had reconciled things with Rock and his mother. He'd made promises to Tara, the kind of promises he'd never made to another woman. And here, tonight, he also wanted to make a promise to God.

For the first time since he was a child, Stone tried to pray. "Help me, God. Help me to find a way to make her love me." Stone lowered his eyes away from the sea. "Help me to find my way back to being a fisher of men."

Then he lifted his eyes up to the night sky. "With Your help, I know I can do this."

And with Tara's love, he could at last put the past behind him and be a better man. The type of man of whom his father would be proud.

Chapter Twelve

"And that's how they lived from the time they were freed until after the war was over. My people have always lived on the marshland. Always."

"Wow." Amanda sank back down on the stack of pillows around Josiah's feet. "I'm going to do my Georgia history report on this, Mr. Josiah. Think I'll get an A?"

Josiah laughed, then grimaced from the pain in his cracked ribs. "I reckon if you set the record straight, you'll gain more than a good grade, little lady. Not many people outside the Bennett descendants know about the story of the free men of color who lived on that land. That's why I have to go back and take care of the chapel—it's the only building left."

Tara saw the worry in Josiah's aged features, then glanced around Rock's cottage to make sure everything was in order. Rock had graciously loaned it to Josiah while he recuperated. His daughter Thelma and her two girls were spending the next week with Josiah here on the island. The girls, twins named Monika and Moselle, were close to Amanda's age, and had instantly hit it off with Tara's two youngest daughters. They now sat with Marybeth and Amanda at their grandfather's feet, listening to the colorful history of the Bennett clan. Laurel was with Cal at Eloise's house, but on a strict curfew to be home by seven.

"Daddy, I told you to quit worrying about the chapel," Thelma said. "We're going to drive out this afternoon and check on things for you."

"And feed that old stray swamp cat that roams around my house," Josiah reminded her again. "Scratch, he gets mighty hungry."

"I'm sure he has plenty to live off of in the marsh, Daddy," Thelma said, grinning and shaking her head at her father's concerned expression. "That cat is as old as me, and still kicking."

"Him and me," Josiah said, and then demonstrated by kicking both his skinny legs against the leather recliner he was lounging in. "Ouch," he said as the actions obviously caused his ribs to burn in protest.

"Daddy!" Thelma rolled her chocolate colored eyes, then tossed her brown curls. "See what I mean, Tara. The man is as stubborn as an old mule."

"But still kicking," Josiah said again. Only this time he didn't move one muscle except to smile.

Tara shook her head. "You are recovering re-markably. I can't believe just a few days ago, you were lying in that marsh—you scared Stone and me." She stopped, telling herself not to spoil the happy mood. "Well, I'm just glad you're getting better."

Josiah grunted. "I appreciate this nice, cozy cottage, Tara, but I sure miss my house."

Thelma shot Tara a knowing look. They'd been huddled together in the kitchen, trying to decide what was best for Josiah. Thelma didn't want him going back to the marsh alone, but Josiah didn't seem to want to live any place else.

Amanda and Marybeth turned back to Josiah. "Tell us some more about your great-grandfather Sudi, Mr. Josiah. About how he made a living from the marsh and the river after he came back from the Civil War."

Monika grinned up at Josiah. "Yeah, tell 'em how he fought in the war then came home and wrestled an alligator so he could feed his starving family."

Moselle gave her sister a long stare. "He didn't wrestle an alligator, Moni. It was a crocodile. There's a difference."

Josiah chuckled, holding his bandaged ribs. "Now you girls probably need to quit worrying about crocks and gators and help your mama and Tara get this place cleaned up. We don't want Mr. Rock to kick us out for being slovenly."

"Daddy, you haven't been slovenly a day in your

life," Thelma said, fluffing pillows and straightening magazines as she went. "And you sure taught me to be neat."

"Hope so," Josiah replied, pride shining in his eyes. "Your mama, now that woman could keep a house so clean, you could eat peas and corn bread straight off the floor."

"Did you ever try that, Mom?" Moselle asked, laughing.

"No, honey. I'll just have to take your granddaddy's word for it." Tara saw the pensive expression on Thelma's face. "But your grandmother Dorothy could surely cook. I wish she was still here."

"Me, too," Moselle said, then turned back to Josiah. "Do you miss her, Granddaddy?"

"Miss her every day," Josiah said, his eyes misty. "But I'm not worried one bit. I'll join my Dorothy in heaven soon enough."

Marybeth glanced up at Tara and the look in her eyes broke Tara's heart. "Will we see Daddy in heaven, Mom?" she asked.

Tara thought about that, about how she should answer her daughter's question. Panicked, she looked at Josiah. He nodded briefly. "Yes, honey, I'm sure we will. Josiah has told me things about your father I didn't even know. And they've brought me comfort. Your father visited Josiah a lot."

"He especially liked the chapel," Josiah said on a low voice. "Chad knew that God was watching over him."

"But we never went to church much," Amanda said, her gaze flying to her mother. "I'm glad we do now, though."

Josiah nodded, cleared his throat. "Going to church is good and I'm glad you're doing that now, but being in church and going to God are two different things, precious. Chad might not have graced the doors of the church, but he knew that God was there in that little chapel. He knew, because he sat and listened. That's all the Lord wants. He tells us to be still and know that he is God."

Amanda rubbed her nose. "So if I lay still at night and listen, God will be there? And maybe my daddy, too?"

Josiah nodded. "Yes, ma'am. No doubt in my mind." His aged eyes shifted to Tara's face, the question lingering there as if to say, "Do you still doubt?"

Tara glanced around the room, feeling as if the walls were closing in on her. "I—I'd better go check on the wash," she said. She hurried out onto the back porch and into the little room where the washer and dryer were stored. Then she heard a car pulling up, and glanced out the window to see Stone coming up the back steps with packages in both arms.

"Hi," Tara said as she came out of the laundry room and onto the back porch. "What are you doing here?"

"Good to see you, too," Stone said, his eyes moving over her face. "Are you all right?"

"Fine." Tara swallowed back the need to lash out at him. It wasn't his fault that her guilt about Chad colored every aspect of her life these days. But it was his fault that she couldn't stop thinking about Stone and the way he made her feel. "I've just been busy and worried and...so much is happening, so fast."

Stone set the grocery bags down on a cedar picnic table pushed up against the wall. "Hey, take a breath. Josiah is doing well and we're going to figure it all out."

Tara waved a hand in the air. "Figure what out? Where my life is going, what other secrets my husband kept from me, whether or not my oldest daughter will ever forgive me?" She stopped, took a long breath. "How I really feel about you? How am I supposed to figure all of that out?"

Stone grabbed her arm. "That's it. You need a break. I know you've been burning the midnight oil, trying to finish up with your commitments at work before you switch over to Stone Enterprises. And while I admire your drive, I also know that you can't handle everything at once, Tara. You need to rest."

"I can't," she said, her shoulders slumping. "I have to get back to Savannah tonight, to finish up some contract work for Monday. Laurel has a term paper due on Tuesday. Marybeth has a dentist appointment on Wednesday and Amanda has twirling practice on two of those days." Hearing laughter coming from the front of the house, she glanced inside. "At least Josiah is safe."

"Yes, he is," Stone said. "And that's one reason I came by. Thelma wants us to try to convince him to either move to Atlanta with her or stay here on the island where he'll have a clinic close by and neighbors to check on him."

"He won't do that," Tara said. "He wants to go home."

"Well, we'll just have to deal with it," Stone said. "I'll go in and visit with him, feel him out about things." He leaned close, assaulting Tara's senses with a clean, spicy smell that only reminded her of his masculinity. "And then, I'm taking you and the girls out to Hidden Hill for a picnic."

"I told you, I can't," Tara said, wishing she could take the afternoon off. But picnics were not part of her job requirement.

"What would it hurt?" Stone asked, his quick-silver eyes drenching her with a challenge. "You could spend time with the girls and we could just talk…about things, about work. Laurel can bring Cal. And if it will help, I'll even invite my mother. She's been hinting for a tour of the house anyway."

Tara shook her head. "I told you, I have obligations."

"The contracts can't be processed until Monday, right?" Stone countered.

"Right," Tara finally said, thinking if she went with Stone at least they could go over a few of the details of her job responsibilities. She thought about it for a minute, then said, "Okay, but only if we stick to discussing work." At his nod, she added, "I'll have to find Laurel first. And make sure Josiah is okay here."

"We'll bring him and Thelma and the girls with us," Stone replied, a light of adventure shining in his eyes.

"How are we supposed to concentrate on work with half the island going on this picnic with us?"

"We'll manage," he said, his gaze moving over her face in a way that made her feel edgy and flushed. "And besides, with all these folks there, maybe you'll relax and learn to trust me."

Tara laughed. "With that many chaperons, I'll be safe with you, maybe."

"Maybe," he said, his tone implying she'd never really be safe with him.

Stone turned to find Rock staring at him.

"What?" he asked before glancing back down to the crowd of people centered on the back lawn of Hidden Hill.

"Who are you and what have you done with my brother Stone?" Rock asked, amazement evident in his blue eyes.

Stone managed a curt laugh. "Surprised?"

Rock nodded, took a drink of iced tea. "More like flabbergasted. I mean, look down there. Mother is here and smiling at Don Ashworth. My wife is dishing out cookies and lemonade with a grin. Cal and Laurel are beaming—Laurel's really pretty when she decides to smile. And Josiah and his family are laughing and telling tales to Tara's girls. Oh, and did I mention that Tara looks relaxed and happy, too? What have you done, Stone?"

Stone turned to lean against the cool bricks of the terrace banisters. He couldn't yet bring himself to discuss his epiphany with his brother. "You don't approve of this little gathering?"

"Oh, I approve," Rock replied. "It's just so—"

"Out of character for a self-centered man like me?" Stone finished, some of that old resentment and hardness bringing the wall back up.

"Well, yes," Rock said, nodding. "Don't get me wrong. I'm very happy to be here and even happier to be helping you get this place in shape for the lighthouse gala next week."

"But…?" Stone asked, thinking that in spite of all his good intentions, everyone around him still seemed to doubt him.

"But I have to wonder why you're doing all of this?"

Stone turned back to watch the crowd below. Instead of having a leisurely picnic with the food he'd had delivered from a local deli, they'd all pitched in and helped the ever present landscaping team with the gardens. He watched now as Tara and Ana sat in the dirt and grass, helping one of the landscapers plant colorful mums and pansies around an ancient cluster of camellia bushes. Off to the side, Cal and Laurel were helping Cal's father, Don, with a wheelbarrel full of compost. Even his mother Eloise was getting in on the act. She was clearing a spot in the center of the garden, directly in line with the restored pool, for the sculpture she'd given to Stone years ago. In storage now, the sculpture would gain a place of prominence in the gardens at Hidden Hill.

"I don't know," he admitted to Stone. "I'm a bit baffled myself." His gaze went back to Tara. He really liked watching her. She was like the wind, always in motion.

He could feel Rock staring at him. "You're falling for Tara, aren't you?"

Stone didn't answer. He looked down at the ice melting in his tea glass. "Maybe," he finally said, refusing to look Rock in the eye.

"Ana was right all along," Rock said, almost to himself, amazement in the words.

"What do you mean?"

Rock shrugged, popped a piece of ice into his mouth. "Ana thought you and Tara would be perfect for each other."

"Does she still think that?"

Rock gave him a grin. "Well, she's wavered some, having heard about your…uh…negotiations regarding Tara's land. But even though she's decided to back off, I think deep down she's still hoping you two will work things out in a romantic kind of way."

Stone let that settle around him, then asked,

"What's the deal with those two and Chad, anyway?"

Rock squinted toward the western sun. "Tara hasn't told you?"

"Told me what?" Stone asked. "She's mentioned that Ana and Chad dated before he married her. But that's about it."

Rock nodded, then glanced down to where his wife and Tara stopped planting ground cover long enough to nibble on turkey club sandwiches. "I don't think I should talk about that. Tara will have to explain things."

Stone appreciated his brother's tact, even if it goaded him that he wasn't on the inside loop regarding Tara's past. "Okay. I guess she'll tell me if she thinks I need to know."

"Yes, she will," Rock replied, relief evident on his face.

Stone watched Tara now as she laughed at something Ana said. She had a thousand-watt smile. He was glad to see her happy. But was she really happy?

He'd abided by their agreement, biding his time until she felt she could trust him. He hadn't been overbearing about her finishing up work for her former boss, not in the way Stone was usually overbearing to new employees. He'd tried not to manipulate her into anything that would make her feel uncomfortable, including coming here today. They'd managed to have a thorough discussion about business, in the midst of all the people roaming around the grounds, then he'd told her to "go play in the dirt" with her sister and her children. Told her to go, then wished desperately she'd invited him to come and play with them.

He was going to try really hard to stay away from her, except for necessary business decisions and discussions. He'd even had Diane place Tara's spacious office down the hall on the far end of the building, away from his own.

Unfortunately, his assistant wasn't buying that.

Still remembering Diane's words when he'd told her he was hiring Tara Parnell, Stone had to smile.

"She won't give in to your charms, so you hired her to work for you?" Diane had asked, grinning.

"Something like that."

"Griffin thinks you're going through some sort of emotional crisis."

"Could be."

"Griffin says you've never been this involved in a deal."

"Griffin gets paid to worry about business, not my personal life. And so do you."

"Right," Diane had answered, not in the least scared about telling him what she thought. "We don't get paid to worry about you either, and we both do. So, Stone, I'd like to say that I'm officially happy for you, *and* worried for you. I think you've finally met your match."

Remembering that her eyes had held a tad too

much open glee, Stone shook his head now. And again felt his brother watching him.

"You haven't taken your eyes off her," Eloise said from the steps, causing him to lift his head in her direction. Apparently, his mother had been watching him, too.

Rock chimed in. "I think my brother is slightly lovesick."

Eloise came to stand between them. "Just as you were earlier this year, if I recall."

"You are correct," Rock replied, his smile indicating that he still had it bad. "You should be proud, Mother. Two down, one to go. Clay had better run for cover."

"I am proud," Eloise said, her turquoise dreamcatcher earrings jangling against her shoulders. "I'm proud that my sons have found two wonderful mates. And I'm very happy that we've all connected again, at last."

Stone felt the yoke of their expectations weighing heavily on his shoulders. "Aren't you two getting ahead of yourselves? Tara and I are friends. We're going to be working together, nothing more."

"Oh, really?" Eloise asked, her winged brows going up in surprise. "And do you stare at all of your employees in that same way?"

"I'm not staring," Stone said, trying to sound detached. "I'm enjoying my guests. *All* of my guests."

Rock gave his mother a warning look. "You are

staring, but you're also doing something that makes me think the old Stone is still warring with the new, improved model."

"Oh, yeah, and what's that?"

Rock lifted a hand in the air. "You're still up here, looking down, brother. Don't you think maybe you should go down and join the crowd?"

Stone looked from his brother's questioning expression to his mother's prim, tight-lipped smile. "I hate it when you're right," he said.

Then he turned and hurried down the steps to Tara.

Chapter Thirteen

A storm was coming in.

Tara stared out at the blackening sky. "Maybe we'd better head back to Savannah."

Stone walked around the granite-topped counter of the long multiwindowed kitchen. Everyone else had left. The girls were watching a movie on the big screen television in the den. Well, Amanda and Marybeth were watching a movie. Laurel was pouting.

"Why the rush?" he asked, seeing the contrast of Tara's feminine warmth in this starkly decorated room.

Tara pivoted from her spot by a floor-to-ceiling bay window in what would soon be the redecorated breakfast room. "Rush? Stone, we've been here all afternoon."

"Tired of me already?"

"No, just plain tired," she said on a shrug and a yawn. "Sorry. I haven't dug in a flower bed in so long, I have muscles screaming in places I didn't even know I had muscles."

Stone rounded the counter to push her down on a tall, steel-encased bar stool. "Let me give you a neck massage."

He saw the protest forming in her expression, but she sank down on the chair anyway. "That sounds too good to pass up."

Outside, a spark of lightning hit the dusk, followed by the rumble of thunder. Tara tried to bolt, but his hands on her neck held her down with a gentle persuasion. "Sit. Relax. The storm will pass."

"I don't want to drive home in the rain."

"You don't have to."

"Oh, and are you going to call me a taxi?"

"No. You can stay here as long as you like."

He pressed his fingers against the soft skin of her neck, just above the pink cotton of her round-necked cashmere summer sweater. "How's that?"

"That feels wonderful," she said, her head slumping forward just enough to allow him a peek of her slender neck. "You could start your own therapy business, you know?"

"I only give massages to special people."

He felt her tense. "Am I special?"

"Of course you are," he said, his eyes enjoying the golden hues of her hair as it fell forward. "Did you have fun today?"

"Mm-hm," she said, "and so did the girls. Laurel even seemed to enjoy herself."

"Until Don took Cal home."

"Those two are becoming too serious, I'm afraid."

Stone smiled to himself. "That's probably what this whole island is saying about us. Do you know we're the topic of the week?"

"Oh, yes. Eloise said that Greta Epperson person keeps buzzing around, wanting the scoop on us."

"Is there a scoop?" he asked, his heart tripping over itself as he took in the sweet floral scent of her shampoo.

She tensed again, then lifted her head. "Thanks," she said as she got up to roam around the work-in-progress kitchen. "All this steel and gray—you need some flowers in here, Stone."

"I need you in here," he said, his hands holding on to the counter as he stared across the room at her.

"We aren't supposed to be having this type of discussion," she reminded him, her eyes darting here and there, her hands fluttering out to touch on the counters and cabinet doors.

Stone sighed, leaned into the counter. "And tell me one more time why exactly we can't have this type of discussion?"

She looked at him then, the blue of her eyes flashing like the lightning outside the windows. "You know why. And you promised—"

"I've been known to break promises."

"You won't break this one. If you do, I'll have to find another job before I even get started at Stone Enterprises next week."

"Right," he said. Pushing his hands through his hair, he added, "What was I thinking, hiring you?"

"Regrets already?"

"If you weren't coming to work for me, would things be different between us, Tara?"

"Do you mean in a romantic way?"

"A very romantic way."

"I don't know." She turned to stare out into the growing darkness. "I don't think I'm ready for that kind of intensity again."

"Is that how it was with you and Chad? Intense?"

She nodded, wrapped her arms against her midsection. "Intense and impulsive. But it burned itself out in the end."

"Tell me about that."

"You know most of it."

"I want to know all of it."

"Okay, I'll tell you because I want you to understand how things have to be between us. Ana and Chad were dating in college, until I came along. Chad and I fell for each other hard. We broke Ana's heart, but she was gracious enough to let him go so he could be with me. We got married on a whim, our whole relationship based on a physical attraction. And we both regretted that for most of our marriage. And for most of the marriage, I believed my husband was still in love with my sister, and she with him. I was wrong on both counts. Chad died thinking I didn't love him. And it's true. I didn't love him enough to fight for our marriage. So I won't, I can't, rush into another relationship, just because you make me feel—"

"You want more," Stone interjected, at last understanding her completely.

"Yes, I want more. I want a real commitment. I want the kind of love I see when I'm around Ana and Rock. And I want my children to heal." She whirled around just as another clash of thunder and lightning hit the night sky. And then the whole house went black.

"Tara?"

"I'm here," she said. "Perfect timing. A power outage?"

"Looks that way. I plan to have a generator installed, but for now, looks like we're in the dark."

"Yes, for now I think we are."

Stone took that to mean he would still be in the dark about a lot of things. Until she learned to trust him.

"Mom?"

"We're coming, Marybeth. Stay where you are, okay?"

"It's dark."

Stone guided Tara through the maze of the hallways. "We've got flashlights and candles, girls. Hang on."

Amanda giggled. "This is fun."

"Speak for yourself," Laurel said, her tone a mixture of petulance and defiance. "This is dumb. Mom, when can we leave?"

"It's not safe right now," Stone said as they came into the shadowy den. "That rain is really coming down."

Tara could hear the storm pelting the old mansion. "I hope you at least had the roof fixed."

"The roof is intact," Stone said, his reassuring smile showing as he held up a candle they'd found in the kitchen. "And you're all safe right here until this storm passes."

"I want to go home," Laurel said, her hands hitting the arms of the plush leather chair she was slumped into.

"Laurel, how do you expect me to take you home right now?" Tara asked as she and Stone sat down on the long couch beside Marybeth. "Let's just wait until the worst of this storm passes."

"We shouldn't even be here," Laurel said, her harsh words echoing out over the still, high-ceilinged arch of the room.

Tara saw Stone's look of concern in the dim light from the candles he'd placed on the glass coffee table. "Didn't you have a good time today, Laurel?"

Laurel shrugged. "It was okay."

"I'm sorry Cal couldn't stay," Tara said, hoping that would diffuse Laurel's anger.

It didn't. Laurel sat up to glare at her mother. "Yeah, he has to leave, but you get to stay here all nice and cozy with him." She pointed to Stone. "Do you think that's fair, Mom?"

"I think that I'm an adult and I think that you need to speak to me in a more respectful manner."

"You can't even be honest about *him!*" Laurel said, her voice rising just as the rain grew heavier outside. "Don't you understand, we know you're in love with him."

"Laurel!" Tara lifted off the couch to stand over her daughter. "You do not know what you're talking about."

"Yes, I do," Laurel said, getting up to glare at Tara. "It sure didn't take you long to forget our daddy."

"Laurel," Tara said on a softer voice, her emotions hitting as hard as the storm. "Laurel, how can you say that?"

"It's true," Laurel said, her hands on her hips. "You never loved Daddy. So it's easy for you to forget about him."

Tara sank down onto the sofa, unable to put into words what she needed to say to her daughter. She felt a soft touch on her arm and saw Amanda staring up at her. "Is she right, Mom? You didn't love Daddy?"

"I loved your father," Tara said, the darkness giving her more courage than she felt inside her trembling soul. "We had some problems and we had some terrible fights, but we loved each other. I want all of you to know and remember that."

Marybeth stayed quiet, but Laurel was just getting started. "Then why are you selling our land to *him?* And why are you always with *him?*"

Tara couldn't speak. She stared over at Stone, saw the heat of anger on his face.

"I think I can answer that, if you'll let me," Stone said, his tone so calm and sure that Tara wondered if he'd heard any of the accusations her daughter had just thrown at her.

"Why don't you, then," Laurel said, as if to dare him.

"Okay," Stone replied. He turned off the flashlight so that the big room was illuminated with only the glow from the candles on the table.

Outside, the storm intensified, battering the trees and garden, probably washing away much of the ground cover they'd just planted, Tara thought in a detached way.

"Before I answer your question, Laurel, I want you to do two things for me. First, I want you to sit down and be quiet. And second, I want you to apologize to your mother."

Laurel sat down. "I don't have to apologize," she said, the words hitting Tara like shards of glass.

"Then you won't get any explanations," Stone said.

The room filled with silence. Tara sat wondering what to do now. Did she grab her daughters and leave? Did she turn down every offer Stone had made to her, including the offer of friendship and maybe something more? She knew she would, if it would help her children.

She was about to go, when Laurel finally spoke on a soft, defiant whisper. "I'm sorry, Mom."

"That's better," Stone said. "Now, before I explain things about your mother and me, I want to tell you all a story. Are you willing to sit still and listen until the very end?"

"I will," Marybeth said.

"Me, too," Amanda replied.

"Okay, whatever," Laurel said.

"Good." Stone sat back in the leather wing chair. "I think I'll build a fire with some of the old lumber stacked down in the basement. Let's all get comfortable. This might take a while."

He didn't know what he was going to say. Stone only knew that Laurel reminded him of himself, in so many ways. And he also knew that Tara was suffering in much the same way his own mother must have suffered. Except Eloise had kept her grief and her suffering to herself and had poured it all out in her art. Her children had needed her, but his mother hadn't known how to offer anything more than obligatory love. He didn't want Tara's girls to feel that way, to feel cut off from the love he saw in Tara's heart. So he had to tell them, had to show them how to heal.

Outside, the thunder and lightning boomed like cymbals, heralding a storm that continued to cover the island in a wash of wind and water. The candles flickered, giving a soft glow to the expectant faces watching him. The fire roared and hissed in the massive fireplace, its yellow sparks casting the old mansion's shadows in a golden hue.

Stone swallowed, said a silent prayer, and hoped he was doing the right thing. He'd never talked about this with anyone. But right now, this very minute, he needed to talk.

The darkness shrouded him in comfort as he cleared his throat. "You all know that I lost my father when I was very young. Tillman Dempsey was my father, and he was a fisherman. He died out there in the ocean in a storm much like this one. We never found his body."

Marybeth gasped, but stayed quiet. Amanda snuggled close to Tara. And Laurel kept her arms wrapped against her stomach and stared at the fireplace.

"But there's more to this story," Stone said, his voice sounding above the din of falling rain. He looked at Tara. "Much more."

"Is this a ghost story? Are you trying to scare us?" Laurel asked in a sarcastic tone.

"No, I'm not trying to scare you," Stone said with a wry smile. "But, yes, there are ghosts in this story. Ghosts from the past, in a figurative sort of way, I suppose."

"You aren't making any sense," Laurel retorted.

"Laurel, please listen," Stone replied before Tara

could reprimand her daughter. Then he let out a long sigh. "This isn't easy for me. I'm not a big talker. I don't like to talk about things, especially about my childhood."

Laurel kept glaring at him, but thankfully, remained silent.

"My mother and father fell in love with each other when they were very young, but my mother came from one of the wealthiest families on this island."

"Did they live in a house like this?" Amanda asked, tossing her blond hair.

"They had several houses," Stone said, the old bitterness coloring his words. "They had a nice mansion in Savannah and a summer house here on the island. That's the house my mother still lives in today."

"I love that house," Marybeth said.

Tara put a finger to her lips, her eyes on Stone. "Go ahead," she said, her interest obvious in the way her eyes held his.

"Okay, so they fell in love. My mother told of how he was walking up the beach and she saw him. And she knew that he was the man she would marry." Stone stopped, his gaze moving over Tara. "I used to wonder how she knew that, how she knew just from seeing him that she wanted to spend the rest of her life with him. But now…I think I can understand that concept."

Tara lowered her gaze, but not before he saw the mixture of fear and awe in her eyes.

"So they got married?" Marybeth asked, her young voice filled with the same awe he saw in Tara's expression.

"They got married, in spite of her parents' protests. And because of that, her parents disowned her. They didn't think this poor shrimper's son was good enough for their society daughter."

"But Eloise loved him anyway, didn't she?" Amanda asked.

"Yes, she did," Stone said, the awe coming from his words now. "She did." He sat silent for a while, then said, "So they lived in the Victorian house by the sea—the house my mother had always loved. She only accepted that one gift from her parents, and it was the only thing they offered, because they rarely came out to the island house. It was always her haven. She accepted nothing more. No money, no friendship, no family holidays together. No communication at all."

Laurel didn't speak, but Stone saw the furtive look she shot her mother. Maybe she was listening.

"Then they had three children. Three boys."

"And Eloise named you all funny names," Amanda said with a giggle.

"Yes, she did. She gave us strong male names, Roderick, Stanton, and Clayton. Then she gave us nicknames that marked us for life."

"Rock, Stone, and Clay," Marybeth said, grinning. "So keep going, *Stanton*."

Stone grinned back at her. "Now you know why

I prefer Stone." He smiled at Tara and was rewarded with a quick, warm smile back.

"Could you get to the point?" Laurel asked, hiding her obvious curiosity behind a cold stare.

"Right, back to the story. Anyway, as we grew up, we heard the stories around the island about the estranged relationship between our parents and my grandparents. We never knew my dad's parents. They died when we were little. But we sure wanted to know our other grandparents. Our mother refused to talk about them, refused to discuss them. Even when they tried to make amends. They wanted us to come and visit them in Savannah. But she wouldn't let us."

"Why not?" This came from Laurel.

Stone gave her his full attention. "At the time, I thought our mother was being mean and selfish. But I think she was trying to protect us. She wanted us to grow up as individuals, to make our own way. She was terrified that her domineering, powerful parents would try to mold us and shape us into something we couldn't be, the same way they'd tried to control her. So we never got to know them."

"Did you ever see them?"

Stone looked over at Marybeth. "Once, I saw them down on the beach. They'd been watching and waiting to see one of us. They saw me and called out to me. How they knew it was me, I'll never know. I talked to them for a long time and they gave me some money. I had to hide the money from my mother, but I never spent it. I saved it and planned on taking it with me when I ran away to make my fortune."

"Did you run away?" Laurel asked, all attitude gone now. She sat up, waiting for his answer.

"I tried a few times," Stone replied. "But Rock always found me and brought me home." He leaned forward, holding his hands together across his knees. "Until I went away to college. Then I turned my back on my family for a while. I didn't keep in touch with them the way I should have."

"You got rich, though," Amanda said on a pragmatic note.

Stone nodded. "I got rich, yes. But—and this is the part I want all of you to listen to very carefully—I came back here and bought this house—a house where I used to work doing odd jobs just to make pocket change. I bought this house thinking I would at last feel some sense of justice, some sense of accomplishment." He looked at Tara now. Her eyes were wide and misty. "But I didn't realize how lonely I was until the day I saw your mother."

Tara's gaze held his, a look of utter confusion changing to a look of understanding. Almost trust.

"Was it love at first sight, like Eloise and your father?" Amanda asked.

"It sure was something," Stone replied, afraid to voice what he felt in his heart. "All I can say is this—it changed me." Then he looked straight at

Laurel. "So, yes, Laurel, your mother and I have been spending a lot of time together. You see, I admire your mother. She's a lot like my mother—a young widow, struggling to raise a family. But there is one very distinct difference between Tara and my mother."

"What's that?" Laurel asked, the dare back in her voice.

"Your mother is willing to fight for you. She's willing to sacrifice for you. She wants you to remember your father—my mother wouldn't even talk about our father with us. Your mother wants you to stay close to both of your grandparents—her parents and Chad's parents. And she's willing to come and work for me, a man she doesn't trust and maybe doesn't even respect, for your sake."

He heard Tara's sharp intake of breath at about the same time Laurel bolted out of her chair. "That's your story? That's what this is all about? She's not doing this for us. She's doing this because she never loved our father, and she probably would rather she didn't have us to worry about! She'd rather work all day long, than to have to come home to us at night. And now, she gets to spend time with you at work and *after* work, too. How fair is that?"

"Laurel, that's not true," Tara said.

"It is true, Mom. Before Dad died, you were never home. And now, it's going to be the same thing. You'll be with Stone, finding excuses to stay away from us. Why'd you even bother having children?"

"Laurel, honey, how can you say that to me?" Tara asked, her voice cracking with hurt and anger.

Laurel was so mad, she didn't bother answering. Then she took off through the dark. Stone could hear her running down the hallway.

"Laurel?" Tara called, jumping up.

"Let me go," Stone said, grabbing a flashlight. "I know my way around this place. You stay here with Marybeth and Amanda."

He headed up the long central hallway, acutely aware of the construction scaffolding and power tools scattered around the old house. Laurel could get hurt if she wasn't careful.

"Laurel," he called, shining the flashlight down toward the drawing room and library. "Laurel, stop hiding."

He only heard the rain softening to a drizzle outside.

Checking the long drawing room and the dark-paneled library, he found only covered furniture and stored books.

Stone wondered where Laurel would go. The girl didn't know her way around this house. It was full of secret doors and hidden hallways. If something happened to her—

He heard a crash upstairs, near the rear terrace. His heart hammering like an anvil, Stone rushed up to the second floor. "Laurel, are you here? Answer me, right now!"

"I'm over here," came the weak reply.

Stone pointed the flashlight toward the sound of Laurel's voice. "Are you hurt?"

She came out from behind a huge armoire centered near the terrace doors. "No. I think I knocked over a vase or something."

Stone didn't know whether to hug her or give her a piece of his mind. Deciding to stay calm, he thought back on the times he'd done the very same thing to Rock. Running away. Hiding out. Pouting. Blaming. So much bitterness, and for what? No one was to blame for his father's death, just as no one was to blame because his mother had fallen for a poor man and married him. As Stone stood there in the darkness, he had a crystal clear image of what he must have put Rock and his mother through.

He laughed out loud. "Okay, God, I can see you have a strong sense of humor." Or maybe a sense of justice, Stone mused.

"Why are you laughing?" Laurel asked, her voice trembling.

Stone walked toward her, letting the flashlight trail over her to make sure she wasn't hurt or bleeding. "Well, sweetheart, I've just figured out one of life's great lessons."

"Oh, so are you going to fill me in?" She looked small and unsure, but she gave him a defiant glare all the same.

"Yes," Stone said, grabbing her by the arm to bring her into the faint light from the paned doors to the terrace. "I think I'm getting paid back for all my shortcomings. I used to run and hide like this myself, when I didn't want to deal with a situation."

"I don't have to deal with this," Laurel said, trying to pull away. "I don't like you and I don't like how my mother is acting."

Stone held her with a gentle strength. "Really, now. Well, you know something? No one likes the way you're acting, either. Have you ever stopped to think that you're supposed to be the oldest daughter? You're supposed to set a good example for your sisters."

"I baby-sit them just about every day," the girl retorted.

"That's good. But baby-sitting and being a sister are two different things." He could be noble now, now that he saw his older brother in a whole new light.

"I don't have to listen to you," Laurel said.

"No, you don't."

He stood there, his gaze fixed on her. She tried not to flinch and look away, but finally she gave in. "I guess I was horrible to my mom."

"Yes, you were. You have been for a while now."

"I don't mean to be. It just comes over me sometimes. I can't explain it, except I just want her to know how I feel—inside."

"I know. We're a lot alike, you and me."

"Everybody says you're mean and rude."

"That's right. I can be both. I have been both."

"Me, too."

"We probably need to change our attitudes, don't you think?"

"Well, tonight *you* were nice." She looked up at him then, her big eyes questioning. "Do you love my mom?"

He couldn't tell her what he felt, since he didn't understand it himself. "I don't know. But I'm pretty sure things are headed that way. Don't you want her to be happy?"

She nodded. "Mostly, I just want some answers."

"Don't we all?"

She didn't say anything for a while. Just stood there watching the last of the rain drip away.

Finally, Stone said, "We'd better get back downstairs. Your mother will be worried. But before we go, will you answer me one question? And please, take this from someone who's been there, okay?"

She shrugged.

"How long are you going to go on punishing your mother for things she can't control or change?"

She didn't answer at first, but he saw the lone tear trailing down her face—saw it in the glare from the single light he was holding in his hand. Then her next words hit Stone with all the force of the wind outside. "I just miss the way things used to be. Even when they fought, at least I had them both there. I felt safe. I don't feel safe anymore."

Stone had to swallow the pain radiating through his chest. That was it, exactly. He'd never felt safe after his father had died. He'd felt abandoned.

"Come here," he said. Then he pulled Laurel into his arms. "It's okay to cry."

She did cry, long and hard, and enough to wet the front of his expensive cotton shirt. But Stone didn't mind. He knew exactly how Laurel felt, had felt that same way himself for so many years. And he'd wished a thousand times that someone would have held him and let him cry.

He hadn't let anybody hold him, though, and he hadn't been able to cry, either. Until now.

Chapter Fourteen

Something was very different.

Tara stared at the work of art centered across from her desk in her new office at Stone Enterprises. But she didn't see the abstract work of Salvador Dali. She only saw the darkness, the thunder and lightning, and remembered the fear on her daughters' faces as Laurel had run away in the night at Hidden Hill.

Thanking God once again that her eldest daughter had been found safe and sound, Tara thoughts turned to the man who'd brought Laurel back to her. Stone.

That same man had become increasingly distant and quiet since that dark night a week ago. He'd emerged from the darkness with Laurel, his arm on her daughter's shoulder, guiding her back to safety. But there had been something different about him then. And something was definitely different now.

She almost wished for the old, calculating Stone back. The Stone who flirted with her and made suggestive remarks, while he tried to keep a business-type expression on his face. This Stone was so quiet, so brooding, she wondered if Laurel had told him something horrible and untrue just to make him turn away from her.

But then, Laurel had changed, too. She wasn't as abrupt in her answers. She wasn't as cynical and sarcastic in her words or deeds. Laurel was being dutiful and obedient, cooperative and pleasant. Which scared Tara almost as much as her daughter's rebellious defiance had.

Neither one was talking about what had transpired between them that night at Hidden Hill. Stone had simply brought Laurel back downstairs, then suggested they could probably go home. The storm had passed and Laurel was safe.

Had Stone said something to scare Laurel?

But no, it couldn't be anything like that. Even though it had been obvious that Laurel had been crying at some point, they'd been smiling when they'd come back into the candlelit den that night. Smiling and almost at peace with each other. Stone had even hugged Laurel goodbye.

Tara had heard his soft whisper to her daughter. "Be kind to your mother. And remember, if you ever need me, Laurel, you call me. And that goes for you, too," he'd told Tara.

Then he'd turned and gone back upstairs. Laurel

had stared after him with a knowing, secretive look that hinted at a deep understanding. And she'd been very quiet on the way home. They'd both been quiet since then. Too quiet.

Had that one statement been Stone's way of saying goodbye to what might have been? Had his talk with Laurel finally changed the way he felt about Tara? So many questions. So many angles. But no one was talking.

This is what you wanted, she reminded herself.

Tara looked down at the preliminary designs for the new subdivision they planned to build on the land. Hidden Haven.

Why did everything Stone Dempsey own have that word *hidden* in it, she wondered. Maybe because since he'd left Sunset Island, he'd kept a part of himself hidden. Maybe because even now when she knew she had such strong feelings toward him, there was still something about him that was hidden and dark. Which only made Tara want to know him more.

"But you signed on to work, not to daydream about your boss." No complaints there. Her office was plush and her job and salary cushy. She had two assistants to help her with everything from client meetings to learning the ropes within the vast corporate structure of Stone Enterprises. She could get home at a decent hour and spend time with her children. She could pay some of her debts. But since arriving here at the lovely home office, she had yet to come face-to-face with the man who'd hired her.

"I guess this is how he likes to operate," she mused out loud. "Behind the scenes and unattainable."

Well, you did want things this way. How many times would she have to tell herself this was for the best?

Her phone rang, causing Tara to jump. "Hello?"

"Hi, Tara. It's Griffin. Could we possibly meet within the next few minutes?"

"Of course," Tara said.

Griffin, a distinguished man who gave new meaning to the term *Southern gentleman*, had been a lifesaver. He'd guided her through the maze of offices in the lavish downtown Savannah building, teaching her all the things she'd need to know in order to get her work done. Griffin had become the middleman again, between Stone and her. Somehow, she'd managed to get through her first week of work without making a complete mess of things. Except with her new boss. The wall was back up between them, and Tara really wanted to know why.

"What did she say?" Stone asked Griffin Smith an hour later. He was standing at the wide solid glass window of his third floor office, very much aware of the woman on the other side of the building. Too aware.

Griffin sighed, then settled down into a leather chair. "She said that everything looks good and she's ready to discuss the rest of the contracts on the transfer of the property. She said the plans look wonderful and she can't wait to get started." Then Griffin threw down his folder. "It's what the woman didn't say that has me concerned."

Stone centered his gaze on his old friend. "What was that?"

"I can't tell you, since she didn't say," Griffin pointed out with a wave of his hand. "What's going on between Tara Parnell and you, anyway?"

"Nothing," Stone said too quickly. "Nothing at all."

Griffin's bushy white eyebrows shot up. "Oh, it's like that, is it?"

"What's that supposed to mean?"

Griffin ran a hand down his thick mustache. "It means that for the last few weeks, you seemed to be a changed man, Stone. You actually got out and got involved, in a way I've never seen you get involved before. You seemed happier. But now you're back to your old ways."

"Am I?" Stone knew exactly how he was acting. And it was killing him. But Griffin didn't need to hear that.

"I'm fine, Griffin. So you can report back to Diane that both of you are to mind your own business."

"We're just worried about you."

"No need for worry, but I appreciate your concern. I'm handling things the way they have to be handled. For the good of all involved."

"If you say so." Griffin got up. "Anything else you want me to discuss with Tara—before the gala tomorrow night?"

"No. I think that just about does it. Oh, she is going to make an appearance, right? You did stress to her that I expect her to be there?"

"She understands her obligations, Stone."

"Good, good." Then because he couldn't resist, he asked, "Does she…does she seem happy, working here?"

Griffin pursed his lips, gave his boss a puzzled look. "Why don't you ask her yourself?"

"I have work to do. Just tell me."

"She seems content. She's a hard worker. As I said, she understands her obligations. Diane had to remind her yesterday that we shut down promptly at five o'clock." He shrugged. "Of course, we haven't told her that our boss never goes home. Wouldn't want her to get the wrong idea there."

"That's why I'm the boss," Stone replied. "I get to set my own hours."

He watched Griffin leave the room. *Her obligations.*

Tara was obligated to do his bidding now. She worked for him. As soon as the paperwork went through, he'd own the land he had coveted. He should be happy, full of glee. He'd won. Again.

But what about the woman he coveted?

Stone felt as hollow as the metal-and-steel sculpture he'd had his mother design for the courtyard below. As hollow and as cold. Because he'd won all right, but he still didn't have the thing he wanted the most.

He wanted Tara. But he couldn't have her. He'd reached that conclusion completely after consoling her daughter there in the storm. He never wanted to hear that kind of anguish in a child's tears again, and he never, ever wanted to open himself up to that kind of anguish again.

All these weeks, he'd been trying to win her over, but that night he'd realized if he pursued Tara, he'd only hurt Laurel more. And probably Tara, too. And especially himself. He'd promised Tara he wouldn't hurt anyone, but he hadn't considered how easily he could be hurt if she didn't want him. Better to resort to the old, safe, hard-hearted ways. Better for all involved if he stuck to the plan of all work, all the time.

He could see it all so clearly now. He'd hidden his heart away long ago, the day his father had died, the day his mother had turned away in her grief. And in all the time since, he'd relied on material things to bring him happiness. But that was just a sham. He was not happy. And now, Stone didn't know if he could ever find his heart again.

At least, not with Tara Parnell.

"Some habits die hard," he said as he stared at

his reflection in the heavy glass protecting him from the outside world.

"What is wrong with my son?" Eloise demanded the next Saturday morning.

Ana and Tara glanced up as she entered the busy kitchen of the tea room. "What's the matter now, and which son, exactly?" Ana asked with a soft smile.

Charlotte and Tina both hurried over to stand beside Ana, their eyes wide, their ears open.

"Are you talking about that big sculpture?" Tina asked, grinning. "The one he's moving—"

"*My* sculpture," Eloise interrupted in a superior tone.

Before she could explain, Charlotte nodded, her brown curly hair bouncing. "I saw it yesterday when I was delivering all those cookies Stone ordered from Ana for the gala. It's beautiful, Miss Eloise. Where have you been hiding it?"

Eloise waved a bejeweled hand in the air. "I gave that piece to Stone when he graduated college. *The Resurrection,* I call it."

Jackie called from her spot at the computer in the office across the hall. "Are y'all gossiping without me?"

Tina answered in a hurry. "Yeah, get in here if you want to hear."

Jackie came scurrying across the hall. "Did I hear something about one of your sculptures, Miss Eloise?"

Eloise shot her a disapproving look which did nothing to quell Jackie's intense interest. "You have mighty big ears, but yes, we're talking about something I created a few years ago and gave to Stone as a gift."

Tara watched as Ana's eyes widened. "Rock told me about that piece. He said it looks like a cross, but you actually designed it to resemble the old pier by the Broken Pier Restaurant." Shrugging, she said, "We went there on our first date."

Eloise nodded. "That's right, dear. It represents a resurrection. It's made of metal and stone, with a waterfall shooting out of the center to represent everlasting life. I made it in honor of my late husband, Till."

The room grew quiet until Tara asked, "What has Stone done with it? Isn't it in the back gardens at Hidden Hill?"

"No," Tina said, her brown eyes widening. "It's—"

Eloise held up a hand. "He's had it put right by the lighthouse. Quite ingenious, really. Every time anyone stares out to sea from just about any hill or bluff on this island, they will not only see the lighthouse restored to its former glory, but they will see the sculpture centered on the rocks and pilings there beside the lighthouse."

Ana quirked her brows. "But Rock told me Stone kept that sculpture hidden away at the mansion. In storage."

"It was in storage," Eloise said, her silver eyes centering on Tara as she talked to Ana. "It was packed up in the garage. Stone said he planned on placing it in the back garden by the pool."

"Guess he changed his mind," Charlotte said just before hurrying off to fill the orders at her tables.

Tina looked from one sister to the other, then back to Eloise. "Maybe Stone decided it was time to bring The Resurrection out of hiding."

"Maybe," Eloise said, her eyes still on Tara.

Ana motioned to Tina to get back to work and the petite woman scurried away, her eyes still wide as she called over her shoulder, "I'll bet Greta Epperson will get to the bottom of this. She's covering the gala, you know."

"We know," Ana and Tara replied at the same time.

Jackie nodded, her chestnut hair touching on her blouse. "She's been snooping around all week, asking about the menu and the entertainment. She's gonna love this." She glanced up to find Ana giving her a keen look. "And I love my job, so I'm going back to my bookkeeping."

Eloise kept looking at Tara, making Tara acutely aware that she'd either made Stone's mother very angry about something, or Eloise didn't approve of her at all.

But Eloise's question to her changed that assumption.

"What have you done to him—for him?"

Tara pushed at her hair. "What do you mean?"

"I mean," Eloise said, waving her hands in the air, "that this is a major step, a very interesting change, in my son's attitude. You see, I always thought giving him the sculpture would somehow make up for the way I responded to his father's death, the way I retreated behind my work. But Stone took the sculpture and hid it away, I think to punish me. If he's willing to bring it out and share it with everyone who visits this island, then my dear, that is a big deal. A very big deal. And I can only assume you had something to do with it."

Not knowing how to answer, Tara glanced over at Ana. "I don't know...I don't think I did. Stone never mentioned to me what he was going to do with the sculpture, except that he planned to center it behind the pool."

"It's not going behind the pool," Eloise replied. "He's put it out there for all the world to see."

Tara heard the implications of that statement. If Stone was willing to bring the sculpture out of hiding, maybe that meant he was coming out of hiding, too?

Then why on earth was he hiding from Tara?

"You look so pretty," Ana told Tara later that night. "Are you ready?"

Tara stared at her reflection in the oval standing mirror of one of Ana's bedrooms. She'd decided to get ready for the gala here with her sister, to help calm her jangled nerves. The girls were safe at the cottage with Josiah and his daughter to watch out for them. "I think I'm ready," she said as she patted the chignon she'd had done at the local hairdresser's this morning. "How does my dress look?"

Ana's gaze moved over the billowing white satin trimmed with a thick span of black across the low portrait collar. "You look stunning. The black contrast around your shoulders is perfect. And I love the way that black bow falls down your back. Stone won't be able to move or breathe when he sees you."

"I didn't dress for Stone," Tara said as she adjusted the pearl-and-diamond brooch she'd placed against the black satin on her left shoulder. But she immediately knew that wasn't true. She'd dressed with Stone in mind, all right.

"Yes, you did," Ana said, echoing her thoughts as she tugged at her own pink sequined formal. "But that's to be expected. He is your boss now. And you don't want to make the boss mad."

"But he is mad, I think," Tara admitted. "Ana, the man hasn't said two words to me since I started work on Monday."

Ana stood silent for a minute, her dainty diamond earrings sparkling underneath her upswept hair. "Isn't that how you wanted things, honey?"

Tara sank down on the four-poster bed, not caring if she crushed her full-skirted ball gown.

"Yes, and no. I wanted him to stop pressuring me, but I fully expected him to at least act professional around me."

"Well, isn't being cold and distant Stone's professional mode of operation?"

"Yes, it *was,* from everything I'd heard. But he never acted that way toward me. Until now. I thought we could at least be friends. What if he regrets hiring me?"

"Have you given him any reason to regret anything?"

Tara thought back over the last week. "No. He started acting strange after he found Laurel upstairs at Hidden Hill. I think they must have had some sort of heart-to-heart talk. Laurel won't tell me anything and Stone won't even come near me."

Ana touched a hand to her hair. "Do you think Laurel said something mean and vindictive to him? I mean, that has been *her* MO lately."

Tara got up and grabbed her matching black-and-white satin wrap. "No, I don't think it was that. Laurel would have boasted about that if she'd done it. She's been so quiet, so nice. It's almost as if she finally understands about her father's death."

"Maybe Stone talked to her—he has been through the same experience. And maybe talking to her brought all of that back for him. The man seems to be struggling with letting go. Once he works through that, I think he'll come around."

"Do you think it could be that?" Tara asked, hopeful even as her heart told her not to count on it. If Stone and Laurel had compared notes, then whatever they'd discussed obviously hadn't helped Stone. He seemed miserable now.

"I think anything is possible," Ana said, smiling at their reflections as they checked their dresses one more time. "Maybe you'll get a chance to talk to Stone tonight and find out what really happened."

"Maybe," Tara said as they headed down to where Rock was waiting to drive them to the gala. Then she stopped at the landing. "Remember when you were so afraid of loving Rock?"

Ana nodded. "I finally had everything I'd ever wanted and I was still scared to accept it."

"I think I've reached that point," Tara replied, her voice low. "I finally have a great job, I can pay off my debts. I've even managed to sell that land, just as I'd hoped. But I'm afraid to take the next step. I'm waiting for the other shoe to fall. It just seems as if…something is still missing."

"Is that something Stone Dempsey?" Ana asked.

"I don't know. I think maybe I'm afraid of being hurt again, or that if I let my feelings for Stone show, I'll mess things up with my children."

"But if you don't try," Ana said, "you'll never know the joy of love again. You and Stone might be able to overcome all of that, Tara."

Tara nodded. "I needed some time. Maybe I still

do. But I want to know where I stand with Stone. I want to know if he even considers me a friend still."

Ana patted her arm. "Talk to him, then. Remember, I went after Rock and found out he thought he was doing me a favor by walking away. He was wrong, so wrong. And I'm sure glad I did go after him, or we might not be together today. You know how men can be. They clam up and refuse to tell us how they really feel."

"But with Stone, it's the exact opposite," Tara said. "He was very honest about things and now he's shut down, and I don't have any explanations."

"Talk to him," Ana urged. "Maybe he'll be honest with you again, if you're up front with him."

Tara didn't know if she could go after Stone, not after she'd pushed him away so many times. But she had to find out what had brought about this swift change in him. She had to find out why he was acting so indifferent toward her. If he couldn't love her, at least she wanted him to know she could be his friend and work with him at Stone Enterprises. But when she thought about the last week and how distant he'd become, Tara wondered how she'd ever live up to that pledge.

When Tara and Ana rounded the stairs, they found Rock waiting in the hallway for them, his expression full of surprise. "My brother sent a limo for us."

"A limo?" Ana asked, giggling like a school girl. "I've got to hand it to him, the man has style."

Rock looked affronted. "And what was wrong with going to the gala in my old van?"

"Nothing, sweetheart," Ana replied, realizing her mistake. "I'll be glad to let you escort me to the gala in your battered old vehicle, if it will make you feel better."

Rock sighed, then grinned. "Are you kidding? I've never ridden in a limo."

"You don't mind?" Ana asked, smiling.

"Of course not," Rock said. "This is my brother's fancy affair. If he wants to send a limo for us, so be it. It's for a good cause, right?"

"Right," Ana said as she turned to Tara. "And how do you feel about this?"

"I'm not sure," Tara said, a sinking feeling in the pit of her stomach. "I just don't know what Stone is up to now."

Rock nodded. "He likes to keep people guessing."

"Do you want to go in your car?" Ana asked.

"No," Tara replied. "He might be offended if his newest employee refuses his kind gesture." Then she turned to Rock. "And I like limos, too."

Rock opened the front door for them. "That means you've ridden in one before, huh?"

"A few times, when Chad was trying to impress someone," she said, remembering how pretentious she'd felt. "It is fun to pretend to be rich, though."

Rock led them down to the driver standing beside the sleek white car. "Well, obviously my brother doesn't have to pretend. He really is a wealthy man."

Ana held a hand on her husband's arm. "Does that still bother you?"

Rock stared at the car, then looked back at his wife. "Not like it used to. Not as long as he learns to use his wealth in a positive way, such as tonight."

"I love you," Ana said, reaching up to kiss her husband on the cheek.

"Even if I don't own a limo?" Rock teased.

"I think *because* you don't own a limo," Ana replied.

"I love you, too," Rock said, grinning. "But mainly because *you* own a tea room."

Ana playfully tapped his arm. "So you married me for my muffins?"

Rock gave his wife an appreciative look. "Oh, yeah."

Tara stood back, watching the sweet scene, and wishing she could feel that kind of solid love in her own heart.

Then she thought of Stone and how cold he'd been lately. Even when she'd denied wanting anything more than a working relationship with Stone, she'd hoped. She'd thought—but her heart was so bruised. Now she knew there might not be a chance for her to ever feel that way again.

At least, not with Stone Dempsey.

Some fears never go away, she thought as she got into the shiny limo that would take her to him.

Chapter Fifteen

The gardens at Hidden Hill were illuminated with thousands of tiny white lights that stretched out like a woman's lace shawl across the trees and bushes. A huge white tent filled with chairs and tables and buffets of food had been set up just beyond the now clean and sparkling swimming pool. The pool itself was filled with fragrant water lilies and floating candles that made the water look alive as they moved with the swirling current.

Up on the first-floor terrace, an orchestra played, the cello, flutes, harps, and violins sending the soft, haunting music out over the trees and flowers like butterflies lifting in delicate sound.

Tara stood near the pool, her eyes scanning the impressive crowd of both Sunset Island's and Savannah's finest citizens. She was looking for their absent host, Stone Dempsey. He had yet to make an appearance at his own party.

"Seen him yet?" Rock asked from her side, then handed her a crystal goblet of sparkling mineral water with a twist of lime.

"No," Tara said, not even bothering to deny it. "I wish I knew what's going on inside his head."

Rock chuckled. "Get in line. We've all been wanting to know that for a very long time."

She turned to stare over at Rock. He looked distinguished in his tuxedo. He was handsome in a different way than Stone. Rock's handsomeness was rugged and straightforward, whereas Stone's was mysterious and distant. Hidden away. "But you and Stone—you've made your peace, right?" she asked, worry causing her to whisper the question.

"Yes, I think we finally have," Rock said. "And I have you and Ana to thank for that. Ana made me see that I needed to reach out to my brother, and you made me see that I'd been judging him too harshly."

Tara nodded, pulled her wrap closer around her shoulders. "I truly think he's been out there all alone for so long that he expects to be judged. He almost welcomes it as a challenge, maybe to keep his bitterness brewing."

Rock chuckled again. "You Hanson women never cease to amaze me. You are both so wise."

"Not wise," Tara said, shaking her head. "We've just learned our lessons the hard way."

"Well, you two had some issues to sort through yourselves," Rock reminded her. "And now you're closer than ever."

Tara smiled, took a sip of the tingling water. It soothed her dry throat. "Yes, and I have *you* to thank for that. You encouraged me to turn back to God, to turn it all over to Him. It seems to be working."

Rock raised his own glass. "And it seems we have a mutual admiration society going here."

Tara agreed, then toasted him in return. "Now, if we could just get your brother on track, we'd really have something to celebrate."

Rock took a drink, then nodded. "Give him time, Tara. It took him many years to build up that wall. It might take a while for us to tear it down. Remember that saying by Edwin Markham, something about 'he drew a circle that shut me out…but love and I had the wit to win. We drew a circle that took him in'?"

Tara bobbed her head, glanced out at the sea. "I've heard it before, yes."

"I think we need to do that with Stone," Rock said. "I think he's shut himself down again because he's come close to finding everything that he's been missing in life."

"And he's afraid?" Tara asked. "You think he's walking away from me before it's too late?"

Rock nodded in silence. "Stone's never opened his heart to anyone. Then you came along and you were the one. That's got to be scaring him to death."

"I know the feeling." Tara looked down at the shimmering pool. "Me, I tried to give my heart to my husband and my children, but it wasn't enough. I didn't know how to love enough, Rock. I'm not sure if I'll ever know that feeling again, or what a complete love is really like."

Rock pointed toward the starlight sky. "Trust in Him, Tara. That's all I can tell you. That's what complete love is—it's more than just physical or more than just a passing infatuation. It takes commitment, work, and most of all, it takes putting God into the relationship."

"Thanks," Tara said. "And speaking of a complete love, go and dance with your wife."

"Good idea," Rock replied with a silly grin.

Tara stood there looking around at the crowd, her gaze moving over the sequined evening gowns and expensive tuxedoes, her ears hearing the clutter of mindless chatter, while her heart was clamoring to run to Stone, find him, tell him she wanted to see inside his battered heart.

What should I do, Lord? she silently asked the heavens. *I made such a mess of things with Chad. We didn't love each other enough to fight for what we needed to save our marriage. I didn't nurture him enough to save him. And now he's gone and my daughters are suffering. I'm suffering, God. I don't want to make the same mistake with Stone. But he needs me. He needs someone to show him what real love means, the way You showed us with Your son. Lord, do I dare tell Stone what's in my heart?*

A noise behind her caused her to whirl around,

hopeful. It wasn't Stone. "Laurel?" Tara squinted as her daughter sprinted down the steps. "What are you doing here, honey?"

"I snuck out," Laurel replied. Then she came rushing toward Tara. "Mom, don't be mad, please. Josiah said I needed to talk to you. But I couldn't wait until you got home."

Fear gripping her heart, Tara said, "What's wrong, Laurel?"

Laurel stood in her jeans and zippered pink fleece jacket, her golden hair shimmering on her shoulders. "Mom, I'm sorry."

"Sorry for what, sweetie?"

"For being so mean to you. Josiah told me everything, about how my daddy came out to the chapel, about how Daddy wanted to love us, but he didn't know how to show it. Josiah said the fighting wasn't anyone's fault. He said Daddy was a very sick man, and a very confused man, but he told me Daddy found God before he died."

"Oh, baby," Tara said, pulling Laurel onto a long stone bench and then into her arms. "Baby, you didn't have to come all the way over here to tell me that."

"But I needed you to know, I understand now," Laurel said. "Stone and me, we had a long talk here the other night. He told me how he'd blamed his mother for a lot of things and how he regretted being so mad all the time. He said that if God gives us another chance to find love, we should listen to our hearts and take that chance. He wanted me to understand that *you* needed a second chance."

"Stone told you that?"

Laurel nodded, wiped at her eyes. "But he told me he wouldn't cause me any more pain, either. He told me he'd leave you alone until I was ready to understand and accept things between you two." She pushed at her hair, then wiped at her eyes. "I think I'm ready now, Mom. Josiah read to me from the Bible, about Cain and Abel, the prodigal son, about Naomi and Ruth, all these stories of forgiveness and love. I've been so mean, Mom. I didn't want Stone to take my Daddy's place. But Josiah said Stone isn't supposed to do that. He said Stone needs us, just as much as we need him. Josiah said God brought all of us together for a reason. And after talking to Stone and really seeing how he feels, I think Josiah is right. So, I'm sorry. You've tried so many times to explain things to me, but I've been so angry and mean. I'm really sorry, Mom."

"Oh, Laurel." Tara pulled her daughter close, rocking her gently. "I love you so much, baby. I promise I'm going to make this up to you, somehow. And if that means giving up Stone—"

Laurel pulled back, sniffing away the last of her tears. "No, you have to tell Stone, Mom. You have to tell him that I'm okay now—that I understand. He won't come back to us unless he hears it from you—he told me that."

Tara nodded, seeing why Stone had pulled away

over the last week. He'd done it for Laurel, to show her daughter that he cared enough to walk away. And he'd probably decided he couldn't bear the pain of rejection if Tara or Laurel never accepted him. The same pain he'd suffered since childhood, that numbing pain that had caused him to turn away from love and his family.

How could she not accept a man who'd do that for her child? The respect and trust Stone had tried so hard to gain was evident now. And now, Tara knew without a doubt that she loved him.

God had answered her prayer.

Tara sat there on the secluded stone bench near the terrace of Hidden Hill, and talked to her daughter for a very long time. And she explained everything to Laurel, from the beginning. Then she sent her daughter back to the cottage, trusting that Laurel would find her way home. Her oldest daughter had matured into a caring young woman.

After Laurel left, Tara stood listening to the music, to the wind, to the sea. She heard all the sounds of God's world here on this island, but she waited to hear the sound of Stone's footsteps coming toward her.

She waited, but he didn't come. Which meant she'd just have to go and find him.

He couldn't bring himself to go out there and find her.

Stone stood in the middle of the solarium,

looking at the rows and rows of orchids he'd grown himself. He wanted to give one particularly beautiful lady's slipper to Tara, but fear gripped him like fish netting and he felt trapped in the darkness of his own doubts. Trapped here in the solarium, behind glass and flowers.

While the band played on.

"What are you doing?"

Stone whirled to see Eloise standing in the arched doorway. "How did you find me?" he asked in answer to her question.

"I wandered around until I did," his mother replied. "You have guests, son."

"Yes, I know. And I have a well-paid staff to see to all their needs."

"Don't want to get too personal with your donors and patrons?"

"The money is for the lighthouse, Mother, not me."

"But you need to show your gratitude. Your benefit gala is a rousing success."

"Then everyone should be pleased."

Eloise walked further into the room, her burgundy wrinkled silk gown rustling like fallen leaves. "Stone, I'll ask again—what are you doing?"

"I'm hiding," he said, not caring what she thought about his actions. "And I'd like to be alone."

Then he heard his mother's gasp, and turned to see what was wrong. He watched as her eyes scanned the orchids.

"Oh, my," Eloise said, waving a hand. "So many colors, so many varieties. Stone, who brought in these orchids?"

"I did," he said simply and quietly, while his heart hammered a roar to equal the cresting waves down below the bluff.

"Well, who's your supplier?"

Stone shook his head, put his hands in the pockets of his tuxedo pants. "I grew these myself, Mother. I take care of them myself. They're mine."

Eloise walked closer, the muted light from the hanging art deco chandelier making her face glisten. "You grew these?"

"Yes." He didn't feel the need to explain.

But then, his mother, ever full of surprises, gave him the shock and the thrill of his life. "I remember you tried to grow an orchid for me once, for Mother's Day. You wanted it to bloom so badly."

"But it never did," Stone said, his voice catching under the roughness of that memory. He stood silent for a couple of beats, then said, "How did you know about that? Did Rock tell you?"

Eloise turned to him then, her hand touching on his face with the gentleness of an artist touching a work in progress. "No one had to tell me, Stone. I knew it back then. And I remember it now. I was always there, son, listening."

Stone took in a breath to push away the lump in his throat. "But you never said anything, never responded."

"No, not in the way you needed me to. I'm responding now, though." She held her hand to his face, her eyes holding his. "Will you forgive me?"

Stone didn't push her hand away. It felt so warm there on his skin. "Do you know, Mother, there are certain orchids that can actually survive growing on rock? They're called lithophytes."

"Yes, I've heard of them. Amazing that they just need rain and humidity to make them thrive."

"They stick to the rocks, but they can't gain sustenance unless it rains, and yet they stay attached anyway, waiting for the water to come."

"Waiting for the rain to nurture them," Eloise replied. Then she dropped her hand and reached out her arms to her son. "I'm here now, Stone. And I'm so very glad you stayed attached. Because I have never let go."

Stone hugged his mother close, savoring the feel of being in the arms of another human being. Then he stood back and took a long breath. "I'm in love, Mother."

"I know, son."

"What should I do?"

"You should go find her and tell her."

"What if—"

Eloise quieted him with a finger to his lips. "What if you don't? We all know there are no promises and no guarantees in life, except that of God to man."

"I guess God is a lot like my lithophytes."

Eloise smiled. "He sticks to us, even when we don't want to allow His love to break through."

"I remembered something the other night," he told her. "My father was a true Christian. He was a fisher of men."

Eloise inhaled a sharp breath, her eyes glistening. "Yes, he was."

Stone ran a hand through his long bangs. "All these years, I've been mourning how he died, when I should have been honoring how he lived."

"If you can do that, darling, you will indeed be your father's son."

They stood silent for a few minutes, the sounds of the distant music drifting up to them, the soft ceaseless waves of the sea comforting them.

"Okay," Stone said. "I've wasted enough time."

Eloise kissed him on the cheek. "Good then. Oh, and Stone, *The Resurrection* looks perfect down on the rocks. Your father would be so proud."

"That's why I put it there," he said. "Pick yourself out an orchid, Mom. And...Happy Mother's Day."

Then he turned and went in search of Tara.

"Are you sure?" Ana asked Tara later.

Ana and Rock were ready to go home, but Tara wanted to stay. She had to talk to Stone.

"I'll be fine," she said, her hand on her sister's arm. "I can call a cab or have that fancy limo drop me off."

"Okay, then," Ana said, worry evident in the expression on her face. "Tell Stone we had a lovely time. Sorry we missed him."

"I will." Tara looked around the grounds. The orchestra was still playing, but most of the guests had gone home. It was late, but the question on everyone's mind had been the same. Where was Stone Dempsey?

"Greta Epperson is even giving up," Rock commented as the blond, bespectacled society page reporter stomped past them with a haughty look, her notebook still in hand just in case the mysterious Mr. Dempsey decided to put in an appearance.

"Well, thank goodness for that," Tara replied. "The woman hounded me all night. I told her about our plans out at Hidden Haven, but Greta only wanted to know what personal plans I had in store with Stone. I couldn't answer that question."

Ana was about to respond, when she looked past Tara. "Uh, can I help you, sir?"

Tara turned to find a formally dressed waiter standing there. He motioned to Tara. "I'm to escort Mrs. Parnell to the dining table."

"Excuse me?" Tara said, wondering what was going on.

"Mr. Dempsey requests your presence at a private dinner, ma'am," the spiffy waiter said with an elegant bow.

"Oh, my, oh, my," Ana said, a smile splitting her face. "I guess it is time for us to go home, Rock."

"Can't we stay and watch? Things are just about to get interesting," Rock said in a mock whine.

Tara looked from the expectant face of the waiter back to her sister and Rock. "What should I do?"

"Do?" Ana pushed at her arm. "Do what you've been wanting to do all night, Tara. Go and talk to Stone."

Tara nodded, her throat too dry to speak. Then she turned back to Ana. "Will you check on Laurel and the girls?" She'd already told Ana and Rock about Laurel's visit.

"Of course," Rock said. "We'll even bring them back to our house, if that will make you feel better."

Tara nodded. "I think Laurel would appreciate that."

She waited until they walked around to the portico on the side of the house, then turned back to the smiling waiter. "I'm ready."

Stone wasn't sure if he was ready for this. But it was now or never. He'd tried to stay away from Tara. He'd even asked God to help him. He'd promised Laurel he wouldn't hurt her or her mother. But mostly, Stone didn't want to be hurt himself.

But he knew that if he didn't tell Tara that he loved her, he'd become the same miserable excuse of a man he'd been up until now. And he didn't want to be that man anymore.

Stone stood on the sandy beach, just a few feet

away from the pounding surf, and looked up the path toward the imposing mansion. To his right, stood the lighthouse. And just beyond that on his left, the stark image of his mother's sculpture shot up into the night from the rocks to meet the stars. Stone could see the water falling gently from the center of the never-ending fountain that his mother had placed in the middle of the steel crossbeams. He'd had the water pipe especially installed among the rocks so the water would always continue to flow out and back into the sea, only to return time and time again, just like the ocean waves.

He'd had a table set up here between the lighthouse and the sculpture. A storm lantern for atmosphere and an orchid for his lady. Dinner for two.

And now he waited for Tara to come. And asked God to show him how to be the man she needed him to be.

Then he saw her. She was walking down the path toward him, her white dress shimmering like bits of moonlight, her wrap falling away from her dainty shoulders, her hair coming out in strands around her face as the tropical wind played through it. The sight of her took his breath, but knowing she was coming to him at last gave him courage.

His heart felt open and full, overflowing, as it sputtered and puttered to a new beat, to a new beginning. He felt a solid wall of fear, but he also felt as if he'd been washed clean and reborn. He couldn't mess up this time.

So he stood there in his tuxedo and held out his hand to the woman he loved.

"You," she said, her expression full of confusion and hope.

"Me," he answered, remembering the first time they'd said those words to each other in such a different way.

Tara nodded, one hand going up to push hair off her face. "I had to see you."

"And I wanted to see you." Stone guided her to one of the high-backed chrome chairs placed at the round, white-clothed table. Then he motioned to the lush bright-pink-and-white flower sitting in a weighted pot on the table. "I brought you this."

"It's lovely."

"It made me think of you."

"Orchids? I remind you of orchids?"

"You're dainty and very ladylike, yes. And a bit exotic, hard to read. You need lots and lots of nurturing."

She smiled and looked down at the table. "Did you have this shipped in just for me?"

"No, I grew this just for you. With my own two hands."

Her head shot up, her gaze touching on him, on his hands. "You always manage to surprise me."

Stone wanted to kiss her. "Are you hungry, thirsty?"

Tara sank down in the chair and allowed him to

push it forward on the soft sand. "No, Stone, I'm mostly curious. Where were you all night?"

"I was around," he said, suddenly nervous.

"But you didn't bother to make an appearance."

"No, I didn't. I don't like parties."

"Then why did you throw one?"

"Just to see you in that dress."

"Well, I've been in this dress all night. But I didn't see you."

"I was around," he repeated, remembering how he'd watched her getting out of the limo earlier. Remembering how he'd watched her laughing and smiling as she moved through the crowd. Remembering while he'd watched her that he'd promised to be patient, that he'd promised Laurel he would cause them no more pain. Remembering that he couldn't deal with his own pain. "I saw you, but I couldn't—"

"You couldn't break your promise to my daughter," Tara said as she pushed her wrap away, her eyes locking with his.

"What promise would that be?" he asked with a nonchalant shrug as he settled back in his own chair.

"The one she explained to me tonight, when she came here to tell me that she loves me and she wants me to fight for you. The one you made to her the night she hid in the darkness of your house up there on the hill."

"What about it?"

"What about it?" she repeated, her voice catching with a mixture of awe and frustration. "You were willing to walk away? You were willing to stay away, for the sake of my children? You'd do that for Laurel?"

Stone felt trapped, like a bit of flotsam caught between the tide and the shore. Almost home. Almost there. He just had to hold on. "I was willing to do whatever I had to do — to make you happy."

She didn't speak. She was scaring him to death. But then he looked over at her and saw a single tear glistening down her cheek. "Tara?"

"Laurel wants us to be together, Stone."

He closed his eyes, tried to breathe. "And how do *you* feel about that?"

"I'm happy," she said, the tears falling freely now. "So happy."

"Because I walked away, or because you're here with me?"

"Both," she said, bobbing her head. "Stone, I respect you so much for what you did. And I trust you. I will never doubt you again."

Stone felt the jagged-edged release of the last crumblings of the wall around his heart. Then a feeling of complete freedom, of complete joy, burst forth inside him, causing him to reach up a hand and clutch it to his chest. "Do you trust me enough to marry me?"

She sat still, her eyes big and blue and as vast as the ocean. The sea crashed at the shore. The wind touched on the trees. The moon laughed at the stars. And Stone knew he'd been put on earth just to reach this moment in his life.

"Yes," she said finally. "Yes, I do." Then she held up a hand. "I thought this was just physical, just a passing infatuation. I didn't want to rush into anything, the way I did with Chad. But Stone, I've never felt this way before. This is so overwhelming, so scary, I've tried to deny it, to hide it."

Stone came out of his chair to pull her into his arms. He crushed her close, his lips touching on her eyes, her hair, her mouth. "No more hiding."

"No, no more hiding," she said as she pushed her hands through his hair to bring his head down to hers. "We're free now, Stone. Free and clear."

Stone held Tara there on the beach, with the ocean waves breaking around them, and knew that he'd come out of the darkness at last. Then he grabbed the lantern off the table and took her by the hand, pulling her along the shore. "I want to show you something."

Tara laughed, followed him to the sculpture called *The Resurrection*. "Read this," he said, holding the lantern so she could see. "It's Psalms 107, Verse 23."

Tara read the King James verse he'd had inscribed in stone at the foot of *The Resurrection:*

"'They that go down to the sea in ships, that do business in great waters; These see the works of the Lord, and his wonders of the deep.'"

She touched a hand on his arm. "You dedicated this to your father—Tillman Dempsey."

"Yes. I understand now, Tara."

Tara turned back into his arms. "Oh, Stone. I never knew I could love this way."

"Me, either," he said. Then he held a hand to her face. "And I never knew I could be loved."

"It's a wonder," Tara said. Then she kissed him again.

Stone accepted that wonder into his heart and felt the joyous burden of happiness and hope and resurrection, at last.

Sunset Island Sentinel Society News
Reported by Greta Epperson

This whole island is all abuzz with news of the upcoming nuptials of none other than that elusive bachelor millionaire Stone Dempsey and the lovely mother of three girls, Tara Parnell. Tara is sister to our own Ana Dempsey, who runs Ana's Tea Room and Art Gallery and is married to Rock Dempsey.

But that's not the best part, oh, no, my friends. This intimate wedding will not take place here on the island, but rather on a spot of land near the Savannah River, in a little chapel in the marsh that apparently holds special memories for the bride and groom.

And there's more. It seems the land, which once belonged to Tara Parnell and her deceased husband, Chad, was sold to Stone Dempsey and slated to be turned into a swank residential development, until Stone and Tara became fast friends with Josiah Bennett, a man who's lived on the land all of his life, was married, and raised four children out there in the marsh. Because of Josiah, Stone Dempsey decided to scrap the idea of a gated community. Instead, he was happy to present his bride-to-be with the plans for just one house out near the marsh— a lovely, rambling, hideaway cottage for his new family.

"I did it for Tara," Mr. Dempsey told me in an exclusive interview I had with the happy couple just this week. "And I did it for Josiah. He wants to stay there to take care of the chapel, and now he will have someone close to take care of him. And besides, Tara and the girls love that spot of land— it was a special place to Tara's late husband, Chad Parnell. I couldn't take that away from them."

And what's to become of Hidden Hill, Stone Dempsey's infamous mansion on the hill here at Sunset Island?

"We're turning it into a grand hotel," Tara Parnell explained. "We want people to enjoy the luxury and history of the house and gardens and to feel free to explore the newly renovated West Island Lighthouse and the rest of Sunset Island. We hope to bring more tourists to the island, and help the economy, too. We've also set up a trust for the lighthouse—for upkeep and continuing restoration."

And where will the happy couple reside?

"We have a suite at Hidden Hill," Tara said, "but we'll probably spend most of our time at our new home back near Savannah, on the river."

I asked if they liked the seclusion out there.

"No," Mr. Dempsey replied, his eyes glowing as he looked at his bride. "We like the openness of the land. We want to be together, but we don't want to hide away from the world."

Well, folks, when Stone Dempsey decided to come out of hiding, he certainly did it in a huge way. Who knew the man had such a big heart? He's asked his brother Rock to perform the marriage ceremony, and his brother Clay to be his best man. Josiah Bennett will give a special blessing at the wedding, too. I'll be sure to give a thorough wedding report.

And I hope to get an interview with handsome but shy Clay Dempsey when he takes a break from his K-9 police duties in the big city of Atlanta, for an extended vacation here on the island this fall.

Details to follow very soon…

* * * * *

Dear Reader,

I truly enjoyed writing this story of a man who showed the world his heart of stone, while he longed for a heart of flesh. Sometimes, it takes meeting one special person to change us and make us see that we need to turn back to God for our salvation.

In the moment when Stone met Tara, he saw the man he had become. But after getting to know Tara and her girls, he also saw the man he wanted to be. This is what love and marriage and faith are all about. Love and marriage mean we're willing to make a lifelong commitment to another human being, so that the two parts can become a whole in the eyes of God. And having faith means that we're willing to put God first in all of our relationships.

At times we're all like Stone. We harden our hearts to God's love and redemption. We harden our hearts to the people who love us, our families and friends. I hope this story will touch your heart and open it to the possibility of God's immense love and grace. And I hope you'll join me for the next story in the Sunset Island series, when Rock and Stone's younger brother, Clay Dempsey, returns to Sunset Island, to find some rest and redemption of his own, in *A Tender Touch.* Also look for my Steeple Hill single title *After the Storm,* a love story about new beginnings, set in the Blue Ridge Mountains of Georgia.

Until next time, may the angels watch over you—always.

Lenora Worth

LARGER-PRINT BOOKS!

GET 2 FREE LARGER-PRINT NOVELS PLUS 2 FREE MYSTERY GIFTS

Love Inspired

Larger-print novels are now available...

HARLEQUIN®

A *Romance*

FOR EVERY MOOD™

Spotlight on

Heart & Home

Heartwarming romances
where love can happen
right when you least expect it.

See the next page to enjoy a sneak peek
from Silhouette Special Edition®,
a Heart and Home series.

CATHHSSE10

Introducing MCFARLANE'S PERFECT BRIDE
by USA TODAY *bestselling author Christine Rimmer,*
from Silhouette Special Edition®.

Entranced. Captivated. Enchanted.

Connor sat across the table from Tori Jones and
couldn't help thinking that those words exactly described
what effect the small-town schoolteacher had on him.
He might as well stop trying to tell himself he wasn't
interested. He was powerfully drawn to her.

Clearly, he should have dated more when he was
younger.

There had been a couple of other women since Jennifer
had walked out on him. But he had never been entranced.
Or captivated. Or enchanted.

Until now.

He wanted her—*her,* Tori Jones, in particular. Not just
someone suitably attractive and well-bred, as Jennifer had
been. Not just someone sophisticated, sexually exciting
and discreet, which pretty much described the two women
he'd dated after his marriage crashed and burned.

It came to him that he...he *liked* this woman. And that
was new to him. He liked her quick wit, her wisdom and
her big heart. He liked the passion in her voice when she
talked about things she believed in.

He liked *her.* And suddenly it mattered all out of
proportion that she might like him, too.

Was he losing it? He couldn't help but wonder. Was
he cracking under the strain—of the soured economy, the
McFarlane House setbacks, his divorce, the scary changes
in his son? Of the changes he'd decided he needed to make
in his life and himself?